Hidden In Plain Sight

Tales From A Secret War

A Novel In Short Stories By J P Claypool

ISBN: 978-1-7308-8620-1

Cover Design by Jessica Reed

ACKNOWLEDGEMENTS

This work is dedicated to:

Lt Col Larry Colvin, Airborne Ranger, Special Operator, Ret.

Who read "One Of Those Days" and insisted I should write more; and reminded me often over the next few years that I should publish my stories. Colonel, I have followed your "order".

And to:

Warren and Sharon Hall

My sister and brother-in-law who read and offered comment on the tales as I put them together. And gave me an occasional prod to keep the project going.

And For:

The "Tweeners" – Those who served and those who went in harms way in Africa, Central and South America, the Middle East, Southeast Asia, and other far-flung parts of the world between the end of the Korean Conflict and the start of the Vietnam War, and came home to no parades, no fanfare and who quietly took up their lives "hidden in plain sight".

Table Of Contents

Acknowledgements

Intro:	Green Dream	1
Prologue:	The Gray Man	2
Chapter 1.	A First Sergeant	9
Chapter 2.	Training Was A Hoot Part1	14
Chapter 3.	Sandbaggers	19
Chapter 4.	Nellis Days Vegas Nights	25
Chapter 5.	Floyd	31
Chapter 6.	Training Was A Hoot Part 2	36
Chapter 7.	3 Guys	44
Chapter 8.	Xmas In A Far Place	55
Chapter 9.	Off The Res	60
Chapter 10.	Spring Surprise	67
Chapter 11.	Fun In The Desert	75
Chapter 12.	An Lac PRICS	82
Chapter 13.	The Boy	85
Chapter 14.	The Gaur	89
Chapter 15.	Sorenson	94
Chapter 16.	Two Jumps	100
Chapter 17.	Turning Point	106
Chapter 18.	Night Engagement	112
Chapter 19.	The Revenue Station	118
Chapter 20.	Revenue Station Aftermath	125
Chapter 21.	Panhead	132
Chapter 22.	Shifting Sands	136
Chapter 23.	The Purloined Notebook	141
Chapter 24.	Ban Ban	148
Chapter 25.	A Kiwi	153
Chapter 26.	Six Big Boxes	157
Chapter 27.	Wet Heat	162
Chapter 28.	Trong Song Road Assault	169
Chapter 29.	A Walk In The Park	176

Chapter 30.	Bolaven	184
Chapter 31.	John	192
Chapter 32.	One Of Those Days	197
Chapter 33.	A Big Change	207
Chapter 34.	Hospital Time	212
Chapter 35.	Dry Heat	217
Chapter 36.	Zero Flys	224
Chapter 37.	Officers and Peaches	230
Chapter 38.	Here Kitty Kitty	237
Chapter 39.	Bo Pen Nyan	243
Chapter 40.	One Cold Morning	250
Chapter 41.	The Wraiths	257
Chapter 42.	Morrisons Deal	262
Chapter 43.	Twilight	267
Chapter 44.	Buster	276
Chapter 45.	Castle Karst	281
Chapter 46.	Bug Out	288
Chapter 47.	Snake In the Pass	294
Chapter 48.	Hole In The Bucket	304
Chapter 49.	The Man	311
Chapter 50.	Smitty's Bar	315
Chapter 51.	The White Envelope	322
Chapter 52.	Xmas in the desert	329
Chapter 53.	Dog Days	336
Chapter 54.	Fear, Anger, Guilt	341
Chapter 55.	String Of Pearls	349
Chapter 56.	Mail Call	354
Chapter 57.	On A Wing	357
Chapter 58.	Buster Leaves	362
Epilogue:	Remembering Day	365

Introduction
Green Dream

In the Green Dream he is running hard, lungs and throat aching, leg muscles burning. He's running through a narrow green tunnel, a bamboo forest under a higher canopy with patches of mist hiding obstacles on the red brown trail. Altitude and heat sucking his energy, roots reach out to trip him, loose rock threatens to send him sliding and falling, every shadowy spot hides some potential danger. As he runs in the dream he knows he is running toward an unspeakable horror. But something, some primal instinct keeps pushing him on and on. Running headlong in a place where every step should be taken with care and caution. The Green Dream is not a dream – it's a nightmare.

The Green Dream is back. For years he hid from it through drugs, alcohol and a series of adventures and misadventures until finally it seemed to be gone forever. But then one afternoon when he was in a dentists' chair it came back. The dentist noticed he was tearing up and thought he had hurt him, but he assured the dentist that the tears were brought on by something else.

Later in the dental clinic parking lot he found his hands shaking and unable to turn the key in the ignition as wave after wave of emotions that he had suppressed for years threatened to drown him.

The Green Dream isn't a dream. It isn't a nightmare. The Green Dream is a memory.

Prologue

The Gray Man

Stillness. Not the frozen-in-place stillness of a sniper but something better, a matching of the rhythms and colors of whatever space he was in. He seemed to have no color of his own always fitting seamlessly into his surroundings and so, and because we never knew his real name, we called him the Gray Man.

Having tea at a riverside shop he looked like a Lowland Lao, drinking vodka in the White Rose he would be taken to be one of the Russians he was drinking with; on a trail with one of the hill tribes he was indistinguishable from his companions. His gait, body language and mannerisms, the way he held a cup, smoked a cigarette, spit or didn't spit, all those small things that give away an impostor were part and parcel of an ability to shift his personality to suit his environment. He was the guy no one noticed when they entered a room, in the field he was invisible unless he wanted you to see him.

He had been running and hiding three days and nights, no chance for warm food or deep sleep. The rains had stopped but the foliage was water laden and the trails, when he was on them, still muddy.

Days earlier finding it impossible to move without leaving a trail he decided he would have to blend in and be mistaken for a porter on his way south to deliver supplies. He had found an old bicycle frame and made an improvised patch to a flat tire, with his trade basket (hiding his radio and other gear) hanging off the frame he looked like one of many soon to be on the paths that made up the Ho Chi Minh Trail. Dressed in dark green shorts, black shirt, Uncle Ho sandals and black slouch hat and festooned with chest ammo belt, bush knife, Elephants' Gut sling and Kalashnikov he should be able to pass if he didn't get too close to anyone.

The plan had been for him to spend a month in the field, three weeks near the Mu Gia Pass on both the Lao and the North Viet Nam sides during the monsoon season (when the Trail would be inactive, the NVA did not like to move during the rains) and map the many routes through the mountains in that area with particular attention to potential truck park and materials storage areas to be marked for future targeting. He would be able to shelter and have cooking fires in some of the caves and abandoned villages if he was very careful: local contacts had cached food for him so although the comfort level was not going to be very good conditions were survivable and he had experienced worse assignments in the past (once living for fourteen days on moldy bread and rainwater seepage in a cellar on the wrong side of the Iron Curtain, the tread of heavy boots over his head several times during the days and nights). His fourth week would be spent working his way east down the mountains to his extraction point in North Viet Nam.

The first two weeks were a little miserable but he got a lot of work done and was content with the product he would be able to deliver to his contacts in Saigon. He had irrefutable proof of the North Vietnamese build up in eastern Laos and had identified and pinpointed good future targets by long/lat coordinates using a bubble sextant and pages from a set of H.O. 249 Star Tables. Boots and/or bombs would be able to find these points at any time despite the dense foliage hiding them. In his own coded shorthand he had taken notes that he could transcribe later into maps to be used by other watchers on this part of the Trail. The detail in his notes included inclines and topo features, fording spots for the numerous creeks and run-offs, springs and other water sources that might be expected to be usable during the dry season, and other information in a 30-kilometer arc around his base location.

Trouble appeared in the form of an early end to the monsoon. The rains stopped and people began to appear on the road coming up from the east, blocking the route he had expected to take to his extraction point. It was critical that no sign of his presence in Laos or North Viet Nam were discovered, the United States Embassy wanted to at least give the appearance of complete compliance with the Geneva Accords saying that all but a small token force of foreign armies would stay out of Laos (the U.S. hadn't signed the Accords but had agreed to abide by them, against the advice of all the "Old Asia Hands" in Vientiane at the time). Equally critical, but never openly stated, was the fact that he could not be taken alive, there were agencies in governments in several parts of the world that would pay a large price for the opportunity to "interview" him. He knew he shouldn't be in the field, he shouldn't be anywhere there might be a risk of his capture, but he had lied to himself (and knew it was a lie) that he needed to see things in person when the truth was that he missed the tension of fieldwork. He was mentally prepared to take his own life rather than be captured.

He had altered his plan to descend east from the vicinity of the border crossing and then turn south in the foothills to a new approach that would take him south across into Laos, moving with other traffic on the trail to a footpath (steep narrow game trail) that would take him east and back into North Viet Nam at a place not far from his extraction point. The distance and terrain would be more difficult to cover but he had adequate time to make his rendezvous if he pushed. Heavy air traffic over the Trail hadn't started yet and most of the land traffic was moving by day, good for him because it meant he could add night hours to his travel time with less danger of being challenged. He would use the early morning and late evening hours as primary operational hours; he laughed at himself at that last thought, he had been at his trade so long even his internal dialogues sounded like something one would hear in a military briefing room, maybe it was time to quit.

On the morning of his second day on the new route he was on a ridge above a steep ravine with fast water flowing at the bottom and a bald spot where he would have to traverse an open area or backtrack several hours to find a new route, he opted to cross the exposed section. Light was still dim, he was going in the direction of other porters, and he didn't have hours to spare; he would risk moving in the open for a few minutes. He was more than halfway across when he heard the hail over the sound of the water rushing in the ravine and saw the men on the other side, one in long pants and pith helmet with a red star on the crown. He waved back and pointed south as though to indicate he would meet with them further down the way after he had cleared the ravine. But he knew that if not full on suspicious the man in the pith helmet would at least question why he was traveling alone. His best option was to disappear for a few hours and give them time to be way ahead before he blended on to the trunk they were traveling, he would have to make up the time tonight.

He slept for a few hours wrapped in a poncho in an almost-dry spot within hearing of people moving by, his sleeping mind registering surprise and alarm at the amount of traffic so soon after the rains had stopped, the North must be going to really ramp up the pressure this year.

Awake and ready to travel again in the late afternoon he waited for a pause in the flow of traffic then started south pushing the bicycle and keeping his gaze down, slouch hat down over his forehead. He hadn't traveled half an hour when he saw something that gave him great concern, there was a boot print positioned where someone had crossed the trail at an angle, other passersby had stepped around the print leaving it exposed to view. The print was large, and the shape and imprint were obviously American. There was a watcher team, probably Special Forces or Marine, already in the area and the people moving south certainly knew it and would have security teams out looking for the intruders. This was a double hazard for the Gray Man, if the watchers saw him moving alone they might decide to take such an easy target and if one of the security teams got close enough to him to see his round eyes the game would be up. He did not have enough time in the bank to go to ground and he was already stressing his body with lack of enough food and proper sleep, he would have to keep going.

He moved on through the night unchallenged, pausing for twenty-minute catnaps every couple of hours, tempted to ditch the bike so he could move faster but certain it was an important part of his appearance he kept pushing the damn thing. By morning he reckoned that he was less than a day's march away from the point where he would leave the Trail and descend eastward.

As he began to come down from a slight rise on a serpentine trail section in the pre-dawn light he was searching for a good spot to hide for a few hours when he realized, too late to stop or turn aside, there was a man standing in the path facing him and motioning him to come forward, AK47 held across his chest in his right hand and left hand out palm up as though to receive something. The man was wearing long pants and pith helmet (same guy he had seen before?). Just off the trail beside him there was a stack of three rifles and two men squatting and drinking tea, farther off the trail under a green bower was the mouth of a shallow cave where there was a makeshift table and a large pot hanging over a fire.

Realizing he was going to be challenged for identification the Gray Man stopped and shifted his AK to his back, to look less threatening and knowing he couldn't risk a shot he moved forward head low to a position between the officer and the tea drinkers, with the bicycle between himself and the officer, thankful for the still-dim light. None of them seemed alarmed, reassured by his dress and the way he moved into the camp, the tea drinkers continuing to banter in low voices as he neared the officer. He fumbled in his blouse beneath the cartridge belt as though reaching for his identification book, nodding but not responding with words to the officer's queries, just another dumb farmer impressed into service as a "dan cong" porter.

As his left hand came out from inside his blouse holding a stiletto he straight armed the weapon into the officer's throat, the Gray Man's body blocking the scene from the tea drinkers, then swept the bicycle in both hands in a half circle knocking the tea drinkers to the ground and finishing them with rifle butt and bolo knife. Just as his tired mind screamed "three rifles!" he caught a glimmer of shadow movement and turned to parry a knife aimed at his neck with the AK barrel. The knife slid up the barrel to the stock, edge catching in the wood and point piercing the Gray Man's left shoulder just as his own knife entered his opponent just below the sternum sharp side up. The two turned and turned again in a macabre

6

"pas de deux", close enough to feel one another's breath and see, even in the dim light, beads of sweat on each brow. They held the embrace, the Viet Cong trying to pull his knife loose to strike again, the Gray Man pulling his knife edge up until the light began to fade from the younger man's eyes and his face settled in to an expression of peace as though he were saying, "I forgive you".

He scooped some of the soup from the pot into his sling over the top of his remaining rice, put the bicycle back on its wheels and started trotting down the trail, no time to even hide the bodies he needed to get as far away from the area as he could in the shortest time.

When the trail came to a fork he took the right branch still pushing the bicycle at a pace between a walk and a trot, suppressing the urge to run at full speed and trying to maintain the appearance of just another porter taking supplies south. He kept the pace all morning, seeing tracks that meant there were people ahead of him but not coming up to any of them until at around noon he found a spot where he could conceal himself, eat and take a short rest. When he moved on he left the bicycle behind and shouldered the pack. He had passed the highest point in the Mu Gia Pass and was well into Laos when he found a spot where he could take a shot with the bubble sextant and determine his position. According to his solution he was now south of the point where the game trail he was seeking would cross the trail paralleling the one he was on, the trail he would have taken had he gone left at the fork.

There was no question in his mind that the bodies at the check station had been found and that there would be security teams looking for him, he did not know if he had a head start of minutes or perhaps an hour but he did know the searchers would probably be better fed and rested than he was, his only advantage might be that they would expect him to keep going deeper into Laos. At the next rock outcropping crossing the trail he carefully worked his way left and slithered rather than bushwhacked east to cross the other trail and move down slope toward North Viet Nam.

He had worked his way back north through the thickets until he found a game trail zigzagging down slope a little before dark. Trying to move further down in the dark was very dangerous and he fell, damaging his already injured left shoulder even more before he quit trying to move for the night. Moving again at first light the forest sounds told him that he was not alone on this part of the mountain, he had to keep a strong pace and kept going, slipping and sliding most of the way down slope until he reached a crossing path and cut back north again where he was sure he was over his extraction point, he could clearly see the river below and the bend where the sawmill should be located but he did not want to go directly there, he needed to keep any trackers in pursuit confused as to his destination until after dawn the next day. At least now he was low enough that the terrain would allow him to move at night with less risk of injury.

He was bone weary and feverish, the wound on his left shoulder throbbing. He would have to fall back on an old survival skill.

Stillness.

Chapter 1

A First Sergeant

It was a hot Friday afternoon when the USAF officer with the sharply creased Uniform- Dacron- Class B -Tropical and shiny new Captain's bars, B-9 bag in one hand and briefcase tucked under the opposite arm, came through the door of the Quonset hut. First Sergeant Kappas' first thought was that he was so glad at the opportunity to relieve the days' tedium he might salute. He immediately dismissed the impulse and waited for the officers' reaction to this military slight while thinking, "How does he keep those creases so sharp in this heat?"

Kappas had started his military career as an enlisted man in WWII, mustanged to a commission before the end of that war and had been a flying officer during the "Korean Conflict" (shot down behind enemy lines twice, walked out on his own twice) but in 1956 the Mosquito Wing was disbanded and Kappas was riffed. His assignments and exploits in WWII remained classified, but his actions flying B-25s in close ground support, and P-51s, Corsairs, and AT6s as a forward air controller (FAC) and as a squadron commander with the Mosquitoes were still talked about in aerial command training centers and officers' clubs wherever military men "in the know" congregated.

After Korea the military services were all required to put forth and execute a plan for "Reduction In Force" (RIF), some officers with less than the time-in-service required for retirement would be offered the option to remain in the service as senior enlisted men until the time-in-service requirements had been met and retire at the highest rank they had achieved. Officers who chose this option were considered to have been "riffed". Lt. Colonel Kappas took the option.

Then followed a series of non-assignments leading to his current position as First Sergeant of a command of the Air Force performing liaison with the US Army Intelligence School at Fort Huachuca in the Arizona desert near the Mexican border. Except there was no command, just MSgt Kappas and two Airmen 1st Class to sign Air Force attendees to the school on and off post, arrange billeting, and perform other concierge duties.

He had developed a routine of running in the morning, then working out with light and heavy bags at the MP gym for an hour, occasionally sparring with some transient war dog. He monitored classes at the Army Intelligence School and used the MARS (Military Affiliate Radio Service) station to stay in touch with the worldwide Senior NCO network – the people who really make the military work – and a few officers he was still close with. On alternate weekends he would load his De Soto with cans of Spam, canned hams, boxes of salt, bags of beans, wool blankets, a few quart bottles of beer, a bag of peppermint sticks, and sundry other goods and drive north to the middle eastern part of the state and a small town called Hon Dah. There he would sit with the old men of the D'Nee and listen respectfully to their stories of the Old Ways and the problems facing the tribe in these confusing times.

After sundown he would leave the gifts with the old men to distribute, helping to maintain their prestige with the tribe, and find some quiet spot to drink his beer and roll up in a blanket for the night. These quiet nights on the mountain were the only hours he allowed himself to think about his dead wife and daughter. Monday mornings would find him back at the fort running over the desert before sunrise.

The truth was, much as he hated the word, Kappas was bored and welcomed whatever small diversion this young officer might bring to the day.

The captain grinned, slid a hip over the corner of Kappas' desk and stuck out his right hand, a large hand with flattened knuckles and calloused on the side, and said, "David Samuels, and I'm here to speak with you Sarge. We have mutual friends in Virginia that tell me you're the man I need to talk to. In private."

After Kappas dispatched the two airmen off to deliver the captains' B-9 bag to the BOQ (Bachelor Officers Quarters) and arrange for his billet and meal vouchers Captain Samuels suggested, "Tell you what Sergeant, if you can arrange transportation I'll buy you a steak and tell you what's up". And that was the beginning of a long friendship based on a mutual respect.

Current Air Force Doctrine at that point of the Cold War held that future wars would be fought by long distance bombers and intercontinental ballistic missiles. The majority of available resources were being channeled toward the Strategic Air Command (SAC) and the new Missile Defense Command (MDC), the new role for the Tactical Air Command (TAC) would be primarily to provide fighter escort for SAC bombers and interception of enemy bombers. Fighter aircraft systems would rely heavily on air-to-air missiles with less emphasis on guns and the close air support capabilities of these aircraft. Some of the lessons of WWII and Korea were already being forgotten or ignored during the nuclear weapons standoff between the Super Powers.

But there were some people in the Pentagon and at Langley who thought that Americas' new role on the world stage might get them involved in small "bush wars" and "police actions" around the globe and some of the Air Force brass did not want to see the job of close air support go solely to the Marines and the Navy (who were also shifting away from gun platforms to missile systems on their fighter aircraft, a decision that would cost a lot of pilot lives in just a few years). And this same Air Force brass wanted to keep the Army out of the aircraft business entirely if possible. There was/is always an inter-service rivalry and fierce competition for funds between the military branches. During the mid-fifties and up into the early sixties TAC was "sucking hind tit" in that competition.

During WWII and Korea airborne troops had proven their value to world armies and close air support had played a key role in every theater of operations. Some of the Wise Men in the various services wanted to keep these capabilities sharp. But where would the funding come from?

Samuels was there to give Kappas the answer to that question and make him a proposition.

The Eisenhower authorized Programs Evaluation Office (PEO) role in South East Asia was expanding, money was pouring through the program, and there was a push to get more people on the ground in sensitive areas of Laos. Then Senator Kennedy was campaigning to have the program broadened in Viet Nam as well. The US Army's Col. "Bull" Simons was pushing to have the Special Forces put into the field (over the objections of the CIA head of station in Laos – he thought the Special Forces were too high profile in their push for a piece of the pie) and the Navy and Marines were searching for ways to participate. The Air Force wanted in as well, this was the opportunity to keep the concept (although not the name) of Air Commandos alive and funded.

The Air Force had a couple of advantages in this scramble for a place at the table. Laos is a landlocked country about the size of Utah with as many wrinkles as West (by gawd) Virginia and a poor road system. The only practical way to move people or supplies around efficiently was/is by air and in-country operators were already clearing landing sites in remote areas. There would be a need for more of these "Victor Sites" (later called "Landing Sites") and someone would have to survey, map and provide communications to these sites. That "someone" would need certain technical skills, be parachute qualified, and be able to survive and function in "Indian Country"- either as part of a team, alone with indigenous peoples, or as liaison to other military entities. This presented a perfect environment for Air Force participation.

The other, less obvious advantage the Air Force brought to the game was relative anonymity; their ground forces would be labeled "Special Operators" rather than "Special Forces" (though entitled to wear the scarlet beret we never did). They would avoid publicity and stay in the background as much as possible (they were successful to the extent that for years almost no one outside the services, and few in them, realized the Air Force had special operators).

Captain Samuels had been assigned the task of assembling the recruiting and training cadre for these special operators under the umbrella of "a guerilla warfare, counter-insurgency study group" (later called 8th COIN) attached to the PEO. He had been told in Washington that Master Sergeant Kappas, Maurice M. was the man he needed to pull it all together, and after spending a short time with the man, he agreed with that assessment.

On Monday morning the airmen assigned as clerks in Kappas' office witnessed something new and unusual – the First Sergeant was humming, and even smiling once in a while at nothing in particular.

On Tuesday morning he was gone.

Chapter 2

Training Was A Hoot, Part 1

When we got off the bus at Lackland AFB we were immediately assailed by white- eyed, foaming- at- the -mouth drill instructors who used language I hadn't even known existed. It was during the week between Christmas and New Year and most of the permanent party training cadres were on leave, those that were on duty were not happy and wanted to make sure all the "rainbows" knew it.

We had our civilian clothes and other possessions taken to storage (never saw them again), got our buzz haircuts, were assigned barracks and issued uniforms and told when and where we could take chow call. Then we were left in the tender care of our barracks chiefs who were told to keep the barracks and areas around them "policed" and handle any disciplinary problems themselves. These barracks chiefs had been "rainbows" with the rest of us just hours before and had no idea what they were supposed to be doing. We would be waiting for a week or more for the training cycles to re-start.

Most of the raw recruits that came on base that week were given weekend passes – I think the on-duty training cadre was hoping some of them would run away (a few did) – but I had had an altercation with my barracks chief and had to stay on base. My new friend Beckstrom stayed as well saying he wasn't much interested in seeing that part of Texas.

During the confiscation of our personal effects the Drill Instructor had allowed me to keep my WSI (water safety instructor) swim trunks and I decided to use them while I waited for training to start. Weather in winter in Texas, that year anyway, is changeable by the hour, freezing cold at night and hot during the day but the pool near our barracks was heated and inviting – and the gate wasn't locked.

I was swimming underwater laps alternated with freestyle laps when I first saw Sergeant Kappas standing by the fence watching. When I got out of the water he motioned me over and told me that I was to be at the pool at 0800 the next morning, and every morning until he told me differently, to give swim lessons to the Colonels' daughter and her friend. He spoke in a soft, even tone but what he said was unmistakably an order. And that remained my morning duty for a week even after the training cycles started again. Until the morning that slick sleeves Bobbie Grimes approached me in the chow hall and asked if I'd like to try out for a really neat outfit where I could learn skydiving, scuba diving and other neat stuff.

As a" worm", "lower than whale shit", "pimple on a real airman's butt" raw recruit Airman Basic I wasn't very familiar with rank and other insignia but I did notice that Sergeant Kappas didn't dress, or for that matter act, like the other permanent party cadre members. There was a diamond in the middle of all the stripes on his upper arm, stripes all the way down his left lower arm and he did not wear the yellow and black stripes on his shoulders or black plastic-white letters name tags the other NCOs wore. He had what I later learned was parachute strap sewn on over the chest on both sides of his fatigues, the one on his right lettered Kappas, Maurice M and the other USAF, 8 COIN, the one on his left side having what appeared to be an ice cream cone with wings and a star in a wreath over the top above the lettering. Instead of the butt can formed fatigue hat (butt cans were empty number ten tin cans, permanent party airmen and NCOs stretched their fatigue caps over these cans and sprayed them with starchy water giving the caps a distinctive shape) the other permanent party were wearing Kappas wore a black baseball cap. He never shouted, screamed or deposited spittle on any recruits. And I never saw him salute anyone.

What I did see was a ropy muscled older (to me anyway) man with a close-cropped sprinkle of red, black, and grey hair and soft brown eyes, I learned later that those eyes could change to something as dark and hard as obsidian. In modern terms I would say he could best be described as

15

looking like a cross between the actors Wes Studi and Morgan Freeman, only condensed and more intense. He rarely raised his voice, but when he wanted, his whisper could be heard clear across a parade ground.

Somehow, after I decided to follow up (and drag Beckstrom along with me) on the exciting possibility Bobbie Grimes was talking about I was not surprised to find myself in front of a desk in MSgt. Kappas' office. During my private interview with Kappas he told me to stand at ease and tell him about my shower room experience (it was customary for the barracks chiefs to take recruits into the shower rooms where there were no witnesses when they thought someone needed a tune up). He told me to give him the straight story and I knew bullshit was not going to fly. So, I told him that I had gone to the shower room because I had balked at what I considered an unreasonable request (chipping ice off the barracks steps with my bare hands) and the barracks chief decided I needed corporal punishment.

"That barracks chief was a big man, how did you come out of that shower room unscathed, Airman?" "I threw my fatigue jacket over his head and kicked him in the side of the knee and he fell down, Sergeant"" Did he get up?"" No, Sergeant"" Did you kick him again while he was down, Airman?"" No, Sergeant"" What would you have done if he got up?"" Run like hell, Sergeant". I wasn't sure but thought I caught a hint of a smile after that exchange.

I knew I had passed the interview when I got orders to transfer to a different barracks. Beckstrom got the same orders and we moved to a different area of the base where there were six barracks facing their own small parade ground. We soon dubbed this area "M&Ms Playground". This was where we met and got to know the rest of the staff in charge of our destinies: Major Bohannon, Captain Samuels, Technical Sergeant Grimes (he of the slick sleeves in the chow hall, easier to talk to potential recruits for the program if they didn't know he was a senior NCO), and a training cadre of ten staff sergeants.

What followed was twenty-one days and nights of Orientation and Evaluation: outside the barracks at 0400 hours for a rousing half hour of physical therapy (calisthenics), then a run to the chow hall, and our day was off to a start- no break in this early morning routine for rain, lightning or frost, luckily no tornados struck while we were there so we didn't have to find out if we would still have been at attention in front of the barracks at 0400 while the storm raged around us (probably). The day generally ended at 20 hundred with lights out at 22 hundred (10 pm). Two hours to shower, shine shoes, ready gear for the next day, write letters home or whatever. We had six hours or so to sleep unless there was a fire drill or other call-out in the middle of the night.

Orientation was about teaching us to do things the military way. We learned to march in step, roll clothes and pack a footlocker, polish floors, scrub toilets, make bunks, and wear uniforms the GI way.

We learned when and where to wear hats, salute, and say "yes, sir" or "yes, sergeant" at the proper times. We learned how to shave in cold water, arrange a hanging locker, and how to fall asleep anywhere. And that the guy from New Jersey (Blaske) liked to shine footwear and was really good at it.

Evaluation meant we ran everywhere. We ran to the chow hall, to our training classes, to the pool, to the firing range, to our testing appointments, resting by slowing to double time. Any time period that found any of us without an appointed place to be, found us doing laps around M&Ms' Playground.

We took IQ tests, aptitude tests, psychological tests, and language skills exams, and were tested for mental and physical dexterity. We ran obstacle courses (some of us found them fun), shuffled through the "burning airplane" fuselage, and crawled through the Gas House (two story building filled with tear gas). We were instructed in the use of .30 caliber carbines and had an introduction to close quarters battle (CQB) techniques. And there was always the pool where we swam laps on and under water, in swimsuits and fully clothed (boots and all), under the watchful eyes of our training cadre.

Some recruits took it all in stride, others took it all too seriously (I think), some got beyond their physical limits or found their nerves frayed. One asshole actually threatened to attack me in the barracks the night after I had bested his score on the rifle range. "Phil-From-Philly" heard his rant while I was still on KP duty (kitchen police, washing dishes in the chow hall) and took the big mouth out between the barracks for a "talk". Must have been some talk, the big mouth looked like he'd been in a train wreck the next morning, he moved out of our barracks shortly after. Never saw him again.

On Sundays we had a two-hour break to attend religious services. Choices were Catholic, Jewish, or Protestant. Animists, atheists, Buddhists, Hindis, Muslims, and others were invited to attend one of the services offered or "pray on their own" in barracks. Two hours of reflection, contemplation, napping (I think we all managed to get a little snooze in), or whatever and then back to training.

Call it gravity, or fate, or serendipity, we found each other; a few guys who were enjoying the challenges and looking forward to more. We found it natural to offer assistance (sometimes a funny quip or a good joke made it possible to get going) and urge one another along. We were forming the nucleus of a team without any exterior pressure or direction to do so. There was Beckstrom (the Norgahoovien), Morrison (Surf's Up), Blaske (Herbie the Jew), Marcotti (The Pasta Bender), Bowditch (Phil-From-Philly), Cerone (The Jokester) and myself (Dimples, damn I hated that nickname). We were already becoming a team.

We were never told that any of our tests or evaluations was pass or fail, never given goals to meet or be dropped from the program, never informed of the training cadres' criteria for selection. But at the end of the twenty-one days two of the six barracks facing M&Ms' Playground were empty.

And the training regimen was about to get tougher.

Chapter 3

Sandbaggers

It's probably not fair to say Marcotti was sand bagger. He just didn't talk. He didn't talk about home, why he had joined the Air Force, what he was doing before that, or any other personal matters. If asked a direct question he might answer, but he was just as likely to make a small noise in his throat and look away. Took us months to find out he had played college football for two years, loved to surf, and "his Mother was the best cook in the world". He looked like he had been carved rather than grown, and if he shaved at 0530 he looked like he needed to shave again at 0930. A solid block, but a solid block with a brain, he scored near the top of all of our scholastic exams. Because he was so solid looking and when he did speak used a measured cadence it was easy to think he would be slow in movement. Until he ran, he could reach full speed in three strides and leave all of us behind in a cloud of dust and maintain a blazing pace all day. If his mother was the best cook in the world he was following in a close second place, keeping the little kitchen in our off-duty house smelling like an Italian bakery. And he could sing. I had never been exposed to opera and could not understand Italian but the warmth of his mellow tenor filling the rooms in "The House With The Blue Fence" made it even more of a home for all of us. I cannot listen to a Pavarotti recording without thinking of Marcotti.

Blaske on the other hand was a sand bagger of a subtle sort, always putting forth just the effort he needed to expend and conserving his energy. If he needed to run a mile in six minutes flat, he would run it in six minutes flat, no quicker and no slower, with or without full pack and web gear. He never pushed for first place (the rest of us were always trying to best each other, every obstacle course was a race, going to the chow hall was a race) and was always happy to finish exactly in the middle of the pack. A little pudgy when we first met him he had "solidified" in just a few weeks of training. So, though he never pushed to stand out he was always there where and when we needed him to be; boat turning over in the surf? Blaske was there to steady it, somebody missing an important piece of gear? Blaske had an extra. The one area where he did stand out was neatness, he was always sharp of creases and clean shaven. He was the first of us to get his uniforms tailored, including his fatigues.

 For some reason Blaske loved to shine boots and shoes, he would first ignite the polish and melt the top layer, then apply the still hot polish, followed by a spit shine with a damp cloth, and end with a pass with a cotton swab dipped in alcohol. Wonderful shine and he volunteered to do all of our "inspection boots and shoes" (that we never wore, if you wore them the shine would split).

And he had a secret. Blaske loved to laugh; he just didn't want anybody to know he was doing it. I learned to identify certain "tells" when he found things funny and Cerone and I would make bets about which of us would be first to make him laugh out loud. Usually had to oil him up with a little booze first and that didn't always work. His other secret wasn't a secret-he loved to be in the middle of the Blue Team surrounded by his comrades in the field, in the barracks, on pass, or wherever we happened to be.

The term "easy grace" might have been invented to describe Samuels but despite the ability he had to make anyone feel at ease and the openness he seemed to radiate we all knew there was something more to him than was visible, Kappas of course knew more but he wasn't sharing. Raised on a ranch in Montana (might have been Wyoming) he joined the Marines as he said, "just to piss off his father", who was a rancher and politician of some sort. He never saw any action in the Corps but during his tour on Okinawa developed a passion for Karate. After two years in the Marines he took an early-out to attend state college then went to graduate school at Yale where he established a lot of useful connections (we suspected he was recruited into the CIA or some other government agency). Despite his easy demeanor, Samuels could be a tough customer on the playground or in a dark alley and he seemed to have political and Pentagon connections to rival Major Bohannon's.

Samuels told us that after graduate school he wasn't quite ready to enter the business world and he joined the Air Force expecting to go into flight training. After he was in training the Air Force discovered some minor physical problem that disqualified him for pilot school. He told us it was because, "his dick was too big, wouldn't fit into the relief tube pilots had to use". Definitely a sand bagger.

Hayes was a grinning, smirking, no-doubt-about-it class one-a sandbagger and the most obnoxious kind of braggart; he bragged by doing. If someone was bench pressing 200 lbs. he would get on the next bench and press 210 lbs., and so on until the other person hit their limit, then he would add 10 lbs. to whatever that number was and press with a smirk on his face. If someone threw a double gainer off the diving platform Hayes would throw a double with a full twist, always just besting whatever had gone before. Then he would raise a pinky finger and say, "Gotcha'" or "That's One", a silly habit we all picked up and imitated whenever we thought we had done something cool.

He was also the most gifted natural athlete I've ever seen and freakishly strong, full of surprises. On one occasion a couple of us were riding a shuttle bus and were amazed to see him passing the bus on an old, rusty English bicycle he had found somewhere, and it wasn't just that he was going faster than the bus – he was riding the thing on the back wheel like a unicycle, smirk in plain view. Until he had broken an instructors' arm during an un-armed defense class we hadn't found out he had lived with an older brother stationed in Japan for four years and had started his studies of the martial arts at the Kodakan Judo Institute, sometimes boarding at the school for weeks at a time.

Hayes had a mean streak and like a cat liked to play with his "mouse", making it think it had a chance at whatever competition he was in, then overwhelming and dominating the "mouse". It was difficult keeping him out of fights off base (we weren't always successful) because he just didn't look all that bad ass and would usually convince his target(s) that they would easily roll over him. Luckily, he never seriously maimed anyone during these escapades, content to show domination. I never saw him even close to losing an encounter or even getting hurt, with the exception of the time that Kappas gave him a spanking, after that he called Kappas "Sgt. Smoke and Iron"; "Smoke when you try to hit or grapple with him, Iron when he touches you". I've never known why he decided to hang with us or why he decided I was his good luck charm.

Cerone, on the other hand looked like just what he seemed to be, an always grinning, happy party animal with no thoughts about tomorrow, or was he? He could show a dark side sometimes. When he met Bill Young in Thailand the two of them hit it off immediately, Kappas said it was because "either one of them would fuck a rope if they thought there was a snake in it". But he was very careful to mind Kappas' proscription against getting too friendly with any of the mountain tribe girls, "fool with one of them and you have a wife".

We spent a lot of time together getting into mischief, playing practical jokes, and keeping off-duty times interesting. Sgt. Johnny Sorenson called us "the piss ants" and Kappas said we were like twin otters; we were playful, liked the water, and could bite. A consummate gambler, he "owned" company clerks and other admin people wherever we stayed more than a week or two. We trained on the same electronics and weapons systems and along the way developed our own shorthand language. In the field I always could "feel" just where Cerone was, an ESP like communication, or maybe it was just that we had learned to think alike with all the time we spent together.

But I learned to be a little afraid of Cerone as time passed and I realized that under the toothy grin and smiling eyes there lay a coldly efficient killing machine. Still, I would rather be in the shit with him than with anyone else on our team.

Beckstrom and Morrison were both just what one might expect of a Minnesota farm boy and a California doctors' son.

 Beckstrom was tall, blond and with clear blue eyes and a gait like he was still walking over plowed rows in the fields. He had grown up with the solid belief that people, all people, were basically good, nature benevolent, and the world wonderful; he was immune to Hayes's pessimism and sparks of paranoia. A likeable guy, and a good listener he was the only one among us who attended Sunday services whenever they were available. He with his Lutheranism and Baphang with his Cao Dai Universalism made for some interesting late-night conversations. He was also the only one of us who had no problems at home, he had joined the Air Force to see a bit of the world before settling down with a local girl and helping to run his family's farm.

Morrison was probably the more sophisticated member of our group, with a slightly aloof air (that I finally decided hid a sort of shyness). As he said, "he had been born with a silver spoon in his mouth and firmly intended to keep it there". I got a hint at why he had joined the service when I went on a four-day pass with him to his parents' house in California. His doctor dad and socialite mom were just too busy to spend any time with him, and his boyhood room had been turned into a library. He smiled a lot but there was always a serious edge to him. Nobody was surprised when he focused on field medicine and later provided medical aid to indigenous people wherever we went. But he could display an awesome physical and mental toughness, once marching ten miles with a broken blister turned to open, bloody sore without saying a word to any of us (I thought that was a dumbass thing to do and told him so).

At five feet six inches and one hundred thirty-five pounds I was much stronger than I looked when I went to boot camp (I grew three inches in the next two years but could only put on twenty more pounds) and had a stubborn streak (my mother would call it determination) that made me keep going when most of the bigger guys had given up. A "cute" guy with curly red blond hair and a dimple I was always being underestimated mentally and physically, which suited me just fine. Sooner or later in whatever group I found myself I would become a "ringleader" doing something I call "driving from the back of the bus".

Being alone in the woods had always given me pleasure and I had trained myself to be comfortable in or under water, swimming the Illinois River north of Peoria with its' currents, undertows, snags and barge traffic, several times while fully clad, and was a good marksman before I went in service. Blessed with unusually good night vision and reflexes I carefully hid the fact that I had a fierce temper and enjoyed fighting, and that I had a "special" way of dealing with fear. I guess I was a sandbagger too.

Chapter 4

Nellis Days Vegas Nights

Las Vegas was a different place in the late 1950s and early 1960s, there was a lot more space between the base and town and open desert between the casinos on the Strip. Downtown tourists and gamblers wore Levi's and Bermuda shorts, Strip tourists and gamblers dressed up; men wore suits, sport coats and ties and the ladies wore dresses and gowns, there was a glamorous air about being in a casino or club on the Strip. There were fewer slot machines and more, free, lounge shows featuring people we heard on the radio.

These were Sinatra and the Rat Pack days on the Strip in Las Vegas and the Hacienda Hotel was way, way out of town toward LA, way out in the desert by the airport.

People still traveled by rail to Vegas and there was a nice depot at the end of Fremont Street that we traveled through often on our comings and goings. Exit the train station and a half a block down Fremont was Roses' bar, usually our first stop in town, even if we had come in by civilian airline or military transport. Roses' was our decompression zone, a real bar as opposed to a miniature casino, a place of dark wood, pickled eggs, roast beef sandwiches and drinks poured with a generous hand; this was where we shook off the effects of moving from one unreal environment to another. In a matter of no time we could be transported from a place where death or dismemberment often walked all around us to a place where people gambled, drank and partied like there were no such things as jobs and mortgages, both twisted realities with no clear tomorrows.

Further down Fremont was Benny Binion's Horseshoe Club, our favorite gambling spot Downtown. On more than one occasion Benny noticed that we had had a bit too much to drink and were losing too much money on his tables and would comp us a room upstairs to sleep, sometimes throwing in a couple of breakfast chits for good measure. Benny was, at least as it concerned us, good to the GIs that came into his casino and I always remember him with a huge amount of respect. He particularly liked Cerone (who didn't?) and was the only person we met who ever commented on the fact that after an absence of some months we would all show up at his club hollow eyed and painfully thin; he commented but never asked how or why we got that way.

Nellis Air Force Base just to the northeast of Las Vegas would be our nominal permanent party station for the years that we were in 8th COIN. It must have been a nightmare for some clerk to put us on the Base rolls, take us off every time we were sheep dipped and went TDY (Temporary Duty) for training or overseas and then re-enroll us when we returned. At Nellis we were seconded to the 7th Armament and Electronics Squadron in the Tactical Air Command and subject to a different set of command and rules than we operated under in the field. The duality of our command structure was somewhat confusing and during any absence of Major Bohannon, Captain Samuels, and MSgt Kappas the First Sergeant of the 7th A&E acted as though he believed we "belonged" to him, the Colonel in charge of the squadron could care less (he had no "need to know") and pretty much ignored us, just signing any orders the squadron clerk put in front of him or countersigning orders from the PEO or TAC Command.

We were assigned our own barracks, old two story open bay wooden buildings with heaters that never worked in winter and a swamp cooler on each floor that could almost keep the people within ten feet of them cool. I built an unsanctioned room at one end of the ground floor of one of the buildings and placed a refrigerator (and later telephone exchange equipment) under the stairs next to my bunk. I also made a small late-night raid on the BOQ (Bachelor Officers Quarters) and acquired a Hollywood size bed and mattress with hanging locker and nightstand to go with them and a window model ac unit that the base engineers were happy to install for me (thanks Floyd). My private room was hidden in plain sight; during barracks inspection visits the entire time I was there no one ever attempted to open the padlock on my enclosure or ask what was inside, even during visits with the 7th A&E's asshole First Sergeant Knight. These barracks across from the classified aircraft hangars remained our permanent on base quarters at Nellis and would be locked up and guarded whenever we were away training or deployed on TDY.

One end of one of the classified hangars was assigned to us and we had our own parachute loft, riggers, equipment maintenance shop and armorer stationed there with a booth at the entrance permanently manned by armed APs. As a suitcase outfit we always had ready-bags packed with military and civilian gear for different climes standing by, these bags were packed with Desert, Temperate, Tropical, and Arctic clothing and equipment ready for immediate deployment and were stowed in the hangar along with our weapons. This was our armorer Zero's domain and no one entered without his okay, even the Base Commander respected the need for security and did not enter without giving prior notice.

At Nellis we attended classes on various electronics systems, worked on aircraft on the flight line or worked in the electronics shops, and participated in development and training exercises at the Indian Springs Gunnery Range, home of the Red Flag aircraft gunnery and bombing training and intra-service competition courses. We practiced at small arms and CQB once a week or more in our hangar "to keep our hands in" as the saying goes. I joined the on base Aero Club for flight instruction in L7s and AT6s and worked on my USAFI (United States Armed Forces Institute) college level correspondence courses in my down time; I carried those grey bound books all over the States and SEA (South East Asia).

Within a week of arriving at Nellis Cerone and I had found a little two-bedroom house for rent just down the hill from Fremont Street near an intersection called Five Points where Las Vegas and North Las Vegas met. The house was on a side street at the side of a mobile home park with a pool we would be allowed to use and was around the corner from the Triumph motorcycle dealer, a twenty-four-hour coffee and donut shop, and a small casino. There were package liquor and grocery stores a few blocks away. Great location for our off-base central for all the time we were stationed at Nellis. We rented the place and with the landlord's permission painted the fence and gate in front to make it easy for our visitors to find the "House With The Blue Fence".

Beckstrom, Cerone and I were having a late-night snack at a deli located in the base of the old Landmark Tower that at the time was about two blocks off the Strip behind the Tropicana when we met the Den Mothers. They were five English lassies who had signed four-year contracts to come to the states and work as showgirls at the Trop and had just finished the last show of the night; the next day was a Sunday and their day off and we volunteered to drive them to a resort about an hour and a half away where there were hot springs, a big pool and a nice bar where they served lemonade and iced tea as well as alcoholic beverages.

I guess we were a welcome relief from the usual hustlers in Vegas and we became regular escorts for the girls, whoever was off duty at the same time the girls were not at work would pick them up in our "team car" (1954 Olds convertible) and squire them around the town or take them to the grocers or drycleaners or wherever. What a contrast between their work personas and the domestic creatures they were when not at work; they would go from glamorous figures strutting onstage in mini bikini bottoms, lots of makeup, false eyelashes, pearls and jewels and outrageous headdresses to girls in jeans or housecoats, hair in curlers and no makeup sitting around knitting or crocheting while something was cooking in the kitchen. They made frequent visits to the "House With The Blue Fence" and would usually arrive with baskets of food; sometimes fresh scones and pots of orange marmalade (still my favorite) or meat pies right from their oven and added a welcome air of "home" when they were around. Four peaches and cream complexioned ladies with reddish blond hair and one violet eyed dark-haired Scots beauty.

None of our group was married and we didn't rate separate rats (separate rations, an allowance for off base housing and meals) but we did have permanent passes for days or nights we weren't training or on duty and were free to come and go from our day jobs at will. Money was sometimes a bit of a problem but Cerone and I both worked part time jobs when our schedules allowed and everyone chipped in, including our visitors. If we were coming up short Cerone could usually be counted on to make up the difference with his gambling skills.

One of the nights Cerone was gambling might have had disastrous results if it weren't for good luck and the familiarity we had established with some pit bosses and dealers. We had a pattern that had become a "known" in the Red Garter (the casino around the corner from the house); Cerone would play cards and I would have a few drinks, dance with the ladies and maybe have some steak and eggs while he played, I wasn't much into gambling myself. Periodically I would visit the table where he was playing and pull a stack or two of his chips off the table, guaranteeing that we would have made some money by the end of the night.

On this particular night we left around one am and walked around to the house where I emptied my jacket pockets of their stash of chips and started counting, reaching $1100 before noticing Cerone looking at me with a strained face. Reacting to his expression I asked what was up and he replied, "I didn't win a decent pot all night. Those weren't my chips". Jeeezus! I had been raking off someone else's chips all night. The pit bosses, dealers and other players were so used to our routine (the players might have been a little drunk) that no one realized what I was doing. If I had been caught the consequences would almost certainly been dire, these were still mob days in Vegas!

Eventually Hayes got a Triumph TR6 motorcycle, I had already traded for one when I was at Lowry, and after "my buddy" Floyd made some modifications to the bikes we spent a lot of off duty hours on mountain fire trails and riding across the desert. The bikes were street legal and we often carried passengers, always ladies (against the laws of nature to have four nuts on two wheels), on our desert excursions or around town. Hayes was a superb rider and gave me a lot of useful tips on the bikes.

We met a lot of interesting people off base at Nellis including Airman 1st Class (formerly Technical Sergeant) Floyd. There was Mr. Sullivan, retired Marine, piano player, and (very patient) landlord at the little house we rented, and the five girls from England who became our "Den Mothers". There was also the beautiful girl who worked in the donut shop on the corner near the house (Hayes became totally smitten), and a number of bartenders, card dealers, and locals (mostly girls, including two future ex-wives) that we became acquainted with in Las Vegas. But we were proscribed from going into detail about our training or later talking about any of our TDY experiences with anyone outside 8th COIN, in a way creating a barrier between us and people "on the outside". As time went by in the next months and years we developed a stronger and stronger "us and them" mentality, we shared secrets that our friends and relatives, wives, mothers, girlfriends and fellow GIs would never know.

And while the house gave us all some sense of "normalcy", there were always the weapons and extra garrison bags waiting in our hangar on base.

Chapter 5

Floyd

It was a Friday night early in our assignment to Nellis Air Force Base and I would have duty the next night so I intended to stay close to Base and have an early evening before going to sleep in our barracks. Las Vegas beckoned but I didn't want to make a late night of it and none of my buddies had passes so I just went to the nearest bar a mile or so toward town from the main gate expecting to shoot a couple of games of pool and have two or three beers before going back to the barracks.

The bar was pretty typical of bars near gates on military posts all over the world, dark, dimly lit and smelling of malt and hops, with a twinge of human sweat and maybe a hint of vomit and urine detectable to a sensitive nose. There was a lady bartender who really needed to wear more clothes, a small empty dance floor, a jukebox, and three coin-operated three quarter sized pool tables. They didn't serve Coors so I ordered a Bud' and checked out the pool tables. On one of the tables was a tall, as in really tall, NBA tall black man shooting a very good stick.

I put a quarter on the rail of the table he was playing on and shot a couple of ho hum games on another table while I waited my turn to play against the tall guy. The handful of people in the place was all lined up to try him and I would have some time before my turn. It didn't take an acute observer to see that this guy was not drinking because he was enjoying the taste of his shots and beer, he was power drinking, a man whose goal was to get soundly drunk in a hurry. His pool game was still hanging in there and he kept control of the table until it was my turn to challenge him. I had more luck than skill at the game but luck was all I needed to beat him because the booze caught up and his ability to play took a huge dive when it was my turn to play.

He paid me the dollar bet and insisted I sit down and have a drink with him, he was too big to refuse and I was curious so I sat with him and had

31

more than a drink. Midnight came and I needed to get back to base, my drinking companion was on the verge of passing out and no one in the honky tonk seemed to be with him. I was still young and new enough to the service to believe that all GIs should take care of one another so I had the bartender call a cab to take us the short hop back to the base, I still had cash, my drinking buddy had insisted on buying all our rounds.

The cabby, grumpy over the short fare dumped us in front of the gate and drove off. Now we had a problem, my very large friend had passed out in the cab and was sitting on the curb outside the gate unable to stand. We were beginning to get too much attention from the APs (Air Police) manning the gate and needed to get on base and out of sight soon. I took my "friends" ID card out of his shirt pocket and holding his ID card and my own between my teeth tipped him over my shoulder stood with him in a fireman's' carry and struggled to the gate with his long body folded in half over my shoulder dragging his feet and hands as I went. Damn it was a long haul!

At the gate the APs couldn't decide to let us through or arrest us for drunkenness. I protested that I was not drunk (I thought I wasn't) and I would get my burden to his barracks. The APs challenged me with the simple question, "What's your buddy's name?" and I was stumped, we hadn't exchanged names at the bar, or if we had I didn't remember it. A deep voice went off from somewhere south of my knees, "I'm his buddy Floyd" and the APs laughed and waved us through the gate. I realized later that the APs knew Floyd, everybody on the base knew Floyd.

He mumbled the number of his barracks and I somehow got him on the shuttle bus, to his barracks and inside where I left him slumped on a wall just inside the building.

The Air Force was officially integrated at the time but people still formed in racial groups, for the most part the whites hung with whites, the blacks hung with blacks and so on. We hadn't seen it ourselves but had heard that occasionally racial tensions would surface so while Beckstrom, Blaske and I were at the chow hall nearest our barracks at noon the day after my pool playing evening out they were uneasy when our table was approached by a one very large and four not very small black airmen. The large man with the big teeth and dark patches on his fatigues where his rank should have been pulled up a chair and sitting next to me introduced himself to the table, "it's okay I'm his buddy Floyd" and smiled a huge shit-eating grin.

The city of Las Vegas was still divided along black and white lines, not including the Indian Reservations downtown and to the north of town, with Downtown and the Strip predominantly white and North Las Vegas predominantly black. Even non-white headliners at the Strip hotels and casinos stayed in hotels in North Las Vegas. The best after-hours music and entertainment was usually to be found on the north side of Five Points, a scary place for young white airmen in those days, but with Floyd as part of our afterhours club hopping group a lot of doors were opened to us that might have been closed (or even dangerous to go through) and we got to meet people like Keely Smith (what a beautiful, nice, talented woman) and other "stars". Everywhere we went on the north side people knew Floyd but he still insisted on introducing himself to everyone by nodding in my direction and saying," I'm his buddy Floyd", I guess out of an odd sense of humor, and then smile with all his big teeth showing.

Floyd was genius with machinery of any kind and was the lead man in the engine shop at Nellis, good with two stroke, four stroke, turbine, pure jet, or any other kind of engine, he had made rank fast and by the middle of his second tour was a Technical Sergeant maintaining engines for aircraft assigned to "The Mad Majors' (Maj. John Boyd)" Fighter Weapons School. Just before Major Boyd left to attend War College Floyd had been recommended to be a crew chief on one of the aircraft flown by the Air Force Aerial Demonstration Team, the Thunderbirds, and was excited at the thought of traveling the world with them. He would be "the man" on a very important plane, rank would come and he would be sure of a good career in the Air Force. Rejection after the selection process hit him hard; he knew he was a better mechanic and that he understood all the F100 systems far better than the candidates that were picked. His morale plummeted and he hit the booze hard, showing up at the engine shop drunk, hung over or both and pushing his NCOIC (NCO in Charge) into having to demote him. I met him when he was near the bottom of this spiral downward.

He was rescued, if that is the word, by someone we all got to know in the future, "Captain Joe". The captain was an acolyte of Major Boyd and had replaced him as head instructor at the Fighter Weapons School and had even adapted his mentor's habit of calling everyone who was not a yank and bank fighter pilot a "puke" as in "bus driving puke" for transport pilots, "mud pukes" for ground forces, and "formation pukes" for the Thunderbirds. When he heard that Floyd had missed the cut with the Thunderbirds and that Floyd was struggling with some bad behavior Captain Joe called the paint shop and had a line added after his name on the side of his assigned aircraft. The line read, "Crew Chief Sgt. Floyd Withers". He called Floyd into the Fighter Wing office and stood him at attention while some new rules of conduct were being explained; Captain Joe's plane now "belonged" to Floyd and Floyd would keep it the best in the fleet or find himself in the stockade. It would take some time to get his rank back, but that's the breaks. Take it or leave it. Of course, Floyd took it; he was now crew chief for the best pilot in the best fighter squadron in the world.

Floyd was a good friend to Team Blue, Team Green, and Team Orange, the three teams that rotated in and out of S.E. Asia, and made sure all our vehicles and equipment, military and private, got taken care of in the shops at Nellis. Any problems with anything mechanical and he would pick up the phone and connect us to the "right guy". Hayes and I both had Triumph TR6 motorcycles and Floyd modified both to have longer suspension stroke, better air cleaners, flat fenders, skid plates, and capacitor discharge systems for the ignition. He turned our bikes into state-of-the art desert machines, even porting and polishing the intake and exhaust on both bikes.

We lost contact for a time when the captain, now a major, was TDY out of Nellis and took Floyd with him, but had a happy reunion when he appeared on the scene at An Lac to make emergency repairs to a downed bird we were watching over. He was at Bien Hoa and Pleiku training Vietnamese mechanics and would be getting assigned to Udorn in Thailand when an F100 squadron came over to be stationed there.

Some of what I knew about Floyd came from stories around the base; some came from Captain Joe who said that "that formation flying puke wouldn't accept Floyd because he was afraid of the way he looked. Chicken shit puke left me with the best crew chief on the base, dumbass." And other info came directly from things Floyd told me.

Already tall at twelve years old Floyd was not going to be overlooked by the gangs in his neighborhood and was "recruited" by the Lords of Harlem under the threat of bodily harm to him and his mother if he didn't join. There were other reasons to join, the gang offered girls, money, and protection on the streets, as part of The Lords of Harlem he would be "somebody". He had the usual juvenile assignments of carrying weapons and drugs and keeping watch for rival gang incursions into the gang's territory until his mechanical skills were noticed and he was put into a chop shop dismantling stolen cars by the time he was fourteen. As he grew taller and stronger he earned a reputation as a fierce fighter and by eighteen was the warlord for the gang, planning raids on rivals and strategizing defense for the territory. Somehow, at his mother's insistence he managed to finish high school and was well aware there were no gang members alive and over twenty-five, he wanted to find a way out of the gang but was trapped; "blood in, blood out", the gang would not allow him to quit.

His chance came when he was arrested during a street fight (the fight that left him with a jagged scar on the cheek) and was given a choice by a judge of "join the military or jail time" and recommended to the Marines. He joined the Air Force instead and lucked out with an assignment to engine school, just where he wanted to be.

Chapter 6

Training Was A Hoot Part 2

Bohannon, Samuels and Kappas had a real challenge; there was a strong pressure on them to supply "technicians" immediately or risk losing support and funding. And while other services' special forces, special operators, and other elite units were going the publicity and media route to garner support, they believed that shadow forces need to stay in the shadows.

The band-aid solution was to break up their training cadre into field units and put them into operation with other services in South America and Southeast Asia, but that meant they would be left with no seasoned, war dog training staff. They had nine months to train and prepare to field at least four ten-man teams of operators for the 8th Counter Insurgency Study Group and conventional training methods were not going to work for that timeframe.

The answer was, I believe, ingenious; wherever possible they would have other units and other services provide the training staff and facilities required to train to the profile they had decided was optimal. And they would have their airmen trained in a parallel rather than linear fashion; they would design the training regimen so that there would be some courses that all the airmen would take and other courses that split the groups into specialties that attendees of these various classes would bring back and train their compatriots on.

The profile they had developed described certain physical characteristics in terms of athleticism, endurance, and height and weight, with some exceptions allowed – I was an inch too short, and Bowditch, Hayes, and Beckstrom were an inch too tall. But more important to the profile were certain psychological and personality traits; something Kappas called Survivability Quotient (SQ).

Kappas did not want to produce "robots, bad-asses, or heroes". He wanted people who could learn technical skills, gather Intel, provide training to indigenous peoples, influence the outcome of certain situations while remaining in the background, and survive under extreme conditions. So, a major (perhaps the major) component of our training was to stay hidden or unnoticed; we learned to stay hidden in snow, desert sand, jungle, forest, and on the local street corner.

We were all to be electronics technicians (with varying specialties), jump qualified, scuba qualified, familiar with small arms, practitioners of unarmed defense systems, and graduates of a list of survival schools. Some would get training as land navigators, field medics, armorers, forward air controllers, air traffic controllers, fire control systems technicians (this has nothing to do with fires, it refers to the electro-mechanical systems that manage gun sight and bombing systems), demolition men, linguists, and in other fields as needed.

Under the plan, if the three of them could pull the proper strings and take advantage of their networks, training would be provided along these lines: Air Force and Army jump schools, Navy dive school, Army and Marine small arms training, Army small unit tactics, Air Force and other survival schools (Kappas had some nice surprises waiting for us with this one), Air Force electronics schools, Air Force language schools, in-unit for CQB (close quarter battle), and so on.

And Kappas added another unusual element to the training and assembly of the new unit; he and his training cadre had carefully selected and recruited candidates for the program; then he allowed teams to begin to assemble themselves, moving or adding people to each team to balance the whole. This was how I was able to stay teamed up with Beckstrom, Morrison, Blaske, Marcotti, Bowditch and Cerone.

Our first stop after Lackland was Lowry AFB (near Denver, Colo.) where we all started learning basic electronics and split into study groups for our various other courses of study and/or training. This was also where we were required to sign certain secrecy documents if we were to go forward with our training to enter 8th COIN. A few people opted out at this point.

Major Bohannon (he of the red Cadillac convertible and endless stream of beautiful women) traveled back and forth to the Pentagon where he waged a fierce (we were told) battle to keep our program alive and well. Captain Samuels worked his political connections (and CIA link?) and First Sergeant Kappas worked all those angles and more. They were already engaged in a war of sorts but got some help and relief when an up and coming Army Colonel joined forces with them in support of the program.

Lowry was hectic and brain-straining with our accelerated courses but the physical demands were lightened up. We could sleep in a little longer, PT and CQB was at 0600 followed by a couple of sprints around our parade ground (free of packs) and a one mile run to breakfast. After that we were on our own to get to our classes during the day with a formation at 1800 where duty assignments were handed out and other information disseminated. Weekends were generally free time and weekend passes usually available. We did notice that we were the only students who had morning and afternoon classes with a Captain and First Sergeant doing PT, CQB and running with them.

We were rotated out of the classroom schedules in groups of forty for two weeks of training at an Air Force Base in Arizona where we attended jump school with newly developed, steerable parachutes. Much better equipment than the T-10D and MC1D models the Army was using (we learned about them later). This was a hoot!

First we spent endless hours learning how to fall. Then we jumped from platforms with harnesses on and learned how to fall all over again and the proper body positions to use in the air. We learned to rig and pack our own 'chutes, main and reserve.

Pre-dawn one morning found me climbing out the door of a light aircraft to stand on a small platform attached to the landing gear and holding on to a hoop over the door with one hand and the wing strut with the other facing into the prop wash. I stepped back on signal from the jumpmaster and placed my hands on my chest, tipping forward to a horizontal position as I fell. The static line looped out, there was a jerk pulling me back vertical, and a lovely silken canopy opened above me. Somewhere below me I could hear a bird calling over the sound of the canopy disturbing the air. I remembered to keep my feet together, knees flexed, and hands on my risers as I made contact with the ground. Three static line jumps and we graduated to free fall.

After we demonstrated we could stay stable in free fall (some never made it past this point) we got to jump with web gear and sally (as in sally forth) packs. This was a washout point for several people who could not manage to stabilize with gear on. And this is where we parted company with Bowditch; he twisted as he landed on his last jump and slammed his hip into a rock suffering enough damage that he was not able to return to the program.

But we still weren't jump qualified! We hadn't gone through a regular course of instruction as per requirements for the badge; we would have to make it up later. So here we were, free fall parachutists before we ever sat on a stick (line of parachutists waiting to jump with static lines, the airborne way).

No matter, Kappas didn't give a rats' ass and neither did we, we had the knowledge and the tool.

Lowry days were pretty good duty since our weekends were mostly free time and we could go into Denver, The Fireside (3.2 bar) on Colfax was a favored spot to drink, meet young ladies, and dance. And the mountains were right there to play in. Cerone and I bought a 1930s something Chevy four door sedan that became the "company car" for exploration and excursions about the countryside. This guy Hayes from another barracks sort of invited himself along on some of our excursions but what the hell, we could always use one more contributor to the gas fund and there were plenty of good times to go around.

We had graduated from Basic Electronics and were moving into studying specific systems. Cerone and I were in a class on Fire Control Systems for fighter/bomber aircraft and the rest of our crew were off learning other systems when Kappas announced an interruption to our classes and sprung his first "spring surprise".

The first batch of forty of us, including Beckstrom and myself (front of the alphabet), were off for three weeks of training at the US Army Pathfinder School at Ft Bragg. We attended classes in land navigation (my favorite class), learned how to clear and manage both day and night landing zones, how to attach cargo slings to helicopters, learned the Army versions of air traffic control and forward air control, and made three static line jumps from five hundred feet – the paratrooper way. Captain Samuels had graduated from the class previously but came along to do it all again with us. We could finally wear jump pins on our piss cutters (flat hat in a belt, peaked at both ends when worn). We got the maroon berets later.

But we still had two more barriers to clear before we could wear the Pathfinder Patch; what was then called "interrogation resistance" and run an escape and evasion course successfully. I won't share the details of the interrogation resistance training except to say, "I never want to do that again." The escape and evasion, or hares and hounds, course was where Blaske revealed his deep thinking, out-of-the-box nature.

We were flown to Hill AFB, Utah where we rested overnight, got briefed and assembled our gear for a three to six-day trek somewhere undisclosed to us. The location could be desert, swamp, rain forest, or any climate and topography in North America. We were allowed to pack anything that would fit into an Alice Pack and were expected to pick our own universal survival equipment. Rations for eight meals would be allowed, other than that we were to live off the land for up to one week. We would be given maps (one each) of a drop zone and surrounding area while in the air to our destination where we would parachute in and find our way out in small groups. And we were each issued a small survival radio tuned to an aviation frequency which was to be used only in the case of emergency.

We would be allowed a two-hour head start, after that time was up instructors could drop in behind us and give chase (some did) or instructors would lie in ambush for us (some did) and anyone caught would have to return to the drop zone and start over. There would be a one-half mile diameter "free zone" around the flag pole at our destination, make it into that zone and you had passed. Caught three times and you would fail the course – no Pathfinder Badge for you.

Blaske had quietly spent some time with the maintenance crews responsible for the aircraft flying us to the drop zone and had learned our destination. The sly dog kept the information to himself, and so while the rest of us were packing shelter halves, camouflage suits, fish hooks and the like, Blaske was packing civilian clothes, a carefully rolled up set of fatigues, cash, and a road map of the state of Washington.

We dropped into a high meadow near a pass in the Cascades National Park in Washington State. We had been supplied with topo maps showing our drop zone and our destination which was a small airport called Stehekin where a temporary tent city, Camp Henry, was set up for the exercise. The terrain was a little difficult but the terrain and the distance didn't present any real problems. The challenge was going to be avoiding the instructors who knew the area and were determined to "capture" as many of us as they could. It was summer in the rain forest, which meant warm in the day and cold at night, and wet both day and night. Plenty of fresh water available, plants to munch on, grubs in downed logs for an occasional snack, what else could we want on our camping trip? Well, a fire for one thing, but that could quickly give away our positions.

We had the option of deciding how many would stay in a pack, we could try to work our way out as a team, paired up, as individuals, whatever we decided on the spot. We choose to move in twos and threes and no one really noticed that after we had secured our chutes for recovery later, Blaske was not among us. Everyone assumed he had gone off with another set.

The terrain offered some advantages and some problems. The valleys were pretty easy going with not too much dense undergrowth or deadfall to cross. Problem was that the lay of the land would tend to funnel trekkers into certain areas if they were not paying close attention – great for our stalkers. And there were several areas of bare rock that would have to be crossed, great for not leaving footprints but exposed to view from a distance.

Beckstrom and I had packed civilian hiking shorts and jackets and had funny hats to wear; we also had grey laundry bags to disguise our Alice Packs. To anyone glassing us from any distance we might look like a couple of civilian hikers.

Our plan was simple, get off the map. We quickly stowed our 'chutes, humped our gear and started double timing for a high mountain pass to the west of our position, we wanted to be high enough to be out of sight of anyone with field glasses at the drop zone in less than the two-hour head start we had. We were over the pass just before twilight and edged carefully down into the tree line to find a place to hunker down for the night. Dawn found us running west to the next ridgeline and after clearing the second ridge we were "off the map" and turned to the south. Cold, wet, hungry and tired we found a stone overhang where we risked a fire the second night and made ourselves as comfortable as we could.

Next day we saw a bear across a draw but he didn't throw stones at us so we didn't throw any at him, did make us feel uneasy and we kept a good watch that night. The rain that started around midnight put out our small fire and didn't help at all.

After running hard the fourth day we reckoned we were far enough south to get back on the map, and crossed a ridge back to the east, too tired to go for another crossing we made a dry (no fire) camp and slept a hungry sleep. Now we were hoping the bear would show up so we could club him to death and eat him. Next day we struck a road at a position that our map and navigation said was south of the airport and dragged our footsore, tired asses to the flagpole an hour or so before dusk.

Blaske was there to greet us, all clean-shaven and spiffy, and although he was keeping a straight face I knew the bastard was laughing inside. What was the joke?

And where was Blaske all the time we were running and hiding so cold and miserable and blisters forming on our feet? In a nice cozy tourist cabin, that's where.

While the rest of us dumb bastards were hauling ass east, west, and south Blaske had hiked five miles or so north to a highway and hitchhiked east to a small town with tourist cabins and a grass strip airport. He enjoyed a couple of days of dining in the café, sleeping on clean sheets and read a good book while the rest of us were shivering and hungry in the woods. On the third day he hired the pilot of a small airplane to drop him at Stehekin Field and arrived there freshly shaven and in clean pressed fatigues.

He hung out there with the airborne guys and greeted us all as we came in with a raised pinky finger and one word, "Gotcha'".

And what was Kappas' reaction to Blaske's sneaky trick?" He's the first one of you boys to get the fighter pilots' credo: if you ain't cheatin', you ain't tryin'!" But Blaske didn't get off scot free, Kappas sent him out with the instructors to round up stragglers at the end of the exercise and he didn't get to shave for three days and got his fatigues all muddy.

Well at least now we were entitled to the little patch with the winged torch. We were United States Air Force Pathfinders.

And Blaske had become the root of a legend, the story of his "Foxing" the Hares in a Hare and Hound exercise made the rounds until people who never knew his name, or even what Service he was in, repeated the story over and over ("I knew a guy who knew a guy who knew the guy") and it became a part of military lore.

Chapter 7

Three Guys

"Buster"

Blaske may have been the bravest of us, a thoughtful forward-looking guy he might have been able to beat Cerone at cards or chess if he had ever tried. What made him brave was the fact that he would calculate the odds of success of any undertaking we attempted then, even if the odds were well against us, do it anyway, if Team Blue went into danger Blaske went too.

He had grown up in a strict Orthodox Jewish community in New Jersey with his future planned by his parents from before his birth. He would take certain studies, he would enter the family business, he would marry a certain girl, and he would stay inside his community for life. He had never driven a car, gone to a movie alone, or ridden in an airplane, much less handled a gun. But he did know that he was hungry for new experiences and wanted to learn about life outside his small, protected world.

When he was 18 and announced to his family that he wanted to explore the world a little before settling down his father was furious at what he saw as an insurrection and said "No!" in emphatic terms. The next day instead of going to his shul Blaske went to a barber shop and had his hair cut short, forelocks removed and took a bus down to the Air Force recruitment center where he enlisted for a four year tour.

Later that evening as he left his home for the last time his father said to him, "you are dead to me" and his mother and sister faced the wall softly weeping as he walked out. His letters to his parents were returned unopened and he never went back to New Jersey on leave. The Team Blue became his family, wherever we were his home.

Despite the fact that we all had training driving various vehicles; 2x's, 4xs', 6x's, tugs, etc. (we even had to be licensed to drive a semi-tractor with a

40 ft flat bed) and the rudiments of heavy equipment operation he never really learned to handle a car very well. But he did go a lot of places alone, rode in, worked on, and jumped out of a wide variety of airplanes, and became an expert shot with small arms. He was one of the first to master our signature "triple tap" with automatic weapons and small caliber handguns.

We tagged him "Esquire" because with his need to debate both sides of every question we thought he should be a lawyer, and because he was such a snappy dresser. His code name was "Buster" as in Buster Keaton the stoned faced actor in silent films.

Years after the event Cerone laughed when he related to me that when Samuels and Kappas made noises about breaking up Team Blue "Buster" took that as an assault on the team and did what he had been trained to do when ambushed, he charged. He cornered the two of them in our operations shack and made the case for keeping the unit intact. According to Cerone who was listening outside, there was some shouting. This was a big surprise as Blaske never displayed emotion, never shouted; and no one ever, ever confronted Kappas head on. The last thing Cerone heard before the door opened and Blaske came out (an hour or so after he went in) was Samuels saying in a loud voice, "okay, okay, okay".

Blaske's biggest obstacle was water; he had never been in water deeper than knee high and he was going to have to overcome any fears of drowning and pass some rigorous tests to be included in the program. He fell woefully short during our initial Orientation and Evaluation and we all thought he had washed out at this early stage until the morning Kappas summoned Morrison and me out of the pool for a "chat". He told us that he was going to allow Blaske to move on for now, he would give him 90 days to be able to pass the swimming quals with help from the two of us. Kappas did not say, "I need him to pass" or "he needs to pass", instead he said (and we caught the inflection), "you need him to pass".

We knew we were the strongest swimmers and best candidates to teach him how to get past the course but did not understand why Kappas was giving him special treatment; here was a guy who couldn't drive, shoot, or swim why were we being saddled with him? What did Kappas see that we didn't see about this guy? Gawd dammit this meant we would be giving up what little "free" time and weekend passes there were to get this hump with the program. And he was already taking up everyone's time needing extra help at the firing range. Shazzbat!

So began our coaching program with Beckstrom, Marcotti, and Cerone chipping in to help at whatever pool we could find during our training regimen. That guy Hayes who wasn't even part of our team helped when he was around. And we began to learn what Blaske was about; terrified of the water at first, he still got in and did whatever we asked of him, that's genuine bravery. And we finally thought we had discovered what Kappas had known about him all along; he was a guy who couldn't drive, shoot, or swim, but he was also a guy who wouldn't/couldn't quit. Several times we had to pull him out of the pool before he passed out and drowned, the stubborn bastard.

We were at Lowry AFB in Colorado part way through electronics training before we were able to tell Kappas we were ready to have a swimming review for Blaske. Cerone volunteered to swim with him and the two of them entered the pool with a lifeguard jump, swam two laps underwater, swam one lap breast stroke, one lap side stroke, and then were handed M1 Garands (they did not touch the side of the pool while being handed the weapons) which they held over their heads while swimming a final lap of the pool. Blaske had passed and then some (swimmingly?).

Foxy Kappas invited Morrison and me to supper at the NCO club (huge honor) and then asked a couple of beers into the dinner, "Can he swim it alone?" As we exchanged glances we knew he had spotted our secret, Blaske needed one of us with him to have the confidence to make the course. We didn't answer and the question died, but we knew we weren't quite finished as coaches.

Blaske was the first to verbalize something we all were beginning to understand, our little team was becoming a family and more, we were becoming a tribe. And as a tribe we all witnessed his coming into himself, we were there for his first hangover, we were there when he got his civilian driver's license, and we were there the morning he came out of one of the bedrooms at our "House With The Blue Gate" face stony but beet red, no longer a virgin.

The morning after the night Hayes went all drunk crazy on us, I walked out on our little porch to find "Buster" sitting in a chair, coffee in hand and a 16-gauge pump shotgun with a short barrel under the newspaper on his lap, protecting his tribe. A man who had "crossed the Rubicon", "burned his bridges", and "sunk his ships in the harbor" he had become a warrior who could only go forward.

"The Jokester"

No matter what the time of day or the weather outside, the sun was definitely shining when Cerone was born. I have never met a happier, more positive, "the sun is always shining somewhere" kind of person. It the midst of "hauling shit" Cerone could always find something funny and positive to say. I spent more time with him than with anyone else on our team and often marveled at his upbeat disposition. He could be down but could never believe he could be beat.

Up to our necks in an alligator wallow during a pause in live fire training, everyone nauseous from the stink of the fetid water and gases oozing up out of the mud, everyone headachy, dehydrated and cranky and a very serious drill sergeant asked if there were any questions. We all knew by then that it was best to never volunteer or ask questions but Cerone's hand went in the air and when the drill sergeant nodded in his direction he asked the straight faced question, "Sergeant, do frogs fuck in this mud? Because I think I feel something humping my leg?" It took the drill sergeant, a Brit, a moment to realize *his* leg was being pulled and then he laughed uproariously. It probably wasn't that funny but the day suddenly didn't seem so bad. Typical Cerone.

Women, children, dogs and other inhabitants of the planet seemed to love being around him wherever we went; he didn't even have to speak a common language with people to have them smiling and laughing within minutes of meeting him. If the situation allowed and circumstances permitted when Cerone was around the party was on.

A California hot-rodder, gambler and inveterate tinkerer, Cerone was always inventing some gadget; usually something to use with one of his pranks. For the most part his pranks were harmless fun and appreciated and taken as good fun by his victims but if someone got on his wrong side the pranks could have a dark side; he was usually so light hearted and fun it was easy to forget he could be a mean little son-of-a-bitch. As early as boot camp Beckstrom and I became his willing co-conspirators and helped him pull off some of his more outrageous pranks.

The target of one of the more memorable pranks was a yank and bank fighter pilot instructor at Nellis who we really liked, "Captain Joe"; who was a prankster himself. He had pranked us on the gunnery range and now it was our turn. Without getting too technical it helps to know that the gunsight image, the reticle that appeared on the windscreen of the F100 Super Sabre Jet ("The Hun") was a light image projected on the screen through a series of computer controlled mirrors that manifested as a circle of ten diamonds with a diamond in the center. The image could be ranged in and out either by the pilot twisting the throttle grip or by the radar. The sight would be "caged" and manually operated during night re-fuel missions to assist the pilot in lining up with the fuel probe. There were certain precisely ordered events that would happen before, during, and after the aerial refueling hookup.

We set up a "Top Secret, Clearance Required" area in one end of a maintenance hangar and went to work making a movie, wiring some circuitry, and modifying a small projector from a cannibalized system. When that work was finished we accessed Captain Joe's plane one evening, removed the floatation kit from under his seat (we were in the desert for chrissake) and wired our device and timers into the aircraft, then went to the base tower to keep the controllers company while night maneuvers were being conducted out over the gunnery range.

As Captain Joe related it the next morning, "I let my wingman fill his bingo (almost out of gas) bird first, then ranged in on the probe and topped off my tanks. I ordered my training wing back to base then pulled some altitude to fly a CAP over the tanker as we orbited in lazy circles back toward the base." "I was flying on autopilot and relaxing a little letting my mind wander a bit (read on the point of being half awake and half asleep) when I suddenly heard stereo clanging sounds in my headset."" The diamond fell out of the center of my reticle and the rest of the diamonds followed right behind."" While my mind was trying to wake all the way up and come to grips with what was happening the clanging sounds got louder, joined by the sound of a train horn and two alternating red lights flashing on my screen"" I flew all over the night sky trying to avoid that damn train crossing!" "If you tell anyone about this the General will have you shot without even a courts martial!" "And I'll be the guy who pulls the trigger."" Now, about that stuck-up asshole F104 driving puke...I have an idea."

When a particular Colonel and his snotty crew chief that were always annoying us finally got on his nerves one hot night Cerone waited until just before flight time, drank a beer and filled the aircraft urine bottle (the relief tube wasn't a tube, it was a bottle with a flapper valve), then watched and smiled while the Colonel positioned himself in the cockpit, started the engine, and taxied out. At some point during his flight the pilot would have to urinate, his choices would be to dump the bottle and use it or wet his pants, in either case the aircraft ac unit would pick up the moisture and distribute it universally in the cabin. As the aircraft taxied away Cerone saluted and said, "Piss on you, Colonel".

Long before we pranked Captain Joe or pissed on a Colonel, a very angry Cerone sent a message to Hayes in a way that only he would have come up with and in a way that made his point crystal clear.

I provided a Polaroid camera and the services of a friend; the rest was pure Cerone.

He was code named "Cisco" as in TV show "The Cisco Kid" and the show tag line, "Hey, Cisco", "Hey, Poncho", "Ha,ha,ha, ha..." I still hear laughter every time I think of him.

"Herc"

When Hayes pushed through the door into the front bedroom of Team Blue's off-base house and kicked the body lying stomach down asleep on a tatami mat he expected to get Jaycee, who would either try to shuck and grin and talk his way out of an ass-kicking or stand up and try to fight him. Both alternates would be okay with Hayes and either would end with fear and submission on Jaycee's face.

What he got instead was a grey-eyed, flat-faced Dave who was pointing a large bore unwavering pistol (it looked as big around as a water main) straight between his eyes and issuing the terse command, "Get. The. Fuck. Out. Of. Here".

He backed out of the bedroom and left through the front room, noticing a couple of girls putting ice bags on the faces of Cerone and Morrison, Blaske still asleep in a chair in the corner, stereo still playing a slow Johnny Mathis album. Booze, emotion, and frustration had driven him to make an ass out of himself and as he made his way out to his car he was feeling something new. Regret, or defeat, or?

Physically talented and physically very brave Hayes would throw his body into the fray with no concern about the outcome, but I intuited that that bravery didn't extend to human relationships and as I got to know more about him I understood why.

Hayes's step-dad was a Charming Irish Boy'o outside the home and a mean drunk at home. Hayes was the kid in not-quite-fitting school clothes barely hiding his bruises all during grade school. When he reached thirteen he thought he was big enough to take on the step-dad. The fight was pretty bloody for him and resulted with the local authorities

50

searching for a foster home to put him in. His older brother had left home and joined the Air Force years earlier but had had enough taste of the step-dad to know what was going on and petitioned the family court to have his younger brother made his ward. The older brother's commanding officer was sympathetic to the situation and authorized him to bring his dependents, including Hayes, to base housing in Japan.

He started high school at the on-base American School on Itazuke AFB and finished at the base school on Tachikawa AFB after his brother was transferred. He learned to speak a fluent "kitchen Japanese" and discovered the joy and discipline of the martial arts at a dojo (martial arts school; technically illegal, certain martial arts studies were forbidden in Japan at the time) off base. He applied himself whole-heartedly to the arts and became a skilled adept at open hand combat before he had graduated from the base school. When he turned eighteen he was no longer his brother's ward and wasn't sure what future he wanted for himself but the military had provided a good home for his brother's family and seemed like the best option at the time. He would be Air Force all the way.

Hayes had never found the peer group where he "fit", always being, or at least feeling like, an outsider; in grade school he had stayed away from other kids because of a feeling of shame instilled by his step father, in school on base he was an NCO's younger brother where most of the other students were officers children, at the dojo no matter how well he did and how much his skill was appreciated he was still a gaijin (round eye, foreigner) to the other students.

We called him "Herc" as in Hercules partly because of his strength and weight lifters physique, but also because it rhymed with "jerk". "Herc the Jerk" was lacking in some social skills and hid his shyness with an aggressive, obnoxious front a lot of the time, but obnoxious was okay with our little group and we welcomed him to our circle whenever our teams were in the same rotation and/or geography. It just didn't occur to any of us that he wanted to be on Team Blue. Morrison maintained for years to come that Hayes had the most complicated psychology of anyone he had ever met.

Cerone and I had rented a little two bedroom house in town just down the hill from Fremont Street at an area where Las Vegas and North Las Vegas met which became off-base central for all the time we were stationed at Nellis. We had painted the fence and gate in front of the house blue to make it easy for people to find and this was an un-official but very real headquarters for Team Blue. Kappas even visited once in a while, always giving plenty of warning before he arrived.

Hayes' rotation had just come back from two infantry weapons and small unit tactics schools, one with Marines and the other with Rangers, and his group had not taken the Pathfinders course so we had not seen him for a couple of months. But it was no surprise when he came to the house on a Saturday night when those of us with weekend passes were partying with a few friends and associates (some young ladies and a few other airmen from Nellis).

He didn't usually drink heavily, preferring to watch other people lose control and make fools of themselves, but on this particular evening he drank a lot and brooded a lot, none of the ladies were taking an interest in him and no one was willing to hear his stories about training with the Marines and the Army Rangers. As he got drunker he felt more frustrated, and unhappy at being on the team he was assigned to (bunch of stuffy no fun guys). He wouldn't admit it but he was jealous; jealous of the black baseball caps and shiny pins we got to wear, jealous of the way Cerone and Jaycee always had a bunch of laughing people around them and along the way to a big hangover he decided to assert himself. He was bigger, stronger, smarter, and maybe even better looking than Cerone or Jaycee, why did people always go their way? He would show those two little smart asses who the boss should be.

Even in his drunken state he maintained a certain cunning; he knew that Beckstrom and Marcotti were pulling duty that weekend and would not show up at the house. Hell, he could take either one of them, but the two of them together might have him over matched; Beckstrom was pretty strong and that damn Marcotti was a rock, a hard fast rock. As he looked around the room he saw that Cerone and Morrison were slow dancing with a couple of girls, a couple of other airmen (guys he didn't know but dismissed as no threat) and their girls were playing cards in the kitchen and Blaske was asleep in a big easy chair.

He walked to the center of the floor, pulled Cerone away from his dance partner and gave him two quick palm strikes to the sides of the head. As Cerone slumped to the floor he turned and before Morrison could react hit him hard right at the point where the temple, ear and jawbone meet. Morrison went out and down and Hayes pushed through the bedroom door, re-emerging quickly and going through the house to his car. He spent the next day nursing a hangover and depressed, he realized that what he had wanted was to be on Team Blue and he had blown it.

Monday morning he woke up in his bunk in the barracks to find my buddy Floyd sitting on a folding chair and smiling at him – the kind of smile a wolf probably has just before it eats the pig. My buddy Floyd was a six-foot five-inch ropy muscled dark black man with a reddish tint to the whites of his eyes and a huge yellow-white smile. A jagged scar ran down his left cheek. Everyone knew he had been the warlord of the Lords of Harlem, a notorious black gang in NYC and that he was the number one stud among all the black guys on the base. We all suspected he was a little crazy and no one, not even Hayes, wanted to find out for sure. In his hand he held a 4"x5" envelope which he handed to Hayes.

Inside the envelope was a neatly hand printed note that said *"Never Fuck With Me Again"* and a Polaroid photo. In the photo was a sleeping Hayes lying on his bunk, in the frame was a gloved hand holding a suppressed High Standard, the muzzle an inch from Hayes's temple.

Seeing the expression on Hayes's face when he saw the contents of the envelope Floyd asked "Any response?" and smiled that big smile again.

Postscript: Shamefaced and knowing his timing was way off and that he had offended a couple of us to the point of near-fatal consequence

(Cerone really was not someone you wanted pissed-off at you, the Swiss Italian lover boy had a seriously serious streak behind his smile) Hayes petitioned Kappas to put him on our team, we were not certain why. Back on base Monday evening Kappas asked us to say yea or nay, would we accept Hayes on Team Blue (a surprising amount of democracy in a military unit)? To my surprise, and probably everyone else's, the first person to speak up was "hang back and watch" Blaske, followed by mumbled assents from behind the black eyes both Cerone and Morrison were sporting. Beckstrom and Marcotti hadn't witnessed Hayes's behavior at the house and abstained from speaking. All eyes in the room turned to me and I looked back over at Blaske who nodded twice, okay Hayes was in. I made no comment based on the fact that I knew exactly what Cerone was thinking; if Hayes fucked up again, well we trained in some very dangerous environments and an accident could happen to anyone. I knew it would take a long time for Cerone to "forgive and forget" meanwhile his modus operandi was "...and keep your enemies closer", his motto was, "Get even Hell, I mean to get ahead!"

Chapter 8

Christmas In A Far Place

The package had traveled a long, complicated way before it reached me. It went to Lowry AFB, Colo., Nellis AFB, Nev., Hamilton Field, Ca., Tachikawa AB, Japan, Clark AFB, Philippines, and Takhli, Thailand where it was put with diplomatic pouches shipping to Laos. Somehow the gift box from home still got to me a few days before Christmas.

There was no possible way for Mom to know where or what we were doing but the contents of the box hit the spot; there was a bottle of V.S.O.P., a smaller box of homemade cookies, an old fruitcake tin containing homemade fudge and divinity, an unusual cocktail glass, and a bone handled bowie knife with an 8-inch blade. The booze, cookies and candy didn't last very long and the glass disappeared but I spent many happy hours bluing the steel and honing the bowie knife.

With apologies to Bob Dylan "the times they were confusing", we were living in the Milton Caniff cartoon "Terry and The Pirates". There were good guys who were bad guys and bad guys who were good guys and one needed a score card to keep track of all the shifting alliances day by day. There was Captain Kong Lee who was a good guy; he trained at the US Army Ranger School in the Philippines. A good guy until he tried to straighten out some of the confusion through a bloodless takeover of the country's capital. His agenda was simple: Lao for the Laos, he was a Neutralist, just what the US government said they wanted. But now as we arrived he was a bad guy who we (the US Embassy) had helped push out of Vientiane with an artillery barrage that killed a few civilians and some livestock and had escaped with all his kith and kin, women, children, and cattle to join the Pathet Lao (sort of inept, bad guys, communists) on the Plaines De Jares in their attempt to oust the Royals.

The Pathet Lao were getting help from the North Vietnamese (seriously tough guys), the Red Chinese (as opposed to the Kuomintang), and the

Russians (who wanted to keep a presence during their almost divorce from the Red Chinese). The Kuomintang were Chinese soldiers left over from WWII who were mercenaries and warlords in the Golden Triangle opium trade and could be counted on to protect their own interests.

There were the Royals who had no clue what was going on outside their capital, and the Royal who supported the communists. There were the Madam of the White Rose who played to all sides, spies, smugglers, Chinese merchants, Indian traders, and Corsican mobsters. And of course, Bill Lair, a CIA Station Head (who had trained the Thai Police Auxiliary Reinforcement Unit) and his small staff.

We were soon to meet the "Gray Man", who had no color of his own but took on the color of whatever background he stood in front of. Also, some characters with plenty of color were on the scene; Jim Thompson ex-OSS, on again off again CIA asset, Thai "Silk King". Bill Young, third generation missionary, party animal and warrior. Soon to arrive: Pop Buell and Tony Poe. Vang Pao was in the hills waiting to come on stage.

There were cutthroats and saints, mercenaries and priests, beautiful women (and a few ugly ones) and wizened old beggars, and darkened aircraft flying to secret bases in the cloak of night.

An entire economy supported by the United States government – the "Meddling Americans". The only faction that wanted us there was the FAR (Force Armee Royale = Royal Laotian Army), we paid their entire payroll and a lot of that money was diverted into the hands of the officer corps. All the factions agreed that they wanted the French gone and for no other colonial power to take their place.

A guy could be stomped by an elephant, bitten by any one of dozens of poisonous snakes, mauled by a bear, flattened by a rhino or even eaten by a leopard or a tiger. Even the water could kill you. Wow, what an exciting place for us to be!

There we were: six greenies in-country. We were in the military, but not of the military; or of the military but not in the military. Sometimes of the military and in the military. On this occasion we had been "sheep-dipped" and were as pure as little lambs, military ID locked away and names removed from military rolls; civilian contractors there to provide technical support to "sheep-dipped" Special Forces guys. As Beckstrom would say, "confusing, eh?"

We had come across the Mekong with three hundred or so Philippine "construction workers" to assist in FAR General Phoumis' return to the capital. Our role was to provide communications equipment and air traffic control for the airlift bringing in men and materials to Wattay Airport in support of the General.

That assignment and the Gregorian New Year over we were sent to a small town near the borders of Cambodia and Viet Nam to prep a Victor Site (later called a Landing Site) and establish a radio traffic listening post for a couple of "spooky looking guys" as Cerone put it – pun intended.

Not much work involved in cleaning up and surveying the airstrip site, it was already useable and we had been ferried to the town in a Dornier 28 (French light twin) and it only took two days to set up radio gear, generator and antenna for the listening post. Easy duty. Why'd they send so many of us?

As civilians, we were not allowed to be armed while in Laos, but we had winked at that proscription and all were carrying side arms under our Hawaiian shirts. I had my 1911 Colt and Hayes his Browning Highpower, Cerone a brand spanking new Colt Python in .357 mag caliber. The other three were still carrying the (sissy, ineffective) S&W .38s that we had been issued as service weapons.

We were in Muong Nong which was a small hillside town and trading center populated with about nine hundred people, one elephant, a few water buffalo, an occasional cow, and the usual herd of chickens scratching out a living in the dirt roads. Below the town is a nice river with a navigable (by small boat) channel through the rapids downstream and slow-moving pools edge the shore. Hey, maybe we would get in some fishing while we were there.

An enterprising local, who must have known the town was going to grow some months before, had managed to have two samoys (or tuk tuks, three wheeled motorized carriages named for the sound of their two cycle engines) shipped up river and had set up a cab stand in front of what passed for a general store just across the way from our quarters in a beautiful old white colonial house.

The hillside roads were steep and the Kip was cheap (local currency, we had been issued bales of the stuff), and we wanted to support the local economy so we rode everywhere in the samoys. Our FAR hosts thought we were crazy.

There was a nice beer garden located in a pavilion at the river edge with an ingenious stream powered evaporative cooler. It was easy to tell that some of the" Philippine contractors" had preceded us, or the locals had had a lot of early knowledge that business was going to boom, or both, because at the beer garden they had a couple of exotic imported beers, Red Lion and Schlitz, and they sold Phillip Morris Gold filter tip cigarettes. Ah, the benefits of civilization.

We loaded up (overloaded) the samoys one evening; Hayes on one side, Marcotti in the middle, and me on the other side of the first, and Cerone, Beckstrom, and Blaske in the second and started down the hill to the river. Hayes commented that he "hadn't seen our driver before, must be a new hire, business for the cab stand must be picking up".

Just below the lamp lit part of the "main drag" the street narrowed and cut back on itself with a couple of switchbacks then ramped on down to the track along the water. At a level point between the switchbacks our driver stopped his samoy, blocking the second, and pantomimed that he had to make water. The driver stepped to a bush beside the street, then suddenly disappeared. Hayes was yelling, "Out, Out, Out!" and diving out his side of the samoy as I went out the other, sliding on the loose dirt and struggling to get my .45 out of my waistband holster. Hayes was up and firing his Highpower (fucking peashooter, you wouldn't have to double tap if you used a real gun) just as a sound I can never forget ripped open the night air; a Mat 49 machine pistol was firing at the samoys.

I was up on one knee and firing at the red blossoms erupting from the top of the switchback but could see that all three occupants of the second samoy were clear and below the street edge firing uphill as well, while Hayes was moving laterally to flank the Mat 49's firing position. I had fired through my first magazine and was fumbling, hands shaking from adrenalin, in my pockets for a second before I realized that Marcotti had not jumped clear.

Somewhere dogs were barking. Everything else was quiet. I approached the ambush firing position from the left, Hayes from the right; no one was there. We did find a blood trail in the morning but no other sign of our ambusher(s).

Marcotti sat upright, half closed eyes staring out at eternity, hands still folded across his lap, with his feet in a pool of blood. I had skinned deer and other game and helped slaughter cows and pigs, but I had never seen so much blood in one spot. I kept thinking over and over, "How can there be so much blood?"

His was the first death in our outfit listed as "A training accident in the Philippines".

Chapter 9

Off The Res

Maurice M. Kappas was named for a French movie actor his mother admired in some black and white movie or other (the name of the movie long lost by the time he told us the story), and his last name came from his Dutch father. When asked what the "M" stood for he said, "Middle". The staff at the reservation infirmary where he was born insisted that he had to have a middle name so there it was; "M" or "M only", or "Middle".

His grandfather had been a Black White Man who came west as a buffalo soldier and stayed on in Arizona when his enlistment was up and took an Apache woman from the White Mountain as his wife (there were stories that said that terrible things happened when anyone dared to call her "squaw"). The tribal elders were happy with the arrangement; the tribe was short on young men, times were tough, his grandmother's father had languished and died in a prison in Florida, and the Black White Man was a good provider for his wife and her family, although there were complaints from some of the old women that he didn't beat her.

They had a daughter who was sent (forced to go) by the reservation authorities (bunch of do-good white men) to the Indian School in Oklahoma where she excelled in her classes and successfully hid her intention to never forget or forego the Old Ways. She returned to the reservation with a teaching certificate and a mission to teach the children of her tribe to read, write, and do their arithmetic in classrooms that taught English but with classes conducted in the Peoples' tongue as well.

She met and married a man who was half Jicarilla Apache and half Dutch and Maurice was the fruit of that union. As he explained it he was Black, Apache, Apache, and Dutch: B-A-A-D. Or as he sometimes said, he was a quarter Black, a quarter Dutch, half Apache and three quarters wild when he was growing up.

His father succumbed to depression, alcohol, and pneumonia when Maurice was seven years old and he said that he might have gone by the same route if it were not for his Mothers' strong will. She insisted he finish high school at the boarding school in Williams when he would much rather have been out hunting, trapping, fishing, and stealing horses from the Navajo at Many Farms with the other teenage boys from the reservation.

He ran, wrestled, and practiced the Apache art of knife fighting, learned to hunt with throwing sticks, bow, and rifle. But he also spent hours reading history and pouring over books and magazines about automobiles and airplanes. He was exposed to a variety of languages including his first language, Athabasca, as well as English, Spanish, and a smattering of Low German, and found it easy to move from one to another.

Even in a matriarchal, tribal society a boy without a father can get into scrapes and Kappas had his share of fights and "misdemeanor behavior". Then WWII happened and put him on an entirely different track than he might have followed had he "stayed on the res" (reservation) as so many of his friends did.

At seventeen he enlisted in the Army Air Corps to be around airplanes and after boot camp was sent to a government contractor run aviation mechanics school in Santa Monica, California. Before he was old enough to shave he was on a troop ship with orders to report to the 91st Bombing Group stationed at Bassingbourn, Cambridgeshire, England.

Then Kismet in the form of a British officer stepped in and took him a long way from the reservation. The officer was struck by how much the young air mechanic looked like a native North African (Berber, Moor?) and arranged for him to be on loan and "volunteer" for an interview with the staff of Colonel Young at the British Commando School at Archnarry. The staff liked what they saw in Kappas and a Colonel Sterling requested of the Army Air Corps that he be assigned for training with the Special Air

Services (SAS) under a Major Roy Ferrin (later famous as the leader of the" Desert Rats" in North Africa).

After Commando School and parachute training near Manchester Kappas was sent on various missions with the British SAS and OSE (Office of Strategic Executive) and the American OSS (precursor to the CIA). He apparently did well on these missions because before the war was over he had been sent to Officer Training School and promoted to 2nd Lieutenant. He had also made some important long-term contacts and picked up a smattering of Arabic, Farsi, French, and Italian.

After the war and some time spent with the Occupation Forces in Germany Kappas stayed on duty in the Reserves and entered college when he returned to the States. He requested and got a billet in the Army flight school at Columbus AFB, Mississippi. After graduation from flight school he was put back on active duty and settled in as a flight instructor in light bombers and transport aircraft at Columbus, received a couple of promotions, and met and married a local girl.

When the Korean Conflict broke out Captain Kappas had a wife and two-year-old daughter and had found a life that made him happy. He had his family, airplanes to work on and fly; he enjoyed his role as an instructor and planned to remain in the service until retirement. Pay was low but his wife worked on base as a civilian bookkeeper and both were used to making do with little; they were content and were planning to give their daughter a little brother or sister.

The newly established (split from the Army) United States Air Force was about to enter its' first conflict as a separate entity and had to get experienced flight crews to the line immediately. They assigned the newly minted Major Kappas to the 3rd Bombing Wing and sent him to Japan as part of the ferry crew on a B-26. He stayed with the 3rd during the early raids over Pyongyang, Korea until shot down on the wrong side of the (rapidly shifting) line. He was able to link up with an understandably wary patrol from the 1st Marine Division which was also caught behind enemy lines due to a rapid shift in positions. The Marines weren't sure about the man in the grubby flight suit who couldn't answer their challenge with a password. Kappas' response was, "For Christ's sake Jarheads, any password you may have had is not in use by now. Do any of you lugs know Chesty Puller (Marine General)? Because I sure as hell do!"

After a short stay in hospital for dehydration and some minor cuts and bruises he was re-assigned to TAC and the 942 Forward Air Control Squadron, he was going to the Mosquitoes. While on this assignment he met a fighter pilot named Captain John Boyd (later famous as "40 Second Boyd" as an instructor at the Fighter Weapons School at Nellis) who he described as "the best pilot in the world who never got to be an ace".

Promoted to Lt. Colonel he instructed and led pilots flying WWII vintage aircraft used to mark positions for bombing and strafing runs for the "fast movers". He also flew P51 Mustangs and other aircraft on tank busting missions. He said later that the B25 was his favorite air to ground attack aircraft because it could be set up to do turns about a point with the nose pointing to the center; with four .50 cals in the nose and two in each wing the B25 could put down a lot of fire power with great accuracy.

Low and slow was dangerous work and eventually he got downed by ground fire while on a FAC mission in a T6 (WWII trainer, slow but maneuverable) and again was stranded behind enemy lines. It was while he was finding his way out that his wife Louise and daughter Lily were killed in an automobile accident back in the States. A tractor and trailer rig had jackknifed on a rain slick highway and the trailer rolled directly over his wife's' car, killing both occupants instantly.

The "police action" was winding down and after attending the funeral for his family, Kappas stayed on at Columbus until he was "riffed". He thought about getting out at that point in his career, but by that time he felt no connection to the Reservation, no connection to any part of civilian life, he would just stay in the military and see where it went from there.

Kappas had made some good friends during his years in service, he had also pissed some powerful people off with his no-nonsense straight ahead attitude. There were a few rings around that he had failed to kiss and his friends had not been able to keep him in the Officer Corps. Okay, being a Senior NCO might have some benefits, he would stay. Or so he thought until his assignment to Fort Huachuca and his mind-deadening duties there.

He was on the cusp of changing his mind and getting out of the Air Force when Captain Samuels waltzed through the door to his office and gave him something else to think about. The first night Samuels was there he went to dinner with Kappas and opened the offer he had come to present with the question, "Who did you piss off to get assigned to this armpit of the world?" (My apologies to those who are or have been stationed there and think it next to the Garden of Eden).

Putting the recruiting and training program together at Lackland AFB with Captain Samuels and Major Bohannon made him feel alive and useful again. He pulled his training cadre together from bases all over the world, Major Bohannon seemed able to get him anyone he asked for that was willing to sign on to this new hush hush program. Several of the NCOs he pulled in were former officers who had also been riffed; he had a great talent pool to pull from.

He was also allowed, with Major Bohannon running interference, to put together the selection criteria and training syllabus based on his own experience and expertise in covert warfare. His entire selection criteria remain a mystery to me, but I do know that he looked for people who were accustomed to, and comfortable with, functioning on their own resources (strongly individual) and turned them into parts of a greater whole. He did once comment years later that in the first few sections of training he had already identified the two hundred or so airmen that would make it all the way through, out of the over six hundred candidates identified in the original recruitment.

His training methods were, I believe, unique in the military environment. His cadre did not bully, which to a greater or lesser degree would not have worked well with most of us, they nurtured. Case in point: Blaske had never held a firearm before we started training at Lackland, the 30 cal. carbines made him very uncomfortable and he kept squeezing his eyes shut just before firing, sending rounds everywhere but near his target. Kappas lay next to him and talked him through each step of loading, positioning, and firing; observing Blaske's' reactions to his coaching and formulating a plan. He assigned a trainer to provide Blaske and two other candidates with individual instruction until they could qualify on the range. All three passed and eventually Blaske became an excellent shot with a variety of small arms.

Another unique aspect; we never had any junior officers as part of our permanent party, the occasional brass bar, silver bar, or RR track, might train with us for all or part of a section but they were never "in charge" and were never a permanent fixture. Kappas intended to field a force of non-commissioned officers who could stay in the background. But he also told us (after Camp Henry) that we were always autonomous in the field and could consider, quietly and to ourselves, that we outranked anyone else in the field in terms of survival and accomplishing our mission. I may have taken that a little too much to heart on a couple of occasions.

The program was rushed, probably more from military political needs than anything else, and he was in a position of having to field some of us sooner than he would have liked. The loss of Marcotti on our teams' first TDY and a man from another team named Phillips ("killed during a training accident at McDill AFB, Florida": we all suspected he was out of No Name Cay, Florida on a survey team in Cuba) struck him deeply. We had just started and he had already lost some of his chicks.

Kappas was not training us to storm the beaches, take the hill, or blow the bridge (although we had the skills and the tools): he was training us to survey the ground, draw the maps, and guide the bad asses in to do the dirty work. We would often have to be the first ones in, but we were to stay hidden if possible and not engage the enemy unless necessary. If we had to engage we were to do so with maximum speed and lethality and get clear "before anyone else knows you are there". We were to "Survive as the first, second, and third priority, everything else comes after." He demanded we stay alive. He was a long way from the Reservation again and we had become his new family.

He was not training us for "Black Ops"; he was training us for "Twilight Ops". In twilight the observers think they know what they are looking at when often what they think they are seeing isn't what they are looking at at all. Confusing? That's the point.

He prepared another training "spring surprise" that he hoped would up the situational awareness and Survivability Quotient for his "Twilight Operators".

Chapter 10

Spring Surprise

When we came back to Nellis after our first TDY Kappas came back with us and convinced Major Bohannon to hold back from sending any other teams or team members overseas; Samuels stayed in Thailand improving his contacts. 8th COIN had lost people in Asia (including Marcotti) and Central America during our first operational season and Kappas felt it was at least in part a training failure. He believed we had been given many of the tools but not enough of the psychology of small or large engagements on the battlefield. He intended to give us more of what we needed to survive.

Forty of us were offered two weeks leave with orders to report to McDill AFB in Florida at the end of the leave time. Blue Team passed on the leave, let the time accrue for later, and hung out at our house in Vegas reacquainting with people we had met before the TDY and chilling out. None of us were over the shock of losing Marcotti, we had been young enough to not believe anything that real could happen to any of us and Marcotti in particular seemed impervious to harm. It didn't help that we were not allowed to talk about what happened with anyone outside our team; no one, no family members, no priest, no counselor was ever to be told the circumstances of his death or even that we had gone anywhere other than Japan and the Philippines, if that. We could only share our feelings with and rely on members of our group. This was a beginning of our becoming isolated from any reality outside our own.

Time to go to Florida and six of us loaded up to travel together, operationally the 8th COIN field teams were supposed to be manned by ten people but Team Blue was never at that strength. So Beckstrom, Morrison, Blaske, Cerone, Hayes, and Jay Cee took three hops on MATS transports and got to McDill in time to get a little sleep and relax after signing in to the transient barracks. Early Monday morning found us being roused by Kappas (gee, it's good to see you too Sergeant, yawn) for a run through the steaming, humid morning and a nice round of PT. Then it was off to breakfast followed by a return to barracks for a shower and change into tropical tan uniforms (we wore the shorts but refused to wear the damn knee socks) and brogans.

Our armaments NCO," Zero", was there to say hello and let us know our weapons lockers had come for the trip, so we knew something was up, but what? Kappas kept us waiting (stewing in the humidity) for a couple of hours before sending a messenger with a shuttle to take us to assemble at a hangar next to a runway. As we stood pinched into the sparse mid-day shade at the hangar door we saw five twin engine high tail unmarked aircraft approaching and passing over the field in formation, at the end of the runway they made a military break and turned back to circle and land with thirty second separation between the planes, a cool maneuver for fighter aircraft, even cooler for transports.

After they landed they turned in trail to the taxiway in front of the hangar where we were standing, as the lead aircraft passed a point just in front of us all the aircraft tail ramps began to come down and they all made a right oblique turn (45° to the taxiway) and stopped. Before they were completely stopped black sweat suit clad figures with soft soled boots and beige berets began to jump to the ground. As soon as the de-barking men were clear the aircraft started lifting ramps, turned left oblique to re-align with the taxiway, moved to the first runway crossing and took the runway and got airborne, still maintaining an even separation. Wow! Who were these guys?!?

Whoever they were they formed a line abreast, crossed the taxiway, came to attention, and shifted to an at-ease posture with feet sixteen inches apart and wrists crossed behind their backs directly facing us. All this was done without a sound other than the pad of their soft soled boots.

Major Bohannon and Kappas appeared at the end of the hangar and we formed up at attention facing the men in the beige berets and black sweat suits. Major Bohannon walked to the center of the space between the lines of men and nodded to Kappas who called us to at ease as well. Major Bohannon addressed us, "Gentlemen (and he grinned) Sergeant Kappas has called some old friends and prepared a spring surprise for you. He will explain the details at the evening mess, for now break ranks and get acquainted with the man across from you, he is about to become your best chance of surviving the next few weeks.". The Major snapped a salute in Kappas' general direction (pretending to return a salute from Kappas) and disappeared back around the end of the hangar.

On Team Blue at least, and maybe universally for all the COIN members, we shared one thought, "Huh?"

My hand was swallowed by the paw of the man facing me who said, "Langdon here" and smiled. I saw the flash on his tan beret was a winged sword pointing up; a ribbon crossing the sword hilt had the words "Who Dares Wins". Before I could reply blue shuttle buses pulled up to take us to the NCO club where Major Bohannon and CMSGT Kappas had arranged an introductory/ get acquainted dinner/briefing for us all.

That was the first time we saw the Dehaviland DHC4 Caribou STOL transport, and the first meeting with some of the best soldiers in the world, the British 22 SAS (Special Air Service).

We were told that we would be joining our new comrades at arms (part of a British Army Training Support Unit) at a place called "Guacamalo Bridge Camp" in a country called British Honduras (later known as Belize), wherever that was, for five weeks of advanced training in escape and evasion, ambush tactics for both aggressor and target, and small arms applications. We would each receive one-on-one training with the Brit we had met on the apron earlier in the day, no trainers were assigned to anyone specific, however the lots had fallen at the first meeting would remain throughout the training; this was the first lesson, luck and serendipity play a part in every military situation. The exception would be for Morrison who would be attending a field medicine workshop part of the time we were in camp. Cerone quipped that he was not sure he wanted to go camping at a place called "Bad Guacamole" but maybe the hot sauce would be good. We would be leaving at 0600 on the transports we had seen earlier, our field gear and weapons had already been loaded on one of the planes.

As part of the briefing we were told to do exactly as our Brit twin told us to do in light of the fact that all their training was conducted with live fire, no blanks, no dummy grenade or mortar rounds, no rubber knives, a guy could get seriously hurt or even killed in the training course (in fact there had been injuries and fatalities at training camps in previous years). If your SAS mate said, "head down" get your head down, if he said, "eyes left, right, up or down" follow the instruction exactly, if he said, "piss up a rope" look for the rope and get with it. These instructions and more were repeated at reveille every morning during our "visit".

The first few days were spent with 0430 reveille and breakfast, CQB (Close Quarter Battle) drills, and chalkboard explanations of the Four Fs of attack; Find, Fix, Flank, and Finish. Diagrams were drawn and explained of different types of ambush including the "L", "V", and "C" shapes and area and subsidiary ambushes. Terms like "enfilade" and "defilade" were explained in detail. Priorities of ambush targets were identified; first the radio operator, second the commander(s), and third machine gunners. This order of priorities gave us pause as we expected to be the communications people in the field in many future operations. Most of this was not new to Hayes but he did say that he was picking up subtleties he hadn't gotten in previous training. Afternoons were spent with familiarization and firing of a variety of small arms and our SAS mates demonstrated the "double tap" as the preferred method of pistol protocol.

The SAS pistol of choice at the time was the Browning Highpower in 9mm caliber which they felt had some advantages over the 1911 .45 Colt Auto I favored; more rounds in the magazine and less muzzle rise between shots. They believed in "head shots, head shots, head shots" and found that with the nine mils greater penetrating power, but less energy exchange than the .45 round they got best results by putting two bullets into the target. They made some converts to the Browning, but I preferred (and still do) the 1911, you only have to hit the target once, and damn near anywhere, to kill or incapacitate an enemy, I did (do) subscribe to the headshot philosophy, but with the .45 round you only need one shot to kill. The tradeoff for a slight accuracy advantage with the Browning is negated by the .45s greater stopping power and (I think) reliability.

Kappas put his own spin on things by insisting on a "triple tap" with all our small-bore pistols (Colt Woodsman and Suppressed High Standard .22s) and all the automatic weapons we fired including the M3 grease gun (surprisingly accurate), Sten SMG, AK47, M14 (my weapon of choice), SK9, and other submachine guns. The "triple tap" was also to be mastered with .30 and .50 caliber machine guns. The principal reasons for this were to improve kill rates with the small bores, improve accuracy and extend weapons life with the SMGs and MGs, and make our weapons positions recognizable to one another during fire fights and through "the fog of war". We practiced the "triple tap" technique (Blaske was really good at it) over and over until it became an ingrained habit. And it worked, the repeated training with this technique for all the 8th COIN operators proved out and we were able to identify one another by sound even during a barrage of noise, very useful for maintaining a situational awareness during a firefight. Once again the "mutha' knew best".

Beckstrom claimed he was having the most fun; his training partner was introducing him to the finer points of mortars, including adjusting range aurally. He was so wrapped in the concept that "Fire One and Adjust" was a phrase he tried to apply to everything even at the bar or in the latrine.

Evenings brought an interesting SAS custom, one we thought we should copy; each man received a daily allowance of two shots of whiskey and a pint of beer at the evening mess. Exacting instructors of martial techniques in the field our hosts were down-to-earth, blue collar types off the field. Journeymen and Masters of their trade, they were to a man affable, friendly companions prone to quiet enjoyment and understated humor rather than boisterous behavior, no braggarts among them.

When the SAS troops took the field there was no "Hooray", "Huzzah", or "Oo Rah", no shouting, no unnecessary noise. No clank of gear was allowed, no "Ki up" during hand-to-hand exercises. This quiet efficiency was a lesson Kappas wanted us to absorb, he also knew that our instructors would sharpen our observational skills; we would learn to see with more attention to detail and we would learn to really LISTEN.

Kappas was everywhere observing, commenting, instructing. Evenings he spent with the officers who showed him a kind of reverence and almost an air of deference. I made some remark about this to Langdon one evening and he gave me a quizzical look and said, "You don't know? Lieutenant Kappas has a plaque on our World War Two Wall of Honor at Herefords (the regiments' home) and a place in our history". I must admit I felt a little vicarious pride at his reaction and couldn't wait to share the information with Team Blue.

Near the end of the training cycle half of our group had been matched with their Brit "twins" and sent on a night march. They would crawl through some mud under live fire, try to identify ambush points on the path of travel (almost impossible in the dark swamp), and crawl through some more mud while grenades went off around them and more live fire would pass over their heads. Next day they would move off with brief rest stops and spend a second night in the field setting up ambushes for the second half of our group for the following day and night.

Langdon decided we (the second half) needed a leg up and pulled me aside after evening chow to come with him while he shadowed the first group. With his expertise and knowledge of the terrain we could sometimes follow and sometimes parallel the first group close enough for Langdon to know where they would likely set ambushes. With this knowledge we should be able to effectively avoid or counter ambushes when our half took the field ("Who Dares Wins"). Langdon's strategy worked and our group made a good showing on our night march and ambush evasion, our opponents were kept wondering how we were able to anticipate and avoid their carefully laid traps and my teammates thought I was a genius or had ESP or both. Neither Langdon nor I ever dissuaded them from that notion.

Cerone had helped to keep everyone's morale high with remarks like, "Excuse me sergeant? Where is that rope they told us about? I really have to piss!" and other Ceroneisms and we had learned a lot from our Brit twins; things like "never risk infection by shaving in the field", "never move through an area closer than three to five meters apart", "never set an ambush without a well-planned exit", "always wear a condom when swimming in tropical waters", "always, even when you are sleeping be aware of your surroundings: look, listen, smell", "in war there is no cheating" and other appropriate aphorisms. I had also learned that I did not like swamps.

I was generally less susceptible to fleas, leeches, mosquitoes and other biting bugs than most people and had laughed when Langdon had said he was glad we didn't have to train during the mosquito season while he wiped the camtec paint off his face trying to get rid of a flight of the buggers, but it only takes one and one of the nasty girls got me.

Early one morning after about nine or ten days and nights (time was a blur) in the swamp, red eyed and sleep deprived, and feverish from the malaria I didn't yet know I had, I told my teammates I was going to the compound to ring the bell that would take me out of the training and send me back to disappear into the ranks of the "regular" Air Force, I thought I had hit my limit and was just done. Hayes gave me a steely eyed direct (scary) look and said, "No. You're not". That settled, I somehow decided I could hack it to the end of the rotation.

Our training in the swamp along the Macal River was cut short because Guatemala was massing troops on the border and preparing to press their claim to British Honduras and our hosts were being sent to deal with them (scare the hell out of them).

Before we got on the plane out of the country I was shivering and alternating between freezing and burning up, my lips were cracked and I was having strange, vivid dreams. For me at least British Honduras represented a quadruple "M" as in "Mud, Mosquitoes, Madness and Malaria".

When we got back to Nellis the rest of my crew got to go play in the hot desert (some transition from hot and wet to hot and dry) while I had to stay in the air-conditioned hospital with an IV drip.

Chapter 11

Fun In The Desert

Day time temps hovered at one hundred and seventeen degrees in the shade, except there was no shade. Night temps stayed near one hundred degrees at the dry lake runway and in our old wooden barracks. We were doing hot, dangerous work in the desert with a four day on and three days off weekly cycle and having a great time. Any kid who had ever had fun shooting off firecrackers would envy us.

Concussion waves from exploding ordinance shook the ground we were lying on and at times lifted us in the air a half inch and squeezed the air from our lungs. The loud chatter of incoming quad twenty mike mike cannon bursts striking targets and the whoosh boom of rockets was all overlaid by aircraft hitting afterburner to pull up from their target runs. An occasional flight of four in fingertip formation would sweep the target area at low altitude at mach 1 plus leaving our ears ringing and heads reeling. No amount of ear protection or hard yawning could keep the deafening roar at bay and we could only call in strike info to the aircraft between drops.

We kept the napalm runs way off in the desert away from our observation positions, it was already hot enough! Bullpup missile (radio controlled air-to-ground missile) and LABS (Low Altitude Bombing Systems) bomb tossing practice made us very nervous; some pilots (Captain Joe) were very accurate with these weapons systems others not so much. Whenever we heard "off the rail" or "pickling" on the avcom we would get a real butt pucker waiting for the missile or bomb to arrive seconds or even minutes later.

We did not have laser target painting or laser guided "smart" bombs, no laser anything was available yet; there were no satellite guidance systems or even LORAN navigation aids for the pilots who had to depend on crossing TACAN radio signals and basic pilotage skills to get them in position for low altitude missions. High altitude bombing runs could be controlled by radar but those kinds of runs were not a part of this exercise.

We relied on identifiable topography features and TACAN navigation directions to get the pilots in position to start a run then used directional headings and altitude calls to begin bringing them in to the target zone. Bright colored marker panels, smoke canisters, tracers and voice corrections from the ground team dialed them in during the day. It got dicier at night when we relied on colored lights, flares and tracer rounds to mark the targets. Some pilots were actually more accurate at night, not as much visual clutter might have been the reason for this phenomenon.

There was nothing theoretical about this exercise; we were making our bones in the deadly arena of fighter/bomber close ground support. The "yank and bank" pilots and "mud puke" ground controllers (us) were getting some serious lessons and learning new techniques as we went. There were some injuries on the ground but none were more serious than some nosebleeds and scrapes and flash burns; the pilots weren't as fortunate, two were lost when they flew directly into the ground (probably reticle fixation) and one banked hard right when he should have banked hard left and hit a sandstone cloud. And that was in just the first week of the exercise.

The old Indian Springs Army Airfield, today known as Creech Air Force Base is a doorway into 12,000 plus square miles of military reservation and controlled airspace, a large part of it used for air-to-air and air-to-ground pilot training and weapons systems testing. This huge test and gunnery range north of Las Vegas takes up a big chunk of the state of Nevada and was the prowling grounds for the Air Combat Training Wing Fighter Weapons School (FWS) with instructors like "The Mad" Major John "Forty Seconds" Boyd and our all-time favorite fighter pilot "Captain Joe".

Major Boyd was called "The Mad" because of his flamboyant personality and "Forty Seconds" because that was all the time it took for him to get on the tail of anyone dog fighting with him using a maneuver he had perfected called "flat plating"; although one well known pilot (an ace and a general) did claim to have fought him to a draw, the Major's acolyte and eventual replacement as lead instructor of the FWS, Captain Finley (Captain Joe to us), swore that the tie never happened.

When the "Mad Major" moved on to a new assignment Captain Joe kept his spirited style alive; referring to everyone not a fighter pilot as a "puke" of some kind and awarding instructor pilots and graduates of the FWS signature yellow and black ascot scarves. He also brought a lively sense of humor and an unorthodox way of making a point to the field; when Cerone and I disagreed with him over some systems operational detail at a de-briefing one night the next morning he led a flight of four swinging low over our ground position and opening their flaps to "bomb" us with toilet paper rolls. Then later that same day he loaded his wing lockers with cases of beer and took them to altitude to chill so that he could offer us a treat that evening. We had to love the guy.

Teams Blue, Orange, and Green had been assigned our own C119s (transport aircraft) and ground support equipment and personnel as part of a Wing Group tasked to set up a temporary operating airbase on a dry lake bed miles into the range where a few old barracks and a water tank were left over from WWII training operations. The temp base in support of air-to-ground exercises would be complete with line maintenance capabilities for F100s and a bird new to us the F105 Thunderchief (the "Thud"). The COIN team members would be responsible for air traffic control and forward air control on the live munitions range and would work as techs on the aircraft fire control systems. We would be dialing in the equipment in some of the same aircraft that we would be communicating with and coordinating onto ground targets and participating in the after mission briefings; a really cool arrangement that redefined (in a wholly positive manner) the term "air crew" but not one that I believe was ever put into practice in the field (too bad, it really worked).

I was in hospital at Nellis for the first week they were setting up the camp (they said I had malaria) and missed all the heavy grunt work. Darn. The hospital staff refused to discharge me and I was afraid I was going to miss the fun so I started a nagging and annoyance campaign that finally got me thrown out of the hospital. I had an interview with the kindly Colonel/nurse in charge of my section of the hospital and I clearly remember the last thing she said to me was, "and don't come back!" I was free to join the boys in the desert before the real fun started and caught a ride out to the temp base that night on a re-supply bird.

Our three 8th COIN teams rotated and overlapped shifts to provide coverage of our duties seven days a week and covered our areas of responsibilities for both day and night live fire practices on the range. On our team Beckstrom, Cerone and I provided tech services for F100 C, D and F models while Blaske, Morrison, and Hayes did the same for the new F105s. We all got our turns in the bucket as Ground Based Forward Air Controllers (FAC) directing fire for a variety of aircraft including aircraft from other fields that would fly in to participate in the exercise and our own First Sergeant Kappas flew with the pilots doing Airborne FAC; fighter pilots took turns in AT6s (two seat WWII vintage trainer used in Korea as FAC birds) and F100Fs learning to identify targets from the air. Although officially a member of the enlisted ranks Sgt Kappas was a former instructor pilot and had flown in ground support roles in Korea, he was the most qualified man for training the pilots in target identification and the technicalities surrounding having an enlisted man train officer pilots were ignored; this was a particularly big plus for me as Captain Joe and Sgt Kappas sometimes acted as my instructors at the base aero club and it didn't take a very large hint to get invited to ride along in the Airborne FAC bird during a few live fire missions. Eventually I got a ride with Captain Joe in a F100F running the targets. There was a wrinkle in my flight overalls under the G-suit and I came away from the target run with a big purple welt on my leg and a huge new respect for the abilities of the pilots flying fighter/bombers.

After the third or fourth rotation of four on (4/24) three off (3/24) we were all getting punch drunk. During the four on we were getting little or no sleep, performing duties that required extreme concentration and getting frequent adrenaline jolts, the three days off were simply not enough time to fully recuperate between rotations. So, the night I answered the phone in the dispatch tent and spoke to one of the pilot Colonels who was having trouble finding the targets my decision-making apparatus was probably not at one hundred percent. Air Force telephone general practice (maybe it was a written protocol) dictated that when anyone under the rank of field grade answered the phone they answered by identifying their rank and last name. Majors and above were not subject to that rule and would often answer with "<insert name> here".

So, when I answered the phone with "Jay Cee here" the Colonel on the other end assumed my rank was Major or above and launched into the problems he was having with the gunsight systems in his ship and complaining that he had reported these problems repeatedly and what the hell was wrong with the A&E shops that they couldn't get it fixed? I recognized the Colonel by his reputation and knew that he was constantly reporting phantom problems to cover his inability to manage the A4 gyro gunsight systems and sort of told him so; that is, I gave him a quick primer on the sequences he needed to use and other information he was supposed to know. Perhaps I came off a bit testy before the conversation was terminated by the Colonel hanging up at his end.

Half an hour later there was noise at the front of the tent and someone was loudly demanding to see a Major Jaycee. I rolled under the back of the tent and made my escape into the dark night. Whew.

After six weeks of noise, confusion and heat (why in the name of all that might be holy didn't they have this exercise in the winter months?) pegs were pulled and tents were folded (literally) and equipment packed for transport back out of the desert.

Collapsing the temp air operations center was night work and our team hid from the sun and slept during the day, venturing out at night to work in the dispatch center helping to coordinate the C119s evacuating the dry lake bed. Everyone's main topics of conversation revolved around long cold showers, sleep in a real bed, cold beer, hot women, and fresh food.

Kappas pulled all three of our teams together to tell us the "Word" was that we had done an excellent job, the Air Bosses were happy, the Colonels were happy, and the Generals were happy and there would be an acknowledgement of our good work at a muster back at Nellis. Privately he wanted us to know that he agreed with comments he had heard us make during the exercise; these techniques would work in tank country or open areas, maybe in thin forest but not in the triple canopy we had seen in the Lao highlands; we were going to have to find a new approach to capitalize on airpower in the jungle.

After the Sgt's talk Captain Joe and three of his instructor pilots joined us for the flight back to Nellis and as we made a turn over the runway setting up to land the Captain (standing in the space just to the rear of the pilot and copilot) spotted something interesting on the ramp. As our transport taxied to a stop the Captain said, "The Thunderbirds are formed up at the other end of the ramp. Let's go see what the formation flying pukes are up to". What the hell, we were up for it and commandeered a ramp shuttle (Blaske insisted on driving the tug) and drove to the other end of the ramp, thirty-odd unshaven, poorly groomed, disheveled, hollow eyed (even Blaske was messy and dirty), smelly men on the trams behind the tug.

The Thunderbird planes with the red, white and blue paint were lined up five abreast with crew chiefs at attention to the left and in front of each bird, a very ordered, military looking display. In a group to one end and in front of the row of planes were the Thunderbird Pilots posing for photographs with five comely ladies dressed in colorful sun dresses and hats.

Just as I was thinking I would rather be in a dark bar with a cold beer in hand than watching this PR (public relations) spectacle one of the ladies, the one with dark hair, started waving in our direction and yelling something my still half deaf ears (we had just finished weeks of really loud noises) had trouble deciphering. Then all five girls were yelling and waving in our direction; they were the girls we called our "Den Mothers" at "The House With The Blue Fence" (my teams' off base rental house) and they hadn't known where we were for the past month and a half; they wanted us to know they were glad to see us!

Captain Joe and his instructors were laughing and chortling (they loved anything that "stole the thunder" from the Thunderbirds) when the puffed up PR Major in the Ike jacket (they were still issued but nobody wore the Ike jackets, the major was trying to look like he was wearing flight gear) charged over and started a harangue that sputtered to a stop when he either realized he was trying to chew out the FWS chief instructor or he saw Kappas' stony look, or both. He half wheezed, half gasped, spittle flying from his lips, "This is the most un-military looking group of men I have ever seen!"

Kappas replied, "Thanks" and nodded at Blaske to start the tug back down the ramp.

Chapter 12

An Lac PRICS

In the few old photos taken with members of the 8th Coin they were the guys standing off to one side of the frame, in the rear, and out of focus. The constant training to stay anonymous, to stay hidden even in plain sight was not easily overcome. But a few members of this shadowy group did receive a certain notoriety among their peers in Southeast Asia - The An Lac Punting, Rowing, and Intracoastal Canoeing Society.

An Lac ("Happy Place"-a common name in Vietnamese) is a hamlet on an island on the Song Ba Ren, a river in the Cam Nan estuary, inland from the ferry port at Cua Dai. For hundreds of years An Lac had been a center for smugglers and during the Japanese occupation and later French expulsion was an active center for the Viet Minh. Not a place an American would want to spend the night alone and unarmed. But that was exactly the situation that was developing for a group of US Embassy personnel after the De Haviland Beaver they were in was forced to make an emergency landing on the road just west of the center of the hamlet.

We had two teams in the area surveying Mourane Field (later Danang Air Base) in advance of the probable US buildup and support of the Viet Nam Air Force. I was with Tom Major and six lads from Team Orange taking observations with a bubble sextant and plotting positions of features of the base while other people in my group were taking water and soil samples and verifying the condition of the runway and taxiways (I believe they added another runway later). The rest of Team Blue were split into three groups; two assisting (okay, riding along with) the US Navy with their survey and soundings in the estuary, the other doing photo recon and aerial mapping of the approaches to the field in another Beaver.

It was around mid-afternoon when the alarm went out from the broken Beaver, with a status update about half an hour later; the Beavers' big round engine had developed an oil leak and the bird was going to be on the ground until a mechanic could come out from Bien Hoa with the parts and tools needed for repairs. This was not going to be accomplished before nightfall and the aircrew and passengers on the Beaver were getting justifiably nervous about their situation.

Tom Major commandeered the helicopter that was on the field and loaded me in with him and two members of Team Orange, the rest of that team would truck to Highway 1 and south to the connecting roads to the causeway connecting An Lac to the mainland. The two Navy boats in the estuary with four sailors and four other members of Team Blue headed for the island, dual .50s locked and loaded. And the other Beaver in the area with two more members of Team Blue aboard headed south to look the situation over.

I've heard it said that timing is everything, and that seemed to be the case that afternoon; the two Navy boats arrived just as we came overhead and the other Beaver arrived within minutes. Hayes had been in a two-truck convoy bringing supplies up to Mourane Field and had heard our radio chatter; he arrived about ten minutes after we got there with twelve ARVNs. Our pilot landed us next to a rice paddy just to the south of the hamlet, then went airborne to keep an eye open for us. The other Beaver landed on the road, taxing up to within yards of the downed bird. About an hour and a half later the rest of Team Orange got there. The hamlet was being invaded by sea, land and air!

We put a defensive ring around the two Beavers and spent a tense but uneventful night in the hamlet. Around 1300 the next day a truck and jeep convoy from Bien Hoa arrived and I was pleased to see a buddy from Nellis AFB, genius mechanic Floyd, was in charge. He had the damaged bird repaired in less than two hours and we were all on our happy way back to quarters in Saigon while there was still plenty of daylight (except the Navy guys, they had to take the boats back to the base at Cua Dai).

Two nights later Blue Team and Orange Team were settling in for an evening of wine, women, and song (beer, whiskey, bar girls and a bad juke box) at our favorite rooftop bar in Saigon when the Embassy types we'd met at An Lac came in and started buying us rounds. They "just couldn't thank us enough" and "if there was ever anything they could do, etc." Somewhere in all the toasting one of them said something to the effect of, "If you're ever caught up shit creek, these pricks'll bring you a paddle!" Cerone immediately latched on to the phrase and ran with it in typical Cerone fashion.

We, at least the Blue Team, had always called ourselves "Kappas' Cowboys", which had a particular appealing irony given that MSGT Kappas was mostly White Mountain Apache (Geronimo's' tribe).

But now we were the "**An Lac P**unting, **R**owing, and **I**ntracoastal **C**anoeing **S**ociety". The An Lac PRICS.

Cerone had patches made up that we proudly wore on our jump suits and Ma-1 flight jackets. Major Bohannon never seemed to notice, Captain Samuels laughed, Master Sergeant Kappas approved.

Chapter 13

The Boy

The boy was seven or eight, perhaps nine years old when his father told him they were going on a long journey. Too young to have been given his man name, old enough to hunt small game for the cook pot and to track and imitate the sounds of the animals in the hardwood forest.

His father packed trade goods on a short-legged pony and filled baskets on pack frames with supplies for the trip and they left early the next day before the morning mists had lifted. The boy wondered at his mothers' tears, he had never seen her cry before.

They walked south, the father leading the pack horse, the boy trailing, for several days before turning toward the morning sun and descending two more days through a narrow pass into jungle. Then the dense jungle opened up onto a wide plain with scattered jungle and rice paddies and several villages visible in the distance. They continued east for most of another day, the trail widening, until they came to an open air market on what the boys' father called a highway. The boy did not know the name of the market or the village surrounding it and was overwhelmed at the sight of so many people in one place, and the sounds of tongues he did not understand all around him.

They sat in the market for two days while his father traded their goods, then arranged stable for the horse and boarded a "bus" (the way the boy remembered it in later years it may have been a train) to take them further south, arriving eventually at the center of what the boy thought must be the biggest city in the world. They wandered the city, sleeping in the open and eating rice and fish from stalls until his father found the place he was looking for. Even in the short time they had been in the city the boys' ear had been starting to sort the sounds of the languages around them and he was beginning to pick out the meaning of some words and phrases.

And so, after they found the Chinese merchant his father had been seeking he had a tiny understanding of the talks between the merchant and his father even before his father told him the meaning; the boy would be staying with the merchant's family who would feed, cloth, and care for him in exchange for his labor in their warehouses. A small salary would be saved for him to be paid after three years of service.

His heart trying to escape his chest, knees weak the boy kept his face from trembling and did not allow himself any tears that might embarrass his father as they said goodbye. His father started to walk away, then turned and grasping him by the shoulders drew him close and spoke softly in his ear, then turned again and walked away without looking back.

His Chinese hosts (indenture owners, employers, or?) soon recognized that he was a willing worker and a quick study and perhaps in the expectation that he would remain in their service, allowed him to attend classes in their garden with their own children where they studied under a French tutor. He was also introduced to the Cao Dai religion and one or two days a week, depending on the workload in the warehouses, he studied at the temple with the warrior monks.

His work in the warehouses was not too difficult, more running errands and helping with inventory than coolie labor, and he was exposed to the many languages around the Saigon harbor. A natural mimic he spoke these many languages in such a manner that people talking with him thought he was conversing with them in his "native tongue".

Life was good with plenty to eat, a nice room above one of the warehouses, new things to study and learn every day, and the river to play in and on in between all his other activities. He knew that one day he would have to choose between a life in Saigon or perhaps return to the mountains and seek out his tribe, returning as a man grown and with a bride price saved. But that day of decision was still far in the future (to his young viewpoint) and the now was delicious.

Then the French Vichy government invited the Japanese into the country. Within three months all of the Wong family warehouses had been looted and the Wongs had arranged with the Binh Xuyen (organized river pirates) to smuggle them out to India. Before they left Master Wong gave the boy a ring of keys to the warehouses and family villa and disclosed a hiding place where they would leave silver and gold coins for the boys' maintenance until they returned, perhaps in two years or less. He never saw or heard from them again.

The years of war that never ended began. He enlisted in the Cao Dai militia that fought as allies with the Viet Minh against the Vichy French and the Japanese until the end of WWII in Europe. When the Brits came in to try to help stabilize the country the boy, now a man called Chan, worked as a guide and interpreter to a Gurkha regiment and participated in battles with them with French and un-repatriated Japanese allies against the Viet Minh.

The Cao Dai and Viet Minh had a similar agenda in that both groups wanted an end to foreign domination (both hated the French in any flavor) which found them fighting sometimes as allies but disagreed about the form of government that should rule, particularly after the last king of Viet Nam abdicated. The Viet Minh wanted a communist, anti-religion government (in North Viet Nam Cao Dai and Catholics were being persecuted alike by the communist government) and the Cao Dai favored a coalition government representing all parties which pitted them one black clad army against another black clad army.

When the Americans backed the Catholic regime of Diem and General The of the Cao Dai Militia was assassinated the Cao Dai lost a lot of their influence in the region and the Cao Dai Militia were conscripted into the Army of the Republic of Viet Nam (South). Many of the militia members choose to flee rather than be forced into an army which they viewed as part of a corrupt regime. Some fled to Ba Den Mountain in the delta and others into the Annamite Mountains to the northwest.

Captain Chan took his company of one hundred seasoned fighters and went north to the mountains of his birth. There they subsisted on game, edible roots and other bounty of the forest. They hired out as guards for traders (mostly opium growers) and other mercenary work and killed Viet Minh and North Viet Nam Army personnel wherever the opportunity arose.

By the time he met the Americans on the trail in the Houaphan District of Laos he had been at war for sixteen years; his company had dwindled to twenty hard-core veterans and he had looked for his village of birth in the highlands on both sides of the Gia Truong Son (Annamese Cordillera) for three years but was never able to identify it; not surprising in an area where slash-and-burn farmers moved every few years. But what was surprising and disappointing was the fact that he was never able to find anyone who spoke his first language.

He did not know if his fathers' last words to him were in reference to his man name, family name or name of his tribe but he could still hear his father softly saying, "Remember, you are Baphang".

Chapter 14

The Gaur

We were in a place with no familiar landmarks, a place of new sights, sounds and smells, the dust on the roads and paths a new and different color and even the texture of the light seemed strange. I felt a relief and reconnection to reality when I smelled and heard something I thought I knew; horse sweat and a low snorting and blowing. There would be horses around the next bend in the road. If there were horses there would be people, I signaled the team behind me and two and two of them melted into the brush on either side of the road while the other three followed me around the bend, weapons at the ready. Damn, why was it my turn to be on point?

The morning before we had crossed a suspension bridge over a narrow but deep river bed and began climbing through a green tunnel in the direction of the Laos/North Viet Nam border into a no-mans-land between two border crossings high in the mountains where the province of Hua Phan (or Houaphan) pushed into Viet Nam. Looking at a map of Laos and imagining the lower provinces as a pistol grip and Sayaboury Province as the trigger, Hua Phan could be the hammer surrounded on three sides by North Viet Nam and is the Lao province nearest Hanoi. With four major mountain passes and a couple of rivers connecting the two, the province lay on the south side of the centuries old route the "Annamese Problem" (the former Kings name for Vietnamese invaders) took to invade Laos.

We climbed most of the morning with the path changing in the early afternoon to an undulating uphill downhill trek for the rest of the day until our guide halted us at a point where the trail fell away steeply to one side and rose just as steeply on the other with a split in the limestone cliff on the uphill side and a flat wooded area making a very defensible position for our night bivouac. The trees were about eight inches around and spaced almost evenly about eight to ten feet apart with canopy fifteen or twenty feet above; we would be able to sleep comfortably off the ground in hammocks and bug netting (we were still low enough for some nasty little swarming "no-see-ums" to be annoying) and with ponchos slung over the hammocks would be reasonably dry in the light showers common this time of year at our altitude.

Early next morning after breaking camp and breakfasting on cold rations I watched the sun light up the mountains across from us while we were still swaddled in shade on our side of the valley. I could see blue mountain ridges marching off north and south and as the mists rose and dissipated a lovely mosaic of terraces and rice paddies appeared in the valley floors below. Roadside Buddhas placed next to the copse we had camped in added to the spiritual feeling of the morning. I placed a flower, a rice ball and a precious small orange for one of the Buddhas as we left. You never know.

Not visible in the idyllic scene before us was the fact that the area we were entering into, similar in size, elevation and topography to Yosemite National Park back in the States, was home to several varieties of poisonous snakes, poisonous plants, poisonous insects and several species of animal that would love to maul us or eat us, or both. Of the fifty thousand or so inhabitants of the small villages hidden in the mountains around and above us probably one third would be happy to kill or capture and sell us, one third might simply shoot us for being "other" and most of the villages would be protected by animal pits, deadfalls or other traps for the uninvited. At any time there could be anywhere from two thousand to five thousand hostile troops (sometimes more) close enough to hunt us as soon as they heard we were near. For our teams and many of the guys who followed us there would never be any cavalry coming to the rescue, no "Jolly Green Giant" air evac heli, probably no acknowledgement by anyone that we had even been there. There was no way to survive very long in this zone in Hua Phan or anywhere up and down the Annamese Cordillera without the "aid and comfort" to be provided by some local "friendlies".

In the west and northwest of Laos friendly connections to hill tribes were facilitated through their relationships with an American, Bill Young, whose family had been missionaries in the region for two previous generations. Our mission was to rendezvous with a man recommended to us as anti-communist, and with a lot of "face" among the hill peoples in the east and south, by a French contact (hotelier, opium trafficker, gun smuggler and father of numerous happy children with a local wife) in Vientiane.

Kappas may have explained to our contact that if any harm befell us on this mission he, the Frenchman, would not live to see any of his grandchildren again. Samuels was supposed to lead the mission (officer grade stuff) but came down with a stomach ailment a day before we were to debark (we had told him to drink the beer not the water) and couldn't cut it. Kappas was already balancing too many balls, Bohannon was in the States and we had already proven we could play in the big sandbox without adult supervision. So it would be six Blue Teamers, a PARU, and a local guide we would pick up on the way in to get the job done. We were not to share the danger or the fruits with anyone else for the time being.

My heart rate was up a little as we moved to the border of and into a deciduous forest at a spot near the rendezvous point marked on my map. I had just folded and put away my map and moved up to point position when I smelled the horses.

As I cleared the corner I saw three short stocky men dressed in black pajamas and with full beards and red turbans standing next to a string of pack animals with bundles stacked neatly in the shade next to the horses. All three were armed but made no move toward their weapons and ignored, or pretended to ignore, our appearance. A few meters up the road a clean-shaven man was squatting in the shade with a horse hair whisk in one hand and an un-lit long-stemmed pipe in the other, a simmering pot of water boiling over a small fire on one side and a Kalashnikov on the other. He was wearing rubber soled sandals, a dark green military cut shirt, a big black wristwatch and a black cloth wrapped around his middle and over his short pants like a loin cloth, on his head was a black rimless hat adorned with red and yellow bead work that looked like a picture I had seen in Life Magazine of a "pillbox" hat worn by that Senator Kennedys' wife. I took a quick mental picture of all that and then froze in my tracks. The three men behind me froze in position as well, and then started slowly backing away.

Directly ahead of me and commanding all my attention was an enormous beast and it was staring straight at me and making a low clicking/grunting noise and swinging its head from side to side. It looked like a water buffalo with a severe case of gigantism. The thing was easily seven and a half feet high at the shoulders, a ton and a half or so of mean with a red Mohawk stripe running down the ridge of muscle on its back. And it was looking straight at me, when I shifted slowly to my left the beast turned so that it was squarely facing me, when I shifted slowly to my right it shifted with me, goddamn I was not enjoying this dance at all.

I hadn't seen one before but knew from briefings and photos what it was and knew its reputation, this mighty beast called a Gaur was said to batter tigers flat and in the lowlands near the coast stomp saltwater crocs to death. It was even said that when they were in bad temper they would gore and batter elephants. And it kept staring at me as if trying to decide if I was worth stepping on. Oh shit, oh shit, oh dear.

Four of my team appeared in my peripheral vision, two on either side on the path and I was hoping to hell they wouldn't decide to fire on the thing and piss it off. I risked looking away and glanced at the squatting man who was grinning on both sides of his pipe stem, the asshole.

Gingerly, my own sweat damn near blinding me, and holding back a strong desire to flee or pee or both, I slid over to the side of the path, the gaur following my move by shifting position and still staring at me. Slo-o-o-wly I took off my 'ruck and placed it on the ground next to the AK47 and squatted next to the man in the funny little hat. Still grinning he took the pipe stem out of his mouth, looked at the dial on his watch and said (in a clipped British accent), "its tea time, care for a spot of Barkley?" then "don't look at that big cow and it will go away" and dropped a handful of tea leaves into the boiling water at his side.

I looked around back down the path and to both sides and saw that no one else was moving a muscle before I nodded "yes". As the tea steeped my companion went exploring in a fold of his loincloth and produced two glasses (real glass) with silver chasing on the bottoms and rims, Russian style, and a small metal box filled with sugar cubes. I reached into a side pocket of my pack and pulled out two melted gooey Baby Ruth candy bars, a P28 can opener and a twelve ounce can of Del Monte Freestone peaches (comshawed from the Naval Mission), being very careful the whole time to not look up the path at the gaur. A hard exercise sort of like "do not think the word elephant for three minutes."

By the time we had finished our first glass of sweet hot tea the beast had ambled off and everyone had semi-relaxed in the shade and broken out some foodstuffs to share, with the exception of Hayes and one of the ten or twelve men who had come quietly out of the forest behind me.

We had seen the Gaur, the Krating Daeng, the Red Bull. And we had made the acquaintance of the man we had come to meet, Captain Chan of the Cao Dai Militia.

The man we would know as "Baphang".

Chapter 15

Sgt Johnny Sorenson

The flower print shirt, tan Bermuda shorts, mustache and sandals were probably supposed to make him look like a civilian contractor or maybe even a tourist. His erect posture, crew cut hair, alert eyes and measured gait all said, "Military"; the snap-link stainless steel bracelet attached to the stainless-steel oyster backed Rolex watch said either "Special Forces" or "CIA". And the fact that he was a foot taller than any of the native populations in Thailand and South East Asia (SEA) meant that he was never going to "blend in with the locals" (Cerone snickered at the thought).

By the time we met him Staff Sergeant Sorenson, John H. had probably attended every specialty course offered NCOs by the US Army, he was a Ranger, a sniper, a field artillery spotter, a Pathfinder, a Master Jumper, and qualified in several other areas that all added up to "Poster US Army Sergeant" and an outstanding representative of the Special Forces. The Sgt was on staff with General Blackburn, the Commanding Officer of the 77th Special Forces Group (became the 7th SFG in May, 1960) attached to the Military Assistance Advisory Group in Viet Nam (MAAG) responsible for the training cadres operating in Thailand and Laos as "Operation Hotfoot".

General Blackburn (WWII Hero of the Philippines) and his number one in SEA, Colonel "Bull" Simons were men who knew that a key to successful insurgency and counter-insurgency operations was a combination of planning and flexibility; they knew the need to monitor and collate feedback and information from the field, then synthesize and rapidly disseminate the information as new procedures and techniques back to operators in the field was paramount to the success of their Special Forces teams.

To meet this need for getting fresh information to the teams in-country SFG Captain Feltzer, operating out of South Viet Nam, was put in charge of an on-the-job refresh and retrain program and was pleased to have Sgt Johnny Sorenson assigned as one of his five "wheelmen", the "war dog" NCOs that would visit and monitor training camps and field operations, in some cases assisting with training programs. The training and operations manuals developed from input from these five "war dogs" were used (and may still be in use) by Special Forces and Special Operators in all branches of the US Services and by some foreign armed forces training cadres.

The Sergeants' reaction to our team members when we met him in Thailand was to dismiss us as a "bunch of kids"; young, green, wet-behind-the-ears Air Force technicians in fatigues that still had a new shine and no rank or insignia and carrying little olive green tool bags. They were there to assist in training the Thai PARU and a few Lao partisans in radio communications and maintenance and stay out of the way of the other training syllabus. He barely acknowledged we were there.

His viewpoint changed a little when we appeared at a jump off point in Thailand heavily armed and wearing our maroon berets with embroidered Jump Pins attached (in lieu of a unit badge) faded fatigues and Pathfinder Patches (Hayes was sporting a Ranger shoulder flash) before changing into our non-descript "civilian" grey jumpsuits. And his eyes were opened further when he witnessed the speed and efficiency we displayed in facilitating ground-to-air communications and directing traffic into Wattay Airport in support of General Phoumis' return to the Laos capital.

The sergeant was curious and wanted to know more about these kids and their outfit. What clues had he missed and who the hell were they? Then we disappeared; scuttlebutt said we were somewhere in Laos east of Savannakhet. By getting on the "NCO net" and asking a few well-placed questions he had discovered a little information about our own Sergeant Kappas and the fact that the MSgt had been a flying officer with the Mosquito Squadron in Korea (it would be awhile before he learned that he had a tenuous connection with another member of 8th COIN), information that only made him more curious.

He had been traveling and visiting SFG teams in Thailand, Laos, and South Viet Nam; places with names like Takhli, Phitsanulok, (Thailand) Luang Prabang, and Pakse (Laos) and places that didn't appear on any maps, and had even visited the radio monitoring station we had established in Muang Nuong, for almost a year before he saw our small group of Air Force techs again.

It was probably just coincidence or serendipity that placed him at Wattay Field when we came back in-country; although anyone with a suspicious nature (Hayes) might remark that Kappas had a knack and a habit of managing coincidences or giving serendipity a shove when the occasion called for it.

Whatever the circumstances, the SFG Sergeant was in our new operations shack (not exactly "in", the shack only had three walls) with two galvanized buckets filled with ice and bottles of Singha beer, followed closely by Kappas' favorite PARU (Tom Minor) who was waving bottles of Beefeater Gin and Roses Lime Juice before we had even finished checking in. Samuels joined the party with additional refreshments and stories were told, toasts were made, and a decision was reached; Sgt Johnny Sorenson was going to take it upon himself to instruct us in some information, skill sets, and expertise we would need if we were going to be trooping around in the countryside. That is, if Samuels and Kappas cleared it with Captain Feltzer.

The idea of having the stiff backed "Old Salty Dog" sergeant as an instructor might have caused a few moans and groans but we had discovered there was a crack in the sergeants' stern exterior, a habit that let an alert listener realize that behind the military face was a warm, caring person; instead of identifying himself as "Sergeant Sorenson" or "Staff Sergeant Sorenson" he always referred to himself as "Sergeant Johnny Sorenson", a clue that took us only a short while to recognize.

He would train us on detecting and avoiding punji stick pits, deadfalls, spring traps, and other surprises we might meet on or off the paths, and most importantly, he would give us much needed training about surviving in areas where there would be land mines and boobytraps.

Land mines are possibly the nastiest weapon in a foot soldiers arsenal, they maim or kill anything that comes in contact with them; man or animal, woman, child, old, young, healthy or infirm. And can go on killing long after the soldiers have left the field.

They could be left behind to be triggered days, months, or years later simply because of the effort and or time (and danger) involved in clearing them or as intentional terror and intimidation tools. Or their location might simply be forgotten, maps lost and the people who placed them gone.

A conventional army might use explosive mines to form a defensive perimeter or to deny access to an area (usually fenced and marked) or they might use them to focus the enemy into fields of fire. An unconventional army, if they mark them at all, may use subtle warning signs such as broken sticks, piles of pebbles, bent saplings, or other hard to discern and easily erased signals. The guerillas will use them as offensive weapons in place of artillery or airpower as an inexpensive and effective means to reach out and strike over distances and to wreak psychological damage on both opposing soldiers and inhabitants of an area they wish to control.

Sgt Johnny Sorenson taught us that the unconventional warriors (at least the ones we would be going up against) will use them (usually in a pattern of threes) as a killing field or to bunch troops together in an ambush scenario, but they will also place them (sometimes singly) on paths of travel, at junctions or in shady, restful appearing spots or other places where they might catch the unwary, they will even place them inside hamlets and villages they control. They will leave minefields unmarked, uncovered by fields of fire and unattended, with no thought or concern about collateral damage (in later years they would use their indoctrination programs to convince the local inhabitants that all collateral damage was our fault).

Part of our enemies' approach to the use of land mines was economics and availability but a part of it reflected philosophical differences: they took to heart Chairman Mao's Long March dicta that "to win territory is no cause for joy; to lose territory is no cause for sorrow". Instead of controlling an areas' geography they were bent on controlling an areas' population. Similar to the later US Army proposed program of "winning hearts and minds", but much more effective.

Starting with Team Blue and continuing on with Teams Orange and Green he began training the Air Force techs in the finer points of land mine and booby trap detection and avoidance with chalk talks and visits to an SFG training camp in Thailand. He continued to keep the training up-to-date through semi-regular visits to their operations centers and teams in the field.

The sergeant enjoyed his role in instructing the SFG and AF COIN teams in the nuances of pressure plates, trip wires, vibration sensors, remote detonation devices, and a particular device we could expect to encounter (and often did), the split bamboo trigger. The bamboo trigger had almost no metal parts and was very difficult to locate with metal detectors available at the time and could be used buried under a thin layer or as a vibration sensor, detonating stake mines, flat mines, or ugliest of all, bouncing mines.

Years before he had gone to Korea as a Private First Class and come back to the States as a battle-wise, old-for-his-age Sergeant and veteran of a war people at home seemed ready to forget. He had gained expertise in survival, small arms and demolition and had discovered a talent for mentoring; adopting and training replacements as they transferred into his unit (saving lives with his on-the-job-training).

When he came back stateside he started taking general education courses at Berkley with the goal in mind of getting a teaching certificate but found it difficult to communicate with non-soldiers or non-veterans.

Other people his age seemed like children and for over a year he foundered not finding a social group he fit into or job opportunities that needed his skill sets in a civilian market.

After a few beers with a colleague who had stayed in the service and was posted as a recruiter in San Francisco he learned that he could get advancement in grade and an assignment as an instructor if he re-upped in the "Green Machine". The services were top heavy after Korea with the ratio of officers to enlisted personnel out of balance. As the lower ranks completed their enlistments or were released from their duty extensions this balance tipped ever further in the wrong direction, part of the solution was to "riff" some of the field grade officers (Reduction In Force, officers were offered early retirement or in some cases were given the opportunity to stay in the service as Senior NCOs or Warrant Officers until eligible for retirement based on time in service, combat duty points, etc., at their previous rank) and another part of the solution was to focus on recruitment and training of a "peacetime" professional military enlisted force.

When we met him Sgt Johnny Sorenson knew he was a lifer, he liked military life with its discipline and structure, he enjoyed the camaraderie among his fellow men at arms, the feeling of accomplishment as he trained men to stay alive, hell he had to admit he enjoyed the rush and thrill of armed conflict, and he had no family or other ties outside the military; besides what could he do in civilian life? He knew he would put in his thirty and retire.

Then he took an R&R (rest and recuperation) in New Zealand and met the beautiful Nan.

Chapter 17

Two Jumps

The 8th COIN were "'tweeners" (between Korea and what was once considered the start in Viet Nam) and had to relearn or become pioneers in many aspects of our operations. The Air Commando had been shut down after Korea and that opening in the fabric of future Air Force Missions was identified by the Generals who sponsored and supported our little wing; these were the upper echelon officers who did not necessarily believe that big bombers won wars by themselves, nor did they believe the entire Air Force should be fighter based, they saw a (very real, very big) need for fighter/bomber squadrons providing close support to ground troops in future wars big or small and saw us as a tool to preserve former ground support tactics lessons and develop new ones. Our Mission Statement was broadened and all the 8th COIN Ready Reaction Teams trained to be what in today's Air Force would be called Special Tactics Squads and Combat Controllers and in a couple of instances Para Rescuemen (for land operations, we were scuba qualified but not combat divers or rescue swimmers).

Jump status and quiet insertions into perhaps hostile areas was key to our methodology and we all got in enough jumps to maintain our qualifications for an extra $35.00 per month. Every jump was unique, no two were ever alike but some really stand out in my memory.

One may have been an Air Force first (remember this was before Air Force Para Rescue protocols and teams were established), it was certainly outside our usual scope and a first for us. We were already packed to go TDY and had stowed our Temperate Zone and Cold Zone Ready Bags in our storage locker at Nellis, we were about to go TDY to a tropical environment when Major Bohannon got a phone call that offered him an opportunity to demonstrate the value of his program, and not incidentally help him garner support and funding, always his principal concerns.

Before dawn a Nellis based training formation of one F100F (two-seater) and three F100Cs had been returning from a base in Kansas and had hit an unseasonably early snowstorm on the way back over the Colorado Rockies. They were fine at altitude but the F model had an engine problem and lost power descending through a rill in the storm clouds. The rest of the formation followed them down and had visibility long enough to see that the two pilots had ejected over what appeared to be a meadow at the high tree line (around 10,000 ft) and get an accurate fix on their location.

Half an hour later a tanker at altitude over the Utah Colorado border picked up a distress call from their handheld emergency set and the message that one of the pilots was injured slightly; the other had a compound fractured leg. They were in need of immediate aid and did not have adequate survival equipment. They were in a remote area in the Holy Cross range and it would be several days before rescuers could reach them overland; there were no helicopters capable of operating at the required altitudes within less than two days distance, closer ones were socked in.

Our transports were already fueled and standing by and we had our supply of packed 'chutes and other gear readily available. Bohannon rounded up an Army doctor with an Airborne Ranger patch who was attending a seminar on the base and Sgt Knight scrounged up arctic survival suits and smoke jumper helmets and gloves. Our riggers filled drop canisters with tents, sleeping bags, alcohol stoves, and a couple of axes, medical supplies and other equipment to be dropped in just ahead of us. One load would wait to be dropped after we were on the ground (in case the first canisters landed out of easy range).

Morrison was picked to go because he was our trauma guy, Cerone and I were just standing too near the door when Bohannon was selecting who would jump, or maybe it was because we were the only ones small enough to fit the remaining survival suits after Morrison and the Army doc were outfitted.

The turbulence was really awful as we circled above the site waiting for a break in the cloud cover and I was in danger of overheating in my layers of clothing and worried that I would start sweating inside the suit, a real danger in a cold climate. The turbulence and heat were giving me a bad ache behind my eyes and the only reason I was not throwing up was that someone might see me. I was anxious to get out of the miserable flying machine and into clear air I thought; until the door opened and the cold air hit me.

I had on so many layers I could hardly move, and suspected if I jumped without a 'chute I would bounce for hours, but the cold still bit right through to my skin, my poor testes were looking for a warm place to hide and I knew my eyeballs would shatter if anything touched them. I waddled to the door, was hooked up and stepped out looking down through wedding cake layers of cloud and blowing snow at white on white, on white, with a puff of orange smoke and a green dye marker to try to focus on through my helmet mesh. Then the wind pulled me around and everything was just white.

It had taken six plus hours to get equipped and gear up and go to the site; a short time to react but not short enough to allow us much daylight when we got there, we had lucked out to get any usable opening in the cloud cover and none of us was willing to let the two guys on the ground stay there overnight with no help. No sane person would have made the jump under any but the most demanding circumstances (gun to the head). I cussed at myself for being a fool all the way down.

I "felt" the ground coming up before I saw it, I failed to "feel" the tree that was waiting for me and just caught a glimpse of it in the dim light before I was hung up in it. I couldn't work my harness release with the heavy gloves on and took one off to free myself just as a snow laden gust hit me and slammed me into a branch temporarily pinning my left hand to the tree with a branch stub stuck in the top of my hand. To hell with the release, I took my drop knife out and cut myself free of the tree and the harness. As soon as I was on the ground in the almost bare protected circle at the base of the tree I had an overwhelming urge to urinate, not an easy task with a damaged paw and in multiple layers of clothing. I told myself it wasn't an effect of fear; I just needed to mark my spot.

It was cold and my hand was numb when it was injured, the painful part came when the Army doc pulled my glove off to dress the wound, which only happened hours later after we had set up three tents, got some soup going and he and Morrison had stabilized the two pilots. We spent about three months inside of two days and nights before a rescue heli' was able to get in and start evac'ing people. Both pilots made full recoveries and one, the instructor, set a record he would probably rather not have made at Nellis, he survived more ejections, including two in one morning, than anyone else flying fighters and fighter bombers.

When my mother noted the scar on my left hand I didn't hesitate to tell her what had happened, I mean the incident was in the US, made the local papers, and couldn't violate any Secrecy Act, could it?

And another jump I still dream about: Sometimes fear reached out to clutch my heart after the fact, some of the things we did were scary before, scary during and really scary after the event when realization kicked in. We were doing a night infiltration jump into an abandoned field near Xam Nua in Houaphan Province. I was carrying a lot of gear that night, my turn to carry the radio and I had my usual weapons and ammunition along with a field pack equipped with supplies for a five day patrol, and two cans of Del Monte Freestone peaches for my friend Baphang who would be waiting on the ground for us. I was at almost double my body weight with all the gear on and my emergency chute was an ankle model that would be useless if the main didn't open, I only carried it to give away to a family on the ground. This would be a static line jump, but with the new (almost) steerable parachutes we would be able to make some adjustments to our glide path.

Hayes, Cerone, and I would be going in-country with four men we did not know and did not like very much, they just smelled like trouble. And they had made it obvious that they did not like traveling with three "techies" who would almost certainly put their, the four hard cases, mission in jeopardy. They had said as much the day before our departure. One of them, a guy named Leon, had taken a particular dislike to me. We had exchanged some harsh words and would have come to blows without Cerone's intervention, an incident I put down to mission jitters. We probably should have called Kappas and asked for a "no go", he was always open to our hunches, but macho prevailed and we didn't say anything. Hayes just put on a half smile and we loaded up at the scheduled time.

Hayes would be our jumpmaster, standing in the door and seeing us all out before hooking up and jumping himself, Cerone would be first on the stick, followed by me with the radio gear, then Leon and the rest of the four we were guiding in. When the ready light came on each man would hook up the troop in front of him and give him two taps on the head to let him know he was ready to go. The jumpmaster would hook up the last man then return to the door and wait for the light that signaled us out. With all the gear I was carrying my jump technique was to cross my arms over my chest (to keep my rifle from taking off my nose) and dive head down so that as I went into the slipstream the shock as I hit the end of the static line would be minimized.

I felt two taps, the light went "go", I got a little shot of adrenaline, the small red light on Cerone's helmet disappeared into the dark, and I dove out. Catching the flick of my un-attached static line in his peripheral vision "Super Human Hayes" caught the tail in one hand and holding on to the aircraft frame above the doorway with the other hand was pulled out where he took the shock of my weight through his body, popping his sternum and cutting his hand but opening my chute. He then had to pull his ripcord manually, and in a hurry, we were jumping at a low altitude.

I don't know if my nerves fooled me into thinking I felt the taps, if Leon thought he had hooked me up and gave me the signal, or what exactly went wrong. Leon didn't show up at the rendezvous point so we never got to ask him. When Hayes straggled in late for the rendezvous he was a little worse for wear but insisted he could hack it for the few days we would be in the field. We dressed his hand and tightly wrapped his chest and he toughed it out for the next five days. When we got back to base he was shipped to Clark for surgery to repair the damage to his sternum, leaving him with a big star shaped scar on his chest. Tough bastard.

Thinking about that incident later scared the hell out of me, it still does. I still get the shivers thinking about how close I came to being a smudge that night. Hayes refused to talk about the jump, or Leon, other than to acknowledge my thanks with his patented smirk, raised pinky and a "that's one".

When I asked Baphang if he or his people had seen any trace of Leon he looked directly at Hayes and said, "An animal got him".

Chapter 17

Turning Point

Cerone was my co-captain for fun; we bought "team" cars, rented off base houses, chased women and generally kept the party going when we were off duty or on R&R (Rest & Recreation). Hayes was my bush partner and self-appointed body guard, Blaske the go-to-guy for out-of-the box thinking. But Beckstrom was my closest friend since the first days waiting for boot camp to start and I had convinced him to come along when Bobby Grimes recruited me to apply for a tryout with "a special outfit".

On our first leave after training I had gone home with him to his family's farm in Minnesota and spent five days there with him and his family. In a way we were like a pair of mis-sized bookends; both blue-eyed and blond but one 6' and 165 lbs., the other 5'6" and 135 lbs. He was my buddy.

But now I was very worried, my buddy and I were having a disagreement (an argument in 15 second bursts over a field radio every two or three hours or so) that I thought could have serious consequences for him. Instead of rendezvousing with Team Green for evacuation from the mountains north of the Plaines de Jares (PDJ) he had decided to "pull a Pop Buell" and escort a party of Mei out of the mountains to refuge at Long Chien. He was convinced that his civilian clothes, beard, and USAAID identification would get them through any encounters with Neutralist troops. And at one time he might have been right, but I was certain that time had passed.

In the earlier days of the Programs Evaluation Office (PEO) in Laos the Royalists and Pathet Lao, and later the Neutralists troops had been, as good Buddhists should be, reluctant to kill, with both sides of an encounter often firing over the heads of their foes. More often than not they let non-combatants pass with perhaps some minor bullying and maybe the exchange of some livestock or perhaps a silver tael (bar) or two. But that began to change with the arrival of Russian and Viet Minh advisors and a greater influx of members of the North Vietnam Army (NVA) who brought new levels of violence and cruelty to the mix.

So, when Baphang interpreted the Yao trackers information early one morning, I went into panic mode. They related that on the "highway" (old trade road through the mountains into Viet Nam to the east, barely passable to motor vehicles in the dry season, impassable to all but the most determined man or animal in the monsoon season) there was a noisy group of three hands (fifteen people) and one French, with children, cattle, pigs, and chickens moving south above the crossroads where our trail cut the highway. To the south of the crossroads was a group of about eight hands (about forty people) including three French, three black suits, two hands (ten) of green suits, and the rest all tan suits. The Yao called all round eyed and tall (to them anyway) people French. The "French" in the first group had to be Beckstrom with the locals he was escorting. The "French" in the second group were probably Russian advisors, the "black suits" Viet Minh, "green suits" NVA, and the balance Pathet Lao.

Beckstrom and company were not going to meet Kong Lee's Neutralists troops; they were heading straight toward some seriously bad guys.

I dropped my ruck', tightened the laces on my boots, attached an extra canteen and three ammo magazines to my belt and started running, Hayes and Baphang in trail. I had to warn Beckstrom and get his people off the highway deep into the forest and safety.

We had a hard 6 klicks (6 kilometers, a little less than 4 miles) to cover on a mountain trail in a part of the mountains where running around blind corners was never a good idea, less so with un-friendlies in the neighborhood. My body was telling me I was pushing too hard, my mind telling me I needed to be cautious but I could not slow my pace. On we ran, trying to keep a sprint pace in an endurance race.

We were a little more than halfway to the crossroads when all the birds around us suddenly took flight, then quickly landed and the always constant background noises in the high forests went quiet for a moment. In that quiet we heard the cork-pulled-from-a- jug sound of mortars, then explosions and heavy machine gun and small arms fire echoing from a distance. "Too Late, Too Late!" a voice screamed in my head and my muscles tensed to push even harder down the trail.

Baphang stopped me with a hand on my shoulder and a nod down off the trail. When I didn't move quickly in that direction, Hayes gave me a not-too-gentle shove and we descended down into a dry watercourse. We followed the sides of the streambed, Baphang in the lead, slowly picking our way, and with tension heightening, stopping only to hydrate and refill our canteens at a small spring in the streambed.

First the smells hit us. I can't, I won't, try to describe the gut-wrenching smell of a mixture of cordite, ozone, feces, human and animal blood, burnt flesh and smoke that assailed our senses. Even Baphang looked ready to puke and we hadn't seen the carnage yet.

Slithering on our bellies, moving carefully one at a time, we moved up the stream embankment through a hollow spot in the foliage to the top of a small ridge where we looked down on a nightmare scene in a clearing on the highway where there was ford across a small river. There were bodies everywhere; bodies of old men, women and children, bodies of babies, bodies of livestock and dogs. And just down-trail from our position, lay the body of my friend Beckstrom, wearing a blood soaked guayabera shirt, pistol in hand. The blue-eyed, apple pie eating, good Lutheran, All-American- Boy, son-of-a bitch had gotten himself killed. God damn I was pissed. How could he do this to us, his team, himself? Then I felt shock at my anger toward him, mixed with a feeling of overweening grief. We watched for a couple of eternities as the "French" and the "black suits" stood off to one side smoking while the rest of their people picked through the remains looting. I felt a sickening twist in the back of my brain and heard a flat, cold, detached voice inside my head. I gave Hayes a look and he nodded his understanding.

We watched and waited as the entire company moved off southwest down the trail dragging the few surviving pigs and livestock and carrying a few chickens by the legs. With a sloppy looking rear guard following, the column moved out of sight.

After a quick whispers-directly- in-the-ears conference, Hayes, reluctantly (worried about my safety? didn't want to miss any possibility of action?) agreed to go back and bring the rest of the team forward. Baphang and I would try to secure Beckstrom's body from depredation from animals then follow the column to wherever they set up for the night.

We did a quick reconnoiter and then went into the clearing to check for survivors, there were none. The bodies were all shredded, blown up, and mutilated even after death, all innocents, all non-combatants, none of soldier age (except Beckstrom), a precursor to the slaughter at Ban Ban a couple of years later. This wasn't a military encounter, it was murder. The Russians and Viet Minh were thoroughly teaching their Lao students. After we wrapped Beckstrom in the remains of a couple of shelter halves and a small tarp we hoisted him into a tree for later recovery and left the grim scene.

Baphang found a sheltered spot on the river where we cleaned up and tried to clear the blood and gore off our boots and trouser legs. I strained to remain alert and sensitive to my surroundings while tamping down the odors and trying not to hear the after-sounds of the killing field behind me, the sounds of swarms of flies and other flying insects, a clicking that I later learned was from a kind of beetle, the rustling of leaves as cooling limbs on bodies now dead contracted, the sound of escaping gases from those same bodies, and the talking between birds gathering for a feast. And I had to hold back my need to weep and mourn, that would have to come later.

We choked down a couple of handfuls of the cooked rice and ham he had the foresight to bring knowing we were going to need all the strength we could muster in the next hours. Grief caught me for a moment and I sat shaking violently until I could push it back down to some level just below consciousness, then we got up, checked our gear, and started down the highway.

We didn't have to track them very far; the clearing where the slaughter took place was only about 3 klicks from an old abandoned revenue station (taxing goods going up and down the highway) left from the days of French occupation. There were a few of the local wood and thatch huts on stilts and a stone blockhouse/residence with a veranda on the south side and an outhouse just to the rear. Some taxman in the old days must have lived pretty well.

We found a lay-up with good cover on a rise to the north of the hamlet right where "the book", and M&M's training, said we should be and settled in to watch the camp. The sun was getting low when I "sensed" the presence of my team mates and felt a slow squeeze on my ankle that confirmed that they were there, they had found our spot just as I knew they would – same training, woodcraft and bush wisdom told them where we'd be. There I lay un-moving, sweat dripping from my headband into my eyes, crouch itching, ass sore from diarrhea, and some insect biting my neck when I saw a chilling sight about a meter in front of me. A snake with an arrowhead shaped head was moving toward my position.

The vipers in this range were territorial and aggressive, and possessed of a deadly bite and like the water moccasin in the States would bite repeatedly when in attack mode. And I was trapped; any sudden motion could give away our position and endanger the entire team. As I was resolving to just let the damn thing close enough to bite and try to quietly pull its head off I saw a green leaf tube moving forward in my peripheral vision. There was a pffft sound and the snake was writhing with a dart through its eye pinning it to a branch on the ground in front of me. I looked to my left and acknowledged Baphang's grin with a loud double blink.

We watched closely while the camp arranged itself, taking careful note of sentry positions and terrain features, the Russians taking the stone lodging just as we knew they would, the NVA and Pathet Lao picking huts, and the Viet Minh picking a campsite off to themselves, again just as we expected them to do. While they were starting cook fires and killing and prepping the pigs and chickens we were planning our assault. Only forty of them and ten of us, we felt the odds were in our favor. When the lao lao (rice whiskey), vodka and beer came out we knew the odds were in our favor.

Somewhere in our training cycles I had come to accept the fact that I might have to take a human life and found that in the heat of a skirmish I could let my training and a certain mental trick take over while I watched myself act from a state of detachment, but I still had not become comfortable with the reality of killing.

And even in my cold anger I had not forgotten the prohibition against our initiating hostile action and the often sternly repeated mission statement that included the words "avoid contact whenever possible". But now a turning point was reached; the "secret war" had suddenly become personal.

I wanted to kill all the sons-a -bitches.

Chapter 18

Night Engagement

When Hayes looked down at Beckstrom's body and the carnage in the clearing below them he didn't feel shock or surprise, only a vague unease and sadness and a detached wonder at all the flies. "If the lame ass had to go off and do something stupid...", "JayCee told the dumb bastard not to try to pull off this stunt..." "Fuck. What will JayCee do now?" He felt a remote sadness at losing a friend, team mate, sparring partner and drinking buddy. Unease at wondering what JayCee would do next – the little fucker was hard to protect sometimes. Then he saw "the look" and knew what was coming next.

Near the beginning of their training Hayes, a religious student of war, warfare, and martial arts had observed that JayCee had that hard to define, but so important element in war that people called "luck". He started quietly attaching himself to edges of the team JayCee was on both during training and off duty hours. After the incident at the party house near Nellis AFB he was even more convinced that JayCee had really good instincts for survival. That was when he went to MSGT Kappas and pled his case to be assigned with the Blue Team.

Hayes, who had an odd fusion of intelligence, superstition and paranoia, he was always saying that "they" were out to get him and his favorite quote was "if you're not a little paranoid, you're not paying attention", was convinced that his survival was somehow connected to JayCee's luck. If he stayed close to him both would make it through the training and whatever came after. He decided it was his job to keep JayCee alive, but it was hard sometimes, the little bastard could be reckless. Although he called him" JayCee" when he was talking out loud, in his internal voice he always referred to him as "the little bastard" or "that little fucker" – with respect and affection, of course.

And now JayCee was putting them in a position to disobey their prime directive "avoid contact whenever possible. If contact is made, disengage and fade away as soon as possible". Which was fine with Hayes who was tired of all the little chicken shit ambushes and counter-ambushes and skulking around hiding in the bush when enemy troops were in their zone – he was ready for a real "let's see who's got it" confrontation.

He had left JayCee and Baphang above the clearing and backtracked along a creek bed to a point where they had left the trail earlier in the morning to find the rest of the team was already waiting. He had Cerone get a message out on his FM set to be relayed to VeePee's command (Vang Pao, commander of Mei/Hmong forces) letting him know what had happened and where the bodies were and asking that a message be further relayed that the team would be a day late getting to their extraction point.

Where the trail met the highway the team broke into three units and slowly leapfrogged down toward a location that showed as a small village on their old French ordnance map. Before they reached the village they spotted the sign on the left of the highway that indicated JayCee and Baphang had gone into the bush to the right. He caught up with them on a rise above the ville just in time to watch Baphang dispatch a mean-looking snake with an improvised blow gun – handy little dude.

While the rest of the team fanned out into hidey-holes deeper in the bush he slid into position next to Baphang and began to assess the situation below. There was no "honey pile" or planted area or other signs of crop production and the huts were all in need of repair, paths to the river overgrown; this place had sat abandoned for a least a couple of years. Pit well in the center compound was being used and troops were busy digging slit trenches at both ends of the ville and lengthening the latrine ditch behind the stone hut. Good, no one would have any reason to go down to the river during the night; the embankment could provide cover later. And the fact that they were digging slit trenches and lining fire pits meant they probably intended to stay awhile. As a security buffer for the airport on the PDJ that the Russians were using as part of their air bridge (the Russians were flying in artillery pieces, arms and ammunition, and food and other equipment to a base on the Plaines Des Jares)? As a supply depot for NVA regulars coming down the trail from North Vietnam? As a bridgehead for an assault deeper into Laos?

No matter, the probability was there that other troops would be moving this way. The assault needed to be tonight; hit them and clear the area before any reinforcements could arrive.

In Hayes's assessment, the officers below them were either very confident they were alone in the mountains, arrogant, or stupid, or all three. Night bombings in Laos hadn't started yet, but the fires could still tell a lot of people where they were. And the sentry positions were not well chosen. And to add to his, Hayes's, satisfaction the officers were obviously allowing the men to celebrate their "great victory" earlier in the day with only the Viet Minh staying sober off to one end of the camp. As he looked down and watched he could almost feel sorry for the jokers partying in what was going to be a killing field. He allowed himself a small smile; they were in his world now.

Weather and time of year were in his teams' favor, there would probably be a light mist in the early morning and moonrise would be at about 0400 local. Cooler air from the mountain tops would slide down and ruffle tree leaves around 0100 giving his team an opportunity to close the distance to their target while the jungle was in motion. Moonrise would give their two long guns (1917 Springfield 30.06s with AN/PUS-2 Starlight scopes) the ability to take out selected targets as the assault began, neutralizing machine gun emplacements in the trenches at each end of the ville and covering the withdrawal. They would have the enemy "by the belt buckle" and their mortars would be useless.

The weakest element below him would be the Pathet Lao, many of whom had probably expended a lot of their ammunition earlier today, at the east end of the camp. Toughest would be the Russians (neutralize them first), then the Viet Minh and North Vietnamese Regulars. The plan would be to stampede the Pathet Lao through the camp to the west end and beyond where the bench the ville was sited on narrowed as the river took a swing north close to the embankment. And lay an ambush at the other end of the narrow point using a new weapon called a Claymore mine, a great force multiplier that Hayes was anxious to try in the field. Create chaos, get the chaos in motion, crush the enemy.

As Hayes laid out his plan the rest of the assault team, even the two Special Forces guys," Murphy" and "Murphy", deferred to his assessment and left him with the lead. The only dissent from the plan as he laid it out was not unexpected: JayCee ("stubborn little bastard") refused to take one of the long gun positions.

They didn't have a heavy machine gun or mortars but did have two BARs and a lot of hand grenades – M26s (BBs), M61s (fragmentation), MK2s (pineapples), and a few M18s (smoke) – enough to create a lot of chaos, six claymores, and a weapons system Hayes had grown to really appreciate; Baphang and his two Cao Dai ex-militia men. And Tom Minor was probably a ten-man army himself.

And although he didn't really know the two "Sneaky Pete" "hunters" (Murphy and Murphy?) he recognized their professionalism and knew they had the most experience with claymore mines.

Troop disposition to start the assault would be as follows: Blaske and one of the Murphys with the long guns would stay in positions midway up the rise they were watching from, taking out machine gun crews and targets of opportunity (NVA leadership if they could spot them), then shifting west as (if) the battle motion below them shifted and cover the road preventing any enemy from escaping up the slope, and provide covering fire as needed when the assault team withdrew. Baphang and his Cao Dai would clear the trench at the east end of the zone and place two claymores on the lip facing the ville (anyone trying to take cover in the trench would have a nasty surprise), two of them would maintain position as a blocking force throwing grenades and firing into the hutches - and Baphang with a BAR would move into a position protected by the riverbank with a thirty-degree angle into the hutches at the east end, he would move west when the flow started. Tom Minor would move into position north of the east trench with the other BAR at the opposite thirty degrees (overlapping fields of fire with enough angles to protect them from each other), he would be free to move to support the assault on either the trench or the stone house or follow the flow as the battle moved. Tom Minor and Baphang would both toss grenades to keep the flow directed toward the funnel. Cerone and the other Murphy (that's what they said their names were) would set up the trap at the small end of the funnel with the four remaining claymores, as the flow moved into the trap the claymores would be detonated most westerly first to further bunch up fleeing forces before detonating the remainder in a chain. After planting the trap Cerone and the Murphy would take cover below the embankment and block anyone trying to turn to the river. Hayes and JayCee would take out the Russians then move to the west side of the stone house for protection from friendly fire and pick off anyone trying to turn to the road.

The two Yao trackers had decided to tag along and Baphang sent them west of the ville to block any stragglers that managed to get through the ambush. They would cover Cerone and his Murphy and guide them out if things went awry and they had to boogie west.

The long guns would start the engagement as soon as they had enough moonlight to register targets through the Starlight scopes. At that signal the Cao Dai would clear the east trench and start throwing grenades and firing at the nearest hutches and the BARs would open up.

Hayes had exchanged weapons with Tom Minor, taking Toms' Thompson in exchange for his BAR, and had a suppressed Browning Highpower and a razor-sharp bush knife for close work. JayCee had a khukiri (commonly called a Gurkha knife, gift from Baphang) strapped to the small of his back, a bone handled Bowie knife (gift from his mother) strapped to his right leg over his boot, a holstered 1911 Colt 45, and his folding stock M14 slung on his back. Both had grenades in pouches carried at the back of their belts.

116

As Blaske pointed out, if they lost the element of surprise, or if the Pathet Lao didn't panic and start a stampede to the west end of the ville, or if the enemy charged any part of their thin line the team would be running for their lives as the sun came up. Cerone and "his" Murphy were in the most dangerous position if the plan skewed as they would be cut off from the rest of the force and would have to either escape across the river or run to the west. Both routes would take them away from the rendezvous position and they could be stuck in hostile territory with a long dangerous walk to safety.

After the briefing the east and west elements moved off to circuitous routes to their assault positions and the five remaining on the ridge took turns eating, hydrating, and resting – they all had long ago learned to go into a rest regime that left senses fully alert but allowed the heart, mind, and muscles to relax, a sort of fugue state.

At midnight Hayes gave each mans' gear a final check and they started the slow crawl down to where they would wait for the mountain breeze to cover their closer approach. They were ready to take on the stone house.

Chapter 19

The Revenue Station

Blaske watched the scene beneath his vantage point, eye straining to pick out detail through the Starlight scope as the pre-moonrise sky began to lighten. He had to grin at what he saw below; a hand slowly waving back and forth at the machine gun placement in the trench directly below him, what appeared to be three bodies lying akimbo to the east of the trench, and the machine gun pointing west into the village. Baphang and his two Cao Dai had already been at work.

He scanned the area below him with the scope picking out a dark piece of brush that had to be Hayes near what appeared to be two more bodies (five down and the action hadn't started?). The dark shadow against the east wall (wrong side of the house for a shadow to fall) of the stone house that might be Jaycee. That thought was confirmed as the shadow slid up around the corner of the building and out of his sight.

With his original target, the machine gun placement, taken out he shifted his attention to the hut nearest the center of the compound where the evening before he had watched an NVA enter; no camo on his pith helmet, pistol belt with shoulder strap- had to be an officer. He would wait for a target to appear in the doorway of that raised hut. The "Murphy" to his right could start the engagement with the first shot.

He allowed himself another small smile at the thought of the "Murphys". They looked nothing alike; ones' heritage had to be from the other side of the Rio Grande and the other would personify the term "Dark Irish". Both had that air of competency that all the SFG guys radiated and he was glad to have them along for this raid.

He was in a position he had picked out the evening before where he was protected on three sides by a swale zigzagging down slope toward the compound below. He had already calculated the variables of range, breeze, and downhill angles, but was concerned about the parallax effects of the light mists rising from the floor below him. With no spotters both long guns might have a little difficulty zeroing their shots in. But this was why he'd spent all those hours on the range, and he was sure the Murphy was an experienced sniper. He would fire one round of tracer, make any sight adjustments he could and be on the job.

In his peripheral vision he caught a glimmer of light from the windows in the stone house, and then it was gone. No time for questions, he settled into a seated firing position, elbows lightly inside his knees, fore stock caressing his left palm, a cheek weld as "firm and gentle as a cheerleader's kiss" (M&Ms' description, Blaske had never kissed a cheerleader and doubted if Kappas had either), rested his eyes for half a minute, and steadied his breathing and heart rate. He was ready.

It was still deep dark when Baphang and his two men reached the east trench. They watched and listened, carefully noting the disposition of the three men on guard then in a silent coordinated move taking all three of them with no more sound than a mouse running across a hardwood floor. They packed dirt in the mortar tubes and turned the RPK light machine gun around to face the compound.

Baphang slid back to where he had left a BAR, reclaimed it and moved to the river embankment and over the edge. Downriver, silhouetted against faint starlight glimmering off the river was a figure in black, light from the fire in the compound liming his head and neck. From his position under the scarp he could hear the man pissing in the river and moved silently up behind him. He clapped a hand over the man's mouth, pulling him backwards and slipping a knife blade into "the window of the soul", that opening at the base of the skull next to the spine, all in one easy motion. He took the rice sling, ammo belt and scarf from the body and glided back to be in position with the BAR.

Snakes, fuckin' snakes; Hayes hated snakes, snakes and leeches. But there was a big advantage in being in snake country. It meant that all the NVA and Pathet Lao would be in the raised hooches up off the ground away from the snakes. This meant they would be crowded together in wood and thatch structures that offered little protection from raking gun fire. Shit, maybe this raid was going to work out.

He squeezed down any feelings of doubt and with his eyes averted from the light in the compound kept his slow, steady pace crawling forward. He knew that Tom Minor was off to his left and behind him and Jaycee off to his right and ahead. It may have been a scent of garlic, ginger and sweat, or some motion against the horizon that alarmed him. The same mountain breeze that was covering his advance prevented him from hearing the approach of two dark forms barely discernable against the night sky moving from his left to right. By their size and gait he knew it was two of the Russians making a perimeter sweep. They were staggered about three meters front to back and one meter apart and moving very carefully. Pros. But the firelight from the camp was deteriorating their night vision and they did not recognize that the clump of brush they were passing was a threat.

Hayes rose silently behind the trailing figure and mirrored his movements, closing the distance with each step. One step, two, three and he was on him. Left arm up over the nose and mouth, right knee hard into the spine, he drew his knife over the exposed throat opening the carotid arteries on both sides. The Russian was strong and tried to resist but was in a vice like grip he could not escape; he spasmed and collapsed, Hayes pulling him gently down to the earth, the smell of hot blood in the air.

Hayes was up on one knee, pistol in hand ready to fire and set off the raid prematurely; the other Russian was walking straight toward Jaycee's position! Then he saw a dark form rise from the ground at the Russians feet, there was a sound like a watermelon hitting concrete as two dark forms merged. He could hear a sharp intake of breath and what sounded like a long, drawn out fart. One of the forms rose and dove toward the rear of the stone house. Was it Jaycee? Had to be, if it were the Russian alarms would be sounding. He watched as the form melted into the base of the east wall of the stone house then started crawling forward again.

The horizon was starting to lighten where the moon was threatening to rise when he saw Jaycee disappear around the corner of the stone house and a moment later lamplight flickered from the windows in the house and went out about ninety heartbeats later. What the fuck?

No time to investigate or even wonder; a shot broke the cool air with a loud C-R-A-C-K and 20 or 30 seconds later a small window into hell opened up at the east end of the compound as grenades went off under the huts closest to that end.

Smoke, a silvery grey in the light of the rising moon, was billowing skyward at the east end of the compound and he couldn't see where the muzzle flashes from that end were coming from but could hear a machine gun start to fire and see red tracers arcing up through the smoke. All sound blended together in a waterfall of noise with men crying out and screaming, staccato bursts of fire, and a cadence of grenades going off. There was a loud B-B-L-A-A-AM followed by another at the east end, some of the Pathet Lao had tried to make it to the safety of the trench at that end. To his left he could see Tom Minor up and firing at the huts and men were beginning to appear out of the swirling smoke, some running, some weaponless, most crawling and staying close to the ground. One runner broke in his direction and Tom Minor picked him off before Hayes could get his front sight on target. A stampede to the west hadn't started. Damn!

I knew who was in the stone house as I crawled through the door, a Russian Colonel we had met and even had a cocktail or two with at Embassy functions in Vientiane, arrogant bastard with an overbearing unmistakable air of superiority, he knew the Russians were going to spread their influence in the region, at a far lesser cost than the Americans were paying. When I finished with him I lay on my stomach just inside the doorway taking in the scene before me. Despite all the noise I could hear Dave chanting, "Kill them, kill them, kill them all, but stay cool, keep it in control!"

The situation was not going as we had planned (hoped), to the left of the fire in the center of the compound under and around the nearest huts I could make out a quivering mass of humanity hugging the ground too low to be caught in the cross fire coming from the east, too far into the compound to be in range of the grenades the Cao Dai were lobbing. The mass moved from side to side like Jell-O in a shaky bowl that any moment could bolt for the river and escape or overrun Hayes and Tom Minor, flank the east trench and sweep us all up. Shit oh dear.

But Dave had a plan; A crazy plan, but a plan. I put on the Russian Colonels' too-big bush jacket and fatigue cap (he wouldn't need them anymore) and walked out of the stone house into the light of the fire. On the other side of the fire I saw Baphang come up over the lip of the embankment waving a red and white checked Viet Minh Honors Scarf (the equivalent of our own Combat Infantryman's Badge), he had the same idea I was acting on.

Hayes and Tom Minor both checked their firing (just in time) and stared at the center of the compound before getting back to work stopping anyone from escaping in their direction. Up in his position Blaske just stopped "squeezing the lemon" on the rifle lined up on the back of the Russian style bush jacket; somehow he recognized those skinny, bowed legs in the green striped pants. He had another inward smile and a cold chill up his spine when he realized how close he'd come to shooting Jaycee.

The three of them watched as Jaycee and Baphang waved at the mass on the ground, Baphang shouting something like "Follow us, follow us, to the west road!" over and over in Lowland Lao, Vietnamese, and French. To their amazement they realized that "they think those little fuckers are with them" and then "those crazy bastards are leading the retreat!" as the mass under the huts turned into a mob following Jaycee and Baphang. Hayes told me later that he was pretty sure he had peed himself at the sight.

I ran like hell, Baphang running with me to my left and jumped over the trench at the west end of the compound, slashing out with my kukhiri at a dark clad form that rose to greet me then we both dove for the lip of the embankment out of sight of the mob following us. The mass ran on west to disappear down the road. Two Judas goats had done what they could.

I climbed back over the edge of the embankment and turned to a sitting position facing west just in time to be assaulted by heat, light and sound as the claymore chain went off leaving me temporarily blinded, deaf and dizzy. As my vision returned I could make out Baphang struggling with someone at the edge of the trench and then, before I could react, two large dark objects flew awkwardly one after another through the air to land somewhere below. Hayes was there grabbing and twisting the body of the man wrestling with Baphang and launching it into the air to follow the other two dark objects. He turned to me and I could just make out his yell, "pay attention, asshole!"

A few survivors of the claymore chain attempted to flee north up the hill or back toward the camp only to be taken down by Cerone and his Murphy partner or one of the long guns firing from above. There were moans and an occasional shout from the huts before Tom Minor and the two Cao Dai went back through the camp. I heard a few single shots from the direction of the east end of the compound, then a silence that hurt the ears. The three quarters moon had just cleared the ridge as we began to sweep the compound collecting weapons and removing items (letters, photos, maps, rank insignia, etc.) from the bodies.

A surprising number of the weapons were US Army issue, a gift from Kong Lee to the Pathet Lao, the remainder mostly Russian and Chinese copies of Russian arms and two field radios of Russian origin. We piled radios, weapons, and ammunition in the center of the compound, reserving what we thought the Cao Dai and Yao would be able to carry off, and covered them with flammable material pulled from the hulks of the huts and prepared to set the pile ablaze. It was the best we could do to destroy the weapons in a hurry.

Hayes checked the bodies of the two Russians at the camp perimeter, removing items that might provide intelligence and with some difficulty pulling out the bowie knife lodged in the spine of the body nearest the stone house. He entered the stone house and found a paraffin lamp on the floor next to a tipped over table and a body lodged against the back wall with a severed right hand still clutching a Tokarev T33 and left hand crossed over the stomach as though to hold in the parts spilling from a slit going from groin to sternum, head lolling to one side and still attached to the body by a thread of skin and muscle. On impulse he tossed a grenade back into the house as he left.

Chapter 20

Revenue Station Aftermath

Word was already out that something had happened at an old revenue station on highway 6 before we got back to Wattay Airport to report in. Instead of being debriefed as a team we were all debriefed individually, including Baphang who had decided to come out of the mountains with us.

Samuel's first words to me were, "Are you trying to start World War Three?" Explaining to me again that the US and USSR had a gentlemen's agreement not to acknowledge the presence in Laos of Russian advisors, never mind that they were supplying the Pathet Lao, the Neutralists, and NVA forces inside Laos, never mind that the Pathet Lao artillery was sometimes surprisingly accurate, never mind that there was so much Russian air traffic mixed in with our own that they were sometimes in the same patterns, just landing at different fields. Never mind all that, our Embassy's position was that they had no advisors fielded with Pathet Lao forces, and now we (you, dumb ass!) had killed some of them, "including a colonel, for chrissake". "I'm going to pull a Pontius Pilate on this one, but you can bet that Kappas is going to have your ass when he gets back down from Tony Poeville!" "I won't be surprised if he breaks up your team and sends you all back to the States".

The moon was full up and the horizon lightening toward dawn as we finished our work at the old revenue station. I went to the latrine and relieved my bowels, puked a little, and let the adrenaline-letdown shakes take over my body for about a minute and a half. Then went down to the river and cleaned myself and my equipment as best I could.

As I climbed back up the hill to the place we had stashed our gear the night before I heard a grenade go off and looked back to see Hayes exiting the stone house and a large fire burning brightly in the center of the compound, everyone else coming up the hill behind me as ammo started cooking off in the fire. I passed Blaske's nest from the night before and noted he was not in position, looked back west and saw that the Murphy on the hill was still on watch, long gun and scope sweeping the road in both directions.

As I came over the lip into the depression we had scouted from the day before I started to laugh at the sight of Baphang and Blaske making sweet tea in a big pot Baphang had scrounged from the ville and doling out breakfast portions of rice and ham, the contrast between what they were doing now and the action just a short time ago seemed comical to me and I just couldn't stop laughing until Baphang slapped me on the shoulder and said, "JayKah, sit down and eat we have a long way to go today". With a tone of voice that was scolding me like I was a silly child.

It took a while for my ear to recognize that something had been out of kilter when Baphang spoke to me. Baphang who spoke many languages, who could imitate the animals in the forest until they talked back to him, Baphang the accomplished linguist suddenly couldn't pronounce the "Cee" sound in Jay Cee. He continued to call me "J'a'kah" for the rest of the time we were together.

Tom Minor and the two Cao Dai had counted thirty-five dead out of an estimated forty enemy personnel in the camp, the count went up when the two Yao came up the road from the west grinning and displaying two severed heads. But there were at least two or three or more unaccounted for and one of the radios we found in the camp had been "up", word of our raid was almost certainly out and we needed to boogie post haste.

Our own casualties were slight, no one killed, no one seriously wounded; one of the Cao Dai was missing the top of his left ear, Tom Minor had flash burns on his arms and face, Cerone had a nose bleed that did not want to stop for fifteen minutes, and I had a large bruise on my right hip and broken knuckles on my left hand. Everyone was tired but mobile and fit for action.

After wolfing down the rice and ham (with crackers and jam, it rhymes) we filled canteens with sweet tea and loaded our gear, we had a long way to go, just as Baphang had said, to retrieve Beckstrom's body and get back up to our extraction point for pick up. We had about a three-hour window before our extraction bird(s) would clear the zone and probably be out of range of our line of sight radio. Miss the call and we'd have to wait another day for a chance at extraction. Impossible with anyone on our heels.

With the two Cao Dai on point and Cerone and the two Murphys as rear guard we had a 3-klick jog back up the "highway" to the tree where we had stashed Beckstrom. The scene was even uglier than it had been the day before, and the smell riper. It was hard to keep our breakfast choked down as we pulled the tarp wrapped body down and fashioned a litter with two tree branches laced through the sides of the tarp.

With Cerone and the Murphys guarding the west approaches to the scene the two Yao had moved up to the east as a fore guard. The Yao came trotting back to tell Baphang that they could hear a truck or trucks coming from further east. Trouble was coming our way and I welcomed it. I had experienced some revenge for Beckstrom's death, but now I wanted more. I wanted to wait and ambush the fuckers coming down from the east, I wanted to kill some more of the sons-a-bitches. Dave was sure we could take them.

But wiser heads prevailed, we were going to be lucky if we managed to get clear today, these weren't the same people who had killed Beckstrom and the civilians, we had no way of even guessing how big the force coming our way was, they might already be alerted to our presence and not so easy to take, and we were completely out of (the lovely) claymore mines. And the biggest point; we had already fucked up and acted as an aggressor force, we shouldn't compound the problem. Kappas was already going to be pissed off.

We needed to clear sign and get hidden up the narrower trail to the north (too narrow for trucks) before they arrived on scene. With luck they would only give this area a quick, cursory glance and hurry on to the revenue station, giving us time to get out and gone before they back tracked.

Finding our trail would not be hard if they came back up the road; so many people moving through in a hurry over the past two days had crushed greenery, left scuff marks and footprints that we did not have time to try and conceal. Worse, the tarp we were carrying had started to leak fluids; the smell alone would be enough for a tracker to follow us with ease. Carrying the extra burden was slowing us down even with men trading off to switch carriers while at a trot, but we were not going to leave the body behind.

We had come up out of the streambed onto the north/south trail by only a few minutes when we heard the whine of not one but two truck transmissions echoing in the mountains. We could hear the pause and clash as they shifted gears in low range. From the sounds both trucks stopped at the site of the massacre and one stayed while the other went on west toward the revenue station. They might already have a party out looking for us. More likely, since they could not know our numbers and would be wary of ambush, they would look for our trail and send out a cautious probe before being reinforced by the troops in the other truck, it was probable a full-on pursuit would not start in the next few minutes.

But we still had problems, if we arrived too late we wouldn't catch our ride out, if we cut it too close and the enemy was too tight on our heels we wouldn't call the bird in under fire; we would have to abandon the body and scatter downhill on game trails and circle back south to rendezvous at the river and start a long walk out to one of Vee Pee's outposts.

While the rest of us kept trotting uphill Baphang squatted with his Cao Dai and the two Yao in the shade next to the trail and hatched a plan that he related to me later; one of the Cao Dai was an experienced mortar man and would be happy to exercise his skills with the tube and six rounds they had taken from the revenue station. The mountainside above them to the east would offer a position that would allow him to strike at sections of the road near and to either side of the trail head at the highway. The two Yao would lay some false trails and set booby traps with grenades along our escape path.

Mortars falling on the (probably) mixed force should convince them that we were a bigger group than we were and make them, especially if there were Pathet Lao in the mix, more cautious about following us. The bobby traps would slow them down further. After laying down a mortar barrage the two Cao Dai would race up and over the mountain to safety, confident that no one could out run them in this terrain. The two Yao would simply melt into the bush under the protection of their animal gods; no one would be able to catch them here in their home.

With no time to sweep the trail ahead, we would just have to chance that there were no "visitors" in the way, we made the uphill run. Cerone was going ahead to get out a message to the bird, Hayes, Blaske, and the Murphys settling in as litter bearers, Tom Minor switching off as relief bearer, Baphang and I leapfrogging behind as rear guard. My body was screaming at me to stop, take a rest break, slow down while my mind kept telling me to keep my gait smooth, find my pace to match Baphang and keep going. The mind won and I kept going, I was not going to fail my team, I was not going to fail Beckstrom, I was not going to fail Beckstrom's family, his body was going home.

We were within a hundred meters of the landing site (a clear spur on the side of the mountain, the bird would have to land uphill, turn around, load, and take off downhill) and could see the plane circling overhead when we heard a distant measured four round cadence of mortar fire then two more exploding rounds. If the trucks were just now at the trail head we had an hour lead on the main body of pursuers but there might be a patrol out ahead of the main body, hopefully if there were the Yao booby traps would keep them off us until we could get airborne.

The ugly, ungainly beautiful Pilatus Porter landed and turned around and we loaded Beckstrom while the Murphys stood guard then climbed aboard. Baphang was coming out with us because he wanted to meet this Vang Pao people were talking about.

I was last to board and saw the two Yao standing on the trail waving and smiling like kids at a carnival each loaded up with an M1 Garand as long as they were tall, an AK47, ammo bandoliers, and crossbows and bush knives. Then they were gone into the bush. I made a promise to myself to try and find them and get them an airplane ride someday.

The Porter rose into the air, circled once to gain altitude and made a slight jog to the south where we could see wisps of smoke still rising from the revenue station and the hulk of a truck at the trailhead.

Samuels did not want to hear these details from me, I would just "have to wait and give my briefing to Kappas next morning, stay in your quarters until then". "But just for your information, every man jack on that raid has taken responsibility for violating your mission brief. The SFG guys said they were acting on their orders and coerced the rest of you into going along with them." " Hayes and Blaske each insisted it was their doing and everyone else had no choice but to go along." "Even Tom Minor and your bush brother Baphang tried to take responsibility."

"But I will tell you something I know for certain, every time some bullshit happens you or Cerone or both are right in the middle of it. And I know you and Beckstrom were buddies from boot camp on so I have a damn good idea who instigated this crap." "I will say the Intel boys appreciate the materials your team brought out, but you did not hear that from me." "Now sit down and have a shot of Jack and a beer and do not tell me what happened out there".

After their debriefing and while they were waiting for me to come out of Samuels's office the guys were having a few beers and talking about the past few days. Blaske asked Hayes, "I saw a light come on in the stone house just before the action started, what was that about?" And Hayes replied, "Yeah, you saw a light." "The little bastard woke up the Russian before he killed him".

130

Next morning I had my debriefing with Kappas and feeling like a whipped puppy dog under his icy gaze I laid out all the details, including the fact that I had let my cold anger go hot and overcome my judgment. The other guys hadn't really had any choice but to come along, they weren't going to let me attack alone and weren't going to try to restrain me. Kappas snorted at that last part. Then told me what was going to happen next.

Travel arrangements had already been made for me to proceed to Clark AFB, Philippines where I would buy a Class A uniform that fit (my arms and ankles stuck out of my old uniforms), get a "real" haircut and either get my beard trimmed or shave it off. From Clark I would travel by MATS to Hamilton AFB, where I would catch up with Beckstrom's body and personal effects to escort them on by MATS to his hometown in Minnesota. I was allowed to travel in mufti as long as I checked in and signed the manifest at each stop in uniform. I would have a voucher to draw funds from our contingency account that I could use at Hamilton.

After the funeral I was to proceed direct to Barksdale AFB, Louisiana where Kappas had arranged with some old friends for me to enter a pistol competition, he expected me to make a good showing. Hell, as long as I beat the Army team he would be happy. He forgot to mention where or how I was going to get a match pistol in time for the shoot. After the shoot I could take a week's leave before hopping MATS flights back to the Philippines and on to Thailand from there. I would receive further orders enroute back to Asia.

Before I left I was to turn all, emphasis on all, my weapons, issue and personal, in to Zero, our armorer. And I was to understand that Beckstrom had "died in a training accident in the Philippines", any breech of our Secrecy Agreements and I would live out the rest of my life under the cellars in some federal prison. "Was that clear?"

An hour before I got on the CAT flight out a bulletin was distributed through the Embassy in Vientiane telling of the great victory FAR troops had had over a large force of Pathet Lao supported by NVA, PAVN, and Viet Minh at an old abandoned revenue station on highway 6.

Chapter 21

Panhead

It was red, white, and chrome; a brand-new Harley Davidson Panhead with longhorn bars, small saddle and pillion seat. Mufflers were not too quiet or too loud, but just right. I rode up and down Collins Avenue, down to Key West and back, and all over South Florida visiting bars and pool halls. Never drunk enough to have an accident, never sober either.

Kappas had made all the arrangements for me to attend Beckstrom's funeral in Minnesota with the strict orders that I was not to give the family any details or information about where and how he had died. The official account was "perished by accident during a training exercise in the Philippines". I would be subject to severe penalties if I broke this iron clad rule.

So I had stood there in my dress blues, shivering under a borrowed trench coat in the cold wind from Canada and lied to Beckstrom's family; adding to the guilt I already felt at not being able to make him stay alive, guilt at Dave's exultation and joy at the revenge we had taken, the guilt at the relief that it was Beckstrom being buried today and not me; I thought I could see in his sisters' eyes that question, "Why are you still here and my brother is gone?".

They were having an early winter in Minnesota and had had to break an icy crust to dig his grave. I kept worrying in an odd way that he was going to be cold and alone in his closed casket. I had given his Jump Pin and Pathfinder Patch to his mother along with some snapshots we had taken together in an earlier, happier time when I was on leave with him at his family's farm. As the minister finished speaking and the family and friends lined up to shovel dirt I dropped his maroon beret on top of the coffin, stood back and saluted with hot tears on my face, steam turning cold as they ran down my cheeks.

That evening I boarded a Trailways bus with my travel bag and a pint of whiskey for company, bound for Grand Forks AFB in North Dakota. I arrived there the next morning in time to sign the manifest and climb aboard a tanker headed for Barksdale AFB, Louisiana where Kappas had me slated to attend an inter-service pistol match (without a match pistol?) which would give me a little more time Stateside without counting against my accrued leave time.

I spent the next three days and nights at Barksdale, which I believe had the highest re-enlistment rate of any Air Force Base worldwide; and I thought I knew why, the chow hall. I was stunned when I checked into the chow hall for breakfast and was asked if I wanted steak, ham, or chicken for breakfast and how did I want my eggs? They had the best shit-on-a shingle (creamed beef on toast) I have ever eaten in my life and the dinners in that chow hall were something better than I would expect to find in a Michelin Five Star restaurant. I basically hung out in the chow hall and NCO club and spent my entire time there sleeping, eating, and drinking; I never made it to the pistol range.

I decided to just take a break from the military for a while, ignoring the fact that I wasn't on leave and was technically assigned to Barksdale for the time period of the pistol match with orders to return overseas after the match. I hitched a ride on another tanker to MacDill AFB near Tampa Bay and rode the bus into town where I found just what I was looking for – A Harley dealer.

I went back to MacDill and arranged shipment of my garrison bag back to Nellis AFB, Nevada; our permanent party station. Then went back to the Harley dealer in civvies and bought the Panhead.

I felt like I'd had enough, we had already figured out that the US support of Phoumi Nosavan was bullshit. The Chinese ethnic Lao General must have been one hell of a politician, but he was certainly no real general. The US was funding his entire army, but most of the pay never trickled down through the ranks and he was never near enough to any frontline to even hear artillery fire. His troops were a joke and almost to a man scared shitless of going anywhere near the mountains or anywhere they might be confronted by real soldiers. And this was the guy our government had picked to back. This was the guy we and our friends were to shed our blood for. What a crock.

Beckstrom's death and subsequent events had rocked my sense of myself and our purpose in S.E. Asia. Putting team loyalty to the side I proceeded on a beautiful binge across and up and down Florida.

I know there were day and night miles on the bike, whiskey and beer in abundance, and a woman here and there. I remember the famous sunset in Key West and a ride in a seaplane, but most of that time was a blur. Until the shiny lieutenant with the two serious faced, hulking APs (Air Police) showed up at my motel room at least an hour before the crack of noon. I had the befuddled thought that I could probably take all three but quickly let that foolish thought drop, especially since the first words out of the lieutenant's mouth were, "I have a message from MSgt Kappas". The message was simple; I had seventy-two hours to report to Oakland Army Terminal for transport back to my unit or be considered a deserter. The lieutenant handed me a manila envelope containing new travel orders and $900 cash, gave me a knowing look that probably meant "I hope you screw up, son. We'll be happy to come back for your ass" and left.

Kappas had a thing with punctuality and often said, "I don't care if your train was derailed. I don't care if your plane crashed, I don't care if you are in a body cast. There is no excuse I will accept for your being late, except, possibly, under certain circumstances, your death certificate".

Well, it was "only" about 3,100/3,200 miles to Oakland and I was still in love with my red, white, and chrome Harley. Given about 48 hours driving time and maybe 12 to 16 hours sleeping time, I could make it in plenty of time to ship the bike back to Nevada and still make my deadline at Oakland. I could buy a uniform in California or just travel in civvies until we got to Clark (sure to be a stopover on the way). What the hell, go for it.

Ride started out okay and I was doing fine across the Florida panhandle and clear to Houston, Texas where I gave myself a four-hour break for a nap and bought a warmer jacket at a truck stop (luckily it was wind and water proof). The rain started and didn't end until I was in Arizona; near Williams the rain turned to snow and I had a forced stop of about twelve hours. Back on the road with the clock ticking I was fatigued and feeling the pressure, peeing beside the road when necessary and dining on candy bars as I rode, ass and back aching, deafened by the constant sound of my (not so long ago "not too loud") pipes, eyes threatening to quit. The fun part was long gone.

Waiting for me at Oakland was my friend SFG Sgt. Johnny Sorenson and one of the Murphys from the Revenue Station, only now the Murphy was wearing a nametag that said Sanchez, Jesse, and my garrison bag. I had two questions; how did my garrison bag get there and how did Sgt Kappas know where I was in Florida? Sgt. Johnny Sorenson laughed and said, "Kappas".

I left the now not so shiny Harley outside the post gate with the key in the ignition in the hope that someone who would really appreciate it would find it. I was done with it.

My escort and transportation were there to take me "home".

Chapter 22

Shifting Sands

Colonel Ross was a man it was easy to respect. He had finished high in his class at West Point but was willing to lose the stiffness and aloof air we associated with most field grade officers as soon as he had spent a little time in the "real world" of Laos. His integrity and honesty were as apparent as the freckles on his nose and we all trusted him to understand what and why we were doing. Kappas had expressed an early, perhaps prophetic, opinion that his basic honesty was going to get in his way if he were ever elevated to the General Staff.

The Colonel's mission was to collect situational information and make recommendations regarding our presence in Laos and Viet Nam up the chain of command, which in his case meant to the Embassy and State Department, he may have also reported to the CIA Plans Department. He was a hands-on kind of leader who got into the mix quite often; as information sources he had a core group of seasoned military and CIA veterans, the "Old Asia Hands", who had experience in the region going back in at least one instance to the OSS during and after WWII.

There were conflicting opinions as to the future conduct of activities in South East Asia, particularly in Laos and Viet Nam. The efforts there were being managed by civil authority rather than military, including the "quasi-military" actions under the umbrella of the Programs Evaluation Office and certain members of the military hierarchy were pushing hard for control of operations.

There was also a conflict over whether we should stay in a limited role ("the least American dollars and personnel equals the biggest bang for the buck") or go full bore ("bomb the little bastards back to the stone age").

"The Old Asia Hands" and most of the "New Asia Hands" (including our operations group) favored the first option and believed the money, training and supplies the US was pouring into the region would be sufficient – if it were distributed and disseminated properly. That was the crux of our viewpoint; not necessarily more resource but better use of the resources already coming. But that was not likely to happen if the US didn't do a better job of picking who it choose to support, and monitoring where the support went. Even at our level it was apparent that General Phoumi and his minions was a money pit, we (the US) had screwed up by not giving Premier Souvanna and his Neutralist government any support, and that the guy we backed in Viet Nam, Premier Ngo Diem was a bad guy, a tin pot dictator.

And we didn't have to be in-country long to learn that Captain Kong Lee's (temporary) coup was founded on his belief that foreigners, including the Vietnamese, had no right to be determining the future of Laos. His actions were further precipitated by the fact that Phoumi and his generals had sucked up all the money coming from the US to support the Royal Laotian Army (FAR) and Lee's troops were unpaid and starving. So, a man we had trained at the US Army Scout Ranger School in the Philippines, and probably the most talented military man in Laos, was giving weapons to the Pathet Lao (Lao communist army) and capturing the Plain of Jars (PDJ) for them.

Our lack of support with necessities like rice and oil for the Souvanna government resulted in an airlift run by the Russian military that continued after Souvanna was gone; they just changed customers and supplied the Pathet Lao and the Neutralists (KL). In one of those funny twists so common in the Laos theater of operations there were occasions when both the Russians and the Americans were airlifting supplies to the PDJ. There were so many uncoordinated flights with planes from different sponsors buzzing around the country we were surprised there weren't mid-airs every night.

We had been briefed that the goal of the United States was to establish a Neutralist government in both Laos and South Viet Nam. But the reality was that "they" meant a neutral government or coalition government that did not include any communists – the Big Boogey Man of the time. This made it all the stranger, and sadder, that Captain Kong Lee was pushed away from the table early in the game.

We learned that Ho Chi Minh had written two of our Presidents asking for friendship and had made overtures to Premier Ngo Diem of South Viet Nam to form a coalition government, all these offers of peaceful conciliation had been rejected out of hand. It gave us something to think about. And there was another issue that picked at the minds of those of us who had had civics classes in school; should the peoples in the region be allowed free elections or should the United States pick the leaders through monetary and political (and military) pressure? Of course, all this involved decisions far above our pay grade; but we couldn't help noticing that "all the cheese wasn't in Denmark" as Blaske put it.

If Laos and Viet Nam weren't enough to watch and try to figure out there was always the action in Burma to give Colonel Ross a headache. After WWII an army of ten or twelve thousand Chinese Nationalist Kuomintang was landlocked in Burma and had found a living as warlords and traders in the opium industry, some seven thousand or so were still there in the late 1950s and early '60s. When presented with a way to evacuate through Thailand and have transport to Formosa they preferred to stay in the Golden Triangle and had been skirmishing with the Burmese Army for years. Our embassies vehemently denied giving any aid and support to these Kuomintang remnants but the truth was that we did supply them with arms, ammunition, and equipment as an irritant and blocking force to keep the Red Chinese from moving into the region.

There were some bright spots; Bill Lair, CIA PM (paramilitary expert, same guy who initiated and trained the Thai PARU) recruited the charismatic Vang Pao to form an army of Hmong tribesmen (we called them Meo in those days) and another PM called Tony Poe and his fellow CIA asset Vin Lawrence were in northwest Laos recruiting and training tribesmen as well. USAF Major Alderholt had re-invigorated the program to create landing strips all over the country and introduced the Helio Courier STOL (short takeoff and landing) aircraft to the theater (we didn't realize this meant General Lemay was getting his fat fingers into the pie). The amazing USAID rep Edgar Buell was in country and or own contacts with mid-land and hill tribesmen were solidifying; we were able to move about the countryside in relative safety (8th Coin Team Blue, Team Green and Team Orange, other operators were at greater risk), even in the Northern Provinces that were strongholds of the Pathet Lao.

The Colonel had cobbled together a comprehensive network of intelligence sources that even included the Corsican and Marseilles French opium dealers and their network of spies. He had street vendors, shop keepers and priests, Lao and Vietnamese military men of both high and low rank, hill tribesmen, mountain tribesmen, disaffected Vietnamese and a whole cross section of the population willing to talk with him. We believed he definitely had his finger on the South East Asian pulse and was quietly in the best position of any American to comprehend what was going on in the region.

So, it was no surprise to anyone when he was summoned stateside to testify with recommendations before a Senate Sub-Committee. The surprise came a few weeks later when the dispatch to pack and ship his gear back to the States came up on the message board, the Colonel was no longer in the Army, he had either been cashiered or had resigned his commission after his testimony; an odd happening for a dedicated career military man. We thought it no coincidence that this occurred at about the same time General Maxwell Taylor was making his report and recommendations for an increased regular services military presence in South East Asia (read Viet Nam) to Congress.

We knew that our Colonel Ross favored the most economical (most bang for the buck) solutions and favored a balanced paramilitary approach; We surmised he had given an honest, thoughtful evaluation to the Sub-Committee that ran contrary to the recommendations given by General Taylor and other members of the High Command and had been dismissed for his efforts.

A lot of change was taking place under the new Kennedy administration and we began to feel a pall hanging over our efforts. When the Colonel was axed everyone in 8th COIN felt the blade touch their neck. Our morale took a big hit.

Shortly after the Kennedy inauguration the Programs Evaluation Office was superseded by a Military Advice and Assistance Group (MAAG) and operational responsibility shifted to the military. Crowley just kept reporting to the Embassy and wherever else he had been reporting. He would conduct "business as usual" until told otherwise. In-country personnel were now to wear uniforms and identify themselves as members of the military. We stayed in civvies and faded into the ranks of technical representatives.

We couldn't even wear our maroon berets and jump pins; Blaske was very disappointed.

Chapter 23

The Purloined Notebook

"We must never let the weight of this combination endanger our liberties or democratic processes" Dwight D, Eisenhower, speaking of the military/industrial complex in his farewell address.   January 17, 1961

"All political power comes from the barrel of a gun".
                    Mao Tse Tung

"You may kill ten of us for every one of you we kill and we will still be here when you have gone"   Nguyen Ai Quoc, aka Ho Chi Minh

"No, No, No. I've get aholt of this Tar Baby an' kent let go!"
                    B'rer Fox (a note added in Cerone's handwriting)

When Cerone entered the rooms in the slightly run-down French villa that had been Colonel Ross's headquarters and living space he noticed a leather-bound notebook that had been left behind by the people who had packed the contents of the Colonel's sleeping room. He wasn't sure if the impulse to take the book from the small writing desk in a corner of the room was based on a desire to have a remembrance of the Colonel or simple curiosity or both. Whatever the motive he picked the book up and carried it around under his arm while the embassy people cleared the rooms.

When he got back to our three-sided shack at Wattay and began reading the contents of the notebook he realized he had stumbled upon a treasure trove he needed to share with the rest of us. The Colonel had kept the notebook as a place to jot down quotes and write notes, thoughts and ideas beginning around the time of his arrival in Vientiane and ending shortly before his departure back to the States, it contained comments on history, the Colonels' projections of the North Vietnamese strategy and his views on how to counter their probable moves. It also contained notes and comments regarding the concerns that President Eisenhower had expressed, the President saying in effect that we should be unwilling to commit to full scale war in Asia (with its millions of people) with the massive manpower that would be required and with a lack of international support.

There were a few clippings from newspapers and magazines tucked between the back pages and the rear cover and notes on the conduct and outcome of former wars with quotes from Julius Caesar, Clausewitz, Sun Tzu, George Washington, and many others (most historical, some still living) penned in the Colonels' neat handwriting, with underlining and penciled notes in the margins.

It has been more or less a half century since I've seen the notebook and I won't pretend to remember every detail but many of the quotations in the book remain in my memory and the gist of the message still rings in my mind with great clarity.

The Colonel noted that US emphasis and involvement had shifted to Vietnam, more so when President Kennedy took office; Laos was a poor land-locked country of little value to US interests and would have been ignored in the grand scheme of world politics if it weren't for the unfortunate fact that the country shared borders with Communist China and Communist North Vietnam and was sited between those countries and Thailand and Indonesia, it was in an ideal position for a proxy war between super powers and in a blocking position to prevent the spread of communism in accordance with the "Domino Theory" (prevalent in those years).

Some of the information in the notebook was factual including references to the training Ho Chi Minh and General Giap had received from the American OSS "Deer Team" where they may have digested the war philosophy of "one slow, four fast" and unorthodox uses of artillery and troop dispositions. It was certainly factual that the North Vietnamese could field a disciplined, well trained and motivated army and they could also field very effective irregular forces. It was also true that the

Vietnamese freedom fighters, the Viet Minh ("free land"), were guerilla fighters on a par with any in the world and their alliance with General Giap would have an important impact on the outcome of any war between the North and the South.

In the years after the defeat of the French at Dien Bien Phu "Uncle" Ho Chi Minh and General Giap enjoyed tremendous "face" throughout Southeast Asia and as President Eisenhower had noted if elections had been held in both North and South Viet Nam Ho Chi Minh would have handily won the Presidency of a united Viet Nam.

Whether sincere or not, no way to know at this late date, Ho Chi Minh had written requests for friendship to President Truman and had offered to participate in forming a bi-partisan government and had the offer rejected out of hand by President Diem (Thiem) of South Vietnam. At the time the Colonel was writing his notes he believed the North Vietnamese would be intent on uniting the country under their banner, any talks of peace or conciliation from this point on would be to gain time and tactical advantage.

Another fact, gleaned from the Colonels' own observations and empirical evidence was that the Royal Laotian Army had proven more than once to be completely ineffectual and it was doubtful they would be capable of the necessary actions to not only defeat the Pathet Lao, who were receiving help from the Russians and North Vietnamese and supplies from the Chinese, but to also keep the North Vietnamese out of their country.

In the Colonel's notes he expressed the opinion that with a large boost from Russian and Chinese aid, equipment, and expertise the North Vietnamese would not stop until they had taken over South Vietnam and as a corollary gain turned Laos (and perhaps Cambodia) into a client state.

Colonel Van predicted that the strategy of the North Vietnamese as lead by General Vo Nguyen Giap, former school teacher and military history student, would be greatly influenced by the teachings of the great

Chinese General Sun Tzu or Ton Tu as he was called in Vietnamese, and the works of other military scholars.

"To fight and conquer in all your battles is not supreme excellence. Supreme excellence consists in breaking the enemies' resistance without fighting." "All warfare is based on deception." "Indirect tactics, efficiently applied, are as inexhaustible as heaven and Earth."
Sun Tzu
"We do not have to win battles. We will hammer the Americans until they leave."
Attributed to Ho Chi Minh

There were other quotes that reflected what the Colonel described as the probable cultural training of both the regular and irregular soldiers under General Giap's command, the same kind of cultural training as was in use by the Russian's Red Army:

"He will win whose army is animated by the same spirit throughout the ranks."
Sun Tzu

"Pursue one great decisive aim with force and determination."
Clausewitz

Critical to Uncle Ho and General Giap's plans was the ancient trade route called the Trong Son Road, later widely known as the Ho Chi Minh Trail, a series of roads and trails running roughly north and south on the spine and western slopes of the Annamite Cordillera starting in the northeast of Laos and ending in Cambodia. The NVA and Viet Minh (beginning to be called Viet Cong) were already increasing the traffic on the supply trails they had opened during the wars with the Japanese and the French. Vietnam was too narrow at the 17th parallel for them to effectively move supplies south without going to the other side of the Annamite Range and there was already heavy traffic by truck, elephant, horse, porter and bicycle in Laos and Cambodia.

"We may take it then that an army without its baggage train is lost; without provisions it is lost; without bases of supply it is lost."
Sun Tzu

"For offensive warfare the constant replacement of troops and arms is the highest strategic principle."
Clausewitz

"Organize recruitment of troops and transport of arms a long time before they are needed."
Clausewitz

According to Colonel Ross's crystal ball Uncle Ho and General Giap would surmise that the United States would have no real interest in Laos other than the area along the Mekong Plain as a shield to keep the communists out of Thailand and Indonesia and would only support the FAR (Royal Lao Army) in efforts to protect the cities on the Plain. In order to keep the FAR off the passages on the trail the NVA would use the Pathet Lao as a proxy to threaten the Lao cities in the lowlands.

The Colonel proposed that the only practicable way to prevent this logistics line from working to the Communist advantage would be to use an old, old military tool; boots. Put boots on the ground backed with air-to-ground support and deny the enemy the six passes through the mountains, make the enemy commit more troops to the mountains thus relieving the pressure in the South or abandon the supply routes entirely.

(Cerone had written in the margins, "Cut 'em off at the passes!" just as we had all grown up hearing the cavalry say in black and white Westerns)

He recommended a paramilitary force supported by Special Forces and US Army Regulars (with air to ground support) and a commitment to secure the border in northeast Laos that would represent the most effective, economical solution to the military problem presented by the "Annamese Problem" (as the last King of Laos had referred to the Vietnamese).

145

He also proposed that we be allowed to attack and harass the enemy wherever we found them and be allowed to pursue them back across the border whenever they committed an armed incursion into Laos.

And he cautioned against being lured into any set-piece battles in the Lowlands or using our irregular allies as regular army, fixed position soldiers. "Own the mountains, keep the enemy off balance, and determine when and where to engage by your own plan, not the enemies', control the action."

"One of the strongest weapons of offensive warfare is the surprise attack."
Clausewitz

"Next to victory the act of pursuit is most important in war."
Clausewitz

In his notebook the Colonel summed up his vision of the mission of counter-insurgency troops:

"Take away the enemies' means of war. Deny them the use of supply lines. Remove their sources of food. Identify them and kill the bastards".

Reading the notebook, we relished the idea of morphing from a Counter-Intelligence Study Group to an actual counter-insurgency, anti-guerilla warfare unit. We had spent a lot of time in the field in the highlands and mid-lands up and down the Cordillera and had garnered allies (we had even made some friends) and intelligence sources and felt we were ready to contribute to a real effort to close out the hostilities in Laos and perhaps short circuit the war in Vietnam (at least one of them, we thought there was a civil war as well as the war from an outside aggressor). We were sure that with just a few of the right resources and an application of the right techniques we could shut it all down before it got too hot.

But that was not the way things were going to go. Our politicians and generals had other ideas about what was happening in Southeast Asia and other plans for conducting the burgeoning wars there.

Our disappointment with the paths they decided to take was immeasurable. The feeling of let-down, a feeling almost of betrayal of the work we had put in was palatable, a nasty taste in the mouth, a bad feeling in the pit of the stomach, and a sinking in the heart.

As weeks and months rolled on and the Colonel never returned Cerone added to the notebook. I can remember a couple of his additions:

Cerone (a Catholic) had this question in his notes: "If Diem weren't a Catholic and Kennedy weren't a Catholic (and hadn't had appeals from a couple of Princes of the Church) would we be doing the same thing we're doing and would our military be ramping up the way it is in Vietnam?"

And this bit of verse...

The bonzes are burning with an awful light

With a greasy smoke that lingers till night

Our politicians are blinded, they have no clear sight

While they support a little man with a nasty wife

And expect me to be willing to give up my life

But I'll go where they tell me to fight

Cause it's my country wrong or right

Still the bonzes are burning in God's early light

Chapter 24

Ban Ban

They were moving slowly, women carrying their babes, toddlers struggling to keep up, and old men and women carefully putting one foot in front of the other on the wet, slick roadbed. It was August and still raining in fits and spurts in the midlands where route 6 came down to meet route 7 near a large bowl surrounded by tall mountains to the north of the PDJ (Plaines Des Jares). People had been coming out of the mountains from side roads, trails, and animal paths to join the refugee columns until their numbers had swelled to six thousand or more before they reached the rest spot at Ban Ban. Some had been walking for more than two weeks; most were Mei or Meo (Hmong) with some Mien, Khmu, Yao and people from other Lao Soung (highland tribes, the French called them "Montagnards"), all were exhausted and hungry.

There were almost no men in the dismal camp, the ones who had not gone off to join Vang Pao in the fight to defend and establish their own tribal homeland had been either killed or conscripted by the Viet Minh or North Vietnamese, leaving behind the very old, very young, and the lame. The old men and women gathered combustible material from dead logs and the bottoms of brush piles, and scavenged wild bananas and banana leaves, some slaughtered chickens and gathered other edible plants from the meadows and hillsides; they would have a few cooking fires and something to feed and shelter the babies with. A small group of the local farmers came up from their village to the south of route 7 and brought food and other supplies but most hid in their homes waiting for the refugees to move on.

The next morning the refugees' Nai Bans and Nai Khones (village chiefs and chiefs of groups of villages) would have to decide if the column should chance going directly through the PDJ or skirt it to the west on their way to the safety of the "Secret Base" occupied by Vang Paos' Mei army at Long Thien. But for this night it was important to get what rest

148

and nourishment they could, either route they took would mean more long days of walking.

The Vietnamese crossing the border and continuing down the old Trong Son Road, now being called the Ho Chi Minh Trail by Westerners, considered them an enemy people who had sided with the French during the early 1950s, and as a lesser, subhuman species, a feeling shared by some Lowland Lao who referred to them as "ka" (slave). The NVA, PAVN, Viet Minh and others passing through their homeland stole the villagers' food stores, put their young people into forced labor, and on some occasions raped and killed at will. The remote mountains that had protected the tribes were no longer a safe sanctuary and many of the villagers knew they had to leave if they were to survive.

More than a third of the country of Laos was already occupied by the communist Pathet Lao assisted by North Vietnamese and Russian and Chinese advisors when the newest Geneva Accords declaring Laos a neutral country was signed by the USA and the Royal Army (FAR) and Vang Paos' army of irregulars were (at the behest of the American MAAG) kept busy defending the lowlands and the major population centers located on the Mekong Plain. The villagers knew there would be no one to protect them unless they could get out of the way of the traffic coming down what we started calling the "Harriman Trail" in response to our certainty that Uncle Ho and General Giap would have no hesitation in violating the treaty.

We knew that when the USA pulled out their six hundred-sixty-six (interesting number) official military advisors the North Vietnamese would leave thousands of troops in Laos, and we also knew, to our bitter disappointment, that despite all the intel available and the wise counsel of the "Old Asia Hands" our military was not going to push for what we all knew was the only correct strategy to possibly win in both Laos and South Viet Nam; that is put boots on the ground to control the five passes over the Annamite Range and stop the traffic of men and materiel going down the Trail before it left North Viet Nam.

If a hose is emptying into a gravel bed the only effective way to stop the flow is to put a stopper at the end of the hose, trying to stop the water after it has entered the gravel bed is a futile exercise and, as we saw it, similar to trying to stop the flow of men and supplies after they entered the wide, many channeled network of roads and trails in the mountains and midlands of Laos.

After the official USA military advisors pullout and movement of MAAG and CIA offices across the river into Thailand a few "civilian contractors", including some of our small group, and several hundred Philippine "construction workers" would stay in the country. A number of mercenaries under contract with FAR would remain in-country as well.

"Operation Hardnose" would start in a few weeks and provide trail watchers to document the North Vietnamese transgressions against the Accords and monitor activities up and down the length of the "Harriman Trail" but in the interim six of the "leave-behinds", including two men we knew from past twilight operations, Sorenson and Sanchez (sheep dipped for the time, we had to resist calling Sorenson "Sgt Johnny Sorenson"), volunteered to man a watch point up in the high ground where the midlands transitioned into the mountains.

Special Forces Group Sgt Johnny Sorenson was a man we knew very well, all our lives on Team Blue had at one time or another depended on training he had given us. He had even grown so close to us that on one occasion he had (out of my hearing, Cerone told me about it later) referred to me as "Peaches", a result of my propensity to hand out canned peaches to various tribesmen wherever we went. Hayes and Cerone immediately set him straight, it would be okay to call me "Peach Man" or "Peach Boy", but "Peaches" would lead to certain trouble, that nickname was reserved for members of Team Blue and even then only under certain conditions and circumstances. Exactly who he would have trouble with if he used the nickname was not made clear but he suspected he might have five or six men to deal with and decided that the nickname "JayKah" fit me best anyway.

Sanchez (or whatever his name, he had many aliases) was someone we had worked with and trusted in the field but did not really know much about. We debated whether he was a CIA plant in the Special Forces, Special Forces seconded to the CIA, or an employee of some other un-named government organization. We did finally ferret out the information (or at least we thought we did) that he had grown up on a subsistence farm or ranch, probably somewhere in the American Southwest; I voted for Arizona or New Mexico as we knew he was fluent in Spanish and had heard him use a few phrases in Athabasca with M&M Kappas. He did tell us that as a child he had lived in a home very similar to some of the planked construction homes of the Yao and felt a certain kindredship with some of the Montagnard villagers. We all agreed that whomever or whatever he was, Sanchez was a consummate field soldier.

The six-man team would be in positions to sound an alert if the North Vietnamese started a major movement in the direction of the cities on the Plain and keep an eye on the activities of the Pathet Lao along an important east/west road. They had been deployed and in position before the moves across the river had started.

Two weeks after they had gone up to their watch post Sorenson and Sanchez were back at Wattay sitting across from one another at a table in our shack, a bottle of brandy between them, at an hour usually too early for drinking even for the hardcore among us, faces hollow-eyed and grim they stared at one another and drank the entire bottle and then another with no visible effects on either man.

Blaske and I were already there when Kappas came into the shack and after a quick look at the two of them quietly told Blaske to fetch Samuels and instructed me to put on a pot of American style coffee. Blaske was back with Samuels in a few minutes followed by the rest of our little group who all sat and waited without speaking to find out what had happened to shake up these two very tough men.

From their hidden watch point they had seen the tide of refugees grow and concerned about their safety had radioed MAAG to ask for C123s to pick them up on the airstrip at Ban Ban or at least send some of the Philippine "construction workers" to escort them on to Long Thien. They got "we'll get back to you on that" as an answer. They then tried to reach Long Thien and Vang Pao directly but could not reach them on the radio frequencies available on their field radios. Frustrated and unable to break cover or offer any help to the slow moving column on the highway their concerns grew as the numbers of people joining the column swelled.

Two hours after darkness the last stragglers in the long thin line reached the bowl at Ban Ban and came in to find what shelter they could and rest for the night. After another hour quiet had descended on the camp with the only sounds a sporadic low coughing and an occasional cry from a baby somewhere in the basin. The exhausted travelers were getting what fitful sleep and rest they could before moving on in the morning.

By 2200 hours the mewling sounds of hungry babies had ceased and everyone in the camp, even the few dogs and livestock, had descended into sleep. A light fog began to form as steam from the ground met cool air coming down from higher ground muffling the sounds of breathing and snoring coming from the exhausted sleepers. The entire valley was still and quiet.

At midnight brave soldiers of the Pathet Lao and a few of their brave North Vietnamese allies descended on the bowl and killed every living creature in it.

Chapter 25

A Kiwi

She was five feet eleven inches tall in her stocking feet, over six feet in her boots, blue-eyed and rounded in all the right places, and wore a crown of red-gold hair and when he turned and saw her come through the door of the bar his world shifted. The out-of-tune discordant noises the band had been making became sweet and melodious, the lights brightened, and the dour faced men casting covert glances at the tall Yank in their midst suddenly became boon companions. The depression that had been hanging over the back of his head and clouding the edges of his vision had suddenly lifted and when her eyes picked him out from across the room he felt a thump somewhere deep inside his chest.

The noisy, smelly bar near the sheep and cattle sheds suddenly seemed as near to heaven as he had ever been. He wanted to know all there was to know about this woman; was she married, what was her name, where was she from, and most importantly, should he try to approach her, try to strike up a conversation? Then he realized she had been keeping eye contact with him and had a small smile playing about her (beautiful) mouth; she might be open to his advances.

There he stood, a tall, rangy veteran of more than one firefight, a Special Forces Sergeant as tough as they come and he was rooted to the spot, blushing like a teenager. Damn, Johnny, get it together!

He watched as she crossed the room to him and held out a warm, strong hand; her smile widening and lips parting to show perfect teeth as she said, "Hallo", "I'm Nan". At that first touch he knew he was about to fall in love.

In Saigon having a few drinks with some Aussies and listening to them talk on about a place called Queenstown on New Zealand's South Island he had decided to take some R&R time he was due (and needed) and visit the little island nation; the scenery was reported to be beautiful, the people friendly, everyone spoke English (he would get used to the accent, he was tired of hearing the ducks-fucking sounds of Vietnamese, Lao, and Khmer), and a visa would be easy to get. The next afternoon he put in his R&R request and the morning after had his travel documents in his pocket and a B-9 bag in hand and was on his way to take a plane ride.

He was tired, tired of long marches and the constant need to stay alert, tired of sleeping in hammocks or on the ground, tired of the constant stomach and lower GI ailments, tired of having to maintain a high energy level and present a positive aspect to his companions in the field; he felt drained, footsore and weary. But more than that, he was mentally tired and depressed at having to realize something that Americans in general found hard to accept; that in this war in SEA (Southeast Asia) there were no non-combatants and no clear demarcation that said, "This is the enemy".

The five or six year old kid carrying a basket of fruit and flowers could be hiding a hand grenade under the basket, and often was; the sweet young girl serving drinks in the local bar was almost certainly trading information for survival, and a red cross on a building, ambulance or helmet made for a convenient target for snipers. As "Others" in a foreign land and culture the sergeant and his fellows would always be at risk anywhere they went at any time day or night.

To add to the stress in both Laos and Viet Nam all the factions at war preyed on the civilian populations, damage to the people in small villages and on farms was not just collateral; they were subjected to terrorism from every side and some of the mindless atrocities perpetuated on innocents he had witnessed had left him feeling sick at heart and cynical. His innate cheerful outlook on the world was turning grey and bleak and he needed to find some way to dispel the sense of gloom and foreboding that was dogging his days and nights.

He knew he needed a new scene and had packed an old sectioned split-bamboo fly rod in the bottom of his travel bag; he would fish some of the streams feeding Milford Sound and stay in an inn with a view of the Sound that offered rooms to let and meals at a reasonable price. And perhaps visit a pub or two in Queenstown.

After four hops by plane to Wellington and a train ride to the ferry between North and South islands by the time he got to Christ Church he wanted to take a break from travel and checked into a hotel before walking out to see the town and finding his way to a working-man's pub on the outskirts of the city near the livestock pens. Not the sort of place where he expected to meet the girl of his dreams.

She told him later that he had looked handsome, out-of-place, and somehow sad and had appealed to her on several levels, but mostly to her curiosity. After she held out her hand to introduce herself she noticed his eyes shift to the figure that had moved up behind her, a man almost his own height but broader at the shoulders. She made a quarter turn, nodded and said, "I'm Nan and this is my brother Devin". He was surprised by the feeling of relief he felt at that announcement and smiled back saying, "I'm Johnny Sorenson", leaving out the word Sergeant he usually included when he introduced himself.

Devin moved down the bar to greet some friends and left the two of them to half talk, half shout over the sounds in the noisy pub. He learned that she taught school in a small town on the outskirts of Christ Church, that Devin was in town to arrange a livestock sale and she was there to meet him and give him a ride to a hotel in the center of town, that her family ran a cattle station a hard hour and half's drive from town, and that they would have time to meet Johnny for breakfast in the morning if he liked. He liked.

Later that night, unable to fall asleep on the soft mattress on his hotel bed he put his head on a pillow propped against the wall and with another pillow under his knees stretched out on the floor to dream of those lovely blue eyes, the red gold hair, the generous mouth and big smile she had shown him.

Over breakfast his plans for Queenstown and Milford Sound were swept away and shortly after he had checked out of the hotel his B-9 bag was in the back of a small cattle caravan and he was on the front seat next to Devin and on the way to the family's cattle station. Nan would join them on the day after next.

As he told the story later (over and over) he probably was placed in the midst of some awesome scenery but the only landscape he could remember from that first trip to the station was Nan. He had met a girl who could ride, shoot, and handle a cattle whip or a skillet with equal ease, a girl who would bait her own hook but could make a plain schoolmarm's clothes look like something from Paris or New York.

Staying on the station fishing, bird hunting, and helping with chores around the cattle pens he began to feel more relaxed than he had felt in years. Rides into the countryside and long evening walks with Nan when she came out to the station had begun to restore his sunny disposition and Nan's mother had made it her mission to put some weight on him.

But soon, too soon his R&R time was drawing to a close; he would have to start the long trip back to SEA. Nan volunteered to accompany him to Wellington and they arrived in that city the evening before his flight out was scheduled to leave having a late supper and checking into separate rooms in a hotel near the airport. At around midnight she came to his room.

Standing at the gate waiting to walk out and board his flight he held her tight and said, "I'm coming back as soon as I can". She replied, "I know" and kissed him tenderly on the cheek.

He surprised himself when he said, "I want to marry you". She replied, "I know" and kissed him again, this time not on the cheek and not tenderly.

Chapter 26

Six Big Boxes

Bohannon found 'em, we needed 'em, Kappas wanted 'em. Cerone and I had to go get 'em.

Major Bohannon had learned that off to one side next to a Quonset hut near the docks at Subic Bay there were four large Conex boxes and 20 additional crates of varying sizes marked "Avia Sud" in big bold letters and "North American" in smaller stenciled letters. The crates had been delivered to the US Naval Station at Subic Bay, perhaps by mistake, sometime in the past. Exactly when and how they got there was a mystery probably only known to some supply officer now long gone from the Navy base.

The Major did an unauthorized reconnoiter and with just the right amount of bluster and a haughty coolness got a civilian workman to break the seal on one of the Conex boxes; when he looked inside his hopeful guess at the contents was confirmed. Now he had to find a way to get those containers shipped to Thailand and into the 8th COIN's possession.

He tried all the proper military channels and could not get beyond a wall of stall and delay. They were in a United States Naval facility but did not belong to the Navy; therefore, the United States Navy did not have the authority to release them to the Major's custody. They might possibly have been consigned to the French Armed Forces as part of an arms exchange; but if that were the circumstance without French proof of ownership and French approval they could not be released to his custody, the French legate in Manila had no knowledge of the containers and therefore could not help. These and other dog-in-a-circle responses were answers to his requests. No one in the Naval Warehousing Office was going to take responsibility for letting them leave the base; perhaps if he could get a General or an Admiral, or maybe even a Senator to approve the transfer?

Major Bohannon might have been able to push the problem up the hill and call in some social and political coinage to break the deadlock but that would take a lot of time; months, even years might pass before the Conex boxes and crates were where we needed them and the contents operational so he sat down with Captain Samuels and First Sergeant Kappas and told them to hatch a plan. Leave him an avenue of plausible deniability and let him know what resources would be needed to get them to a secure location in the north of Thailand; this was tricky shit and could get someone in trouble, so naturally First Sergeant Kappas selected Cerone and me to tackle the problem.

M&M Kappas liked to smile and kiddingly say that he considered the Blue, Orange and Green teams as his small Fast Action Response Teams; or maybe he wasn't kidding and that was just his kind way of saying he considered us a bunch of little FARTS. But one thing for sure, whenever he needed a job done that would require out-of-the-box thinking and perhaps a willingness to color outside the lines he would pick Cerone for the job; and if he sent Cerone on one of these grey area missions it was a sure bet that I would be picked to go along.

One of the Philippine "civilian contractors" we worked with at the new secret air base being put in at Long Thien (Long Chin) had previously told Kappas that he had several family members working in various capacities at Subic and he was more than willing to accompany us there to act as interpreter and middleman, for a small profit, on whatever scheme we came up with to "rescue" the containers.

It took a couple of weeks for our new ID badges (including background paperwork) identifying Cerone and me as civilian contractors for the USAF Logistics and Supply Depot at Clark AFB and a badge identifying our Pilipino companion as our official interpreter to arrive at our shack. While we were waiting we had some beautifully painted hardhats and clipboard covers crafted by a local artisan. We even had printed forms and official looking letterhead to stuff in our clipboards. We were ready to look like a couple of young eager-beaver civilian clerical types let loose on Subic to find some misdirected cargo containers.

158

Mindful of Krebb's directive and showing unusual discipline we avoided the bars and fleshpots outside the gates at Subic and had our plan within a day of arriving on the Naval Base. Three factors played into our plan; it is sometimes easiest to hide large objects in plain sight, cigarettes were (and maybe still are) the best across-borders currency in South East Asia, the locals working on the base considered a grand theft as the highest form of machismo.

We took a flight to Saigon and then on to Vientiane the next day and on our arrival at Wattay Field informed our leaders, Bohannon, Samuels, and Kappas of our plan and the resources we would need to ease the Gordian Knot holding up our acquisition of the Conex boxes and crates. Then we waited for several weeks until we got word that a shipment of six Conex boxes slated for delivery to a shipping agent for the US Air Force at Udorn Thailand and routed via Subic Bay had arrived at Subic.

The three of us, Cerone, me, and our interpreter/co-conspirator, were back in the Philippines a few days later garbed in civvies and hardhats with our ID badges prominently displayed and armed with a flat case containing stencils. We were accompanied by a Pilipino crew of stevedores to "our" Conex boxes on the docks with large lettering on the sides that read PM USA, ATC, and RJR and smaller lettering that read Phillip Morris, Lucky Strikes, and Camels. The stevedores conveniently "lost" our delivery containers and moved them to the same dock area as the containers and crates containing the objects of Major Bohannon's interests. Somehow the Major had gotten by all the questions about why he needed such an enormous order of cigarettes for the small number of American personnel in Thailand and Laos and had been able to expedite the delivery to this point.

The second night the six containers were on the docks the contents of two of them were placed on trucks and in "Jeepos" and disappeared into the night, the twenty crates marked "Avia Sud" replacing the contents. And then the stencils and paint pots came out. The large Conex boxes originally marked "Avia Sud" and "North American" now were marked "PM USA", "ATC", and "RJR" and the cigarette containers re-marked as well. Switched number plates identifying the individual Conex boxes were braised on and were "aged" to pass an indifferent inspection. Now if no one looked close enough to see the numbers were changed and that twenty crates that had been there the day before were missing we would have our goodies on the way to Thailand rickety-tick-tick.

The next morning the two young civilian USAF contractors were barely able to disguise their impatience and dismay at the Naval Yard's incompetence in losing six large containers bound for the port of Laem Chabang in Thailand. After a certain amount of name dropping on one side, "you know, Ambassador Unger personally ordered this shipment" and some 'ems and 'ers on the other side and a few phone calls transportation was summoned and the two civilians escorted to the docks to locate the "missing" containers. Two days later the containers left Subic Bay on a US Naval Transport headed for Thailand. Six days later they were on rail cars and rerouted from Udorn to a railhead not far from a small town in the north of Thailand. From there they were trucked (a huge logistical effort) to a plantation headquarters located between the villages of Phrae and Nan near the Lao border.

MAAG and the CIA had their "not-so-secret" base established at Long Chin (Long Thien) in Laos where an entire small city complete with shops, churches, bars, and brothels was built around an airstrip with an eventual population of forty or fifty thousand people and was a secret only from those who paid for it; i.e. the United States Congress and the US taxpayers. It became known as "The Most Secret Place on Earth" although the Lao government, the Pathet Lao, the Vietnamese, the Russians and the Chinese and a myriad of traders, pimps, prostitutes and mercenaries knew all about it. By contrast our little base of operations at "Camp Sammy" (named for a friend, his mother owned the plantation) was never known to more than fifty people from outside the plantation.

Our armorer "Zero" was brought over from Nellis to direct construction activities and "my buddy Floyd" was given leave from his duties at Udorn and was at "Camp Sammy" (named for our friend whose mother owned the property) to direct assembly of the contents of the six Conex boxes.

Floyd would stay and perform maintenance and service to the birds. Within weeks we had a serviceable airstrip, a fuel dump, and a munitions bunker hidden in a steep walled valley. And we had four Fennecs (modified French versions of the T-28 prop driven air-to-ground aircraft) with slotted holders on the sides where insignia of the Lao Royal Air Force or of the Thai Air Force could be inserted as the need arose. Ex-USMC and former Anzac mercenaries would pilot the planes and re-fueling points and emergency strips and procedures for flights over Laos were provided for.

Now we had a tool we had long needed; an off-the-books, at-our-direction, armed, ready, and very dangerous "Phantom Air Force".

Chapter 27

Wet Heat

Fear is a smell, a taste, a buzzing in the ears, a narrowing of vision, an acceleration of heart rate. It had become such a common state that I almost welcomed it early one miserable morning when it helped me ignore the little ants that had found a way inside my pants cuffs and were exploring up my leg. After a long three-day uphill slog through muddy terrain and more than a week in hiding on cold rations in a stinking green hole we were a sullen, sorry lot who had trouble remembering the excitement we had felt when this mission was first laid out for us. Hard to maintain a level of fun when you are eating nothing but cold food, drinking nothing but cold tea, and having to shit in a rubberized bag (we would leave nothing behind when we left this spot).

I could feel the tension in my companions and knew they had all gone on alert as well and tried to reach out with all my conscious senses to figure out what had caused the fear spike in all of us. I fought to hold back a sneeze while we listened and began to pick out the low murmur of voices from the forest sounds and heard the whine of a truck transmission; we were going to have the visitors we had been waiting for.

Traveling from one climate to another was a little hard to adjust to; one year we went from moderate rain forest to deep snow to tropical monsoon in a few weeks. Another year we went from wet and hot to dry and hot and back to wet and hot and rounded out the year wet and cold mixed with dry and cold. My poor nose never did get fully caught up with the climate changes.

The searing dry heat of the practice range in Nevada was hard to survive but, in some ways, the wet tropical climate in SEA was even more miserable, despite the thermometer registering lower temps than in the desert the humidity made the heat less tolerable, especially in the Lao Lowlands and along the Mekong Plain.

Boots and leather equipment would be covered in green fuzz; even the infrared light bulbs we installed in our lockers couldn't control it. Any item of clothing we wore was wet within minutes of putting it on. I spent a lot of effort and made several "almost authorized" trips to the Philippines just to make sure we all had an ample supply of socks, foot powder and athletes foot medication.

I once had an Army Colonel tell me that he thought it unethical that some of his troopers found ways around the regular supply channels to procure extras for items like socks, heat tabs, canteens, certain rations, and ammunition. I almost laughed as he spoke because we (especially Cerone and I) were always "comshawing" items we knew our team would need (and sometimes a few luxury items) and I had to wonder how much time the Colonel had spent deep in the field running out of critical supplies. I could surmise he must have depended on aerial re-supply for his troopers' needs; telling any enemy where and how many they were. I guessed that his troopers were proponents of the "recon by fire" (spray every bush a bad guy might hide behind with automatic weapons) philosophy and probably needed re-supply often. If we'd had him along on one of our missions we would have had to carry some extras to be able to take care of him after a few days in the bush, we didn't believe in re-supply whenever it could be avoided; to paraphrase a hot rodders' expression we, "Had to run with what we brung".

To give the Colonel the benefit of the doubt perhaps he was like some of our allies among the Cao Dai, Yao, and Wa who could leave home empty handed and like any good guerilla warrior come home with a bag of rice, a quarter of a pig, and an AK47 with ammo bandoliers; and in the case of the Yao and Wa perhaps with a head or two hanging on a string.

In Laos the lower and mid elevations were particularly uncomfortable, some might say maddingly uncomfortable, during and just after the monsoon season. An observer could actually watch the vegetation grow and at the same time see and smell fungi taking over everything not moving. We could not only see and smell the rot; we swore we could hear it at night. Heat rash got us all with tiny pustules forming in our armpits, crotches, inner thighs and everywhere clothing could rub against skin. People got short-tempered in a hurry during this time of year and I believe that it was one monsoon season when we started hearing, "Patience hell, I want to go kill something".

This would also be the peak season for mosquitoes, ticks, and leeches, and flies that could take chunks of meat wherever they bit so baggy long pants and long-sleeved shirts, tight at the cuffs and collars and chaffing wrists, ankles, and necks, were de rigueur for the field. We were never issued tropical boots that ventilated and would wear thick socks soaked in repellant with rubber soled sandals (they had the added advantage of leaving tracks that might have been made by locals) whenever conditions allowed. Neck scarves and head bands and sometimes shaved heads topped with shapeless hats completed our ensemble.

To add to our misery there were two kinds of mosquitoes: day mosquitoes that carried dengue fever and night mosquitoes that carried malaria; either disease could incapacitate or kill. We all religiously took doxycyclene (an anti-malarial medicine) and quinine tablets and hoped for a mission in high country; there would still be leeches and mosquitoes but not in such great numbers and in such large clouds.

I had an anti-pest technique that helped, (I was never as susceptible to bug bites as my team mates) I tried to maintain a balanced gin intake, drinking just enough to keep the critters off my skin and not enough to smell like a rum pot. Other team members tried this approach with mixed results (probably not maintaining the proper balance), but all reported that consuming a little gin made the itching more tolerable.

Our team was understandably excited one soggy October morning, so humid you couldn't tell if it was raining or not for hours at a time, then it would rain so hard the bouncing raindrops made it look like it was raining up, to learn we were going to re-visit a spot we had mapped on an earlier trip in high country. South of the Ban Karai Pass on the Lao side of the border was a large open spot under a double canopy where it would be possible to hide a park full of trucks, elephants, other pack animals, and a few hundred bicycles, complete with drivers and freight. There were several long trenches that would service hoang cam stoves (the trenches would dissipate the exhaust smoke from the stoves) and prepared camp spots under overhangs and in shallow caves near a water crossing. This was definitely a spot that would be used repeatedly as a layover and distribution point for taking supplies south into Viet Nam and would almost certainly be occupied as soon as the trails dried up from the monsoonal rains. We needed to get there and establish a couple of secure watching posts before the place got busy.

Adding to our excitement was the knowledge that we were going to be allowed to use a new ambush technique, we were going to "Bring Some" to the bad guys. In place and waiting to spring our trap we were still wet, miserable, itchy and sore but not sullen or sorry; this was all going to be worth it and the additional two days we lay in wait while the park filled up with people and materiel didn't seem like much of a hardship.

As we watched trucks came in twos and threes and off-loaded bags of supplies that were transferred to be carried by modified bicycles; a quarter of the worlds' bicycle population must have been stacked up on that trail waiting for porters, or at least so it seemed. The bicycles were modified with a wooden over-frame for hauling heavy panniers and a long wooden steering handle attached to the handlebar on one side; they would be pushed by one or sometimes two people and could carry loads of two or three hundred pounds at a time (sometimes more). Even in these early days when the trail was busy there were probably twenty thousand people pushing bicycles over various routes through the mountains and south to the jungles in South Viet Nam. Once they were dispersed throughout the trails that made up the "Trail" it would be hard to damage the flow of supplies; the best idea (if they were allowed over the passes into Laos) was to hit them at logistics re-distribution points like the one we were watching.

We were going to use air-to-ground in our own fashion; not to soften up an objective in preparation for an assault, not in support of ground troops engaged with an enemy, not as a relief for beleaguered soldiers taking hostile fire, but more in the manner of pre-registered artillery triggered when the enemy enters a kill zone. We were going to set off an ambush and if all went as planned the enemy would not even know we were there when it went off.

We had carefully mapped and made scale models of several locations that were likely to be used as rest areas and/or redistribution centers, and where trails funneled in to choke points. We were certain our pilots could readily find IPs (Identification Points) based on the models and without any electronic navigation aids or ground based aids. All we had to do on the ground was transmit a "yes" signal to a small plane flying a grid about thirty miles away when the location we were watching was target rich and the message would be relayed to armed aircraft nearby.

The plan came out of necessity, the techniques we had learned at the Nellis gunnery range were not going to work for us here; there was no practical way to set colored panels on the high canopy (setting colored panels would not work in open country either without a significant force to provide distraction and covering fire), flares and smoke grenades would tell the enemy that we were there and where, and tracer fire presented the same problem as it marked both ends of the tracer stream.

We were set to give our plan of action its first test and had set up a hidey-hole where we could rest and stow our gear in a spot beneath a low escarpment to the west of the parking area we planned to strike. Our camp was about a hundred meters from the LP (listening post) where we watched and monitored activity through artillery glasses. Three men manned the LP and were relieved one at a time by rotating one man every four hours during the night, day watchers were stuck for twelve hours at a time, we couldn't risk moving anyone during the day, we were starting to think and operate more and more like the Viet Minh.

I would have felt more comfortable with Baphang and Hayes in our camp, and perhaps Sgt Johnny Sorenson but Baphang and Hayes were fifty klicks to our north with a group of Mei irregulars preparing to blow down a slope on a narrow section of trail used by PAVN trucks and the SFG Sgt was somewhere out of the country. Morrison had come up to join us after guiding Team Orange to a position to our west (they were to provide cover for our withdrawal if needed) and Cerone, Blaske and Tom Minor had made the uphill slog with me, being joined on the way up by Mr. Sanchez (Jesse Sanchez, aka Mr. Davis, Mr. Murphy, Mr. Alvarez, and several other names) and a new Mr. Murphy we hadn't met before rounded out the watcher team.

On the morning of the third day of activity in the supply dump Cerone, Sanchez and I were in the LP and observing the high piles of supplies in the park we answered the wordless open mike clicks from the scout aircraft with a coded "yes" and the operation was on in pre-dawn light.

 The first attack aircraft in (a T6 with Kappas in the front seat) placed a smoke bomb just to the south of dead center in the park and I spotted while Cerone called corrections from the plume for the follow-on attack, hoping our brief carrier wave would not be noticed and located during the confusion. Sanchez was busy with a Leica and telescope lens trying to record the scene in the dim light.

The distinctive sound of big paddle props and rotary engines announced two T28Fs (F for Fennec, these aircraft were supposed to belong to the French) the first blind firing rockets and 20 mike mike cannons down through the canopy followed by the other releasing a five-hundred-pound bomb that hit almost at the base of the smoke plume and left us partially deafened in our muddy green hole.

The sound of the aircraft faded then returned as they circled to come back on the attack; this time they dropped two canisters of napalm splashing everything in the clearing beneath the canopy with liquid fire and setting off secondary explosions as the trucks and fuel and ammunition stores ignited. Sanchez had plenty of light to take some extraordinary photographs of the action and the aftermath before we withdrew down to the west.

The raid had followed the guerillas' dictum, I believe first codified by an American captain during the Revolutionary War, of "one slow, four quick". Our planners had gone slow, taking the time to wring out the details before solidifying the plan, we had advanced quickly and gotten into position without being discovered, the attack had come quickly, and we both cleared the field and withdrew quickly.

The raid had destroyed tons of materiel, bloodied the enemy, and as we learned from stragglers picked up by Mei (Hmong) patrols demoralized (read scared the hell out of) the survivors. It had all been done on the cheap and without loss of life or injury to our side.

It should have been considered a very successful operation; except it had occurred under the wrong officers' command.

Chapter 28

Trong Son Road Assault

We had been in the field twelve days slogging around in mud left over from the monsoon and hiding in smelly wet holes before we launched our first air ambush. We caught the rascals by surprise and caused a lot of damage (documented on Sanchez's camera footage), withdrew without their even knowing we were there and moved south to set up at our next target.

Sanchez and my two favorite Yao tribesmen moved on ahead to the next spot on the trail we planned to hit. They would get there a day ahead of us and staying hidden observe and map enemy defensive positions, trenches or bunkers, cook areas, vehicle parks, store piles and other features. The detailed information they collected would tell us where to set up for our marshalling zones and where we would advance to in order to be in position when the trap was sprung.

Hayes and Baphang with ten Mei (Meo, Hmong) irregulars would be following us, catching up from a position fifty klicks north of our first ambush. They would have to move carefully to form our rear guard and protect their group from pursuers from the place where they had poked a hornets' nest with explosives when they had blown down a section of bluff to block a truck road at a narrow spot.

 When they reached a point down slope from our first air action they would rendezvous with New Mr. Murphy and eight guys from Orange Team with another squad of ten Mei and lay ambushes on several trails leading in our direction. If this rear guard and blocking force came under heavy fire we would abort our primary ambush plan and divert our air resources to cover their withdrawal.

Coming up from the west and south would be Samuels and a Mei captain with a company of thirty men who had been training for an action just like this one for over a year. They would fill out our trail assault force with a clear mission statement that said our objectives were to disrupt the flow of men and materiel, to cause confusion, to harass and interdict the enemy, to bleed the enemy but not to engage in a pitched battle. We would strike and withdraw then bloody any pursuers who got between our main force and the blocking force to our north. Air power would be available to cover the withdrawal if needed.

We had made three-dimensional models of several target spots (places we identified as depots and re-distribution centers) for our pilots of the "Phantom Air Force"; places we and Tom Major had mapped on foot and Kappas had reconnoitered by air. This second target area was not bunched up in a single park but was a place where several trails converged on a north south line wide enough for trucks and was about one kilometer long. After careful study of the model and repeated detailed briefings our fly boys were ready. They just needed the call to "Come on in!"

The long thin shape of our target area dictated our strategy; ground forces would strike at the ends, far enough apart that neither end could see what was going on with the other and confusing the people in the middle as to which direction to go to assist their men under fire. Then the air resources would take out the middle. If they bulged east the enemy could escape, losing their supply dumps and equipment. If they attacked our ambushes (as they should) we would bleed them as we withdrew, calling in air support on any concentrations. If they bulged west at the center we would catch them in a pincer action then withdraw.

Our first air ambush had taken place at dawn, giving us plenty of time and cover to get into position undetected; this hit would be at dusk to give our force the advantage during the withdrawal but making it more tedious and dangerous getting into position. One element in our favor was that the Viet Minh, PAVN, and NVA were not expecting to get hit this far up the trail and, hopefully, would not have made any adjustment to our new tactics yet.

We would use red and green flares to mark the ends of the target zone this time, Cerone and a small team taking the south end and me taking the north end with three Mei companions as guards. When the planes came in they would keep the line between our flares to the left and begin laying down ordinance as they passed the first flare and pulling up and away as they passed the second flare. The planes would be monitoring a pre-determined frequency that matched with our three PRC-9 sets. Cerone would man one radio at the south end of the line and Morrison the second from Samuels's hidden CP (Command Post) near the mid-point of our assault line, Hayes would have the third at the north end of the line. Kappas would orbit above and to the east of the linear area and act as FAC (forward air controller) for the flights coming in on target.

We would be well armed for a hit and run with three heavy machine gun crews, two mortar crews (they would fire a flat trajectory, rounds probably exploding on tree limbs but still doing damage and adding to the havoc), three BAR men (including Hayes and Tom Minor), sixteen M14s and an assortment of M1 Garands and M1 carbines, and a couple of M3A1 grease guns, plus a few AK47s (I didn't like having them on our side of the line because the sounds confused my sense of where the players were), at least twenty handguns and a lot of grenades. The problem would not be arms but might be ammunition; some of the Mei loved hearing their weapons and would keep firing even when no targets presented.

While we were finishing our work hiding our rucks' and non-combat gear in the marshalling areas, memorizing our routes into and out of our assault positions and withdrawal routes, eating and hydrating, and attending to all the small details that had to be covered before twilight Kappas was aloft in a T-6 on his way to refuel at a small strip carved out of the side of a mountain to our west. Two hours later the first flight of two un-marked Fennecs (French model T-28s) were leaving a base in the north of Thailand to be followed twenty minutes later by a second flight of two. A Dornier D-28 was orbiting about twenty miles from our position waiting to relay the "go" signal. Our "Phantom Air Force" was armed and on the prowl, ready to drop aux tanks and attack on schedule.

An hour before sunset I took my three men and moved over a ridge then back and into a spot that would allow me to get to my position to fire a flare in less than thirty seconds, anyone that spotted us making our dash in the twilight would have to be picked off, noise at that point would not make any difference. As soon as I got the flare off the four of us would back up about twenty meters and watch the fun begin.

While we were waiting I realized that although I was not comfortable with so many of our people skulking about in the bush waiting to be discovered and disclose our presence to the enemy I was comfortable enough to be suffering a dangerous feeling. Boredom. Not anxiety, not eagerness to get started with the action, just boredom. The days and nights out in the field, the hours on and off adrenaline, the monotony of the humidity and cold food had left me tired and flat and daydreaming about places anywhere except up on this damn mountain. I needed to get my focus back, I needed to, "get my head out of my ass and get with the program!" The minute hand on my watch was creeping toward straight up; it was time to dash to the hummock where I would fire my flare.

I thought I could hear aircraft in the distance as I ran and was still three long strides from the hummock when I heard gunfire start to my right (south) and then closer and to my left (north) as I got my flare up and started back to my protected position.

I slid/dove back into cover and had rolled on my belly, rifle pointed down range before I recognized that my three Mei were not there! Twilight was fading fast but I had just enough light before dark rolled all the way in to see the three of them creeping forward toward the enemy positions. Was it teenage bullshit, training failure, excess of enthusiasm? The dumb bastards (just kids really) hadn't stayed put and hadn't noticed the eight or ten men in camouflaged pith helmets approaching the hummock where I had fired the flare. In less than half a minute all three Mei were dead. The NVA patrol would be trying to find me next!

172

I could hear the firing to my left intensify and could distinguish the sounds of a ma deuce and a couple of BARs and thought I heard the three-round spacing of M14s from Team Orange before it was all lost in the roar of T-28s in trail firing cannon and dropping napalm canisters along the line in front of me.

In the sheet of fire before me I could see dark shapes writhing and pulsing and a large dark object that came out of the curtain and ran south and I remember thinking, "where the fuck did that elephant come from?" before spotting bodies low and moving toward me limed against the fire light.

Hayes and Cerone were having the most fun, chatting with the aircraft and reporting to Samuels, the machine gun crews were working the hardest, picking up and moving to new firing positions as the fluidity of the action required. Samuels was happy with the results he was hearing in his CP and Blaske and Morrison were in their professional modes, doing what they had been trained to do. Baphang and Tom Minor were as usual practicing their skills with great efficiency. Sanchez and New Mr. Murphy were alternating between firing their weapons and documenting the action with their cameras. I was looking for hiding places and having the least fun.

I was sure the NVA squad that had killed my escort knew I was there and would try to flank me and had started a crawl back toward my boogie route when the second flight of Fennecs came in dropping five hundred pounders and splashing the burning napalm into orange red fountains. Shit, the stuff was coming down around me!

I had been bored less than an hour before but now I skipped Fear and went straight to Terror mode. My logical brain was telling me to stay down, crawl out to a lower trail leading south and follow it to hook up with Samuels at the CP (follow the plan), or if that route didn't look good move on to find Cerone's withdrawal route.

My reptilian brain was screaming hide, hide, hide! Coming over a berm and looking back I could see a darker spot up under a root system where the last rains had washed away some of the earth under a tree. My logical brain was telling me the small cave might have snakes, spiders, or poisonous bugs; that I could find myself trapped in the hole, I needed to keep moving! But my alligator brain took over and my limbs moved without my volition, in seconds I was pulling my feet and weapon up after me and trying to get really small.

Over the crackling roar of the fire above me and over the sounds of shouts and screams and exploding trucks and munitions strewn out for half a klick (approx. a quarter mile) north and south of my position I could hear the small arms fire at both ends of the target line punctuated with occasional noise from claymore mine, hand grenade, and heavy machine gun fire shifting westward. Our teams at both ends of the ambush site were withdrawing. Later Hayes described the withdrawal at his end as, "Playing at Gopher Holes (an arcade game where gophers pop up out of holes to be hit with mallets) with machine guns"; they would hopscotch and set up ambushes as they were being pursued, when enemy troops appeared they would let the first two or three point men go by to be picked off later and when a squad sized group or larger popped up, "hit them with .50 caliber mallets". The Vietnamese tired of the game and quit following after the third or fourth encounter.

The popcorn popping noise of firefights became sporadic and dimmed out entirely leaving me with the sounds of the fire and men moving about above me; and leaving me with the smells. The smells of wood smoke and burning oily brush, of truck tires and upholstery; the gasoline and soap smell of napalm providing a background to the olfactory symphony with the odors of cordite and human flesh as soloists.

I started to drop out of my hiding place but froze again when I thought I heard a noise on the path below me. There it was again, a low swishing sound interspersed with a soft padding. Someone was cautiously coming up the path from the south, the direction I intended to go to quit the area, maybe one of my team mates. Then through a root lattice I saw three men with the wrong silhouettes and stayed frozen in place; luck and my old friend Fear had saved me from meeting them on the path. I would stay where I was until I was sure an escape route was clear.

The dim twilight that signaled the return of the half-light that passed for daytime in under the canopy was just coming on when I decided the activity around me had slowed to the point where I dared chance my retreat. My cramped legs didn't want to work but that was okay, I planned to slither for at least a hundred meters before poking my head up anyway. Finally, I felt I was far enough away to risk standing against a tree trunk while the burning pins and needles in my thighs, knees and ankles subsided. Then I sat back down and removed my boots and washed my feet with dribbles from my canteen, put on fresh socks, re-laced my boots and started walking.

Feeling very much alone.

Chapter 29

A Walk In The Park

Gawd damn, son of a bitch. Not gonna' do, another hitch.

Gawd damn, son of a bitch. Not gonna' do, another hitch.

I kept a non-verbal cadence making up new rhymes as I went along, the lyrics helping to keep my pace even and non-threatening here in monkey country. Baphang and Tom Minor had taught us that if we moved too slowly the monkeys would alarm, if we moved too quickly the monkeys would alarm, the trick was to keep at an even, un-hurried sort of glide in groups of less than two or three. If it was done right the brown monkeys with white and red ruffs and no tails would stay on the ground and the grey leaf eating monkeys with the white faces would keep gossiping in the trees. If one moved just right the birds might tell one another a human was there but not sound loud alarms and then go silent.

Hair standing on end and senses on full alert as I worked my way over a ridge to the southwest I was depending on the forest early warning system to tell me when someone else was near. If the monkeys had a sudden change in their behavior or the bird calls and other forest sounds changed, or worse went silent, I would suspect I had company and needed to hide.

At dusk the night before I had been part of a ground/air raid on a supply column and depot on a major artery of the old Trong Son Road (Ho Chi Minh Trail) near the crest of the Annamite Cordillera where supplies were coming over the mountains from North Viet Nam for transport down to the south end of Laos and northeast corner of Cambodia and back over the mountains into South Viet Nam.

As dark slammed down I had found myself alone (the three men who had been with me dead) and the probable target for an NVA/PAVN patrol search just as an attack on both ends of the column erupted. I found a hole under a tree and attempted to pull it in after me, spending the night peeking out of a root lattice watching the onslaught on the column while dark forms, some silhouetted against a sheet of fire, passed on all sides of my lair.

Hours after the attack fires were still burning, the light bouncing off trees and a low hanging cloud cover that rolled in around 2200 hours. In the eerie glow I could see men moving about, and some that would never move again and at least a dozen truck carcasses still burning fitfully in my narrow range of view. Occasionally pockets of ammunition or other ordnance would cook off and send roman candles in the air to disappear in the cloud cover.

I stayed frozen in my hole, the refrain of an old folk song playing over and over in an endless loop in my head, "In the pines, in the pines, where the sun never shines, I shivered the whole night through" and time passing like "treacle through a pin hole". Twice I started to leave my hiding spot and some instinct kept me where I was, watching people go by on the path below me minutes later, breaking into a cold sweat at my narrow escapes.

Finally, a little before what would pass for dawn deep under a triple canopy I crept out of my spot and rolled across the path below me and crawled into the brush on the other side, not standing until I had found a spot in the shelter of a wide tree with an undergrowth enclosure at its base.

I checked my pockets and web gear to assess my weapons and supplies situation, if I didn't have it on me I didn't have it. It would not be safe to go back to where I had stashed my rucksack the day before even it if it were still there, which was doubtful.

For weapons I had my M14 with two 30 round magazines taped together, my holstered 1911 .45 cal pistol with two extra magazines, an M6 bayonet slung upside down on my web gear suspender and a khukiri (Gurkha knife) in a sheath at my back. In a shoulder bag I had two MKII frag grenades, a flare gun with three flares, and two more full magazines for the M14 wrapped in two pair of clean socks.

I was dressed in khaki cargo pants and a four-pocket shirt that had been washed with a fresh set of OD green fatigues, giving them a non-descript mottled grey green color that I thought made for perfect camouflage in the forest. For headgear I wore a floppy grey green full brimmed hat over a drab green bandana that protected the back of my neck and for footgear I had a pair of Redwing boots that had been taken apart and reassembled with a thin steel plate between the outer and inner soles to protect against spikes and punji sticks. These boots had water proofing and a mud-shedding sole far superior to anything our military had available at the time (and came with a life-time warranty).

In one pants pocket I had my soap dish survival kit (a metal bar soap container covered with electrical tape to keep it from clanking or shining) containing a one-sided razor, a small magnet, fish hooks and line, two condoms, a small wax candle, water purification tablets, dysentery meds, four fuel tablets, a couple of feet of electrical tape wound on a pencil stub, three feet of thin wire also wrapped on a pencil stub and a dozen water-proofed strike-anywhere matches. In another pants pocket was my Zippo lighter and a pocket knife with a serrated edge blade, a wad of baht (local currency), and a small tin of green camtec face paint. On my web belt was two canteens and a pouch with a small first aid kit.

In one upper shirt pocket I had an un-opened, crushed pack of Lucky Strikes and in the other a brass cased engineering compass and a folded up section of a topo map. I didn't really need the map, I had been in the area before and had committed the prominent terrain features to memory but I might need to use it to get a fire going or something. In my lower shirt pockets I found some crackers, and a handful of hard candy, two chocolate rounds, a packet of dried fish, a tube of foot ointment, and a small oiled-paper bag containing leaf tea and sugar cubes. I was already half starved after two weeks of cold rations and would need to find some protein calories somewhere soon or run completely out of energy.

With enemy patrols certain to be in the neighborhood (they might even pick up my trail) I would have no time to try for fish or set up snares and could not risk a gunshot at a deer or wild pig. With a little luck, speed and cunning I might be able to catch one of the red, black and yellow half-wild chickens that were to be found all over the forest floor but I would not have time to clean and cook it. There was also a better than even chance that any hunting activity would probably get me off rhythm and set off the jungle monkey and bird alarms.

The need for a good food source would have to influence my decisions determining which evasion route to take on my way out of the mountains.

I sat down and took care of my feet while I formulated my plan of action.

The raid elements attacking at each end of the column we ambushed would have withdrawn at least ten hours ahead of me leaving by separate routes and headed for two different landing sites for air extract by Porters and Helio Couriers down to an old airstrip left by the Japanese after WWII. There they would have boarded C119s or C123s for the flight back to Wattay. I thought it unlikely that during the confusion and darkness of the night withdrawal that they realized I was not with them; each element probably thought I was with the other and they would not miss me or my three erstwhile companions until they took roll call at the extraction points and communicated by radio.

The lead time they had on me would get bigger as I had to move more slowly than they would have traveling on my own and in daylight. I would still make my way to one of the sites on the chance that Kappas would expect me to go that way if I were alive and un-captured and might send an aircraft to look the places over a couple of times in the next few days.

If I failed to get picked up at the landing site I faced the prospect of a five or six-day trek over uneven terrain before I could get to a region I knew to be controlled by Vee Pee's men (Vang Pao, commander of the Meo/Hmong irregulars) and effect my own rescue. Either way I would need food and had an idea where I might get some.

179

There was a Khumu (one of the hill tribes) village not too far off of my route to the more northerly of the landing sites and I had visited there with Baphang twice in the past year. I would put myself at the mercy of the villagers, counting on their good will and respect toward Baphang to work in my favor. At least I now had a plan to work on and it boosted my spirits and made the god-awful feeling of loneliness I was experiencing a little less burdensome. I was well armed, well clothed, in good health, and had a plan; fuck it, this was going to be a walk in the park. Now I just had to keep myself on pace, resist the urge to hurry and let the klicks roll by. I stuck a hard candy in my mouth and started walking.

The rains had stopped weeks ago but the humidity was still high and I was at altitude, and I had been highly stressed for hours on end so about three hours into my walk I had to stop and rest and found a nice little place next to a running stream a few meters off the game trail I was on. I was dreaming of the fat-meat-patty hamburgers on white bread with mustard and slices of dill pickle that my uncle used to make when we visited my grandmother's house but didn't even know I had fallen asleep until I woke up alarmed. It took a couple of seconds for me to figure out what was wrong, the monkeys weren't gossiping, the birds weren't talking.

I couldn't see them but I could hear them, a group of men moving up the game trail from the direction I was going. I pulled back the hammer on my .45 (a round in the tube) the quarters too close to swing a rifle and waited until the forest sounds came back. As I eased the hammer back down on my pistol I noticed my hands were shaking and I was really, really thirsty.

I made slow progress, stopping often to take rest breaks and check that no one was following, I even stopped and made a half canteen cup of tea and ate a chocolate round and some powdery crackers before I reached the Khumu village in the late afternoon. At the village gate, a footbridge crossing into the village compound, I waited for someone to call the elders to grant me permission to enter, protocol must be followed, good manners observed.

My life would be in their hands and I needed the villagers to feel well disposed toward me and in no wise threatened by my appearance at their doorstep so I had left my rifle slung on my back and had holstered my pistol. I had even stopped by the water edge a few meters up the path and removed the camtec paint from my face and the backs of my hands, feeling but not seeing someone watching. My message was simple, "No threat here". Three old men approached and I pantomimed my hunger and displayed a few bahts to indicate my willingness to pay, my hammy acting amusing the old men and some curious children watching from the other side of the bridge. When they beckoned me to follow I crossed into the center of the village and was led to the communal kitchen.

One of the old men kept patting me on the shoulder and saying, "Baphang" over and over until the other villagers surrounding me nodded their understanding, they recognized me and knew I had been there before with the trader and would favor me with their hospitality. I think what was left of the entire village (I had noticed a lot of empty huts in the compound) gathered to watch me consume one of the best meals I have eaten anywhere. There was a pudding made from a yam-like root baked with bananas and chopped papaya leaf seasoned with some savory spice and the usual sticky rice with a fish paste sauce. But the best dish was minced chicken mixed with seared rice, garlic, eggplant and peppers and steamed in a banana leaf wrapper. I offered my packet of dried fish to the ladies preparing the food and it immediately went into a green vegetable, onion and egg drop soup as an extra flavor and texture ingredient; wonderful stuff.

I knew the villagers could not chance my staying overnight, the risk of a Viet Minh patrol (they were particularly active at night) finding me there would put them all in danger and after I ate (and burped) I pantomimed my need to move on. I put my bandana (cleanest side up) on the ground next to where I had eaten and placed my Lucky Strikes, Zippo lighter, two needles and some thread from my med kit, and half my wad of baht and, well fed, prepared to leave. The cook ladies tugged at my arm motioning me to wait while they wrapped six of the minced meat packages for me to take with me.

What the hell, I took the two grenades from my shoulder bag and added them to the pile of gifts on the bandana, watching some eyes light up and a few grins spread among the men. I stuffed the minced meat packages in the bag and prepared to leave a little before dusk and get well clear of the village before I found a secure place to sleep, unwilling to try to travel too far on unknown trails in the dark.

The village elders anticipated my problem and appointed two young men (I would guess thirteen or fourteen years old) to guide me over the game trails to the northwest, the direction I indicated I needed to go and they took me to a spot about a two hour hike from the village where I could shelter for the remainder of the night in a small limestone cave. They checked the cave for unwelcome inhabitants, gave me some reassuring pats on the shoulder, and disappeared back up the trail leaving me alone in the pitch black of the cave. I took care of my nightly ablutions and fell into a deep sleep, waking a little cold but refreshed just before dawn.

I breakfasted on the contents of one of the leaf wrapped packages and a cup of tea then set to work with the engineering compass figuring out where I was in relation to the landing site I was heading to and what route I should take to get there. I would just have another day walking in the park.

And the path I was traversing that morning was in fact in a park like setting, the thick forest and dense undergrowth of the day before giving way to evenly spaced trees about six feet in diameter sited several meters apart with ten or twelve inch diameter saplings spaced between them and fan-like shrubs dotted here and there with sunlight filtering down giving an illusion of peace and safety. I did miss the monkeys though, that piece of my early warning systems wasn't to be found in this part of the woods.

I set a quicker pace than the day before and made good progress, skirting the open areas and checking carefully before crossing any water, I could see further here but so could the bad guys and I didn't want any ugly surprises. Traveling I heard and saw a couple of light aircraft and was tempted to use one of my flares, but with no place to be picked up immediately at hand I decided not to risk exposing my position to any un-friendlies lurking in the neighborhood.

In this more open landscape I had holstered my .45 and held my M14 at the ready when I heard a branch break just off the trail to my left. I switched the selector switch to full auto and was swinging the muzzle in the direction of the sound when I heard the first part of a corny old joke, "Hey, Tonto, are you lost?" Relieved I answered, "Indian not lost, Indian here, teepee lost!" Blaske stepped into sight long gun in hand, big grin on his swarthy puss and said, "Hayes was worried about you".

Cerone appeared out of the bush next, radio pack on his back, followed by Baphang and Morrison, and then Hayes stepped out onto the trail. I could see that Cerone was talking on the PRC-9 and he turned to me and said, "M&M says you're late", "a Porter will be here to pick us up in thirty", and "Blaske was worried about you". Wow, I had a whole welcoming committee worried about me and waiting at the point where Cerone had insisted I would appear. Blaske told me that Cerone and Baphang refused to leave the un-named, un-numbered, un-marked landing site certain I would show up there in a couple of days and the rest of the pack decided to stay with them. I felt touched by everyone's concern and flattered by their certainty that I would have the woodcraft and skills to survive and show up.

Baphang summed it up with a dose of reality when he said, "I was not worried about you, J'a'kah, I believe in your luck".

Chapter 30

Bolaven

Down in the southern part of Laos is an area that Eden may have been modeled after. It sits on a plateau surrounded by craggy peaks formed in the crater of a long extinct volcano and higher, and with more temperate weather, than the provinces down in the Mekong Plain.

This beautiful land with its fertile soil and industrious peoples was at the south end of Baphang's trading routes and he kept a small house there within sound of a waterfall that fell perhaps a hundred meters before crashing onto boulders and continuing to flow east, then south and finally back westerly to join the Mekong. He had placed his raised, wooden plank house at just the right distance so that the falls were a melodic background sound that blended with his brass chimes when a breeze came through his kitchen garden.

Down the road to the west a few hundred meters from his house were two more houses, one occupied by an elderly couple and the other occupied by a shining faced, almond eyed beautiful woman and her three young children; it took a while but I finally realized the woman was Baphang's wife, he kept his family in a house separate from the one where he entertained friends and business contacts.

Behind Baphang's "business house" to the east and toward the waterfall was a small wooden house with faded red paint and red tiled roof placed on a raised stone foundation, looking like it may have been a miniature "Wat" or holy place at some distant time. Inside was a small kitchen area with a wood burning brazier and a raised sleeping platform of polished teak. This would be my quarters whenever I was Baphang's guest.

Behind the little red house and past the privy was an almost invisible track that led to a series of caves hidden in dense foliage. The caves opened at the other end at a point on a cliff face halfway down the waterfall we could hear from the kitchen garden at the main house. The hidden path and caves were to be my escape route and refuge in the event that any Pathet Lao or Vietnamese, regulars or irregulars came near.

I spent many pleasant hours in the safety of Baphang's compound studying my dog eared USAFI (United States Armed Forces Institute) correspondence courses and reading from the works of Flaubert and Victor Hugo (the only books written in English in Baphang's library) but remained mindful of the admonition to keep my weapons at hand and to waken without a sound. The two red-turbaned Cao Dai that were always somewhere nearby, they took turns sitting outside the door of the little red house at night, reminders that danger was always at hand.

The French in the 1920s had brought new cash generating crops to the plateau including two kinds of coffee stocks, teas that had not been grown in the region before, and even potatoes and strawberries which grew well alongside the wet and dry rice fields, cardomon and cinnamon trees, yams, bananas, durian (I was told that the durian from the plateau was prized for its creamy texture and taste, but I could never get past the rotten smell to find out why) and other fruits and vegetables that thrived in the orange soil and temperate climate.

Baphang had acquired a small coffee and tea plantation from a French planter who they both knew was anxious to get out of Asia and was happy that Baphang had offered what they both considered a fair price for the property and its warehouses and a modest inventory of farming equipment. He used the plantation as a base for his trading sending some coffee and tea to Pakse and on to docks on the Mekong for export and packaging some for his own trade following ancient routes north up the foothills and eventually to the highlands of the Annamite Range in the northeast of Laos.

The Shan Silver Tip and Black Dragon teas that he carried north were particularly prized by the Lao Soung (highland tribes) and they also enjoyed trade talks with Baphang while drinking kafeh thaong, a dense brown coffee sweetened with condensed milk and sugar cubes, and telling stories and sharing gossip from other villages. For some villagers the news he carried about the outside world was more important than the shiny needles and brightly colored threads he brought to trade. Sometimes even more important than the flat bars of steel, ammunition of different calibers or other dry goods his pack animals were laden with.

With the French and their aircraft gone and the lowlands in the northeast provinces patrolled by Pathet Lao the hill tribes were virtually cut off from outside communication, and more importantly from the buyers of their principal cash crop, opium tar. There were still a few caravans from China, Thailand, Burma (Myanmar) and the Lao southern provinces coming to a new trade center in Ban Houei Sai in the Lao northwest, the old trade center in the PDJ was now occupied by Pathet Lao, but getting their products to the new trade center was dangerous work, and a windfall for Baphang and his trained fighters. He provided armed escorts, made up primarily of men from his old Cao Dai company who had fled Viet Nam with him and settled in with various hill tribes, to and from the new trade center.

Baphang hated the military, irregular and regular, of both North and South Viet Nam. Both sides killed women and children and old people just because of their religious beliefs or simply because they were in the way on the wrong day; political beliefs didn't even enter into the motives for killing, most of the victims had no particular political view, their loyalties were to their families, their clans, and their tribes.

He hated them and he killed them when he came across the invaders in Laos. His ambushes were carefully planned and executed, he never lost a man to enemy fire, and he was careful to avoid engagements that would result in repercussions to local villagers. And now that the Pathet Lao were murdering Catholic priests and their parishioners in the northern provinces they were fair targets as well.

When the Corsican sent the message that the Americans would like to meet with him he arranged for the meeting to be held far to the north in the mountains of Hua Phan, no reason for them to know he had a base in lower country. He agreed to meet with the falang (white people) partly because he knew they had a common enemy, partly because he knew they had airplanes, and partly just out of curiosity, what were these Americans like?

He thought he would be met by an officer, probably a captain, maybe a major, possibly a lieutenant. Instead the first person he met was a fresh-faced boy barely old enough to shave, with curly blond hair sticking out behind his ears under the shapeless green hat the American was wearing. He was amused by the timing of the boy's arrival; he came around a corner of the trail just as a guar (a huge water- buffalo- blown- way- up looking beast) stepped out on the trail coming from the opposite direction. The beast and the boy stared at each other for a long moment then the boy crossed over and squatted next to Baphang who was just dropping tea leaves into a pot of boiling water. He was amused, but also impressed by the boy's composure, and by the way the rest of the American team silently appeared out of the forest, alert but not threatening.

He allowed the tea to steep for a few minutes before producing two glasses, offering one to the American squatting beside him, and noting that the tall American with the blank eyes had remained standing in a position that commanded a view up and down the trail and that the rest of the team members, while bantering in pantomime and exchanging foodstuffs with his men, had placed themselves in positions that would be advantageous if a firefight broke out, either from within or without the perimeter of the camp. He was pleased with what he saw and signaled the ten men in the forest behind him to come out into the open; the Americans knew they were there anyway.

While the tea was steeping the gaur wandered off, bored or perhaps uncomfortable with the smell of the pack horses, and the boy beside him opened a package with some kind of gooey confection that he spread on the paper it was wrapped in before opening a tin can and passing it to Baphang. The contents of the can mesmerized Baphang.

Baphang liked peaches but they would not grow on his plantation, it didn't get cold enough to cause the trees to bloom properly, and they were a rarity even in the high country where it did get cold enough, the soil conditions just were not right. The peaches he got from Thailand got over-ripe very quickly and the fruit was too soft for pickling (or canning). And here were some tinned peaches that were firm and flavorful and had a beautiful color swimming in a balanced liquid that was neither too sweet nor sour. He was intrigued and wanted to know more about these wonderful fruits and the boy who had brought them to him.

The six Americans and their Thai companion were dressed in civilian clothing similar to that worn by their Lao Theung (mid-land) guide with no symbols of rank or distinction so it was not possible to readily identify who their leader was; they moved as though they had no one commander and positioned themselves with no audible or visual signals he could detect, these were a well-coordinated group, he was well disposed toward them and after observing them for a few days decided he would teach them, "which bugs to eat and which bugs were poisonous" and "to never drink un-boiled water, always drink tea".

The Cao Dai complement included several experienced communications men so training with the com gear wasn't an issue, arrangements would be made to supply them with the equipment, codes and schedules they would need to maintain contact with this "Blue Team". Other details such as equipment needs, payroll (Baphang would only accept payment in silver or gold, no script or paper money) were discussed and Baphang agreed that he would provide guide services and introductions to hill tribes and offer his aid and protection to these Americans. This was not to be mistaken as a blanket agreement to assist all Americans or their allies (Baphang was a little leery of getting too involved with the Mei).

To quote Bogie in "Casablanca", this "was the beginning of a beautiful friendship". Baphang was true to his commitment to help and it was due to his influence that many villagers opened their gates to the Americans, warning them when enemies were near and giving other cooperation that allowed them to move about the mountains and to even form friendships among the tribal peoples. Without these relationships it was doubtful the Americans could have completed their missions or even survived in the mountains with PAVN, NVA, and Viet Minh/Viet Cong all around. In time he expanded his protection to assist the Blue Team with an evolution in their missions that had them acting as guides and bringing other assets, usually mercenaries or US Special Forces, into the mountains.

Baphang would often accompany them on missions himself, sometimes alone but usually with some of his Cao Dai or Yao tribesmen to scout and fight alongside the Blue Team. It was after a particularly memorable mission that he decided to fly out with them to meet the Mei leader Vang Pao.

But when he got to their base at Wattay Airfield he forgot he was to go on to Long Chen to meet Vang Pao, instead spending most of his time with (the amazing) "Pop" Buell discussing farming problems and techniques. Baphang's Arabica coffee trees were suffering from some kind of blight, the Robusta trees seemed to be immune, and he wondered what he could do for them. The sad answer was that he needed to cut the trees down and dig up and burn the roots to kill the fungus infection causing the problem. If he wanted to grow Arabica beans he would have to import new stock.

He decided he liked this boy they called "Jay Cee" and after many days and nights in the bush, and many ambushes and quick firefights together, and after a night when the boy killed at least two Russians and probably several other enemies with a knife Baphang had given him he began to call the boy J'a'kah, which in Baphang's home language meant "little brother" or "younger brother" (the closest most of the falang would get to pronouncing the new name was "Jay Kah") and even invited him to come to the plantation on the Bolaven Plateau.

And that was how I found myself in the little red house on the plateau named for one of the tribes, the Laven, that had lived there for hundreds of years (Bolaven = home of the Laven) and being awakened in the middle of the night by a stocky man with a red turban. Viet Minh and NVA were nearby taking chickens, eggs, and rice and other foodstuffs from the farmers and it was time for me to go to my hiding place in the caves.

This was becoming a regular occurrence, the fertility of the plateau and its position on the ancient north/south trading routes was making it a favored stop for porters and soldiers going south on the Ho Chi Minh Trail. Elements of the Pathet Lao were staging raids and stealing anything they could find unprotected now that the presence of the North Vietnamese emboldened them.

As Pathet Lao and Vietnamese activity increased on the plateau the remaining French plantation owners and managers, and even some of the Buddhist and Catholic priests, had fled ahead of the assassinations that were sure to come. The snake was loose in paradise.

The listening post and communications center the Blue Team had set up on our first mission to Muong Nong (where Marcotti had been killed) had become too dangerous to the operators and to the town people sheltering them and had been moved to a position on a high mountain located southwest of the town and near the northeast corner of the plateau. I had gone with SFG Team Feltzer for a visit to the new installation and was waiting with them for their airborne extraction from one of the straight gravel surfaced roads that ran through Baphang's plantation south of Thateng (locals would brush the road and remove all traces of the aircrafts' tracks as soon as it took off) when an H34 appeared coming from the northwest.

The big helicopter landed sending a cloud of dust and chickens in every direction and the door popped open revealing Cerone's smiling face. I was being given a ride to a new mission. After a brief conference between Captains Samuels and Feltzer it was decided that Sgt Johnny Sorenson would come with the Blue Team on an excursion (incursion?) over the border and re-unite with his unit later.

As the helicopter lifted off taking J'a'kah away to the east Baphang was ready to begin to implement his plans to move his family away from their home on the Bolaven Plateau to a safer place, perhaps across the river to a place in Thailand.

The war was already coming to his home and he knew an old saying was true:

"When the elephants fight, the grass gets trampled".

Chapter 31

John

He had carefully chosen the spot where he could crawl in under the elephant ear leaves without leaving sign that he had passed this way visible to any but the most keen-eyed observer; wouldn't fool dogs though and he had heard some baying in the distance a few hours ago. He was completely hidden from anyone on the ground but could still see an arc of sky where his extraction heli should appear at dawn, and from his position once he broke cover he would have a clear sprint to the LZ. Not perfect but the best he could do in his deteriorating physical condition; days without proper food, water, and sleep had taken a heavy toll on his reserves and the wound to his shoulder was red hot and oozing pus. His hips, knees, ankles and elbows had taken severe beatings, he was certain at least one rib was broken and his entire body was a giant, worn out ache.

There he sat bone weary and wounded watching the sky predawn lightening and tapping out on his radio handset long, long-long-long, long-long then repeating the signal (T-O-M pause T-O-M), waiting thirty seconds and starting the cycle again, ear straining to hear an answer and to hear the sound of the extraction bird. He sat repeating and listening and shivering in his green cave while the light turned from pre-dawn to dawn. Where the hell was his ride out?

Down at this elevation the groundcover was dense and provided good camouflage and he could hear the Song Long Dai River on the other side of the woodlot clearing near him, he could also hear birds and other jungle life and that told him the watch birds were not alarmed by his presence; any change in their cadence or tone would tell him when other people were coming near to his spot. He had already taken off his pack and booby-trapped the radio and bubble sextant with three MK-2 grenades, saving one to carry if his extraction team didn't show in time to pull him out ahead of his pursuers (or at all, he shivered at that thought), if the enemy got too close to him and capture was imminent he would pull the pin, release the spoon and hold the grenade to detonate under his chin. He had spiked his AK 47; he would not need it if he was pulled out or tried for plan "B", and pulled the wide checkered black and white scarf from under his blouse and tied it around his waist, his stiletto still in its sheath tied around his neck and bush knife ready to hand.

He was in a feverish zone somewhere between awake and asleep when an old boyhood nightmare (a scene in a Tarzan Movie) grabbed him - a constrictor snake was falling from the limb above him ready to wrap him in a deadly coil –when he snapped back to wakefulness he realized he was still tapping out his signal, pausing and listening, signaling again.

Plan "B" would be to run across the clearing and jump into the river, now swollen at the end of the monsoon season and in full roar, ground pursuers would not be able to keep pace with the rushing waters and if he could survive the currents and deadfalls pushed along by the torrent he might be able to ride the cresting waters south to the point where the river turned left and headed east near the DMZ. Or he might be smashed to pieces against boulders in the river.

If he managed to stay afloat he would have to get out of the water before it tumbled through a series of cataracts just after turning east. And he would have to be very careful about grabbing onto floating logs or other debris, that's where the snakes would be riding. There was a chance, slight but still a chance that if he survived the river and still had any energy left he could move south across the 17th Parallel and find an ARVN and/or American patrol, then he would only have to hope they didn't shoot first and ask questions later. A shitty plan but the only one he had.

Some tired part of his brain was telling him to just give it all up, let it go and he began to feel a strange sad sorrow and regret mixed with a calm acceptance of his impending death. He told himself that was just the fatigue and hunger trying to shake his resolve; he would not give in as long as there was a chance he could survive to get the intel he had collected on the Ho Chi Minh Trail out.

All he could do now was stay still and wait, he would give it an hour or until he heard sounds of his pursuers getting nearer. Meanwhile he needed to focus and keep his mind off his pains and the hunger gnawing at him; he had finished the rice and soup mixture in his elephant gut yesterday and his last meal had been the rice paper from his notebook, he didn't need the notes, if he got clear he would be able to reconstruct them from memory. His camera and rolls of film had been sacrificed days ago.

The mission had been to monitor and map locations on the Trail to be able to forecast future movement and activity during the dry season. He had been in the area expecting the monsoon rains to provide a cloak for his operations and later extraction from inside North Viet Nam. The rains had stopped two weeks earlier than predicted leaving him "high and almost dry" (ha) and if he survived he planned to have a few choice words with a certain USAF meteorologist (ha again). Thousands of NVA, PAVN, Viet Minh, Viet Cong and porters were already active on the Trail before he could make his departure, a big push was going to be coming and he needed to get that message back to the Embassy in Saigon.

The sun was well up and he was mentally steeling himself to execute plan "B" when he finally heard a welcome squelch and the scratchy word "Tonto" in the handset; the chopper was near and coming to pick him up at the pre-planned point. Straining his ears he was soon able to hear the telltale whop, whopping sounds of one or more helicopters, at the same time the birds in the bush changed their tunes, some went quiet, some became raucous, and others changed the message they were sending. Alarmed by the approaching big, noisy metal bird(s), or by something closer and on the ground?

Knowing the extraction bird was in the area and would land to pick him up in minutes he very carefully pulled the pins on the grenades balanced in and under the pack with the radio and sextant arming the surprise for whomever jostled the pack and stood against a tree trunk waiting for the circulation in his legs to come back after so much time in a cramped position. Through the opening in his green surround he could see what

194

appeared to be two H34 Choctaws coming toward the woodlot in front of him.

One chopper hovered just touching the ground across the lot while a team of soldiers poured out to secure a perimeter at the LZ then rose and flew by almost directly overhead and turned west to disappear behind the karst to the rear of his position followed by a second bird that landed in the skid marks of the first and disgorged another team who fanned out through the perimeter guard in his general direction. His ride had arrived; time to let them know where he was.

Just as he broke cover to start a run across the open space in front of him he saw what he assumed was one of "Kappas' Cowboys" motioning the second team to take cover and starting to run for the cover of a log. He heard a shot from behind him to his right and saw the trooper in the sage green fatigues spin and dive for the safety of the log. Was the trooper hit? How did the shooter get so close without his knowing it?

Now fully committed he had to go forward and get across the open to protection as fast as he could, soggy ground pulling at his feet, wet grass wrapping around his ankles, energy almost completely spent and clutching the grenade in one hand bolo knife in the other he was making a last desperate effort to stay alive.

He was halfway across the open space when he felt what might have been someone with a ten-pound sledgehammer driving a red-hot poker through his left side. The force of the blow spun him completely around and deposited him in the grass and mud on his side, losing his knife but still clutching the grenade. He looked toward the log across the clearing and saw a figure starting to crawl in his direction; he tried to call out for the man to stay back, the man coming toward him would be an easy target for a sniper but he could only get out a hoarse croaking sound. He flopped over on his back and asked himself if it was time to pull the pin on his grenade and the answer that came back surprised him, "not yet, not yet, not yet". Everything around him seemed to stop for a moment and he was intensely aware of a beetle climbing a blade of grass, the green wet grass in such sharp focus he could see its vein pattern, then his attention shifted back to his surroundings with a stunning clarity. He was on the edge of going into shock, he needed to fight the effects and stay alert.

Twisting his neck, he could see the grinning face of the kid who was always giving out canned peaches, almost in reach. Bullets pocking the ground all around, the two of them alone together under some invisible umbrella he began to believe he might survive the day.

Chapter 32

One of Those Days

It wasn't the last or first, best or worst, but I can still clearly remember a day after over half a century:

"Gawd... Damn... V..iet... Nam" the whole team hated coming to this side of the mountain - we'd all rather be in the high forests on the other side of the Annamites and not here in an H34 going north along the edge of the coastal plain.

On our first TDY to Indo-China we'd arrived thinking we were Boy Scouts with guns. All the children and dogs, and even most of the grown-ups would love us (Kappas and Samuels knew better of course, but we were young and invincible and didn't really hear their warnings). And our view seemed to be true while we were at a PARU camp in the south of Thailand teaching operation and light maintenance of com and nav equipment to hill people from across the river. The locals did like us, beaches were close, food and beer were cheap and good, and the women were beautiful. Compared to the training regime we'd gone through for most of the past year this place was super light duty and as close to heaven as some of us were likely to get. How bad can it be when the nearest large town is called Phukett?

Then we were "sheep dipped" and sent across the Mekong to a small city called Muang Nong and Marcotti was killed in an ambush while we were riding samoys into the beer garden area of the town. Training, and the fact that we had all managed to arm ourselves saved the other four members of our team in the samoys. The Boy Scout mentality was gone.

But on this day we were all seasoned veterans of many ambushes and hit and run operations – sometimes contrary to our mission to Survey and Observe. As we clattered, banged and shook along on our way north we all knew we were headed for a cluster fuck. But M&M Kappas had briefed us to pick up an asset from a tricky locale and when Kappas said jump it was wise to jump. Some of us pretended to jump when Kappas said to

197

because they were afraid of him or felt constrained to follow orders, all orders (not likely with our group). But we all did what Kappas said without hesitation because we all knew the "the mutha' knows best".

The asset was someone most of us had seen before and called The Gray Man, or Tom Major, or Tom Tom. I don't think any of our team (other than Kappas and probably Colonel Billy and Tony Poe) ever knew his name, but I did overhear M&M call him John one night when the whiskey was flowing.

Kappas and the Gray Man had already decided that when the Gray Man was due for extraction from his listening post on the "Harriman Trail" he would head east over the mountains just south of the McCullough Pass (amazing how many places had Scots names on the old French topo maps) and rendezvous at the tree line just west of a wood lot a couple of klicks from a small ville. Timing would be tight and we'd have to be close to hear the "okay squelch" on his handset.

Kappas had "borrowed" the chopper and its' "ex" Marine pilot and co-pilot from CAT/Air America on the grounds that if they didn't make the loan he would take his request to Bird and Sons. He didn't exactly tell the dispatcher what he planned to use it for but promised to have it back in a few days "in show room condition". Which I guess translated to "back in a couple of weeks with a missing wheel, lots of daylight showing through the hull, an engine ready to cough and quit, and a very thirsty pilot".

The mission brief was simple. Hayes, Cerone, Blaske, and Samuels would board with weapons and web gear at Lon Chien then pick me up at the north rim of the Bolaven Plateau and cross into Viet Nam enroute to Dac To for an overnight stop to refuel and to pick up a Navy corpsman as a ride-along. Tom Minor would come as interpreter and an additional BAR man. Our next re-fuel point would be set at Dac To. After the second fueling we were to proceed to the pick-up point, extract the asset and deliver him to Saigon for a de-briefing. We were to stand by, in quarantine, until the Gray Man gave us further orders. Uniform for the mission was to be OD green fatigues with no insignia, no dog tags, jewelry, family albums, or other identifying paraphernalia (SOP for us). Black baseball cap for the R.O. and boonie hats for everyone else was spec'd. We never decided (time in grade, coin flip, etc.) who was going to be R.O. (sniper bait) so we all wore boonie hats. It was that kind of outfit.

A mission imperative was that our ingress and exit routes had to be from and to South Viet Nam. What wasn't stated was that we would be going north of the 17th parallel (border between North and South Vietnam). Once we crossed into Viet Nam all communication with our command base was to go dark and stay dark until we delivered our passenger.

The ever-thoughtful M&M knew I would need a set of fatigues and told Hayes to pick up a set, and a re-supply of socks and underwear from my locker (read mildewed closet). Hayes didn't find any ODs in my locker, nothing but sage green and civvies, so he grabbed a set from Blaske's locker instead. Blaske was always a fussy dresser so Hayes didn't bother him with the information that he'd borrowed a few items from him for my use, just boarded the 34 and waved at Kappas and Samuels as it lifted off.

I was com/nav liaison with Special Forces Team Brandon at the time and when the team arrived to pick me up and give me my briefing my counterpart, Sgt Johnny Sorenson, late of the 10th Mountain Brigade, via the 82 Airborne (I never could call him Johnny, or Sgt Sorenson – it always came out "Sgt Johnny Sorenson"), an original "Sneaky Pete" (our name for Special Forces guys) volunteered to come along to "keep me out of trouble". What the hell, we had the room and we could use another warrior. Captain Brandon gave his okay and we were off.

As AF snake-eaters we usually communicated with voice, coded voice, and micro burst transmissions while SFG Team Brandon's' primary com link was Morse. We could talk to, and about, and provide direct traffic control, for aircraft and they could not. This situation put me in repeated contact with Sgt Johnny Sorenson, who seemed to be a wheel man (OJT trainer) for the 77th SF Mobile Training Teams and popped up all over Laos, Cambodia, and sometimes points west, and the older man (must have been thirty-something) took it upon himself to mentor us in war craft (my woodcraft was damn good) and act as my bodyguard when things got hot.

Hell, man, I felt pretty good about things. I was with a team I knew and trusted and had two bodyguards along to keep me alive, Hayes had decided that was his avocation somewhere in our early training days when he somehow attached himself to our team. Our team was 12 when we started but by now had been whittled down to the survivors – guys that I knew could survive anything.

Then we got to Dac To and the shit began to circle the basin.

No Gas. Dac To had been mortared the night before and the fuel dump had taken a direct hit. There was mo gas available but no av gas. Our tanks were low and the pilot had no choice except to take on some mo gas - knowing engine performance would be degraded- and divert south to Pleiku to top off.

We arrived just after dusk at Pleiku and were met by a character straight out of Hollywood casting – a SVNAF colonel with a thin mustache, ascot, pearl handled revolver, and an honest-to god swagger stick who informed us that there would be no fuel available unless and until we followed his directive that we have a Vietnamese pilot aboard. And a squad of his Tiger Teams and two members of the press corps were to come along on the mission. His attitude was "My country, my war, my airspace, my gas". Otherwise scrub the mission and get out of his country "pronto". He actually said "pronto". It was obvious that too many people knew we were there but the clock was ticking and we'd already had time added to our flight in the morning, we had to go along with the directives. Samuels probably could have made the right calls to the right people at our Embassy but that would cost even more time and alert more people to our presence. "Adapt and Overcome".

As the day started at 04:00 local we had turned into a god damn parade. Our bus was full with our team, the Navy corpsman (Tom White, we immediately named him Tom Other), our former co-pilot, and Sgt Johnny Sorenson. The flash colonel had appointed himself as co-pilot of our bird. Our original H34 was now accompanied by another H34 and an H19. Three birds in a row – noisy, internal combustion powered, shaky, and unarmed and under-armored beasts all.

With the limited range of these three birds they would have to top off again to be able to get to the pick-up point and then fly non-stop to Saigon. And with three birds instead of one the re-fuel time would be a lot longer. But the good news was our flash colonel was able to prioritize our mission and have fuel trucks standing by when we arrived at the fuel point. Bad news was that everyone in the neighborhood knew something was up.

While we were topping off I had a chance to look over the Tiger team: No laughter, chatter, or horse play, or transistor radios and clanking gear. Half the Tigers cleaned and checked their weapons while the other half stayed on alert, then the two halves switched places. These were serious troops. If I didn't know better I'd have taken them for NVA Regulars.

Dawn was breaking as we "streaked" (at a mind numbing 100 mph) across the DMZ; we were going to arrive late and in daylight at the pick-up point. Not good. I hated helicopter inserts and extracts because I always felt too exposed with no place to hide on the bird and no way to hide the bird itself. As far as I was concerned they were big flying billboards with the message "Here we are!" I understood their value but did not like to be on them. I would be much happier skulking around in the bush with Bill Young and his Lahu and Mei tribesmen.

And now instead of one chopper going in "nap of the earth" in pre-dawn darkness, picking up the asset and making the dash south we were a minor invasion force arriving in daylight. The NVA were not going to see the humor in our situation.

I was out of my seat, copper taste in my mouth trying to spot the landmarks that would tell me we were arriving at the pick-up point, headset on listening for mike clicks. Sgt Johnny Sorenson was at the port on the opposite side tapping the Perspex with his left hand; our erstwhile co-pilot slouched against the forward bulkhead looking forlorn and miserable, while Tom Other checked his med pack again and again. Samuels kept checking his watch, Blaske sat composed, neat, creases all straight, Cerone looked bored and Hayes and Tom Minor exchanged crooked grins while they stroked their BARs.

We were late for our appointment and had no way of knowing if the Gray Man would still be at the designated spot or even if he was still alive and un-captured. We were late, god-dam-it.

Ears straining in the headset as we neared the pick-up point I heard the squelch we were waiting for: long, long-long-long, long-long on the prick 9 frequency. I keyed the mike and said "Tonto", and got the answer "Tom, Tom". The Gray Man was at the LZ.

Our target area was a spot where the Song Long Dai River, swollen now at the end of the monsoon season, ran due north and south between a limestone karst to the west and a 300-meter ridge to the east. Good news was that the site was well hidden from the east or west; the birds would be out of sight of any nearby villes as they dropped into the pick-up zone. Bad news was that we would be funneled into a tight space with high ground on two sides and dense cover on the other two sides. More bad news; the only clear spot to bring in the birds was an area next to a water-powered sawmill (unused during the high-water season) with little room for our entire parade. Perfect spot to get ambushed and have our asses handed to us.

As we passed to the west of the small settlement of Thu Lu our pilot reported spotting two trucks on the road paralleling the river, almost certainly signaling the presence of troops. They were on the other side and the roadway was muddy but they could still mean a danger to us.

"The Ugly Duc", our flash colonel, Colonel Nam Duc Ngyuen, took control sending his H19 to hover and appear to land at a spot across from Thu Lu and just out of small arms range from the parked trucks. The decoy might split the attention of any watchers. His H34 went ahead and dropped into the LZ and Tiger troops poured out to secure the perimeter then the chopper took off and flew north circling around the karst to our west. They didn't draw any fire as they passed over the canopy and circled back around behind us. So far, so good.

Our turn. As soon as our bird set down the team was out, through the security perimeter and crossing the wood lot toward the tree line. No sign of the Gray Man. Then things started to get really interesting. I think it was years of squirrel hunting as a kid that alerted me – I saw a branch with the leaves turned under and already had my right hand out flat and pumping a warning and had started to run to my left when I saw the first pressure wave at the tree line. We were taking fire.

Running right to left when under fire was something I had learned from Sgt Johnny Sorenson; experience had taught him that most soldiers under fire would run left to right so they could fire to their left as they ran, that made them predictable. Also, it is usually easier for a shooter to track a target moving from the shooter's right to his left, increasing his/her odds of hitting the target.

Three things seemed to happen simultaneously: I saw the Gray Man materialize at the tree line (just like a magic trick), something banged into my left ankle hard, and my sphincter let go. As I fell I managed to get behind a log pile between my position and the tree line. From my vantage point I could see the other members of my team angling off to the left and right to flank the point the incoming fire was coming from. And I could see the Gray Man sprinting straight at me like a wide receiver smelling the goal line. No hat, no weapon and no radio pack; the black and white checkered scarf tied around his waist identified him as a friendly and I remember wondering for a millisecond if the big rust colored blotches on his black pants and blouse were camouflage.

I watched as he came across the soggy field and then did a slow-motion pirouette and fell to the ground. I remember thinking, "why is the silly bastard just lying there in the open?" and "M&M Kappas is not going to be happy if we don't get him to his destination" just before I slipped into hyper alertness and became aware of everything around me with an amazing clarity. I could pick out the lovely sound of the BARs providing suppressive fire to my right and left, the spaced three round bursts from my team mates' M14s, and the sporadic bursts and single shots from the Tiger team. From the tree line I could hear the clatter of two old French MAT 49 submachine guns (the clatter from their actions louder than the muzzle blasts) and pick out two rounds per minute bolt action fire at three different locations in the trees.

Without thought I had placed my weapon next to the tree trunk and as I rolled, crawled toward the Gray Man I could hear the measured cadence of Dave's voice chanting "steady on, stay cool, fetch the whistle from the pool" while my own internal voice was saying "what the fuck are you doing? this is not in your MOS!". I rolled him on to his back and placed myself next to him shoulder to shoulder then reached across to his opposite arm, pulled it across my chest and rolled away from him pulling him onto my back. I remember thinking "why am I so tired? Maybe I can rest a minute" when I heard Dave's voice again "it's okay, you're in the bubble, bring it on home. Move, move, move" and I started a three-point crawl, two elbows and a knee, my left leg refused to obey my commands, the ten yards back to cover.

A certainty and calmness took me forward-none of the whir-buzz rounds going zzzutplp into the soft ground around me were going to hit us. I knew this as an absolute and just kept inching toward safety. There was a lull in the firing and the Gray Mans' weight was off my back. Sgt Johnny Sorenson had him in a fireman's carry and was trotting toward our H34 and Hayes had me lifted by the web belt and was loping in the same direction. I could see Blaske in the middle of the Tiger team calling targets and Cerone was running alongside Hayes with my weapon in one hand. Tom Other was running for our bird as well. The firing from the tree line started again and had an added sound I did not like coming from the north end of the valley, AK47s - at least four or five of them. Fifteen to twenty figures in green/brown uniforms and pith helmets came out of the green wall. We were now taking fire from two directions.

Samuels and Tom Minor pulled us all aboard then Hayes and Tom Minor lay prone in the doorways, BARS at the ready.

As we lifted off the engine began to sputter and backfire – overheated from the long hover or fuel contamination? Oh shit. Two corkscrewing white streaks came at us- RPGs – one hitting our right main and exploding on contact, the other bouncing off the windscreen and exploding in air, breaking the screen and temporarily blinding our pilot. The Ugly Duc took the controls and instead of turning south, he flew north just skimming along the ground and with our ungainly, magnesium skinned, engine sputtering, right tire burning, unarmed hotel three four charged the enemy!

Hayes and Tom Minor were firing out the doors and Samuels and Sgt Johnny Sorenson were lobbing grenades out over their heads as we closed on the tree line. Metal rain was splattering the hull and holes were appearing all around, the rounds by some miracle missing everyone inside. Hayes told me later that it was comical watching the NVA troops scramble to get out of the path of the wreck that was about to happen. Then the Ugly Duc pulled collective, the engine caught and we hopped over the trees slowly gaining altitude as we circled the backside of the limestone karst.

Looking around the bay I noticed something missing and looked a question at Hayes who bent over and yelled in my ear "Blaske is okay, he got out with the Tigers on the other bird". Then I slept for a few minutes. When I woke up Tom Other had cut off my left boot (damn I was gonna' miss those boots, a gift from my Mom) and pant leg and cleaned the area of my wound. He told me that Tom Major/the Gray Man was going to need all the available painkiller but that he, Tom Other, needed to set the bone in my lower leg and it was "going to hurt like a sum a bitch". It did. I went back to sleep for a while.

Somewhere on the flight back the three birds formed up and all arrived together at Bien Hoa where we were greeted by M&M Kappas who put us all into shock when, as the Gray Man was being put on a stretcher, he came to a rigid attention and saluted (Kappas was famous for never saluting anybody!), getting a slow nod in return.

Blaske ran over as I was being lifted out and wrinkling his nose said, "damn Jay Cee, you've shit your pants!" To which Hayes replied, "No Herbie, he's shit your pants." This became the byword that would send us all into laughing uproariously anytime and anywhere we gathered for years to come.

And we renamed "The Ugly Duc" as "Big Brass Ones Duc".

Chapter 33

A Big Change

If the ivory yellow telephone in the lobby of the Hotel Continental was worn out too soon it was probably Sgt. Johnny Sorenson's fault.

Every time the SFG Sergeant was in Vientiane, which was often and probably more than necessary, he was placing calls to a small town in New Zealand, usually leaving a message but on some sweet, sweet occasions actually talking to Nancy Braithewaite - cattle station owners' daughter, horsewoman, school marm, and the most beautiful, delightful woman he had ever met.

The GRC-109 radios the Special Forces teams were using had limitations that meant even in secure areas he couldn't use them to do anything but send an occasional message to be relayed to the MARS station in the Philippines and on to ham operators in New Zealand for delivery to Nan, the sets could receive both code and voice messages but could only transmit in code. Mail took too long and cablegrams offered no more privacy than on-air broadcasts, and what he really wanted was to be able to hear her voice.

A loner outside of military environments and uncomfortable in civilian social settings for most of his adult life he found he had an itch, an ache and an almost overwhelming desire to be in the same time and space, breath the same air, as Nan. To eat at the same table and sleep in the same bed. Sergeant Johnny Sorenson was in love.

He had fallen hard during an R&R (Rest and Recuperation) trip to New Zealand and when he returned to the theatre in SE Asia went straight to Captain Feltzer and put in a leave request. Two months after the R&R visit he was back on the cattle station near Christ Church, New Zealand for two weeks leave.

The third night the sergeant was on the station Dad Braithwaite looking down the long dining table at his daughter and her American suitor paused for a long moment and with what might have been a wink or a frown or both said, "So, that's how it is then". And Nan blushed and said, "That's how it is Dad".

During the following year or so of long distance romance and a lot of long conversations they came to some realizations and made some decisions; the sergeant wanted to share his life with Nan and have marriage and children, a state of mind he would not have recognized in himself before he met her. He did not want his wife and children living in military housing somewhere waiting (and worrying) for him to come home from some assignment that he probably wouldn't even be able to discuss with them. He would have to find a job that would allow him to be present in his wife and children's lives, a civilian job. They agreed that he would have the best chance at finding work in the United States and they should start their life together somewhere in the States at the end of his current enlistment.

And they had another decision to make together, wait for the process for getting approval to marry a non-American from his military chain of command or get married in New Zealand and start the paper work after. They choose to do both; they would use a two-pronged approach and see what developed.

Their choice meant that until he received approval from his commanders Nan would not be entitled to any benefits as a military dependent and would receive no assistance from the military channels with her immigration status when they moved to the United States, but they did not see this as a major issue after the sergeant's decision to get out of the service. Nan would apply for a student visa and admission to graduate school at a university in California. Getting married in New Zealand would give them an earlier marriage date for the civilian immigration process if he was out of the service before he got the military approvals. But they still couldn't just run down to the magistrate and get married; Nan had her family to consider.

Her Dad liked the Yank soldier and knew that his daughter had made up her mind to marry him; this after a few years of worrying that she would never find the man that suited her. But he was saddened by the decision they had made to move to the United States and the distance that would put between them, still it was probably for the best, the cattle station would go to his two sons when he passed and the Yank's prospects for employment were probably better there than in New Zealand.

Her Mum was both sad and happy at the same time but insisted on two points; the young couple must be married in the same church where she had exchanged her vows years before and family members and friends should be there to witness the event and if they were blessed with a child Mum would have to be informed of the estimated delivery date in plenty of time for her to make the trip to America and be on hand at the birth.

A chance encounter during a four-week assignment to the 8th Special Forces Group at Ft. Gulick, Panama put him on the path to finding a civilian job opportunity when he ran into an old friend he had first met years earlier when they had shared a small cold, very cold cave and a few even colder foxholes behind the lines in Korea. He had just stepped out of the mess hall and was watching a deuce-and-a-half (two-and-a-half-ton truck) with USAF markings being unloaded, the unmarked crates stacked on pallets awaiting transfer to smaller vehicles when he recognized USAF Technical Sergeant Bobby Grimes standing off and observing the unloading.

There was some grinning and backslapping and they agreed to meet for dinner and a couple of beers that evening and catch up. After a little, "whatever happened to so and so?", "and do you remember old whatzit and his "moose"?" and a few "where-ya'-beens?" Johnny started (no surprise) talking about the beautiful Nan, their plans, and his concerns about finding a civilian job. Bobby gave the problem some consideration and before they parted, Sgt Grimes back to Nellis and Sgt Sorenson off for a couple of weeks in the swamps, jotted down the name and phone number of someone in Los Angeles who he thought might be able to help.

A few weeks and a few MATs (Military Air Transport) hops later and Sergeant Johnny Sorenson was at March AFB near Riverside California. After a hot shower, a meal, and a nights rest in the transient barracks he boarded a train for downtown Los Angeles and after arrival at the station walked to the Alexandria Hotel in the center of the business district. He checked in and as soon as he was in his room asked the switchboard operator to connect him to the number Grimes had given him. "Yes, Sgt Grimes had called with a recommendation. Yes, the man on the phone was looking forward to speaking with Sgt Sorenson, and would he be available for an appointment at 9AM the next morning?" Yes, he most certainly would.

Next morning, dress green uniform freshly cleaned and brushed, shoes at a mirror gloss, and green beret at just the right angle he walked to the address for his appointment, then paced up and down in front of the building to use up the half hour he had arrived early, entering the building three minutes before nine and within seconds of announcing himself at the desk was ushered in to his interview.

An hour and a half later he was back on the street anxious to get back to the Alexandria and a phone where he could call Nan with the good news; he had found a job that could use his military background and talents, the interviewer had offered to have a job opening for him at the end of his enlistment. The pay was good (especially for someone accustomed to military wages), there were good benefits and they would even credit his service time toward his retirement. And the gentleman who had interviewed him had even offered to help with Nan's immigration process when they were ready to come to L.A. How he wished he could be in the same room with her when he gave her the news!

The Special Forces Group Sergeant probably was not even aware in the beginning that his behavior had changed in the time since he had met Nan, but the first thing we noticed was that the confidently quiet smiling sergeant had become talkative whenever we got a few drinks in him regaling us with, "Nan said this, that, or the other thing", "Nan could do this, that, or the other thing". And his previously firm plans to be a "lifer", he would put in thirty and retire then try for a job as a Forest Service Ranger, had been completely forgotten, or at least no longer mentioned.

When he got back from the training assignment in Panama there were other subtle changes that might not have been noticed other than by people who were tuned-in observers and who knew the sergeant well. Blaske was first to comment that he noticed the sergeant wasn't enjoying some of the fun things we did as much as he had seemed to relish them when we first met him; there was a half heartbeat pause and a deep intake of breath just before he stepped out a planes' door and "hit the silk", a blink and a tightening around the mouth just before he stepped out of cover onto a pathway in the forest. He took a little longer setting booby traps and paused longer before disarming them.

While wedding plans and arrangements for his future with Nan were being made Sergeant Johnny Sorenson still had his military duties to perform, he could only monitor the results from long distance and wait (im)patiently, putting further wear and tear on the phone in the hotel where he was quartered.

Waiting for his enlistment to be over Sergeant Johnny Sorenson was having the "short-timers jitters". This would not be a good time to get careless or unlucky.

He was "So short he could sit on the edge of a dime and dangle his legs."

Chapter 34

Hospital Time

When I was air-evac'ed out of Saigon I arrived in the Philippines at the hospital on Clark AFB with no identity papers, dog tags, or other means of proving who I was and my situation was rendered even more complicated by the fact that I had been sheep dipped prior to the TDY rotation; all military records that might prove my identity were erased or sealed.

The phone number I had been given to use in just such an emergency went to an operator Stateside that (after several calls) verified that I was a civilian contractor (under a "legend") on assignment to a military program and confirmed that I was entitled to treatment for the damage to my left ankle caused by a "motorcycle accident". I was to be put into a private room and kept isolated from other patients in the hospital. Damn, I started getting bored in a hurry with no one to talk to and nothing to keep me occupied except some old magazines, some dog-eared musty novels with pages missing and an itchy cast on my left lower leg.

Relief came in the guise of one U.S. Air Force Staff Sergeant Hayes and one Army of the Republic of South Viet Nam Captain Chan; Baphang had donned an old uniform and an old name, Cerone (at Kappas' instruction and with his help) had acquired travel and identity papers for the pair and they had come to check up on me, and escort me back to light duty if the hospital was ready to release me, bringing some cash and box of candy. And a small silver flask secured in Hayes' inside breast pocket.

I was up and on crutches and the doctor in charge of my ward released me to the care of my friends for the day while my discharge paperwork was being prepared and as I was leaving the ward met me at the door of my room and displayed a quarter sized flat lead disk with a bit of copper fused to one side of the rim. He handed me the object and smiling said, "Here's a souvenir from your motorcycle accident".

The object he had handed me opened up some questions and conjecture to be discussed with my friends; how had I been hit in the left ankle when I was running right to left, right side toward the enemy? Was the round that hit me a ricochet with lowered energy when it hit and broke a couple of bones without going all the way through and doing more damage? How did the round cause the spiral fracture above the ankle? Who was using copper jacketed ammunition that day? Bo pen nyan; it didn't really matter and we dropped the subject.

While we were sharing the contents of his silver flask Hayes told a story of going down halls in the Bien Hoa infirmary looking for an orderly to clean me up (a nasty job) and a doctor to care for my wound, finding one of each and holding them in place until I was taken care of and staying with me on the ambulance ride to the transport that would carry me to Clark. I didn't remember any of that and it may or may not have been true, but the way he told the story had all three of us laughing as we got some sun out between two of the hospital wings. The silver flask helped enliven the tale I am sure.

That evening the three of us flew commercially to an airport in Viet Nam (I don't recall knowing which one) where we changed clothing and I.D. cards before debarking on a C123 for the flight west over the mountains and on to "home".

John had been aware of his surroundings when he was lifted into the Hotel Three Four (helicopter) at the woodlot near the Song Long Dai River and despite all the pain killer he was injected with by the Navy corpsman had stayed at a level just above unconsciousness for the ride to Bien Hoa.

He saw the extraction team gathered around the stretcher Jay Kah was being loaded on and heard a raucous peal of laughter before his vision shifted and focused on M&M Kappas. His old friend was standing at rigid attention and saluting him. Damn, Kappas never saluted anybody, "does the old son-of-a-bitch think I'm dying?" He tried to acknowledge the salute with a smile and a salute in return; all he could manage was a small nod.

Then, realizing that if Kappas was there he was safe, John allowed himself to go all the way under, loosening his grip on reality, letting his mind slide away from the pain he had used to stay aware and going into a dreamless sleep.

He almost woke up several times over the next (few, many?) hours but never swam all the way to the surface always lapsing back into deep sleep. When he did wake up he remembered having vivid dreams but could not remember what they were or what they were about. The darkness he could see through cracks along the edges of what he thought were window curtains told him it must be night, but which night he could not tell. He was relieved to see that Kappas was sitting under a lamp across the room reading from a manila folder and drinking something (coffee?) from a large mug. M&M must have heard or sensed his awakening because he put down the manila folder and mug and beckoned to someone outside John's blurred field of vision.

As John's vision cleared he saw that there were three men sitting around his bed, two husky (almost fat) and one thin. All three wore short sleeved shirts and navy-blue neckties over wrinkled chinos, and all three were wearing brown shoes with laces and hard soles (John called them "banker shoes"); none smiled when they saw he was awake.

To his left was a closed door flanked by two armed men in fatigues, from his right he was being approached by a smiling white-clad figure he assumed was a doctor and two ladies in scrubs, probably nurses. The bow trusses overhead, the size of the space he was in, and the sounds he had been registering with his sub-conscious told him he was in an aircraft hangar somewhere. Peeking over the top of a cloth partition at his far right was the top of an operating room light and he could see a portable x-ray machine and other equipment at the far wall. Seeing that his was the only bed in the space, he realized he was in his own private hospital.

His left arm was pinned across his abdomen but he was glad to see his legs moving as he tried to shift position on the bed, he hurt like hell all over but was glad to think all his parts were still attached. When he raised his right hand to his face he felt smooth skin where he expected rough stubble, someone had shaved him while he was sleeping. One of the ladies in scrubs gave him a big toothy smile and held up a small mirror, the face that stared back at him was gaunt, almost skeletal, and tired looking.

After the to-be-expected, bedside manner, "Glad to see you can join us", "You gave us quite a scare", "You must have the constitution of a mule", etc., the doctor got down to cases:

The bullet that had hit him from behind was a through-and through that had passed through his left side just missing his hip and doing almost no damage to anything internal. It would take a little time, but the wound should heal without complications. He had gotten a mean bruise on his right hip and some other bruises and scrapes that would leave him sore for a few weeks and had suffered simple fractures to a collar bone and cracked three ribs that would contribute to his discomfort but should heal properly.

Of more pressing concern was the infection in the open wound he had suffered to his shoulder and the pathogens inhabiting his GI tract, probably from the un-boiled water he had had to drink on the mountain, both were life-threatening problems and the doctor would have to monitor the treatment results for at least a week. But overall the prognosis was good and with the proper medication and rest and recuperation he should be fully recovered in a few months.

He slept again and this time when he woke up, still attached to wires and tubes, he could see daylight around the edges of the window curtains across the room. The three men in "banker shoes" were at a desk near the door having breakfast on metal trays, two armed guards still flanking the closed door. Kappas was sitting on a chair beside his bed; he was there to say goodbye and farewell, holding a brown paper wrapped package that he said was, "from the boys".

What followed was two or three days (time was still subjective for him) of medical treatments, lots of sleep, and visits from a "member of the Embassy staff" John knew from Virginia who was there to de-brief him.

His innate talent and trained memory allowed him to reconstruct the maps and notes he had made in the weeks he had been up on the Ho Chi Minh Trail and he was able to make corrections to the old French ordinance maps of the area he had traversed. He was able to dictate a report outlining his observations and conclusions about enemy troop composition and probable future concentrations, including his prediction that the North was preparing to significantly ramp up their efforts. Sorry, no photographs, his camera and film had been lost during his E&E (escape and evasion) run.

After his thorough de-briefing and with the doctors' blessing he was airlifted to the hospital at Clark where he would undergo some additional surgical repairs to his left shoulder before being shipped back to the States where he would complete his physical therapy and recuperation. He was assigned a private room, complete with a Marine with a holstered sidearm posted at his door.

He was sitting on a chair looking out a window and contemplating his options, remaining in service or retiring, perhaps retiring and getting a contract as a consultant with the company he worked for, when he noticed three men talking outside the window. He could tell by their body language they were sharing something from a flask and laughing.

He recognized the one on crutches as Jay Cee (or JayKah) and tapped on the window trying to get his attention, he wanted to thank him for that day in the woodlot; he had an overriding, un-characteristic urge to thank him. But the distance was too great and none of them heard his tapping.

Soon the three walked back toward the building and out of his sight.

Chapter 35

Dry Heat

"Yeah, but it's a dry heat"

By 0800 hours it could already be hot enough and dry enough to make the back of your throat ache, lips begin to crack, and you could feel layers peeling off your eyeballs. The air was so dry it was a race to drink enough to keep pace with dehydration, perspiration evaporated as quickly as it appeared leaving behind a salty residue on any exposed skin. And the day was just beginning.

Air temperatures could get higher at our training facility north of Indian Springs but all the concrete and asphalt paving at Nellis meant that surface temps stayed high all night and any moisture in the air was squeezed out and pushed up over Sunrise Mountain to the south of the base leaving the zone between the runways and the mountain as arid as a drying oven.

When we were at Nellis and far from Kappas' protection, the First Sergeant of the A&E squadron we were nominally attached to would delight in finding shit details for Cerone and I if he found us unassigned on any duty roster. MSgt Knight was probably afraid of Hayes, loved super-squared-away Blaske, and Morrison always got himself assigned to duty at the base infirmary, so that left Cerone and myself to suffer his attention. Knight was a strange man, a Titless WAF for his entire career he was very interested in finding out where we went and what we did on our TDYs, and what was really in our secure hangar; and frustrated at not being able to find out he would ride the two of us when the opportunity arose and then try to inveigle an invitation to our off base house or invite us to come and have drinks and a cruise on a cabin cruiser he kept at Lake Mead. He never got an invite to the "House With The Blue Fence" and we only made a lake cruise with him one time, Cerone and I roaring up and down the lake in the dark trying to find something to run into and sink the boat while Knight was passed out on a locker in the stern. We knew we could swim to shore from anywhere in the lake, we were pretty sure MSgt Knight couldn't.

In summer conditions aerial warfare training flights usually took off at 0600 or earlier with most aircraft back on the ground by 0900 with a few stragglers from air-to-air refueling exercises or aircraft coming in from other bases landing as late as 1100. There might be a few takeoffs in ones and twos during the day and flight ops would pick up in the evening and stay busy until midnight. There would be dispatch trucks stationed on either side of the runway 24/7 to provide transport to any pilots who found their aircraft stalled for any reason on the runway or one of the taxiways, or as we learned later in the scrub brush hummocks on either side of the paved surfaces. The worst detail on the base was being stationed in one of the trucks on the far side of the runway during the day, even a four-hour shift was almost unbearable. Just the sort of detail Knight liked to put us on.

The dispatch trucks were 6-cylinder Ford pickups painted a dark Air Force Blue (what were they thinking?) and came with a dispatch radio and two un-insulated ten-gallon water cans as standard equipment, savvy drivers were always careful to check that the water cans were full before leaving the dispatch center, there was no air conditioning in the trucks.

Late one morning when the sun was high and there was not enough shade to hide in and the inside of the truck was like a furnace I was standing outside the truck in my non-regulation desert uniform (loose white shirt and loose white draw string pants and a wide brimmed straw hat) pouring water from an evaporation bag over my head (hat on) and wondering where my relief was. He was already over an hour and a half late and dispatch kept telling me to stay put, he was on his way. The glare and the heat had me in a somnambulant state and I was struggling to get enough oxygen from the hot thin air I was gasping for through a moist bandana over my mouth and nose. My level of awareness was down to the heat, the glare and an occasional radio transmission coming through the window of the truck. Heat waves were making close objects seem far away and distant objects seem close; an occasional miniature tornado would throw a blast of heat and super-fine desert dust my way to add to the misery of the morning.

An apparition appeared and grew larger in the simmering air toward the downwind end of the runway and before my half cooked befuddled brain could register what it was I was assaulted by a blast of sound, hit by a hot stream of air smelling of kerosene, and submerged in a dark wave of reddish brown talc. My straw hat went aloft never to be seen again and even the bandana covering my lower face was blown away. A landing F-100C had veered off the runway crossed the taxiway and plowed to a stop in the desert less than fifty feet from where I was standing.

As the engine whine spooled down the canopy opened and the pilot disappeared over the side away from me, reappearing at the front of the bird walking toward the dispatch truck. I walked around the rear of the vehicle (not blue anymore) to meet him and tried to ask "what happened?" but my ears were plugged with fine sand and still ringing from his noisy jet and the sound that came out of my throat was more a croak than speech and what came out was, "**WHAT ARE YOU DOING?**" or something like it.

The understandably nervous pilot gave me a startled look and started backing away turning and half walking, half trotting in the direction of the runway. A totally stupid thing to do, there could be other traffic on short final and the tower would not want to chance directing a go-around on this hot hot day. The guy was going to risk standing in the sun with no hat and no water waiting for a crash truck or worse try to cross the runway on foot. He must have been really rattled by his off-runway desert excursion.

I radioed the tower that the pilot was okay and I would deliver him to the operations shack and that there was no fire, no fuel leak, just a jet stuck in the sand and needing a tow truck. I drove alongside the pilot telling him to "get in the truck, Sir" several times until I finally pulled ahead and stopped the truck in his path, got out and said, "**Get in the truck, Sir. Do**

it now, Sir." And he got in. After a few minutes wait the tower flashed me a green light and I drove across the runway and delivered my passenger.

After I dropped him off I went into the washroom under the tower and almost backed out in a hurry before I realized that what I was looking at was my reflection in a mirror. My hair, longish for the military, was standing in caked orange spikes, my face plastered red brown except for the reversed raccoon mask around my eyes, rust colored streaks running from my head down my shoulders and clinging to my once-white clothing. A great look for Halloween, not so good for meeting and greeting a stressed out young pilot. I started to wash the mess off but had another idea; the boys would have to see this!

And that is how Polaroid snapshots of my "bloody body" found their way to a posting on the bulletin board in front of Knights' office the next morning just in time for the Colonels' inspection. The Colonel was not amused and gave MSgt Knight an earful.

After that miserable (but interesting) morning Cerone and I made a pact, every time one of us drew the dispatch truck duty the other would come out and relieve him after two hours (in a truck that was not exactly checked out from the motor pool). Sometimes we would just sit out under a big umbrella (borrowed from the enlisted pool deck) on Adirondack chairs (missing from the officers' pool deck) and drink Kool Aid from a ten-gallon insulated container (missing from the mess hall). We would park the trucks in the shade of an old drogue chute (missing from aircraft misc. stores) and visit for a spell.

We were sitting out one morning making the best of the situation when we noticed a jet starting the break to turn downwind with the landing gear still up. The bird completed the turn, turned crosswind then lined up with the runway and flew by the tower gear still up. We learned later that there was a gear malfunction and the fuel tanks were down to fumes, the pilot elected to eject and let the bird auger in on the desert at the east end of the runway. We were parked nearest the point the man in the parachute was headed for and got to him ahead of the emergency

220

vehicles. Captain Fitzsimmons, the pilot and an old acquaintance, was happy to accept a cup of our cold "bug juice" and a ride back across the runway, radioing to the tower that he was okay and in no need of medical attention (the docs would be at the ops shack to check him out anyway) and expressing his surprise at meeting us again.

Late that same afternoon it was Cerone's shift and it was my turn to visit, bringing a fresh container of the lemonade (that's what the label on the packet said) with a block of ice in the container (there may have been a bottle or two of Schlitz in with the ice). We both turned at the "wrong" sound of a two-seater taking off (F-100F) and watched as it mushed forward in the high-density altitude of the super-heated air over the runway, we couldn't hear or see the afterburner needed to get it to altitude and ran for one of our trucks, the F model was not going to gain any more altitude.

As we raced up the taxiway (if one can be said to "race" in a six-cylinder pickup on a very hot day) we watched the canopy blow off and two seats take the rocket ride, holding our collective breath until we saw two chutes open. Both men drifted toward the scrub at the base of Sunrise Mountain and I started off pavement in their direction bouncing over hummocks and keeping the truck speed up to avoid getting stuck in the soft stuff beneath the brittle shell of the desert floor. We were relieved to see both men up and getting clear of their parachutes no more than a hundred feet apart and picked up the student pilot first, instructor second.

When we picked up the instructor Cerone just couldn't help himself and blurted out, "Gawdamn Fitzsimmons, those fucking things cost a million dollars each, you can't just keep throwing them away! Sir. Captain Sir. Two in one day, Sir!" and offered both pilots their choice of beverage from our cooler.

After both pilots had gulped down some cold liquid and had a satisfying piss, and still waiting for the emergency vehicles to come across to our location Captain Fitzsimmons said, "Men, I think we are going to need something a little stronger, take us to the Officers Club" and called in to the tower with his intention. Who were we to argue? We bounced back across the hummocks, Cerone and the student pilot holding on for dear life in the back of the truck, and on to the paved surface and I started to the turn to go back to where we had left the other truck but was ordered to proceed directly to the other side of the runway (green light was already flashing from the tower), someone could retrieve the truck and our other gear later. Captain Fitzsimmons had a thirst on.

At the door of the Officers Club the looks thrown in the direction of Cerone and myself were brushed aside by Captain Fitzsimmons with a brusque, "they're with me" as he headed for a phone to call the Officer of the Day (OOD) at base ops and inform him that he, Captain Fitzsimmons, would come in later to fill out the incident report unless the OOD wanted to bring the forms to where he, Captain Fitzsimmons, was in the midst of administering some self-medication. The OOD, a fighter pilot himself, passed his duty to a junior officer and came over to join us; he wanted to hear the story of Captain Fitzsimmons's day while it was still fresh.

The party kept growing as other officers gathered to hear about losing two jet fighters in one day and eventually we were joined by a couple of Colonels and our favorite fighter pilot Captain Joe (he was a major now and lead instructor at Gunfighter School but we still called him Captain Joe); no one seemed to mind the non-officers in their midst and the liquor flowed as other stories of adventure, reckless adventure (there is a difference), and derring-do floated in the smoke filled, booze scented room.

Eventually Cerone and Fitzsimmons got around to a laugh filled story of a serious adventure that took place on a snow-covered meadow high in the Rockies. When we had first met Captain Fitzsimmons he found himself in dire straits, hurt and in a place, "so cold a yeti would freeze his balls off" and now we were re-united in a place, "so hot the coyotes had to keep standing or burn their balls off".

222

Sometime after the steaks and fries had come out and been consumed (we didn't tell our hosts that the food was better in the NCO Club) Captain Joe asked what a couple of NCOs were doing pulling Airman Third Class duty and we let him in on our relationship with MSgt Knight. His response was to tell us to have the First Sergeant call his office and verify that we were on a "special assignment" with Major Finley (Captain Joe) and unavailable for any other work details, the two Colonels still at our table nodded their assent.

We were happy to relay that message to MSgt Knight early the next morning and when pressed for details we just smiled and said, "Need to know, First Sergeant. Need To Know".

Chapter 36

Zero Flys

Like many other people who went into the service I could come up with a dozen reasons for my enlisting; probably none of them would be completely true. There were a lot of factors that led me to decide to go visit my local Navy recruiter and sign up, like a train wreck it was a buildup of several events and conditions that contributed to my decision. It was an accident of timing (the Navy recruiter wasn't at his desk yet that morning) that put me in a conversation with the Air Force recruiter, who told me that if I could pass the proficiency exams (I didn't see that as a barrier at all) I could get into the Enlisted Pilot/Warrant Officer Program and get military training as a pilot.

The Air Force recruiter either didn't know or didn't care to tell me (perhaps he had a quota to meet) that the Air Force was starting the process of phasing out Warrant Officers and replacing them with the new "Super Sergeants" ranks. There would be no more flight training for anyone other than officers in the United States Air Force. I was several weeks into basic training and had already met M&M Kappas before I learned about this very disappointing (to me) change in Air Force policy and mentioned it to him during the evaluation interview that helped determine if I would be accepted into his new training program.

The sergeant didn't forget my disappointment and within hours of my first arrival at Nellis AFB had introduced me to Lt. Donahue, the man in charge of the Nellis AFB Aero Club. I would have to arrange for lessons on my own time and pay (a pittance) for the fuel I used, but I could take lessons and learn to fly with some of the best instructors available anywhere. In addition to the very patient Lt. Donahue there were officers on the base who liked to stay proficient in light aircraft, and some who just liked to teach (they would even charge off the fuel costs), and best of all there was MSgt Kappas himself (on active duty as an NCO he still held his flying status and military licenses as a Lt. Colonel in the Reserves) and Captain Finley, "Captain Joe", top pilot in the Fighter Weapons School, who eventually took some time off from the jets he flew every day to get upside down in a T-6 in the Grand Canyon with me.

As I got qualified in a variety of aircraft I added to the fun and helped defray my expenses by getting members of the Blue, Orange, and Green Teams from our Group to fly with me and chip in for the fuel costs. Everybody went along with the program, except for our armorer "Zero". I mentioned to Kappas one afternoon that I was unable to convince, coerce, or inveigle Zero to fly with me and Kappas simply looked at me said, "Zero flys" and gave his attention back to his coffee mug.

His name was Macintyre but he was called "Zero" because that was all he ever had to say. Reticence did not begin to cover Zeros' reluctance to talk; he never, ever used two words when one, preferably a monosyllable, would do. We sometimes referred to the older man with the funny British sounding accent as the "Jack in the Box", convinced that some day when his handle was cranked to just the right spot he would pop out, show himself and make a loud noise.

He would sometimes sit quietly and have a beer with us but would not stay too long or late or share any personal information. We knew right away that he was a master of small arms and gradually learned he lived off-base with his wife and two children, had known M&M Kappas somewhere in the past, and was in the Air Force as a short cut to the US citizenship (at that time there was a policy that if a prospective émigré served in our armed forces they were eligible for citizenship at the end of their tour) he needed to qualify for a high-security-clearance-required job in the States.

As our armorer he and his crew of two ex-Navy "retreads" were in charge of maintenance for all of our weaponry and field gear and he was "boss" of the secure hangar where our parachute loft and weapons lockers were located and ready-bags stowed.

When I complained that the length of my M14 made it clumsy to jump with, especially for a short guy, and hard to carry or track and train on a target in close quarters Zero just looked at me with a blank expression and waited for me to stop talking before he checked the weapon in. The next time I checked it out the front sight had been repositioned, the barrel shortened and threaded to fit a set of flash and sound suppressors, the fire selector switch given a positive feel, the trigger pull set at an even rate pound and a half, and a folding stock installed. Pretty soon everyone on my team would have to have one just like it.

And when I brought in a personal weapon, a well-used and worn Model 1911 Colt .45 he looked at it, grunted, and disappeared with it in the direction of his bench. Two days later it appeared in my locker re-blued, re-barreled, tight and tuned and looking brand new. Even the magazines looked new.

The quiet, accommodating armorer would have been the last person any one of us would have expected to be a part of one of Captain Joe's pranks.

We had laid out a ground-to-air practice course that required a lot of low level, high g-pulling, grunt, groan and yank and bank flying with the ground as hard deck and a 1500'agl (above ground level) ceiling way out on the gunnery range and the pilots were practicing dry runs through the course (no guns or other munitions, that would come later) with most of the fighter pilots clearing the course in seven to eight minutes, some in under seven and Captain Joe at six minutes flat.

A particular Colonel could not best nine minutes with his first three runs and that positioned Captain Joe to make a bet with his fellows that with just the tiniest coaching, which Captain Joe would provide, the Colonels' plane could make the course in under eight minutes, and to top it off the Colonels' plane would be his usual mount, an F model (not the most maneuverable in the F100 series).

Losers of the bet would have to finance a steak and beer feast for the one hundred plus enlisted men and officers involved in the exercise. A little one sided as most of the officers would bet against the Captain even if some of the shrewder pilots knew he was bound to "have an ace up his sleeve".

Kappas and Samuels were in on the prank and requested of Colonel Foster, air boss for the exercise, that some of their people be allowed on ride-alongs in two-seater F100Fs to experience the g-loads and observe the pilot workloads under high stress conditions. This would give the electronics techs and forward air controllers a better understanding of how their jobs fit into the big picture. I've been told the Colonel was smiling and had a twinkle in his eye when he said yes. Could he have been wise to the plot?

The exercise was shut down for a three-day break to give the pilots a chance to attend briefings, digest the lessons they had just learned on the range and get some rest. Hanging around on the flight line (no passes this weekend) and listening to the tower freqs we took note of the fact that Captain Joe checked out an F100F at least four times over the three-day break. What was up with that?

What was up was that Captain Joe was bringing in a ringer and was using the F100F to familiarize him with the practice course out on the gunnery range. In a couple of days if all went according to his plan he would plant the ringer with the Colonel in the Colonels' bird for a run through the traps (radar timers) at under eight minutes.

On our second morning back out on the range the ride-along program was initiated and it was no surprise to see an F100F model or two in every series of flights. On the third morning after the first series of planes had run the course all of us lucky enough to be hiding in the air-conditioned temporary control/dispatch shack heard the Colonel at the center of the bet call in that he was standing by to make his first run of the day.

We waited with fingers crossed, some for and some against Captain Joe's bet, for the field phone connecting to the radar shack to ring and bring us the trap time. The phone buzzed and the lieutenant who was Officer of the Day in the operations center picked it up, grinned and wrote the time on the chalk board in front of the shack - 00:08:05 -, way better than any previous time the Colonel had posted but not low enough for Captain Joe to win the wager. Still, some of us kept the faith, we would never bet against Captain Joe.

We were enlisted personnel working as part of the exercise crew and we would win either way; however, the bet went we would be in for steaks and beer. But of course, Cerone could not pass a chance to make a little money gambling and was taking book, with this first run at over eight minutes the odds were shifting against the Colonel making the course in less than eight minutes. It looked like the trading floor of a stock exchange in front of the ops shack as Cerone stood in the center of a group of men (yes, there were some officers in the knot of men) jotting down bets in his little black notebook with a pencil stub.

When the Colonel called in a second run a lot of loud arguing broke out when the time was posted. Was the time of 00:08:00 under eight minutes or not? We would have to wait for the third run of the day and if that run was not decidedly under eight minutes take it to the air boss for a decision (unofficially of course, the air boss could not be involved in any gambling).

It was late morning and already getting really hot out when the Colonels bird with its Tech Sergeant ride-along went through the traps a third time. Some loud cheers, some loud cursing, and some stunned expressions were evident when the time was posted. The Colonels plane had gone through the traps at 00:07:15 and radar confirmed it had not busted ceiling going through the course. We had a winner!

Within minutes an F100F was landing on the dry lakebed in front of the ops shack and taxiing up to turn and stop starboard side to the shack. As the engine whine got lower and quieter the canopy began to open, the words "Lt. Col. Simonsen" stenciled on the canopy sill telling everyone whose bird it was.

I had climbed up on the shack followed by Cerone and Morrison, joined a few minutes later by First Sergeant Kappas, and from my vantage point could see that the man in the back seat had a handkerchief sticking out of the sides of his oxygen mask and a yellowish stain on his collar and ascot before pilot and passenger disappeared over the canopy rail on the far side of the aircraft.

The Colonel reappeared crossing in front of the bird with his ride-along, helmet still on, trailing a few feet behind. While the Colonel was being met with a lot of loud, hearty congratulations, and a few loud moans, the ride-along ringer, the ex-RAAF fighter pilot/test pilot and future Edwards AFB civilian test pilot/consultant walked toward the shack, pausing just before the door to take off his helmet.

My jaw must have dropped as far as my knees as Kappas chortled (chortled!) and punched me on the shoulder saying from behind a big grin, "Zero flys!"

Chapter 37

Officers and Peaches

Major Bohannon never came into the field with any of us and only rarely got as close to our operations as Thailand. His role in 8th COIN kept him busy shuttling between Clark AFB, Philippines and the Pentagon and "keeping the home fires burning at Nellis". He was effective at his job of keeping our units funded and equipped while staying below the radar with the press. We dubbed him "The Cocktail Party Warrior".

Colonel Ross, US Army was another story. As commander of the all services Counter Insurgency Study Group he had been liable to pop up anywhere there was a Victor Site (small airfields we were putting in all over Laos) and would parachute in to visit us in remote sites with no strip. He spent several days on more than one occasion walking out of a zone with us. We liked him. He didn't bother with a lot of the spit and polish we associated with other ring knockers (West Point graduates) and was very "field savvy". Everyone knew he had been on his way to becoming a good (maybe great) general.

Captain Samuels became Samuels as soon as we were in-country on our first TDY (temporary duty), after all we were civilians now and it would make no sense for us to go around saluting and calling people sir, and somehow that was who he remained for us unless we were Stateside and there were other, ranking officers around. In the field he let us practice our crafts with rare interruption, instead he generally "got with the program" even if it didn't seem to follow military dictum. He was our brother-at-arms.

We worked with members of other services and their officers on occasion but our training geared us more toward working in the field responsible for our own conduct and mission accomplishment. We worked singly, in twos and threes, or as six to ten-man teams with other armed forces units (where we stayed in the background as much as possible, nobody remembers the guy who comes to fix the radio after he is gone) and/or indigenous peoples. We got along fine with Special Forces officers and most of the Regular Army (RA) officers who came through. Marines we saw were mostly noncoms and Navy personnel were usually warrant officers.

But we did have notable run-ins with two RA (Regular Army) officers: one resulted in a (perhaps unkind) practical joke and the other could have had serious consequences if it had happened at another time.

On both occasions we were moving overland from Nam Yu in Northwest Laos into the Yunan Province of Southern China, a tricky insertion into a country that was not going to treat us well if we were captured, we could either be used as political coin or beheaded on the spot; Nerve wracking stuff. Bill Young had grown up walking these trails with his missionary father before becoming an employee of the CIA and had an intimate knowledge of the territory and its' people, thirty or more tribes considered him kin, and we relied on his expertise and followed his "book" when we were in the bush.

On the first occasion a young man with new civilian bush clothes, I think the tag was still on the back of his shirt (Abercrombie and Fitch?) and his new boots squeaked, was to accompany us. He resisted, but we finally got him to oil the damn boots, we couldn't afford for him to go lame on us on the trail. As soon as he told us he was a lieutenant with "Army Intelligence" we might have known he was going to be a pain in the ass.

I was told later that he was given the standard Kappas speech which was to the effect that on the trail "JayCee is in charge, follow his lead, do as he does, sleep when and where he tells you to sleep and you'll be okay." He didn't listen.

We had a long, hot hike on a dusty trail made slower by the lieutenants' insistence on looking at a map and waving around an engineering compass at every fork in the trail, didn't he realize that to our guides and porters this was as familiar as the path to the outhouse down on the farm? Hadn't anyone told him that maps of this area were notoriously unreliable? That was annoying enough, but then he insisted on making noises about where we should bivvie for the night, disposition and rotation of guards, and all the other stuff he had gotten from reading comic books or something.

We set up the camp pretty much as the lieutenant "ordered", ate our rations and waited for the puppy to fall asleep. After a long walk at a high altitude that didn't take long. As soon as he was solidly snoring we stole his sidearm and then followed Bill Young's Book. That is, we picked up and quietly moved to new locations twice during the night. Nobody had bothered to tell the Lieutenant about the Book.

It may have been that I felt some sympathy for him, or more likely the knowledge that Kappas would tear off a piece of my ass if I didn't bring him back, in either case I had two of our Wa tribesmen keep watch over him so he wouldn't get lost or eaten by a tiger or something. He was not in very good mental health when a couple of us stepped out into the road where he could see us at about midday.

I sent him back with an escort to be Tony Poe's guest at Nam Yu until we could pick him up on the way back out. As far as we would tell anyone he had accompanied us on the mission. Well, except we had to tell Samuels and Kappas the truth.

Fortunately, we were still sheep-dipped when the second incident occurred or I could have been in deep, deep shit.

An RA Captain flew into Wattay (airport near Vientiane) still in uniform, a big no-no, new Ranger patch on his sleeve. He was there to "look the situation over" which we took to mean, "log some field time to look good for my next promotion". We immediately tagged him as a "political" officer and a blustering windbag. Did we really have to take him into Indian Country (areas of hostility)? Apparently someone he knew had juice because the answer was yes.

I would have happily foisted him off on someone else except Tom Minor, Hayes and I were the only ones available. Cerone was already in the field

232

with Young waiting for us to bring equipment and supplies and the rest of the Blue Team were scattered on other assignments. We were "it".

Bird and Sons (aviation contractors) provided transport to Nam Yu where we linked up with our guides and porters, Lahu and Wa tribesmen, and we hit the trail early the next morning with the Wa on point, pack animals in the center, Lahu next with Hayes and Tom Minor (a Wa from a tribe in Thailand) bringing up the rear guard. The Captain, now in soft, used civvies and I stayed a little ahead of the pack animals.

The captain was too nervous (my take) to give us any trouble on the trek in, but we surmised from the way he walked and in general carried himself, that he must have bought the Ranger patch and had it sewn on right before flying in to Wattay. We didn't say anything out loud but silently agreed to keep to a pace that he could maintain without difficulty.

We were on a rugged trail just inside Yunan and skirting Myanmar which we followed to a point where the Myanmar border turned back west and south and where we were to rendezvous with Young (and our pal Cerone), good news was that there would not be any Vietnamese near us, bad news was that elements of the Chinese Red Army might be nearby and the KMT (Kuomintang) warlords would probably show up to be paid off. Our protection would be the Wa tribesmen whose guests we would be.

Our mission in this part of the world was to maintain and monitor four or five radio listening posts, which had to be moved often, to tap into telephone landlines, and look for signs of road building and any troop build-up or activity from the Red Chinese Army.

We set up inside the Wa encampment to wait for our fellows to join us; no need for a dry camp (no fires) here and we sat down as guests to a nice repast of young dog, hot peppers, and rice mixed with some green vegetables and garlic. The whipped green tea was particularly welcome. The captain was obviously feeling more at ease in this larger population, although he didn't eat any of the food, a slight our hosts were sure to have noted, and was beginning to regain some of the swagger he had lost

233

on the trail. I should have known something stupid was about to happen. Damn.

Tom Minor, Hayes, and I left with one of the locals to reconnoiter the area leaving the captain napping in the camp. Actually, we were going sightseeing in this wonderfully beautiful land of lakes with cool, deep pools surrounded by limestone cliffs. We were on a part of the ancient Horse Trail which had seen Timur-a-lanes' Army pass through centuries before, The Wa claim to have witnessed the event.

The Wa had migrated to this remote area from "someplace cold" and lived by hunter-gathering and some agriculture, but their main avocation was as mercenaries; they had had a wonderful windfall when the Japanese were occupying the territory, taking heads with the Gurkhas during the Burma Campaign.

They start their martial training at around age three or four and are seriously good soldiers before they hit puberty. The form of Muay Thai that they practice is deadly; a knee to the chest from one of their fighters means a broken breastbone for the opponent. Small in physical stature, large in ferocity, but also large at heart with their friends, a Wa will go for days without eating to be sure that a guest has enough to eat.

So, when we came back into camp I was appalled to see the captain, hands on hips, intimidating posture towering over a small wizened old man squatting in a loin cloth. What the fuck did he think he was doing?

The little old man was a tribal elder with years of killing behind him, on other visits he had talked to us through the interpreter and told wonderful tales, probably all true, of tracking and killing men and other dangerous animals; he had earned the respect of his tribesmen and their enemies lived in fear of his visit. And now his hand was on the hilt of his knife and he was looking directly at the captains' eyes.

Completely without thought and on pure reflex I did the only thing I could have done, I touched Tom Minor on the upper arm to say "I've got it" and sprinted across the camp and kicked the captain in the side of the head, catching him right at the point of the jawbone hinge just below his left ear. He folded into himself and went down like a limp sock. The crouching man focused on something about six inches to my left and smiled.

Hayes deposited the unconscious asshole at the base of a tree and waited for him to wake up. He would probably never understand that I had just saved his life (and maybe ours as well), but Hayes would keep him from getting into any more trouble until we could send him east. I think Hayes would have probably broken his neck if that was what was needed to keep the captain quiet (I'm not saying that was a bad thing).

The air in the camp was ominous, we were not forgiven for the behavior of our bad mannered lowland ward, we should never have brought a man who would behave so badly into their midst. I knew this because the Wa were usually touchy-feely friendly people, they like to touch knees when they squatted next to us, tap us on the back, throw an arm over a shoulder and never, ever look directly at one's eyes.

Now they were standing off and looking at us, probably waiting for some word from the tribal elder who had been so rudely treated. Luckily, I remembered that I had a secret weapon in a pack near where I was standing: canned peaches.

All ambassadors and other people hoping to spread good will should be armed with canned peaches. I have never been anywhere in the world where canned peaches weren't appreciated as a gesture of friendliness.

Keeping my eyes on the ground near where the elder was still squatting I moved laterally to my pack, reached in and pulled out four cans of Del Monte Freestone peaches. The old man grinned, the camp relaxed and all was well with the world again (at least for now). Thank you, Mr. Del Monte, wherever you are!

We put together an escort of Lahu, it would have been dangerous to the captain to include WA, to escort the captain back to the tender care of the former Marines' Marine and current CIA officer in charge of the north end of Laos, where I was later to learn the captain had a very uncomfortable stay. Bully for you Mr. Poe.

I thought the incident was over but apparently the RA officer did not. He wanted me court-martialed for striking an officer, he wanted me hung, he wanted me shot on sight. He wanted me turned over to the Marine Corps brig in the Philippines awaiting trial.

But, as Samuels and Kappas reminded him, technically I was a civilian, not subject to the UCMJ (Uniform Code of Military Justice). Sorry.

Chapter 38

Here Kitty Kitty

The Troung Son Road, or Harriman Trail as we called it in the early days after a Geneva Accord affirming that Laos was a neutral country, became famous as the Ho Chi Minh Trail. It was not really a road or a trail, but a network of roads and trails used as the major supply route from North Viet Nam through Eastern Laos and parts of Cambodia to South Viet Nam. After the Geneva Accord was signed the US pulled most of its' assets out of the country, CIA offices moved across the Mekong, uniformed and non-uniformed Americans all but disappeared as the US prepared to honor the neutrality agreement.

The North Vietnamese flooded the northeast provinces of the country with 5,000 troops (some estimates said the number was as high as 20,000) and started improving conditions on the trail(s), just as we knew they would. It fell to our lot, back in civilian garb of sorts, to introduce trail watchers and hunter teams from other services to the area and to our contacts with the hill tribes.

Tom Major had already surveyed the area during a previous monsoon season and we had a rudimentary map of the zone we were to observe and assess. Following his map, we had selected a stream crossing near a clearing at ground level that was covered by a high canopy, perfect place for a truck park, logistics dump, or relay point, as a place to observe traffic and help the "hunter team" we were escorting into the sector.

To be clear, these "hunter teams" were not hunting game big or small, they were hunting people who had been ID'd through intelligence networks as "targets of value"; i.e. people important to the North Vietnamese war efforts. Failing to identify specific targets they were authorized to take down NVA officers or Viet Cong (new name for some of the Viet Minh) at their discretion. Dirty, dangerous work, and after introducing them to a zone and/or some of our contacts we were supposed to get clear of them and get out of the zone they were working quickly, before the NVA was aware they were in the neighborhood and called in the trackers and dogs to chase them. It was never clear (and didn't have to be) whether these team members were SFG or CIA or SFG/CIA, but a few had Australian accents and we met one guy who had to have been ethnically Korean.

Our mission brief stated that once we were well clear of the "hunter teams" we were to observe and gather Intel on enemy troop disposition and movement (especially movement patterns) before going "di di mau" to our extraction point or walking out to a safe zone. It didn't always turn out that way; as field conditions sometimes dictated changes to the plans.

We were transported by C34 (Beech 18) to do an infiltration drop at a location in Houaphan Province that we knew would be hot, hot, hot. And not the weather; the province was always crawling with NVA and their allies. There is a common misconception that all of the Montagnards (mountain tribes) were allied with, or at least friendly to American operatives. Not so, a few of the Mei (now known as Hmong) tribes in the northeast part of Laos were sympathetic to Ho Chi Minh and the NVA and many other locals were bandits or mercenaries who would be happy to capture us for sale to the highest bidder. The guy you had a meal with in the evening could be trying to kill or capture you in the morning. The kid you gave a chocolate bar (chocolate round) to could blow you up or cut your throat at any moment.

And to add salt to the soup, Houaphan in the time before the French came was not a part of Laos, shifting between independence and being part of Viet Nam from time to time. Blood ties, cultural ties, and language roots, and the common fight against the Japanese (and any other non-native invaders) kept many of the people in these forested mountains friendly with the North Vietnamese.

While some loin clothed denizens of the mountains were later portrayed as romantic "Innocents in Eden", as far as we were concerned most were sly, cunning, hardcore survivors. We didn't blame them, but we didn't trust them either. So Baphang, known and respected by all the mountain factions, had gone in a week ahead of us to ensure a safe landing at our arrival point.

The Blue Team was spread all over; Cerone helping Bill Young at Long Chien, Blaske assisting Kappas and Tom Minor at Wattay, Morrison somewhere with Pop Buell giving kids shots, and Hayes on liaison with an SFG A Team at Phitsanulok, Thailand. I had politely demurred (flat out refused) from bringing a replacement to our team with me on this sortie telling Kappas that, "Baphang and I will have too much to do to try to stay alive without bringing along an unknown". I guess the guys' feelings were hurt but that was better than being dead or captured or getting one of us wounded, captured or killed. Besides he hadn't had time to learn the JayKah (used to be JayCee) rule for the bush, "step where I step, drink when and where I drink, sleep where I tell you to and you will survive, deviate from this rule and you will not". It was just one part of a deal I was confident I had made with the war gods one night, "don't let mortar rounds, artillery rounds, machine gun fire, sniper fire, or sappers come into where I am sleeping" and they didn't. My old team mates knew of this and always had me pick our bivvies at night and listened to my instincts on the trail, I was lucky and they knew it but this new guy wouldn't have a clue and I didn't think he would have time to be a believer under real field conditions. He was killed later, stepped on a mine, not with me at the time.

Some months after, back at "home" at Indian Dunes (part of the Nellis AFB gunnery range) we had a chance to discuss the subject of replacements with other teams and all agreed on a pattern that had emerged; as the teams whittled down and lost members they hit a point where original members survived over and over, the replacements (no matter how well trained) did not. I believe this is probably a universal rule for men (and women) who are exposed to dangerous circumstances. I do know that I began to be unable to remember the names of the replacements. Too much guilt.

Dropping in with me to meet Baphang were two "hunters", one I had met before when his name was Murphy, now it was Sanchez, and his mate a guy named Culver. They had a PARU interpreter with them (all insertion teams in Laos at that time had a PARU assigned to them) with yet another consonant filled, unpronounceable (to me) name; I called him New PARU.

After a dry breakfast and a hurried conference, I realized we had gotten ourselves into the middle of a hornets' nest. The entire province was swarming with troops, trucks, and artillery pieces. There was a strong possibility that they were massing for a move west into the heart of Laos rather than stock piling for delivery to the south, they were too far north for a logistics base to be practical when there were so many better options south of this province (we were north of the Mu Gia Pass, the usual top entry into the Trail). Baphang agreed with this assessment and had perhaps even steered me to it. This was Intel that had to get out, but first we needed to get a real handle on the scope of the operations in the zone. I wouldn't risk even a microburst transmission until I had more information, we would stay dark and watch for a while.

We had a bit of a conflict going with Culver when I told the "hunters", "do not fuckin' kill anyone!"

Technically, from a military standpoint, Culver outranked me but Kappas had told us that in the field, and in pursuit of our mission we outranked anybody on the spot and I took that to mean that in this case I was the final word. He started getting pissy with me until Sanchez shut him down. Although never lacking in self-confidence and a belief in his abilities, Sanchez had seen Baphang in action and didn't want to tangle with him, or more to the point didn't want Culver to learn the hard way what it might mean to cross the two of us. New PARU agreed the info we could collect was far and away more valuable than "striking fear into the enemy" with some "assassination bullsheet". Sanchez may have saved Culvers' life that day.

The information we gathered over the next few days resulted in a blocking action of H&I (Harassment and Interdiction) by Vang Paos' Mei forces that kept the NVA and PAVN from striking southwest to Vientiane, instead squeezing them west northwest from the vicinity of Xam Nu to near Louang Namtha and into Phongsali Province. Sometime later the Royal Laotian Army went up to meet them there and got scared shitless, retreating (dropping their weapons and running) a hundred miles and more. But the capital at Vientiane was secure. I was back in Kappas' good graces (?).

To collect the info we had to stay hidden in the bush for a few days and we decided to find a hidey hole near the stream ford Tom Major had mapped. After I changed out of my boots into my Uncle Ho Shoes (tire tread sandals) and we waited for dark it took us a long scary night to get there and find our spot. Overlooking the ford was a stand of hardwoods with a complicated root system (similar to giant cypress knees) reaching twenty-five to thirty feet up and the lower branches of the canopy starting at about thirty feet, with the tree going up to a hundred feet or more to form a top canopy. There was a concave structure at the top of the root system providing cover and an overlook of the ford just big enough for two people at a time, the other three would hide farther up between the canopies and we would rotate watches from the root system.

We had been in place about two hours when we first heard the sound of trucks slowly approaching. The trucks, ten in all and accompanied by men on foot, crawled into view and crossed the ford to come to a stop in an opening under the canopy about fifty meters from our lookout. They began to set up camp and set out perimeter guards and were joined by three more trucks during the day; we were going to be stuck in our tree for a while. Traffic flowed beneath our watch point almost non-stop for the next two days and nights, leaving us on cold rations and no opportunity to comfortably relieve ourselves, the heat rash alone was getting me cranky.

An ELANT (electronic monitoring and counter-measures) bird was scheduled to be over our zone twice in every twenty-four hours and on the third night in our tree house I sent out a message to be relayed to Samuels for decryption and delivery to the Embassy brass that he reported to. I wasn't on the air long enough for anyone to get an accurate triangulation on our position but just signal strength and proximity of enough listeners would give some clever little bastards the information that a broadcast was originating nearby and give them a rough idea where it might be coming from. They would be out with the dogs looking for us soon.

Later that night I was intrigued when I was able to just make out a dark form crossing the stream, stopping at the near edge and gently splashing at the water, then I heard a cough and a growl that made the hair on my neck stand up and my blood freeze – I was looking at a black panther. Even tigers at two or three times their sizes were known to back off from confrontations with these stealthy beasts. It was well known that panthers are superior tree climbers, often dining on monkeys and other life to be found in the forest canopies; was this beauty looking at us as lunch? Because I knew he knew we were there. I swear he was staring straight into my space as he approached the base of our tree, grunted a couple of times, coughed, and had a long, drawn out, smelly piss at the bottom of the root system we were hiding in. Then the dark form glided back across the stream and out of sight, looking back over his shoulder at us just before he disappeared. Later that night I heard a loud roar and a scream from somewhere on the other side of the ford.

A little after first light the next morning, justifying our fears, we heard and saw a security team with three dogs move into the clearing beneath us. As we steeled ourselves for the confrontation sure to come (we didn't have a plan B for getting out of the tree), the dogs began to whine and whimper, then pulled loose from their handlers and disappeared down the trail. The panther urine odor had sent them into a panic!

That damn cat had saved our lives.

Chapter 39

Bo Pen Nyan

Sammy Thonasauvaupat (best I can do to remember his name and the spelling) was a princely fellow. Or more correctly a princeling fellow, he was one of dozens, perhaps hundreds of grandchildren of the last King of Laos, his grandmother had been one of the King's Thai concubines and must have pleased him because he left the family with properties on both sides of the Mekong. I was never able to discover who and where Sammy's father was, or if he was alive or dead but his mother was still residing in a French colonial home in Nong Khai, Thailand across the river from Vientiane. He seemed to have a lot of uncles everywhere in both Laos and Thailand.

Most of Sammy's close relatives were civil servants or military men in both Thailand and Laos and when it became time to pick a career path for him his family chose the Royal Lao Army and he attended a military academy prep school. With the Americans and their Programs Evaluation Office in Laos that would be where the money was so at a young age he was given a position roughly equivalent to the British Subaltern or Midshipman ranks as an officer-to-be. After a year of being errand boy for junior officers he complained to his mother and she petitioned one of his uncles to make him an officer ahead of schedule and find him an assignment whereby some cash might flow into the family coffers.

This teenager on staff with the Lao Royal Army Paymaster was handsome, charming and full of fun. He was also lazy, scheming, and arrogant with anyone he saw as his social inferior; he liked to refer to all the upland peoples as "Kah" meaning "slave" or "subordinate person" (Baphang considered the word a compliment and said it meant "member of the brotherhood in several mountain languages).

Sammy liked to hang out with Americans, I was never sure he recognized we were NCOs and not officers in our civilian attire, and particularly liked

243

smoking their cigarettes; Camels were his favorite but he also liked Lucky Strike and Phillip Morris (filtered Phillip Morris Gold were a better than good substitute for money everywhere we went in Asia). He rarely had anything even approaching duty time and was almost always available as a guide when we were at Wattay and often invited us to his mother's house across the river and accompanied us on excursions to visit friends in Chiang Mai, Thailand.

He learned our English quickly, he'd had previous exposure to the (East) Indian version and taught us a common Lao phrase "bo pen nyan" mostly by accident; it was something he said often. The phrase was a sort of Alfred E. (what me worry?) Newman expression that meant "it don't matter", or sometimes "too bad" or "who cares" and was a good way to demonstrate the usual Lowland Lao lackadaisical attitudes. We would often hear him rattling off in French with Cerone and one or the other would repeat the phrase and they would both laugh loudly and look around to see if anyone else knew what they were talking about. The rest of us picked up on the phrase and used it often; something didn't go just right? "Bo pen nyan". Boots all moldy? "Bo pen nyan". Bad news from home? "Bo pen nyan".

He thought of himself as a lady's man (he was) and a great drinker (he wasn't) and knew he would be a great general someday, just how he was going to accomplish the last part I have no idea, he never spent any time on the range (too noisy), wasn't interested in practicing with small arms of any kind, was bored with artillery tables and would bow out of our morning calisthenics and unarmed combat drills after a few minutes saying, "bo pen nyan" and finding a shady spot for a nap. He was probably right; by Lao standards he was learning all he would need to know (including how to skim the payroll) and had all the right family connections to become a Lao general.

Our own Tom Minor (Thai PARU member of our outfit) was somehow distantly related to Sammy through Sammy's mother but I often got the feeling that the distance was not great enough for "Our Tom". Tom Minor was a serious man in the field and not really a barrel of laughs off duty, thinking back I realize that he was probably never "off duty". Sammy on the other hand never seemed to take anything seriously but was careful not to piss off the older man if it could be avoided.

When we were in the area and the weather was fair Sammy's lovely mother would frequently send us invitations to cross the river and attend one of her informal evening garden parties that she used to promote her family, I think having Americans in attendance somehow added a kind of spice to the mix of Thai, Lao, French, Chinese and Indian businessmen and politicians and other attendees who were regular guests. We would don our best chinos and least loud Hawaiian shirts or guyabera shirts, shave or trim our beards and hair and do our best to make a good impression, usually leaving around midnight to catch the last ferry but sometimes staying over and bunking in hammocks in a sort of screened cottage at the rear of the property.

When we stayed over Sammy's mother would have breakfast with us and the cook would fix several dishes including my favorite; a bowl of thick hand-pulled rice noodles topped with poached eggs, small red peppers and bean sprouts and cilantro as a garnish washed down with a creamy sweet chai, often followed by a cold beer. After all we were guests of her (obviously) favorite child and she wanted to ensure that we enjoyed our visits. Her experiments with something she called "hamburgers" (she had heard they were the Americans favorite food) were not quite as successful; the ingredients were questionable and they never tasted the same twice in a row. If we were to stay for lunch Cerone would half-jestingly start counting the cats on the grounds before meal time.

There would be card games, dice games, and tile games, Samuels's game was in noting who was talking to whom and for how long, but my favorite game was trying to guess which lithesome beauty was which attendee's wife or mistress (I believe Sammy's mother had an introduction service of sorts, or at least provided a venue for wealthy men to meet potential mistresses) and trying to keep track of Sammy's brothers and sisters and numerous cousins, the ladies might change clothes two or three times in an evening and it was hard to keep them sorted, especially after a few drinks.

Jim Thompson, former OSS, on-again, off-again, on-again CIA asset, arms dealer and the man who was bringing back Thailand's silk industry (we heard him called the "Silk King", we called him "One of the Old Asia Hands") was a regular and once remarked that, "In the States I do business on golf courses, here I do business at garden parties and social affairs. Madame Collette's soirees are a great place to meet people and make a deal". He was also a regular at Bill Young's house in Chiang Mai (where the parties were more raucous) and we would occasionally see him in Laos, sometimes accompanied by the mysterious American we christened "Dicky".

On one of our visits to Sammy's mother's home a buddy from Nellis was TDY at Udorn and had arranged to come over to Wattay for a gam so we brought him along for the evening. In a part of the world where 5'6" was taller than average Floyd's 6'5" or so made him a real standout. Few people in the region had seen anyone as big and black as he was and although very few ever stared at him directly, everywhere he went he was, as Cerone put it, "being marveled at". Sammy's mother saw him as a great addition to her party roster and when he came back over for a longer duty assignment at Udorn she kept him on her list and he became a frequent guest at her events. She also decided he needed a wife and would giggle and in her French accent make suggestive comments when she told us she intended to find him one.

Our visits over the river were a welcome relief from the realities we faced in-country in Laos and we sometimes felt we were visiting a movie set or had taken a ride in a time machine. The gracious hospitality we received gave us hope that a genteel civilization really existed somewhere in S.E. Asia.

Sammy pestered, wheedled, and almost begged to go into the field with us on one of our trips to the eastern provinces of Laos, I think more for bragging rights than from any desire to experience whatever it was we did on those trips, but we were able to forestall any such requests simply because he was not jump qualified, our usual means of ingress in a country with few serviceable roads. Every time he brought the subject up Tom Minor would frown at him and look a "No!" in the direction of Samuels and/or Kappas, Sammy had no business in the field and would be a danger to himself and the team.

But he finally got a highly placed relative in FAR (Lao Royal Army) to assign him to accompany the officer in charge of the delivery of a payroll for officers and soldiers who had been in "battle" with the Pathet Lao for several months; lobbing a few shots and the occasional artillery round over each other's heads, a situation that was beginning to change as North Viet Nam sent in NVA and irregular forces to buttress the Pathet Lao.

Sammy was all bright eyed and excited the morning we waited to board the Porter that would fly us in near Luang Prabang (always a dangerous landing site for us) like a kid going on his first carnival ride and told us it was his birthday, obviously this would be a day of great import. I gave him my Zippo lighter that he had always coveted and wished him a "Happy Birthday" as we attempted to strap him into a seat and we were off the ground a few minutes later.

There was always turbulence over the mountains to the north and this morning was no exception. We had gotten in the air early enough to miss the worst of it but the motion was severe enough to give even the experienced passengers un-easy stomachs, for Sammy it was torture and we could see the bright-eyed joy and enthusiasm fading fast. I gave him some soda crackers to hold on his tongue and to his credit he was able to keep his breakfast down and didn't engage in too much whining or complaining.

From the air the area we were going into looked like the colors and texture of the hide of a piebald horse; dense rain forest spotted with brown, bald hills and mountain tops, the result of years of over-timbering and slash and burn agriculture. We would be landing at a doglegged

Victor Site (later called a Lima Site) on one of the bald spots between two forested ridges and could see our greeting party already waiting on the rodent-potted field. The pilot changed prop pitch, pulled power and set his flaps in one continuous motion as we turned short final and prepared to land. We were on the ground and almost at a stop when the hole appeared in the fuselage just above the pilot's head. Sniper fire was common here and for our pilot getting on and off the ground at this site was just SOP. Made us nervous though and we got out of the tin can as quickly as we could, our waiting party had already taken cover.

Cerone pulled and I pushed and we hustled Sammy into cover while Tom Minor, Hayes, and Blaske helped the payroll officers to a secure spot then began to maneuver to find and deal with the sniper or snipers. The ground party was able to point out the general location the fire had come from and Tom Minor and Hayes began to play hedgehog, moving brush and exposing just enough of themselves to try to draw fire without getting hit so that Blaske could get in position and zero in on where the fire was coming from. Nerve racking game, I was fine with the fact that it was not my turn in the barrel (my turn to draw fire) and satisfied to lie next to Cerone in a tree lined hollow where we could see without exposing ourselves, Sammy prone in the grass under a tree just to our rear. I had time to almost feel sorry for whoever was out there being stalked by our three deadly hunters.

The plane started it's take off run and we all watched the surrounding green carefully but the sniper did not chance a shot and it disappeared over a mound to the south without incident. The boys would take their time playing the stalking game and for the three of us in the hollow the plan would be to stay alert and quiet until we got an all clear. Patience and discipline would win the day.

Blaske had narrowed down the possibilities and was carefully watching the green where he suspected the sniper was hiding. He was gratified to see his analysis was spot on when the sniper fired again at a target back up the field and he was able to take the shot, watching the sniper's body slump and slide from a small brushy promontory he had been watching.

Tom Minor and Hayes gingerly approached the position and found the sniper's body; she had taken a clean shot directly through the throat. They removed her ID book and a snapshot of her posing with another young girl, both dressed in pressed white and black school uniforms.

Right before we heard the first shot Cerone and I had heard the "ping" of a Zippo lighter opening and smelled the odor of a cigarette (goddamn Sammy, we never smoked in the field, a sure way to give away your position) and turned to see him sitting up leaning one shoulder on a tree and smiling with smoke coming out of both nostrils just before we were sprayed with bone, blood, and grey matter.

Sammy Thonasauvaupat was eighteen the day his head exploded, the girl who killed him around the same age. When his kinsman Tom Minor saw the body his eyes turned a soft, wet brown and the lines around his mouth deepened, he would have to be the one to tell Sammy's mother. For now there was work to be done and we were all still in a dangerous position, we needed to get moving.

As he turned away from Sammy's body there was a sound something like a sob and we heard him softly saying, "Bo pen nyan".

Chapter 40

One Cold Morning

Sanchez was pissed off, he was mutha' fucking mad at those MAAG maggot assholes and startled everyone when he stormed into the riverside den where they were having a late morning break and kicked a chair out of the way as he headed for the corner where Samuels and Kappas were playing a quiet game of gin.

To see the unflappable (we thought) Sanchez stomping around mumbling a string of obscenities was strange enough to start them all following him to the corner; until he turned around and glowered at them. They couldn't hear what he was saying to their leaders but watched and saw Samuels's lips go thin and the skin around his eyes tighten while Kappas' eyes turned into the black agate they all knew meant trouble.

Sanchez had somehow gotten an advance peek at the report on our activities of the past few months, and the evaluation of the results of those efforts, that the Military Assistance Advisory Group was sending forward up the chain of command with recommendations.

While Sanchez was displaying his temper and disgust down on the Mekong Plain I had my scarf over my mouth and with teeth chattering was trying to prevent the moisture cloud from my breath from giving away my position. I was lying in a spot that on an earlier, much warmer visit had been covered by tall lush green grasses. Now the dry season grass was brown and brittle with sharp edges ready to open any bare skin that came in contact with them. Any movement Tom Minor or I might make would be accompanied by a loud rustling noise and a wave of motion in the grass tops. Even our shivering in the unexpected cold wind from the north could mean the enemy would know we were there.

They had almost caught us unaware; we had not expected to see any Pathet Lao up this high in the mountains and had gotten no warning from any local tribesmen that the twenty or so men on little shaggy jug-headed ponies were near. We had been out in the open when our Mei guide had warned us with a bird whistle that something was amiss just before we heard the muffled sounds of unshod hooves and blowing horses. No time to make the safety of the deep forest, we had sprinted into an area that had been clear cut years before and was now filled with almost leafless small trees, scrub brush, and the tall dead grasses we were using for cover, our guide disappearing into the taller trees in the opposite direction.

Usually the Pathet Lao stayed at lower elevations leaving the higher ground to the mountain tribes; their presence probably meant there were North Vietnamese of some ilk lurking nearby potentially adding another element to our predicament. As I lay there with a stone digging into my thigh and the cold earth under me sucking calories out of my body two problems, besides the need to stay hidden, were at the forefront of my mind.

We were up in the high ground waiting to meet a two-man survey team who would be coming in later in the day by Helio Courier to look over the clearing that had been grubbed out for a landing strip on a narrow bench on the mountainside and we had no way to warn them off except one short range, line of sight radio. If it came to it we would have to expose ourselves to wave the plane off before it landed and then fight our way to safety, there would never be any consideration of surrendering.

The other problem facing us was not a new one, but our need to stay hidden did give it an added dimension. Water.

In Laos there was always either too much water or not enough water and never much of it drinkable for someone who had not been reared on it (the locals were not always immune to the pathogens and parasites in the water either), we had to boil it before consumption and usually added a few leaves to make a weak tea before we drank it.

During the wet season a small rill could become a roaring torrent in the time it took to cross a stream bed, everything stayed wet or at least damp and people tended to get grouchy after a couple of weeks of having their boots or sandals sucked on (or off) by the muddy roads and trails. The only advantage to the rainy season was the fact that the Pathet Lao and the Vietnamese enemy did not like to move about in the wet and the mud that did not bother our tribal allies all that much. Air operations got a little trickier but regular flights were still made carrying supplies and ferrying troops around the mountains.

During the dry season perils particular to the limestone mountains injured a few unwary people and animals every year; solid looking flat rock surfaces in dry streambeds had often been undercut during the rainy season leaving a thin limestone shell over an empty space with a nasty fall for whomever or whatever broke through, and trees that had had their root systems undercut during the rains could suddenly come crashing down without warning. As Cerone put it, "This is a land that is always coming up with new ways to maim or kill a guy". For Hayes it was all a part of the "they" that were out to get us.

Laying up in the tall grass and waiting to see how our situation would develop we were subjected to a cold dry air that was going to dehydrate us quickly, we needed to back out carefully without shaking the grasses to even get to a place where we could drink from our canteens and then we would need to replenish the water in them soon. A fire to boil water (if there was any to be found in the streambed below our position) was totally out of the question; even using heat tabs would be risky with the steam plume and odor that might be detected by an alert patrol. It was going to be a thirsty day.

Landing sites, originally called "Victor Sites" but now called "Lima Sites" were being grubbed out all over Laos to facilitate airborne movement of men and supplies, primarily to the highlands, and eventually there would be between 180 and 190 named and/or numbered sites (example: Lima Site 20A). Well over a hundred other sites were prepped but rarely or never used and went unnamed and unnumbered and it was hard to keep track of where they were and what condition they were in. On our mission on this trip up country Hayes and I and our PARU team mates were to locate and map some newly cleared sites and then guide in and assist survey teams and we had split up before dawn to work two sites about 8 klicks (kilometers) apart, planning to rendezvous at the strip Hayes was working before sunset.

The BOGs (Blue, Orange, and Greens) were enthused about the program because we expected/hoped the strips would be used as part of a rapid deployment and re-supply for aggressive actions against the traffic on the Ho Chi Minh Trail, the key to defeating the enemy in both Laos and Viet Nam.

We had already used some of the sites to get in and out of border areas where the Trail came across high passes from North Viet Nam into Laos and had used our "Phantom Air Force" in conjunction with a few of Vang Pao's Mei (Hmong)irregulars to successfully ambush the NVA, PAVN, Viet Minh and their porters at supply depots; killing hundreds of men and destroying tons of supplies and equipment, it would take weeks for the enemy to recover and re-supply in the two places we hit at chokepoints of the supply route. Our tactics had caused a lot of damage to the enemy in terms of both men and material lost and the morale of their troops at a very low cost in men, munitions, and dollars on our side.

We felt that we had demonstrated that we could successfully, "cut 'em off at the passes!" but the politicians, that is the politically oriented military men who commanded MAAG and whomever they reported to, were not happy with our efforts. The operational planning, permission from the Embassy (the US Embassy in Laos had to approve all air missions in the country), and execution of the plans had not originated or been carried out under the MAAG flag and at the instigation of the Embassy they had not been in the information loop until after the raids were fait accompli. Just the idea that a small sheep dipped Air Force unit orphaned when the PEO (Programs Evaluation Office) was closed down, and whose members had probably "gone native", could, with the help of a few mercenaries and a couple of Special Forces NCOs, be allowed the planning, command, and control of an offensive strike was enough to give a few officers apoplexy. "And where in the hell did they get that air support?" " And who left those fucking civilians in Vientiane in charge of this war?"

The report they were forwarding to the Pentagon suggested that we had done minimal damage to the enemy (this despite the evidence in the photographs Sanchez had taken), had "only created a six-day delay at one spot on the enemy's supply route", and had put the cities on the Mekong Plain at risk by pulling needed troops from the defense of those cities. They recommended that the ground resources needed to harass and interdict (H&I) the supply caravans would be put to better use protecting the Lowlands and that all future H&I could be better managed from the air (only). It looked like Captain Samuels's Operational Reports were buried and would never go up the military chain of command.

What a crock, we had used less than one hundred men including pilots, loaders and aircraft service personnel, dispatchers and ground troops and had caused a major portion of the damage to the enemy by blowing up his own munitions.

This was all bad enough but Sanchez had even more disgruntling news: Air operations based out of South Vietnam had started dropping chemicals over a wide area of Laos to the north of Muang Nong, ostensibly to deny cover and food sources to the enemy bringing supplies down from the north but with a more sinister back motive, the planners of the operation wanted to force the populace in the country into the cities and towns so they could be more easily watched and controlled. The story released to the American news correspondents included the statement that, "nobody lives there anyway" a lie that was extended later when the mass bombings and planting of air delivered land mines began.

The reality was that the area was occupied by friends, allies, and intelligence assets we had been cultivating since our first visit to the country; all the chemical defoliation, poisoning of water sources, and spoiling of food crops was going to result in was clearing the area for the benefit of our enemies. Once this part of Laos with its numerous caves, proximity to the passes into South Vietnam, and wrinkled topography was rid of its pesky vermin natives (the Viet Minh viewpoint) it would be (and became) the perfect place for building logistics support facilities. One huge depot impervious to air raids and out-of-bounds for ground assaults.

And in an ugly twist of irony the chemical agent used to defoliate the jungle canopy was called "Agent Orange"; the chemical agent used to destroy food crops was called "Agent Blue".

But Tom Minor and I didn't know any of that as we waited, barely breathing, for the men on the little ponies to trot off before making our way out of the grasses and into a jumble of windfall beside a trail the width of a man's shoulders. The forest noises hadn't come back and we stayed still waiting for the sounds and rhythms to return to normal.

The first black clad man in a six-man patrol coming from the direction of the field where Hayes and New PARU were working was betrayed by the sounds of his rubber soled "Uncle Ho" sandals on the dry mud and stone trail. As he neared our position out of the corner of my eye I saw Tom Minor melt into the bamboo cane break in front of the windfall, no chance to move where I was now standing, the rustle of dry leaves would give me away. I froze in position and tried hard to think like a tree.

I stood stock still, wondering if my camtec and charcoal paint job was covering all the white of my face and neck and ears and trying again to keep my entire exhale in my scarf as the first five men passed close enough that I could have reached out and pinched their cheeks. As the last man came directly in front of my spot his head swiveled in my direction and I tensed, hand on the hilt of my kukuhiri ready to chop at his throat the instant his eyes registered that he had seen me. Then two Muntjac (small funny looking deer with goat like antlers and protruding canine teeth) broke from the grasses where Tom Minor and I had laid up just a short time before and the man in front of me swung his head to see what had caused the noise and commotion in the patrol ahead of him. Mountain wildlife had just saved me for a second time up on the Trail.

By the time all our unwelcome visitors had cleared the area the sky was too bright for me to get any star sights and fix the position of the field, I would have to wait for evening twilight, or maybe until the next morning. For the rest of the morning there was nothing for us to do except follow our guide to a fresh running spring and eat, hydrate, and refill our canteens.

We were back at a hidden spot that gave us an unobstructed view of the landing site and waiting for the Helio Courier to arrive and I was thinking that "we had had a pretty good day all considered, we hadn't been killed and we hadn't had to kill anyone" when we spotted New PARU and a local coming out of the edge of the clearing followed by a hatless Hayes carrying two large bundles, one in his arms and the other attached to the back straps of his web gear where his rucksack should have been.

As they got closer I could see that New PARU was carrying Hayes's weapon and that Hayes's hair had been charred and his eyebrows were gone. What the fuck? Over.

Chapter 41

The Wraiths

The six men had traveled at a slow, tedious pace all through the cold night halting often to look and listen for other travelers in the dark and now were having a welcome rest in a tiny sunrise lit glen. They had scooped out a spot where they could fill their water bladders one at a time in a small trickling stream that would have been a roaring river just a few weeks before. Two men worked to fill the bladders and a dozen canteens, three sat at ease in the red morning sunlight on the stream bank just downstream, and the sixth man stood guard with an automatic rifle. They were in no great hurry to finish filling the containers and rejoin their main unit waiting a half klick uphill from the stream.

When the green and black striped wraiths suddenly appeared out of the dense foliage swinging dark knives almost invisible in the twilight the guard was first to die. In less than a minute five of the men were dead and one unconscious, awaking a few minutes later to find his knees and ankles tied together hands bound behind his back and a stick laced through his elbows, another stick, rag wrapped, tied in his mouth by a cord running around his head and neck. Another cord encircled his neck in a slip knot with the long end passing through the bindings on his knees and legs then tied to the partly pulled pin of a grenade lodged under a root just in front of his sitting position and buried under some dead leaves and grass; if he moved the pin would be pulled the rest of the way out, spoon fly off, and grenade explode.

He sat, cramped and terrified that he would topple over or start to shake, sweat running down his brow and evaporating in icy streams in the cold dry air, then watched in horror when three men from his detachment appeared on the path coming down the hill, no way to warn them of the three shadowy forms that emerged on the trail behind them. He wanted to scream but could only make a grunting sound as the dark knives sliced through bodies again and three more of his companions were dead, their weapons carried off into the dark green and brown beside the path.

The day before a grandmother, her daughter, and the daughters' two children were working their way to the southwest when they stopped at the abandoned village to scrounge for food and find shelter off the ground for the night, in the morning they would be able to catch and cook one or two of the half wild chickens running around the compound and perhaps find a small cache of rice in one of the huts. They were awakened before dawn by the sound of a cock crowing, then squawking, and a low murmur of men moving about. Peering out of the latticed walls they could see perhaps fifty men milling around and talking in a language the women could not understand. Fearful, the women very carefully lifted a panel in the floor of the hut they had been sleeping in and lowered the two children down into an animal enclosure below them then made themselves as small as possible while they waited in dark corners of the room for the men outside to go away.

Hayes was standing in the pre-dawn light under a clear sky and had just finished taking observations with a bubble sextant of four of the fifty-two navigational stars listed in the HO249 Star Tables when he smelled the smoke.

Scanning the area around his position he identified thin tendrils of a whitish smoke rising in the direction of an abandoned Khamu village three or four klicks away. Looking to his right and left he saw that New PARU and their local asset were looking in the same direction. Wordlessly, he packed his equipment away and the three men hoisted their 'rucks and began a stealthy approach to the abandoned village site. They needed to know what was going on in the neighborhood before they got any surprise visits from un-friendlies.

The three of them watched the men in the village from a concealed spot a safe distance away and saw them pull the two women out of one of the raised huts not yet ablaze. And watched grim faced, stony eyed and helpless, the odds were too long and the timing wrong for them to be able to help, as the women were raped and beaten and thrown limp and lifeless back into the hut they had been dragged from. They continued to watch while the remaining village huts were fired and the men in the tan/green uniforms moved off in one direction and a patrol sized group in black moved off in another.

Hayes thought he saw movement in the stock pen under the hut the women's bodies had been tossed in and when he looked at New PARU got a nod; something was alive in the pen, probably pigs. Then he heard a scream and thinking that one or both of the women might be still alive ran toward the village at an angle that offered concealment from the departing troops. Reaching the hut, he took the three steps up and tried to enter but was forced back by a wall of flame and jumped back to the ground to look for another way in and saw two small people in the pen under the hut trying to get out.

He kicked at the wood and bamboo slats until he got an opening in the pen and grabbed at the sides of the hole he had made pulling the enclosure apart with his hands until he was able to reach in and pull out two wide eyed children, New PARU taking them one at a time from his grasp and beating out the fire and embers in their clothing, the local tribesman standing over to the side watching up the trail, weapon at the ready. New PARU grabbed Hayes's hat and swept it off his head, it was on fire, and pulled him back with a tug on his shoulder; the hut was fully engulfed in flame, there would be no survivors inside.

Back in a place of concealment the three men gave the children water and tried to offer comfort, holding them tight and patting them gently, until sure they wouldn't try to run when released.

Concerned that the patrol that had peeled off from the main group of NVA or PAVN was moving in the direction of the site where two of his teammates were working Hayes tried to raise them on the small field radio he was carrying for this assignment. No luck, his mates were on the other side of a ridge and the batteries in his radio were low, he would move in their direction and hope for the best.

After coaxing the kids into eating a small meal of sticky rice balls and tinned sardines, the little party started working uphill away from the burned-out village, the kids keeping a surprisingly good pace before they tired on the downhill slope about five klicks from the field Hayes was making for. Anxious to keep moving, Hayes stripped his rucksack from his web gear, stuffing a few essentials in his pockets, and handed off his BAR for New PARU to carry, then loading up the local Mei with his extra ammunition had New PARU lift one child onto his pack frame and picked the other up in his arms.

It was well after noon when they stopped to rest and water, eating another small parcel of sticky rice balls and something from a tin can labeled "Lima Beans and Ham". Not feeling refreshed, but at least hydrated, Hayes reloaded his burdens and began double timing the short distance toward his goal, New PARU scouting ahead and the Mei bringing up the rear.

After a happy reunion with his team mates, sooo glad to see you alive, and a quick conference, Hayes set off with Tom Minor and the two local guides; they would track the Viet Minh patrol that had passed by earlier following them through the night. New PARU would stay with the kids that were clinging to him (he had a smattering of their language and could understand some of what they said) on a flight out in the Helio Courier that had just landed with a survey team and Hayes's other team member would fly out as well, returning early next morning with supplies and more people.

The man sat chilled by his own sweat with a sun that offered hardly any heat on his back and waited for someone to come. His inner elbows were chaffed and his shoulders ached with a dark red pain that threatened to make him scream, except he was gagged and bound and couldn't make any loud noises.

He fought to keep the pain down and stay conscious enough that he wouldn't fall over and set off the explosive device at his feet, focusing on half-awake dreams of his former life and of being warm again, it had never gotten this cold on his parents' farm.

He sat hoping that someone from the unit he was attached to would realize that he and his five companions had not rejoined the larger group, or that someone would wonder what had happened to the three men he had watched slaughtered on the trail in front of him. Spurts of raw terror coursed through his entire body every time his cramping legs started to tremble as he fought to stay still and keep upright.

He thought he heard the familiar sounds of AK47s in the distance, and a lower slower beat that he couldn't recognize, but it might have just been his imagination, or the rising breeze playing tricks.

A rustling and a shuffling sound behind him brought a new realization and a new fear, there was a heavy smell of blood in the air and hungry beasts abounded here high in the mountains. Here were big cats, bears, and most fearsome of all to him, wild pigs. All would smell the blood from a long way off and be attracted to the scent. If wild pigs came he would jerk the cord around his neck and set off the grenade at his feet as the gruesome alternative to being eaten alive.

A movement flickered at the edge of his vision, and then a figure came into view filling him with a strange mixture of dread and relief.

The wraiths were back.

Chapter 42

Morrison's Deal

Hayes took my hat, my M14 and all my ammunition, both of my canteens, my two grenades, my partner for this assignment, Tom Minor, and both of our local Mei guides and disappeared down a narrow trail to the south saying over his shoulder just before going out of sight, "I'll leave sign for you to follow if I'm not back here by noon tomorrow".

Leaving me to board a Helio Courier with Hayes's BAR and New PARU and with two black eyed, bowl haircut boys that looked like twins, or at least siblings no more than a year apart, clinging to New PARU and looking about wildly as they were ushered (pushed) into the aircraft. Except they weren't boys, as we discovered when we got back to Wattay and tried to clean them up.

We learned later that their mother and grandmother had taken away the coin decorated headdresses and heavily embroidered clothes that the girls usually wore and cut their hair and dressed them in a plain boy style to help protect them while they traveled. Their young woman clothing had been left behind in the burning animal shelter where Hayes had found them.

Language presented a problem, New PARU could understand only part of what the children said and they did not seem able to understand much of what he was telling them, not surprising in a country with at least four root languages split into one-hundred-thirty or so tribal variations. Based on where Hayes found them we could (perhaps) assume they would be from a tribe in the Miao-Yao speaking group, which narrowed the problem down to forty or fifty likely tribal variations. Luckily Morrison and one of Dr. Weldon's nurse/interpreters were on hand to bring on the scene and gently coax them out of the corner they had hastily retreated to when we tried to salve their burned skin and give them baths.

Whatever the nurse said and the sight of Morrison's kind, crooked face calmed them down, especially after the nurse reassured them with speech and pantomime that Hayes (their savior) would be back to see to them in a couple of days; meanwhile they should eat and rest, the French (generic for all white foreigners) would protect them from harm until he got back.

Morrison wasn't exactly ugly, but he was far from handsome, his face looked somehow like it had been taken apart and reassembled by someone who was not completely sure where all the parts fit. One eye was higher than the other; his nose had a mid-slope bump that slid off to one side while his mouth twisted a little in the opposite direction. But he had bright eyes and a big, big smile and was always humming or singing softly when dealing with children. The overall effect was that of a big happily used, slightly threadbare teddy bear with perhaps one button eye a little loose. We had all witnessed him chiding, cajoling, and joking kids (who may not have understood a word he said) into taking vaccinations with smiles instead of tears.

A "stoked" California surfer stuck in a land-locked country Morrison had kids and some of the local ladies going around uttering (twittering) things like, "Cow-A-Bunga Buffalo Bob" (never did figure out what that phrase had to do with surfing), "Big Kahuna", "Hoo Daddy", and "The Ninth Wave". And eventually he had people all over Laos going around calling each other "Dude". The first English exchange some of the locals learned was the question, "How's the weather?" answered by, "Surf's up, Dude!" followed by peals of laughter.

While the handsome Cerone made friends everywhere we went with a smooth charm, Morrison won people over with warmth and enthusiasm; far from being what would later be called a "hippie", he could be one tough, mean sumbitch when he needed to be, but he genuinely loved people and was never really happy in the field where violence (some of it ours) lurked.

When we got out of the Helio Courier at Wattay we had skipped stopping at the operations shack and took the kids directly to the little noodle house northwest of the field where the Blue Team stayed; I was hoping to delay talking to Kappas until I could decide what I was going to say about Hayes staying in the field and the baggage I had brought back with me. No soap, the First Sergeant was at the door less than half an hour after Morrison had started feeding the kids and wanted to know just exactly what we were doing up in the mountains to the east, forgetting our primary mission, running a refuge rescue operation? What? What? What?

Somehow, in the First Sergeant's view, I was the party responsible for the whole cluster fuck, despite the fact that Hayes had rescued them and that they (the kids) adopted Morrison as their favorite uncle during the next few days, I was the one that brought them into our company on the Helio Courier, they were my problem. As if I had had any choice in the matter, was I going to just leave them in the bush? Did anyone on the planet believe I could tell Hayes what to do when he was in a "mood"?

My original plan had been to take them to Long Chien and deposit them there in Pop Buell's refugee camp, now swelling with thousands of people, mostly women and young children fleeing the mountains while their men were off somewhere training or fighting (or dead). But I just was not able to bring myself to dump two relative-less, pre-pubescent young girls into a place where they would have no protection and might get lost in the swarm.

Morrison gave me a cold dash of reality when he reminded me that the most likely future for these un-protected kids would be for them to wind up in one of the many brothels at Long Chien or in Wattay at "The White Rose" or "Lulu's House of Specialties", or worse. He was not going to let that happen and what was I planning to do about them? They were following him around like ducklings chasing their mama and even he was pretending to make them my responsibility the minute I came back from my next few days in the field. Hayes just snorted and winked when I told him they were his problem. Kappas didn't let up and although he never gave me any specific instructions about what to do with them he would ask me, "What are you doing about your pets?" at least once a day; meanwhile he was teaching them to play checkers.

But while everyone was making noises about the kids being my responsibility the reality was that they were becoming Morrison's mission, he began dedicating all his determination (stubbornness) to finding a way to keep them safe. His first step was to make an effort to find family or at least tribal affiliations among the refugees but that became a futile effort and we reached the sad conclusion that the girls probably belonged to one of the small mountain tribes that been driven to extinction (there were many) by the "troubles" in the northern and northeast provinces.

As Morrison looked at it there were four options available for the girls; turn them over to Pop Buell's camp and hope for the best, send them to the mother of our dead friend from Thailand where they could perhaps join her pool of servants, find Baphang and ask him to include them in his family, or find a way to get them to the United States of America.

He analyzed the options (or pretended to) and came up with these conclusions (a bottle of Beefeaters and a few liters of Lucky Lager was consumed while he debated with himself, we were in the room but not allowed to interrupt his monologue): the first option was the quickest and easiest, just take them to the camp and drop them off. Don't look back and see the fright and disappointment on their faces as you walk away (no volunteers for that one). He just couldn't picture leaving them in a life as servants and second-class citizens in Thailand so that ruled out the second option. Where in the hell was Baphang anyway, we hadn't heard from him since he began moving his family out of the Bolaven Plateau and into Thailand. "We" (waddaya mean "we") would just have to get them to the States.

And not just smuggle them over the pond, get them there with legal status and in a good home where they would have a chance at a safe life away from war zones, where they could get an education and have the possibilities of becoming mothers and even grandmothers themselves (Goddammit).

Samuels helped by putting Morrison in front of the person at the Embassy who needed to be nagged about US entry visas and our friend Sammy's mother had the girls as guests at one of her evening garden parties across the river where she pled their case to some senior American officials, she also arranged to have the girls declared orphans and given official permission to leave the country by some minister in the Lao government.

Bill Young contacted someone in the Baptist Overseas Ministries located in Oklahoma (I think) and they came up with a family in California that would be happy to sponsor the girls and provide them housing until they could be adopted or put into a permanent foster home.

Morrison had one more resource he was loathe to use but he put aside a few years of resentment and unhappiness and made the calls he needed to make to his father. His father agreed to help based on certain conditions and after extracting a promise from his son and assured that they had a deal put his political connections (he was a well-known surgeon and political contributor, and frequently spoke at political events) in the mix and provided an immigration attorney who would insure the girl's legal status, then later trumped that move by finding a couple in Orange County, California who would love to adopt the girls.

Kappas got orders cut for Morrison to take a leave and accompany the girls on the long voyage hopping across the Pacific and on to their new lives. Morrison's dad picked up the costs of the trip and would be waiting at the airport in Los Angeles to meet them.

The stage was set, the play ready to be put in motion - the two little girls would get their shot at the "American Dream".

Chapter 43

Twilight

It was always twilight deep in the ancient, three canopy forest where Hayes and Sanchez were hunting with their Cao Dai and Yao tribesmen allies. During the daylight hours sunlight would penetrate the thick cover here and there in a random pattern with hazy shafts of light tricking the eye and confusing depth perception. These shafts of light could make it seem to an observer's eyes that the space under the tall hardwood trees was open when in fact the screen of smaller trees and ground hugging broadleaf plants reduced visibility to five or ten meters or less along the main routes through the forest, on the lesser routes the openings between the plant life was often barely shoulder wide.

Even during the day colors were sucked up by the gloom, a brilliant red and gold flash of a bird passing through a shaft of light would turn dull and grey as the bird moved out of the light and the only colors left in the forest after its passing were a dark, dark green, black, a rusty red and many shades of grey.

At night, when the moon was not up, the phosphorescence from rotting vegetation could create an eerie, dim light that coupled with the almost constant rustling of dead leaves by passing small animals, insects, and reptiles, made even the most hardened skeptic believe that there could be ghosts walking the trails. The occasional crash or thump caused by a large animal (or was it something else?), a loud screaming bird call, or a cursing monkey only adding to the unease people felt as they struggled to stay on the trails in the gloomy darkness.

It could be somehow even scarier when the moon was up, the moonlight that made it through the canopy making dark spots darker and silvering a tree trunk here, a patch of fern there, tricking peripheral vision into seeing motion where there was none. Maybe.

The people from the low coastal plains of North Viet Nam were familiar with the patches of thick jungle abutting their rice paddies, fields, and villages, but here in the highlands it was different; different sights, sounds, and smells, and the dense foliage was unrelenting, they could walk for days without ever seeing a clear path to the sky, day or night. And someone or something was killing them, then leaving unseen. They began to whisper among themselves in low frightened tones about ghosts and demons; some claimed to have seen "Yeu Quy" (Ghost Demons) at their awful work but would not speak aloud about what they had seen when political cadre members or officers were in earshot for fear of stern reprimands or even punishment; but still the whispers spread.

The Ho Chi Minh Trail was more than a series of interlinking roads that made up a broad highway; it was a long spread out, sprawling city with many characteristics and features of any big metropolis, there were roadway builders and maintenance workers, traffic directors, public kitchens and baths, infirmaries and hospitals and midwifes (some babies were born in the city). Under trees and in caves and tunnels there were rest stops and food stops, caravansaries, entertainment centers, commissaries, and materiel storage and distribution centers. At any time there were porters, soldiers, police, truck drivers, mechanics, animal handlers, cooks, tailors, and an entire range of people and professions in the city; paramount among them the political cadres that gave lectures every day to keep morale high and keep the people in the megalopolis focused on the work they were doing.

These political officers just naturally became favorite targets of the Hayes/Sanchez/Tom Minor team, "nail one of them in the middle of a lecture and you scared the shit out of everyone around them". The places where people would gather for their evening meals were easy to predict and the political officers giving their lectures were easy to spot at these sites; they were the ones standing and talking and looking important. A single shot would come, report and echo swallowed by the dense forest, then a dead lecturer and silence. "Welcome to the Twilight Zone" as Rod

Serling would say (the host of a popular television show of the time back in the States).

But the political officers weren't the only targets, no one was safe. Singly, in small groups, or even in company sized units they would suddenly and brutally be attacked, the raiders disappearing soundlessly into the twilight just as abruptly as they had appeared, never staying for a pitched battle or seeming to attempt to claim any objective, just spreading death and fear and vanishing. Like ghosts.

As the whispers spread about ghosts in a certain section of the trail/city, an area beginning to be referred to as "Cai Chet Nui" (Death Mountain) by the whisperers, security forces comprised of NVA Sappers and dog handlers and their tribal assets (not all Mei or Hmong sided with Vang Pao and his irregulars, many, notably those from the Red River drainage, sided with the North Vietnamese) were dispatched to rid the mountains of these pests, whoever or whatever they were, and quell the rumors.

Hayes and Sanchez and their team had often been tracked by the Viet Cong cadres and NVA regular force patrols and had made a game of eluding the searchers, ambushing them at every opportunity, but the Sapper security forces and their dogs and mountain tribe trackers presented a new set of problems and in the beginning they avoided any contact with them.

The NVA Sappers were particularly bad-ass, trained in part by Viet Cong and the left-over-from WWII, un-repatriated Japanese training contingent in North Viet Nam; they were highly motivated seasoned professionals similar in operational scope and philosophy to the US Army Special Forces and other elite forces. These were the guys who would slide in under concertina wire at night and generally do scary stuff; it was said of them that, like big predator cats, if eye contact was made or they thought they had been seen they would attack without pause. They were definitely a bad-ass bunch; jungle warriors with a kamikaze attitude.

On a break from their "field exercises" back at a well-hidden base camp Hayes and Sanchez and company began to plot about what to do with the ten-man sapper security squads and their trackers and dogs in "their" territory, should they roll up and leave, continue to avoid contact, stop the guerilla terror attacks and go back to the primary mission of survey and observation and reporting of enemy strength and movements? Should they stay hidden and continue to coordinate the occasional air ambush, or just cede the territory to the North Vietnamese Army (NVA)?

Hayes had been feeling an unfettered new freedom operating with no supervision or limits in the high country and Sanchez was just doing what he was paid to do in his chosen profession (I suppose). The slight-of-stature, calm faced Tom Minor was one of those people it was dangerous to piss off, if angered he would come after you and when you were dead go after your whole damn family – and the North Vietnamese had done something somewhere in the past to really piss him off. Besides, it was protocol at the time that all Westerners operating in-country had to be accompanied by a member of the Thai PARU, if Hayes and Sanchez stayed in action he would be duty bound (?) to stay with them as long as they stayed in the field.

The Cao Dai, a philosophy and religion rather than a tribe (most of them had come from Viet Nam), and the Yao tribesmen who lived in the mountains where the raids were being performed, their families all relocated or dead, or worse conscripted as laborers by the NVA, hated the Viet Cong and North Vietnamese with a smoldering passion, they would stay and fight as long as they could draw a breath.

It was an easy consensus, they would trap and kill the security teams that were trying to find and kill them.

Hayes had designed the "treeland 'tigues" they wore up in the high elevations, sage green fatigues with broad green and black vertical stripes interspersed with a few thinner rust red vertical stripes and random darker green and rust blobs, he had extra sets made up for the Cao Dai when they weren't wearing black pajamas to blend in with enemy Viet Cong (a tactic they used often). The Yao that worked and fought beside him remained dressed in loin cloths over short pants, but also wore the long sleeve shirts he provided. Dressed in these treeland 'tigues and with camtec painted face and hands and a floppy dark green hat with a couple of sprigs in the headband a wearer easily became invisible in the forest background.

He also supplied knives of my friend Baphang's design and manufacture, an eighteen-inch blade as thick as or thicker than a Bowie knife, half leaf shaped, chisel honed edge, and a handle at about a six degree angle to the tip. An eight inch section across the curved top was hollow ground razor sharp and the center of mass was about six inches forward of the full tang riveted wooden handle. A deadly weapon that could easily slice meat off bone or cut through both meat and bone, it only took guidance and speed and the knife would do the work to take off a head with one swipe. I once witnessed Baphang behead a water buffalo with one easy swing of one of his knives.

Hayes foreswore his Browning Automatic Rifle (BAR) and the only automatic weapons they used on their highland raids were Chinese made AK 47s taken from the enemy. Sanchez carried a M1917A1 Springfield 30.06 with a Weaver scope and Tom Minor an old, ugly British Lee-Enfield .303 with open sights, Hayes said T.M. could hit a moving butterfly with it at one hundred yards; both rifles could be fired through improvised sound and flash suppressors of our armorers' design. In addition to M1911 Colt Auto side arms both Hayes and Sanchez carried a .22 caliber Colt Woodsman with sound suppressors and wrapped with rubber electrical tape to muffle the noise from the actions. Tom Minor stuck with his suppressed Browning Highpower.

In the field everyone on "Team Blue Squared" (TBS or Tango Bravo Sierra, it could also stand for "Team Bull Shit") as Hayes named it carried an additional knife or two, K-Bars and F&S stilettos were favorites, at least two grenades of Chinese manufacture, a guitar string garrote with weighted wooden handles, and the Yao usually packed an M1 Garand and a crossbow.

Good weaponry for the stalk and kill raids they had been pulling off but they would need something a little heavier to take on the sapper security teams that were hunting them now, and some careful planning and painstaking preparation would be needed; stay within the "one slow, four quick" dictum.

"One slow" meant they would take the time to very carefully plan and prepare for whatever action they were going to take and after somber deliberation they came up with a simple plan, but one that would take a lot of preparation, based on previous experience and "gut feelings" they were sure the Sappers would try to herd them into a closed area, bring in additional regular NVA to encircle them and then rain down boatloads of over kill; the smart thing to do. They would let the Sappers trap them, at least to outward appearances, but first they would have to pick the terrain where they would allow themselves to be "surrounded", and then prep the area as a killing zone.

TBS had a definite home turf advantage, the Cao Dai had been living and fighting in the area for years and the Yao, hunters and trackers nonpareil, had grown up knowing every wrinkle, roadway and game trail in their mountains; no matter how good the trackers were that the NVA brought, the Yao would be able to confuse and frustrate them. And the Yao were accustomed to dealing with animals of all kinds, they did not think that dogs were a very big problem, if the dogs stayed on leases they would slow down the pursuers and leave a broad noise trail, if the dogs were loosed the Yao would trap and kill them; maybe eat them later. Hayes was not so sure and the dogs worried him but he decided to "trust the little fuckers" (he said affectionately).

For three weeks there were no assassinations, no raids on the traffic on the Trail, TBS wanted this part of the mountains to stay calm while they were busy, busy setting animal traps and laying mines and explosives at strategic points. After a few trips back to Wattay Field they had the equipment they thought they needed and had placed some of it in well concealed spider holes near a narrow game trail. Other equipment they cached at a spot about a kilometer (.62 miles) away in a small pocket hidden from the kill zone by a low ridge. The Yao ran up and down narrow paths dragging sweaty old socks to create scent trails and subtly bending and breaking small branches at random intervals, leaving animal scat undisturbed as they passed.

According to the plan when preparations were made and the kill zone ready they would begin raids again and draw a security team up over the pass to the north and lead them on a merry chase south into the trap. When they heard the trap go off from their watch tower to the south Cerone and JayCee would call in an air strike further south on the Trail to create a diversion for the TBS withdrawal.

Plans finalized and equipment in place it was time to bait the trap; the old stalk and kill program was ramped back up with quick bursts from submachine guns (SMGs), single shots from a distance, and the always-thirsty-for-blood knives. Team Blue Squared was ready and waiting for security teams to come up through the pass to the north and start chasing them.

Timing would be critical, once the trap was triggered TBS would have to get in position quickly, attack, clear the field, and withdraw just as rapidly – the "four quicks" of their tactical dictum.

Ready for action, some instinct had Sanchez scouting south with two of the local Yao and tired, sweaty, dehydrated and grouchy he had just finished roping to the top of a tall tree where he would have a clear view over the canopy to the south. With bare eyes he could make out the ragged line of karst where Cerone and JayCee would be hiding, Buster (Blaske) and New Paru acting as bodyguards somewhere on the slopes below them and further down slope the opening in the trees that would be above the river crossing below. He was just settling into a safety sling and opening a canteen when a flicker of motion caught his eye and squinting he thought he saw two H-19 Chickasaw helicopters approaching the opening; that couldn't be, not at these altitudes and at that location!

A quick view through his old Wehrmacht (WWII German Army) artillery glasses made his hair tingle at the back of his neck; the helis were Russian MI-4 Hounds and as he watched they landed and disgorged, by his count, twenty black-clad men, three men dressed in NVA officer "pinks" (I don't know why we called them "pinks", the uniforms were a light greenish tan), and four large black and tan dogs, to be joined a few minutes later by another half-dozen or so black-clad men who came into view from the edges of the clearing. Shit! It looked like there were going to be security squads coming up from the south instead of or in addition to squads from the north! He had to get this Intel back to Hayes and the rest of the TBS team ASAP!

He watched while the men in the distance squatted in a circle talking and then as the light began to fail started his climb back down the tree. He was too far away and the light was too dim for him to see when three of the four black and tan dogs looked like they had been hit by an invisible sledge hammer, then shuddered and died. He had just missed some of Busters' finest work.

In his haste he made a rookie mistake and let his left wrist get caught in a twist of the rope he was rappelling down; he heard and felt a pop as the wrist pulled free and he skidded down the last ten or fifteen feet scrapping his face on the bark, unable to slow his descent with only his back, lower, hand to use as a brake.

Even un-injured he wouldn't be able to race through the dark forest as fast as the Yao and he sent one of his companions on north to take the word to Hayes and Tom Minor and the rest of Tango Bravo Sierra, the small handheld radios they were carrying were strictly line-of-sight gear (junk) and he did not want to risk making any radio traffic or static this close to an enemy that was searching for him anyway.

He tucked his injured arm against his chest inside his "elephant gut" sling and started scout walking (double time fifty paces, walk fifty paces, stop and listen, repeat) to the north behind his remaining Yao companion. Two hours later he found Tom Minor waiting for him beside the path, three quick blinks from a red-lens pen light identifying him as a friendly.

Tom Minor had a simple message, "Improvise, improvise, improvise, adapt and overcome; make a very noisy attack on any targets of opportunity they could find at 22:00 hours. Attack again ten or fifteen minutes later at a point further north. Start drawing the security team in the south back north away from the Blue Team members at the watch tower and back toward the prepared killing ground". "Stay alive and make your way to your Tango 2 (his weapons position for the trap)".

Chapter 44

Buster

Buster was content inside his well hidden lie-up. He had spent considerable effort making it comfortable and the effort had been paying off for the three days and nights he had been waiting and watching. He had plenty of water and a convenient pee bottle at hand and when it was dark he was able to back out of his spot and stretch for a half hour or so a couple of times in the night. He was not bothered by being on cold rations and would be okay with staying out another three or four days if that was what was needed.

We all had either taken or been given field monikers based on movies and television shows and our favorite name for Blaske was "Buster", as in Buster Keaton, the stone faced actor in silent movies. We thought the name fit because it was almost impossible to tell what he was thinking, but we knew that he was indeed always thinking about something just a half step out of kilter with the "normal" world.

He may or may not have been the best shot in our group but he was the best sniper; partly because it was work he liked, particularly when he was providing cover for an extraction or other team activity, but even more because of his patience, situational awareness, and unique approach to problem solving.

He had demonstrated some of these traits when Sgt. Johnny Sorenson had run a training exercise in Thailand that was intended to revive the almost forgotten (at the time) stalk and shoot skills that differentiate a sniper from a marksman. Being a good or even excellent shot was not enough, a sniper has to be able to close on his target unseen, take the shot, and disengage still unseen; that was the point of the Special Forces Group Trainer's exercise.

There were no grades, no pass or fail for the attendees of Sgt Johnny Sorenson's class, but there were pride and bragging rights at stake and as an extra incentive a bottle of White Horse Scotch would go to the attendee who scored the highest points. We knew that Buster felt honored to be invited to attend and would quietly take the training seriously. We noted that before he went across the river for the five-day class Buster spent a lot of time talking with and studying a man we all called "The Gray Man"; A field operative known (by us at least) for his ability to blend and disappear into any background.

At the culmination of the exercise the attendees would be given a map and a pencil drawn sketch of a rough draft of the area where a stalking target was positioned and they would be released ten at a time to find the area, fill in details on the rough draft, and "kill the target" all unseen by spotters and roving patrols in the practice area. It was left completely at the trainees' discretion to pick the distance and position to make the "kill" on an "enemy" silhouette positioned in a wide clear spot in the jungle, remembering that they would not only have to hit the target, but also to clear the area without being tagged by a patrol. Or stepped on by an elephant.

Buster wasn't able to carry his long gun (sniper rifle) back and forth across the border but he did take his "Magic Cloak of Invisibility", his version of the Ghilley Suit; a camouflage suit named for the (Ghilleys) Scots gamekeepers who invented it. Busters' version was made from a four by twelve foot piece of thin camo netting that was grey/green/black on one side and grey/tan/brown on the other and completed with a similarly sized and patterned loose woven cloth. The entire rig could be folded and rolled into a figure eight package slung over his shoulders and crossing at his back under his day bag or worn like a cloak over his body and equipment. He could tie it over branches as a cover, pitch it as a shapeless tent, pile it to look like leaves, alive or dead depending on the background, and add foliage or other material local to the site where he was using it as desired. A cunning, versatile piece of equipment, I even saw him sling it as a hammock and sleep in it a few times.

On the day he was to stalk and "kill the target" he had his own "Blaske Plan" all worked out and in addition to the Springfield rifle, field knife, canteen and other equipment he had been issued for the exercise was carrying his "Magic Cloak" and was ready to shift the game to his advantage.

That evening as the day was being reviewed by the instructors and roll call taken Sgt Johnny Sorenson had an "Aw shit" moment. Of the thirty men that had gone out on the course that day only twenty-nine had come back. The Air Force guy must have gotten lost (A Pathfinder lost? How ironic was that?), he would have to get a search party and trackers out to find the missing man at first light.

What they found after a two hour sweep was the draft sketch of the area with measurements and topical features filled in with great attention to detail and pinned to the forehead of the enemy silhouette target by a K-Bar knife. A note at the bottom read, "Sgt Sorenson, you owe me a bottle of Scotch. See you at the shack. Bring my knife. Buster."

In his lie-up Buster was already breaking a rule, in his vest pocket was a small package wrapped in oiled silk containing three photographs (a no-no, we were not supposed to have any items of a personal nature with us in the field); one had been cut from a promo shot taken at the Tropicana Hotel in Las Vegas and showed a girl dressed in pasties and g-string with a long train behind and with out-stretched arms balancing an enormous feathered head dress, another was of a red-haired, lightly freckled pretty girl dressed in a man's white shirt and jeans standing next to a horse corral, and the third, his favorite, was of the same red-haired girl all sleepy faced wrapped in a blanket and holding a cup of tea. In behind the photos was a section cut from a thin papered letter written with purple ink saying that Anne, the girl in the photos, was coming to the end of her work visa and might have to return to England. Every time he read that piece he had cut from a long letter he felt saddened that he had never told her how he felt, that he had never said those three little words, "I love you". The worry that she could be gone before he got back to the States gave him a shiver of foreboding and loneliness.

And now he was about to break another rule, the proscription against taking any aggressive action had been side-lined but there was a new protocol in place that said 8th COIN teams were not to reveal their presence in the field to other American sponsored operatives. "Operation Hardnose" would have Army Special Forces to the west and south of Blaske's position and Marine Long Range Patrols (LRPs) would be coming up from Khe Sanh to monitor the trail. The new protocol said that we were not to contact these teams or interfere with their activities in any way, even if we thought they needed help; he was about to disobey the second part of that protocol.

Early in the day he had been surprised to hear and then see two Russian MI-4 "Hound" helicopters (probably flown by Russian pilots) land at the far left of his field of vision and disgorge what had to be North Vietnamese Army (NVA) security teams and dogs. His first spurt of alarm was the thought that JayKah (aka JayCee) and Cerone might be exposed to view from above in the stone fort on top of the ridge to the north and above him where they were doing "radio stuff". Naw, they would be more wary than that. But the trail watchers (probably Marines) he knew were nesting down to his right might not know the dogs were out and would be looking for them after dark fell.

New PARU was at a fallback position over the ridge guarding the team's evac route with a Browning Automatic Rifle (BAR) and Hayes, Sanchez, and Tom Minor were out on patrol looking for someone to quietly murder as part of their own brand of terror against the NVA. If anyone were to alarm or aid the team of trail watchers it would have to be him.

He had already put the combination spotter scope/range finder that Hayes had taken from a Russian artillery advisor to good use and had plotted the adjustments for deflection and bullet drop he would need to put accurate fire down on five killing zones. His Starlight Scope, filter in place, was pre-set for one of the zones where the dog handlers were posted with their charges and he had picked out the three targets he planned to try for as soon as conditions were favorable.

279

He wanted it to be light enough that the flame pattern around his sound suppressor would not be visible, but dark enough that people in his targeted area would not be able to spot him when he pulled out of his lie-up. He would take three shots at the 5 handlers, then send one round into the trees just above the watchers' nest as a warning, pack his gear and boogie to a new hide, being careful to stay downwind of the dogs, almost sorry at having to leave such a comfortable, well-hidden spot.

Wrapped in a mantle of lonesome and hidden under his "Magic Cloak of Invisibility" he tried not to think about the red-haired girl and ignoring the itches and muscle aches, and the smell of his own body odor, he waited patiently for the right moment to arrive.

He would wait to take his shots in the twilight at dusk.

Chapter 45

The Castle Karst

It stuck up like a lower canine, a one-hundred-meter grey-white limestone fang rising from the high forest floor and connected at the base to the green-grey-brown mountain ridge behind it by a thin land bridge; one of a series of seven tooth-like karst (limestone formation) on the east face of a wrinkle in the Annamite Range somewhere to the north of Muang Nong.

Looking from the west side, the side toward the mountain, there appeared to be a crack near the base of the tooth. A hard scramble to the crack revealed that it was an opening into the hollow center with a dry cave and a chimney open almost to the top. At the top of the chimney was an opening on to a sloped gully surrounding the spire on three sides and hidden from view from the forest floor and the mountain behind by a lip that varied from one to two meters deep. Like a watch tower in a medieval castle it provided a protected view of the surroundings and a defensible position – a castle keep. And a great spot to operate a clandestine radio transmitter.

Baphang had taken me to this spot on an earlier trek and pointed out the lack of bat guano, bird or animal droppings, or signs of previous fires in the cave, and that erosion had created a water runoff lower than the cave floor; this was a place where two or three men could hole up indefinitely in any season provided they were careful not to leave any sign of passage over the connecting land bridge. When or how he had found this spot he never shared with me, just pointing out its features with a big grin and leading me on a climb up the chimney to the hidden ledge above. On that first trip to the spire I had decided not to share the location of the cave with anyone other than my mates on the Blue Team, if I could find it again.

Of all the hideaway spots Baphang had shown me (I wonder if he would have shown it to anyone other than the person he called "J'Ah'Kah" or "little brother") this airy and dry chamber with the look-out above became my favorite; the only drawback being that there was only one way in and one way out.

Up in the depression near the top I wondered at the toughness of the plants that had found root in cracks and spots where a little dirt had blown in, wondered and was thankful, the bits of foliage gave us places to shadow the lenses of our binoculars and rangefinders and even provided a little shade during the hot season. And the view was magnificent, to the east a couple of ridges away was Viet Nam and back to the west a line of misty ridges lay between the tower and the Mekong Plain, wild country in between. During the slash and burn season the mists coming up from valley floors mixed with the smoke from hundreds of fires and created a cloud layer that threaded through the mountains and turned every color of the rainbow as daylight moved from morning to night; beautiful but making tough work for pilots trying to find Identification Points (IPs).

I don't believe I have ever had a cup of coffee or tea that tasted as good as it did up on that tower while savoring a few minutes of calm, alone or with a boon companion or two.

Cerone and I were having one of those quiet moments up in the tower just before dusk on our fourth evening of this trip to the "Castle" when we heard shots muffled by the forest but still distinct enough to recognize as probably coming from a 30.06. First three evenly spaced shots, a pause, then a fourth shot. Blaske must be up to something but we hadn't heard any return fire and took that as a good sign that he had gone undetected, we'd know for sure by morning.

Earlier that afternoon we had had a disquieting moment or three when we watched two large Russian helicopters land men and dogs in a small clearing on a ridge between us and a spot where several arms of the Trong Son Road (Ho Chi Minh Trail) converged on a river ford below their landing spot (a target rich loc for sure). We knew they were probably NVA security teams called in to track down Hayes, Sanchez, Tom Minor and the eight Cao Dai working with them. Dumb bastards were taking the bait. Ambushing and eradicating a security team would put a lot of fear into the porters and fighters on the Trail and that was the plan Hayes and Sanchez had cooked up. And now it looked like they were going to have two security teams to suck into traps. Up in our lair we hid our worry from each other and told ourselves that our guys were very, very competent and would pull off their plan "no sweat".

Although Hayes, aka "Herc" (sometimes "Herc the Jerk"), aka Lone Ranger, just like the prototypical GIs we had all grown up seeing in movies liked kids and was protective toward them (except maybe for the kid soldiers and terrorists that tried to kill him) he was basically unable to talk to them, either trying to communicate with goo goo ga ga baby talk or speaking like (we imagined) a college professor. He never said so but I sensed that his feelings were hurt when two little girls he had rescued and brought down from a high mountain village attached themselves so readily to Morrison.

I knew he had tracked and killed at least some of the men who had raped and murdered the girls' mother and grandmother; he just didn't want to talk about it. But a blood-lust door had been opened that would be hard to close; he was in a punishment mode whether from outrage at what he had witnessed or guilt and anger at not being able to rescue the mother and grandmother. He did once mention in a whiskey-soaked moment that he often wondered if the two women were still alive in the burning hut when he pulled the girls from the animal enclosure beneath; a question he would never be able to answer.

He launched his personal campaign of terror with the willing assistance (complicity)of Sanchez and Tom Minor who were always up for some action and some of Baphang's' contingent of Cao Dai former militia who had been fighting the Viet Minh (now called Viet Cong) and North Vietnamese for years before we got there.

With small groups of six to eight men they would ambush random targets with gun, grenade, garrote and knife taking out porters, foot soldiers and officers in quick attacks designed to instill fear up on the trails in the mountains. Sometimes they would cut a few throats of sleeping enemy, bodies left to be found when their "comrats" woke up. Sometimes they would take heads and leave them in a neat pile along a well-traveled path. Other times they would leave behind a man (or woman) trussed up but alive.

A man who stepped behind a tree or bush to relieve his bladder might never be seen again. A group huddled in a hidden spot eating their rations could be attacked by grenades and automatic rifle fire, the antagonists disappearing just as quickly as they had appeared. Splinter groups moving through tight undergrowth away from the main flow of traffic would fall prey to their own mines or be suddenly attacked in brief firefights, or simply disappear. Attacks could come by day or night; they could happen at any time and at any place in this part of the mountains where Hayes and Sanchez and their raiders practiced their arts. Our local contacts told us that this area began to be known as "Cai Chet Nui" or "Death Mountains" to the North Vietnamese. Fear was traveling up and down the trail, people looked constantly over their shoulders and spoke in whispers of the wraiths attacking and then vanishing and referred to them as the "Yeu Quai", or the "Ma Quy", - the "Ghost Demons".

Samuels and Kappas might not be happy with the actions of this little group of guerillas when they learned what they had been up to but Kappas had been summoned back to the States and hadn't yet returned (we were all nervous when he wasn't there to tuck us in after a time in the field, where the fuck was he?) and Samuels was up to his ears in a constant political battle with the MAAG offices across the river in Thailand, too engrossed in his daily paper war to notice what Hayes, Sanchez, and Tom Minor were doing, or maybe he didn't care, or even approved.

One benefit of the actions they were taking was that it brought the enemy into tighter concentrations, the people streaming south stayed closer together for protection (even though the more experienced among them knew that was a bad idea) and stayed off some of the smaller trails resulting in better, richer target areas for air raids and ambushes. Too bad we didn't have a strong presence of ground troops to take advantage of the situation, but we could raise some hell with air strikes at places like the stream ford and truck park beneath us.

But the "Ghost Demons" created a problem for Cerone and myself while we were trying to "Survey and Observe", bringing a lot of heat with extra vigilance on the part of the "ants" trying to find them, and by extension us, or any other American sponsored teams in the mountains. The security teams looking for them might find our sign and track us to our lair. And now that Blaskes' long gun had spoken they would be actively searching the area near us.

We had a quick decision to make as night fell; stay where we were and hope to remain undiscovered or risk a running gun battle and stay mobile, don't get penned in. We both voted to stay mobile, which would be our best chance; if we got surrounded in our "Castle Karst" there would be no reinforcements, no cavalry to the rescue. But with New Paru in position guarding the approaches to our land bridge we could expect some warning before any trackers got too close and decided to keep our radio gear at the ready to call in an air strike before we evacuated. Moonrise found us willing the radio to click with a query com, but no squeaks, squawks, or clicks came from the T-28s we called our "Phantom Air Force".

We did not have any way of knowing it at the time, but they weren't coming.

Perhaps the "secret" successes with the ambushes on the Trong Song Road (Ho Chi Minh Trail) we had coordinated with our "Phantom Air Force" had come to the DOR/USAFs' attention and were part of the undoing of our tight knit little group. These and a few other actions had proven out the "low investment, high yield" approach advocated by Colonel Van and "The Old Asia Hands" but had engendered jealousy and outright hostility on the part of some senior officers of all the major military commands who were able, after the Military Assistance Advisory

Group (MAAG) took the lead in Laos, as we learned later, to shut down our unofficial air arm.

At 2200 hours and followed again about ten minutes later the sounds of small explosions and automatic weapon fire came from somewhere to our left (north), the "Ghost Demons" were probably at work and we hoped that would pull any searchers in their direction.

At 0100 hours the three-quarter moon was sliding toward the horizon but we could still see (and hear) the dark shapes of twin engine prop driven aircraft running in to drop ordinance on a ridge three wrinkles toward Viet Nam from our position. We watched the green tracers and orange-red-blue explosion flowers bloom on an area we knew to be devoid of any enemy activity and assuming them to be A-26 bombers operating out of Takhli, Thailand tried to reach them on the assigned frequencies for the day. No luck, they were probably part of a new group starting to operate out of South Viet Nam.

There we were, two Little Jack Horners, sitting in our corners, with no thumbs to pull plums out of the pie beneath us.

At 0300 there were more small explosions and small arms fire seeming to come from even further to the north and the moon was almost down, time to boogie.

We set our punji stick trap, a loose slab of limestone carefully balanced so that the unwary would either fall into the trap and on to excrement coated sharpened sticks or fall the other way off a twenty-meter cliff, either way if on any future visit we observed that the trap in front of the crack in the karst that led to our cave had been moved we would know our hide-away had been compromised.

It took us two trips across the loose rock on the land bridge to get all our gear across, New Paru would help pack it out and Blaske would carry some of it if we managed to rendezvous with him. But getting it across the narrow spine was tricky work and on the second trip I let my attention lag and damn near took a long ride down, only New Paru's strong grip kept me from dropping into the dark below.

It wasn't fear that had gripped me and almost sent me careening down the slope, hell I was scared all the time, being afraid was "situation normal" for me and I suspected (we never discussed it) for my team mates as well.

It was "Frustration" and "Anger" that had made me lose my concentration. I tamped them down, shouldered my load and started trekking to our extraction point, New Paru in front and Cerone bringing up the rear.

Chapter 46

Bug Out

It must have been light somewhere, the moon out, or the sun up, people talking and maybe laughing, all the day and night sounds all around and coming from every direction in a world full of life. But not where we were under a triple canopy, surrounded by darkness so complete and thick you could feel it on your skin; the black, black darkness a heavy blanket squeezing the body and mind. The forest around us preternaturally still, no sounds of movement, no night noises in the forest foliage or rising from the jungle floor four hundred meters below us. The mountain was holding its breath.

Staying still in the thick dark was scary and hard enough, moving around blindly, knowing there were creatures waiting to maim and kill, and people hunting us with bad intentions had been terrifying.

We had been moving through a huge "M" with one peak, the one to the west, higher than the other, going north in the "vee" formed by the steep slopes toward an opening in the higher ridge to our left, the pass that would take us over the mountain and toward an area controlled by Vang Pao's Hmong irregulars. Further north beyond the pass the "vee" would drop steeply then widen into a deep bowl about fifty meters wide by a hundred meters long with thin flat rims on both the west and east side before narrowing again, the wide section part of a killing ground Hayes, Sanchez, Tom Minor, and their local allies had prepared as a nasty surprise for anyone who followed them into the zone.

The hidden path we were on was one we had taken several times before and had carefully committed to memory, and of course New Paru, our Thai scout, probably had a name, and a personal relationship with every rock, tree, and bush along the trail, an advantage any followers would not have. Blaske caught up with us at our rendezvous spot, a place where even a crawling man would be outlined against the horizon and identified himself with a wave of his hat against the lighter sky behind him. He had taken a long, circuitous route to the spot, doubling back now and then to observe and confuse the five or six men and a dog that were tracking him, but never getting a good chance to set up to safely take a shot at one of the pursuers. He gauged that they would be about a half an hour behind him, moving warily through the unfamiliar (to them) terrain, but not as encumbered with radio gear and equipment as we were. We needed to get moving before night fell away, we wanted to still be in the darkness when they caught up with us.

We moved on up and down over rock falls and scree under brilliant starlight where we were clear of the brush, plunging into dark tunnels on pebble strewn dirt paths where the route took us back beneath the canopy until we came to a barrier, a four-meter rock face that we knew had a dense, tangled wind fall on one side and a steep, loose rock covered slope with sparse vegetation on the other side. A slick rock barrier hidden in the deepest dark, a barrier it would take hours to go around, the only other choice would be to scale the face in the dark and continue down the trail. Perfect.

New Paru was the first to scale up over the rock face, reaching down to help Blaske ease over the rim, dropping a double strand of para cord and hauling up the gear and equipment we were packing in three or four stages, all with barely a sound.

Cerone eased into the windbreak, I couldn't see him but I knew what he was doing, while I found a place with good footing and a flat spot to sit on against a stumpy tree trunk in the loose stones on the other side of the path, and waited, the only sound the noise of my heart beating and the rush of blood in my veins and my own breathing; how could that be so loud?

I sat waiting, my eyes adjusting (I was blessed with much better night vision than anyone else I've ever known) but smelled and heard the dog padding and huffing as it strained against its leash before I made out the dark forms sliding along the narrow path, the dog pulling straight to the "present" Blaske had squatted and left at the base of the rock barrier. I felt a twist in the back of my brain right at the spot where neck meets skull and could hear my long-dead friend Dave telling me, "Steady... steady on...keep your finger off the trigger...(the safety on the Swedish K SMG was clumsy and I didn't use it)... wait..."

Cerone and I were both armed with the 9mm Swedish K/45 as a favor to our Special Forces pal Sgt. Johnny Sorenson who wanted an evaluation of the weapon in the field, we both preferred the folding stock M14 with its auto/singles selector switch and greater effective range but the Swedish SMGs (sub machine guns) we were using came with a very effective fixed suppressor designed and installed by our armorer, were light, and were easy to hold on target. And we had learned on our practice range to easily fire our signature three round bursts.

I could see the dark forms of the enemy patrol as two stood guard, and two gave an assist to a fifth man scaling the wall. A lower to the ground form was lunging and pulling at a sixth man, the not too well trained, excited dog pulling at a lease. Just as the man on the wall disappeared over the top Cerone and I began our "magic dance", a dance we had performed many times and in many places to the amazement and maybe a little awe and wonder of those who witnessed it.

There was no synchronized watch to look at, no agreed upon signal, no outward communication at all, just training and similar mind set, or maybe ESP. I stood and turned silently and the dark curtain we were all standing under was torn open by the muzzle flash and loud dry fart sound of two suppressed SMGs simultaneously firing three round bursts, and then firing two more bursts, again in perfect sync. Cerone and I had done the "magic dance" again. A few quiet shots from a Colt Woodsman (suppressed) and the moans and dog whining stopped. I dared a look with my hooded flashlight in time to see a headless torso fall from the top of the rock wall.

A rush of electricity jangled my body as a strong jolt of adrenaline hit my system (I knew it was coming, I was addicted to it) and I wanted to scream and curse (where were some more of those nasty little cocksuckers that needed killing!) and do my best Tarzan impersonation, instead I turned and danced in a little circle looking around at nothing and pumping my SMG in the air. Until that voice in the back of my brain said, "Calm down, calm down, you aren't home safe yet" and I started a series of long slow exhales and quick shallow inhales until my heart rate came down and my hands steadied.

But we still had ugly work to do going through the pockets and back and chest packs of the dead men collecting anything that might provide Intel and itemizing details of their rank, weaponry, clothing, food supplies, and general physical condition. I filled a Musset bag on my web gear with personal items from their pockets without looking at the contents, a crumpled letter, a pressed flower in a notebook, or a snapshot of a family member made it all too personal, made the enemy human when I needed them to remain a faceless threat. How do I explain what I could not understand about my conflicted feelings? I could kill; I would kill, and feel joy in the moment, but I didn't like doing it or like myself for that sheer joy I felt in the after moment. I needed the enemy to remain anonymous and evil.

Feeling tired and raggedy-assed we trooped on north leaving Blaske behind as a rear guard, if no one else was following he should catch up with us before we got to the pass, stopping in a sheltered spot just as the sky lightened to swallow some thin, cold tea that tasted a little too much like musty canteen and down some hardtack and jam. We were still "taking ten" and enjoying the relief provided by a light pre-dawn breeze when a series of loud explosions, the thump of a couple of mortars and the sounds of automatic weapons fire, followed by heavy machine gun fire, erupted from the direction of the Team Blue Squared (Hayes's name for his hunting party) kill zone.

Our first reaction was to want to move in the direction of the battle to observe and possibly lend a hand to the "good guys", if we could spot their positions, and not get shot approaching. But our mission was to deliver the information we had collected over the past days and nights at an observation post sited above a main intersection of trails and a water crossing. We had been watching the major buildup of a depot for fuel, munitions, and other supplies; a ripe, ripe target we hadn't been able to guide any "friendlies" in to attack. The "boys" "back across the river" would need the high value information we were bringing.

We cleared the bare hump over the highest ridge in the pass on our evac route one at a time, leap-frogging to a hidden position in a stand of trees and took turns napping while we waited for Blaske to appear. The sun was well up behind him as Blaske cleared the ridge sprinting in a low crouch, to be followed by two more figures that were walking half erect, one of them limping, Blaske hissing, "Don't shoot, they're ours!" before we recognized Tom Minor and a somewhat-beat-up Sanchez.

It was an all-day trek, thankfully mostly on a downhill slope and with frequent rest stops, New Paru and Tom Minor alternating on point and Blaske staying on drag, Sanchez in the middle of our little column as we made our way to our extraction point (I think it was labeled LS38 later in the game, but I could be mistaken about the number). It was late afternoon when Hayes and his band of Cao Dai caught up with us (his Yao guides would be staying behind) while we were prepping to set up our com gear and scout the clearing where our transport would land.

One handset was broken and the other wouldn't work so we didn't have voice com but Cerone had a good "hand" with Morse (I was never any good at it) and got the message out that we were ready to go, getting confirmation that our ride was on the way a few minutes later. We stayed alert but rested and hydrated while we waited, and talked about girls, beer, whiskey, and hot showers, and girls.

We were surprised to see not one but two C130s circle and land uphill on the airstrip, and shocked by what we saw when the rear door opened on the plane that had landed in trail. Another kind of danger, a quintet of news people, poison to us, debarked on the loading ramp, cameras and notebooks poised for action. Just the year before we had had trouble avoiding a writer and photographer team from National Geographic

(National Geographic in a war zone 'fer crisake!) and now these pukes were on top of us!

Hayes was gently letting the news correspondents know that if they took any photos of us he would strip the film out of their cameras and "cram them up their arses" when one of them noticed a beat up, strange looking Sanchez and pointing asked, "What happened to him?"

The usually quiet, monosyllabic Tom Minor answered, "He fell out of a tree" and started laughing so hard tears were running down his cheeks. While the correspondents were standing around looking puzzled and our entire team, even the Cao Dai, was having a good laugh (relieving some of the stress and tension from the past couple of weeks) I noticed something that gave me concern.

I had to get us away quickly (as in right now!), one newsperson was female (I think her name was Jane) not too pretty, maybe a little plain, but we had been in the bush for a while and she was a round-eyed girl from home, I had to get us out of there before Cerone got a hard on and started wooing her.

Chapter 47

The Snake In The Pass

In many parts of the Orient the snake is regarded as a symbol of wisdom, and oftentimes as a symbol of cunning and guile, so North Vietnamese Army Captain Trinh Ngo was pleased that people called him "The Snake". And he was happy to be deployed with these hard-case men for his present assignment; he was tasked to rid a section of the trail of the so-called "ghosts" that were interfering with the stream of supplies going south on the Truong Son Strategic Supply Route. These "ghosts" or Yeu Quai (Ma Quy to some) were an annoyance that was making morale problems in a key part of the mountains; his orders were marked as a high priority and three squads of sappers had been put at his discretion, he enjoyed the thought that there might even be a promotion at the end of this mission.

French schooled and reared as one of the few privileged members of the Trinh family the Captain, like many converts to a "cause" pushed hard to prove himself. And although proud when he was appointed as a political officer and given this opportunity to shine he was barely able to suppress his disdain for the superstitious people who believed in ghosts (uneducated peasants, they needed leaders like him). He would find and eliminate the raiders that were interrupting operations up and down the Trail and put the foolish rumors to rest. If possible he would take one or two of the "ghosts" alive to show the people that the raiders were merely humans and not of the spirit world.

A proof of the importance of his mission was the allocation of two of the big Russian helicopters for transportation of his men and equipment, including four large guard dogs, to the jump off point for his mission. As further proof in his pocket he carried a letter stressing the necessity of eradicating the problem signed by Vo Nguyen Giap - the great general himself.

The plan was simple; the in-place security teams, augmented by the sapper squads, would approach the portion of the Trail that the frightened whisperers were starting to call "Cai Chet Nui" (Death Mountain) from the north and south and spreading out into wide fans, close on the area in a pincer movement with dogs and trackers searching for signs of the enemy raiders. When found the enemy would be isolated from any escape routes, surrounded and captured or killed. The only worry gnawing at The Snake came from news that there had been no "ghost" raids for almost a month; he might be too late for a chance to gain a reputation in the field as something more than a political lecturer.

But the plan was off to a shaky start the late afternoon the big helicopters dropped him off with two sapper teams and four large dogs. His comprehension couldn't keep up with the action in the clearing where the big noisy machines were just taking off as first one, and then two more of the dogs were shoved sideways by an invisible force and he was pulled to the ground by one of the officers in his greeting party, his brain barely having time to form the thought "sniper" before he was pushed/pulled to cover behind a berm.

Choking down his fright, hoping that the half-light of dusk would conceal any sign of fear on his face from his companions, he ordered a full-scale chase of the sniper using all available personnel, this insult must be answered!

The NVA 559 Transport Group Captain in charge of the supply route at this critical junction of two main sections of roadway and a vital river ford refused to commit any of his troops to the chase, insisting that keeping them on guard against attack was more important and tactically sound than having them run through the bush at night chasing a sniper (he almost said ghost). The captain was defying the directive from a member of the political cadre (!). The Snake made a mental note to deal with this act of political insubordination at a later date and, calmer now, reassessed the situation.

As dark slammed down, the three-quarter moon adding only a dim light that would last for an hour or less, he made a new decision and dispatched four of his sappers and two of the mountain trackers and the remaining dog, darkness would be a familiar operating environment for them, to find and kill the sniper. Secretly, he took some comfort from being in the midst of the remainder of his men in the dark.

Sanchez was having a shaky start to his evening as well. He had missed his footing and twisted his wrist rappelling down a tall tree and as he moved through the dark behind his Yao guide (Sanchez had named him Barbarossa because of his red-dyed beard and general pirate-like demeanor), Springfield in its canvas bag at his back rubbing against his hip, AK47 slung barrel down over an ammo pack on his chest, leaves and branches tugging at his hat and clothes, and arm throbbing where it was pinned against his chest over the Kalashnikov by his "elephant gut" food sling, he realized the wrist was broken. His face was stinging where it had scrapped against the tree trunk and his left knee was swelling and aching, he must have slammed it against the tree trunk too.

Stopping to rest and slake their thirst, he took a moment, with help from his guide, to fish out a tube of anti-bacterial ointment and smear it on his face where it stung the most and gulp down a few aspirin, tempted to use a morphine syrette but knowing he needed to stay sharp, he would just have to, "grin and bear it". By reflex he smeared on another layer of camtec, three broad stripes of green/yellow across his checks and nose. He had not slept in more than twenty-four hours as they started warily back up the trail, alert for any enemy patrols.

He was relieved when they connected with Tom Minor and he learned that Hayes had gotten the word that there were security forces south of his position. Tom Minor said that when Hayes got the word that there were two security forces on the mountain, coming from two directions, rather than the one they had planned for Hayes just grinned and said, "that's two" and held up two middle fingers in the air, then made a small modification to their original plan to trap and kill security forces. And he was relieved to be able to snatch twenty minutes of sound sleep before they moved on.

At 2200 hours the little group of three had threaded their way through the armed troops moving south on the smaller trails to a location above the main trail where trucks were rolling on one side and bicycle streams were moving on the other, all carrying supplies south. From the position overlooking the main trail they fired AK 47s and a RPD light machine gun that Tom Minor had taken away from two surprised men earlier in the day (the two men did not survive the encounter) and dropped a couple of grenades before shifting position a few minutes to the north and got ready to poke the beehive again.

After a tough crawl to a brush pile conveniently placed by the laborers keeping the roadway below clear Sanchez assumed a seated firing position, it was a bitch firing the AK one-handed, left hand against his right chest under the rifle stock pushed on his right shoulder, bi-pod hooked on a slim tree trunk in front of his left knee. When Sanchez was in position Tom Minor threw one, two grenades over his head to roll down the slope between him and the truck route below and he threw up his hand in front of his face to preserve his night vision against the glare the grenades would make, and he got lucky. Sorta'.

The hot envelope of expanding gases when the small gasoline dump below him exploded was deflected by the hand in front of his face and the medicinal salve and camtec paint protected him from a flash burn on his exposed flesh, the paste-like covering melting in the heat and leaving behind a residue buried in his skin, a green and yellow tattoo running transverse with two big black blotches around his eyes and three vertical red/black stripes down the left side of his face, a four day old stubble of beard charred black.

The shock wave that followed a milli-second later rolled the brush pile, with him in it, back a few meters as it caught fire. His hat was gone and small holes were burned in the top of his green headscarf with spikes of burnt hair sticking out when Tom Minor pulled him out of the smoking brush pile, body aching, head aching, throat sore, ears ringing, and only able to see bright spots dancing in front of his eyes. In the confusion that followed the three of them walked out unchallenged; with Barbarossa as a guide in front and Sanchez holding onto his collar with his good right hand, Tom Minor in back holding Sanchez's shoulders, the three of them in train disappearing back into the darkness above the main trail.

The Snake was pleased when he saw and heard the gunfire and explosions to his north, he was sure it meant the raiders were still attacking the NVA convoys, he would get his chance to engage them. A hissing message on the Chinese 102-E com set confirmed that raiders had attacked the column in several places and disappeared, typical tactics of the "ghosts" causing disruption along the supply lines.

The patrol he had sent out earlier to track and kill a sniper hadn't returned, he would leave a porter behind to tell them to catch up while he radioed the security teams to the north and organized some of the armed soldiers moving south into a fighting unit to accompany his sapper squads and tribesmen as they trotted toward the fire-lit scene of the attack. They would fan out and get these "ghost demons" between the two forces and herd them to a spot where they could be eliminated.

The moon was dropping behind the horizon when The Snake reached the scene of the latest attack and his team got the com gear operating again, one man scaling a tree to hold up the antenna lead and another man cranking the portable generator. He was pleased (excited!) with the report from the team to the north, their dogs had picked up a strong trail and they were tracking the enemy to the south and west toward a blind canyon higher up on the mountain side. Map coordinates would follow.

The little caterpillar-like column of Barbarossa, Sanchez, and Tom Minor made a slow slog up the steep terrain toward Tango Two, a previously cached weapons position in a depression behind a low swale on a ridge above the killing ground prepared by Tango Bravo Sierra in the previous weeks. Hidden at the position were an 82 mike mike mortar of Soviet make with three rounds and an old 60 mike mike mortar with another three shells left behind by the French. There was also a Ma Deuce .50 caliber machine gun with three boxes of ammo in the cache.

Barbarossa led them up the mountain guided by feel, instinct, and memory, pulling them to a halt twice as groups of ten or twelve men swished and padded by in the dark. Both times it took an enormous act of will for Sanchez to get moving again, so dark he didn't know if his eyes were working or not.

When the trio arrived at the site Sanchez was feeling worse than, "a horse that had been rode hard and put away wet", lungs on fire, left arm and left knee throbbing, blisters forming on the top of his right hand, his entire body protesting the abuse it had received by sending him messages of red hot pain. Tom Minor was tired as well but Barbarossa seemed ready to go on for another twenty-four hours, the fucker had legs of spring steel and lungs bigger than a blacksmiths bellows.

Two of Baphang's Cao Dai, experienced mortar men, were already in place and a third man had hot tea boiling in a cave just up the hill from the firing position, the front of the cave carefully protected against any light seeping out. As the tired trio entered the cave the tea maker looked at Sanchez and with raised eyebrows asked, "What happened to you?" Sanchez tried to answer but could only roll his eyes and get out a croak/grunt before his voice gave out completely so Tom Minor answered for him, "He fell off a tree" and made a sound that might have been a laugh.

Determined to be in the midst of the action Sanchez refused to start toward the evac point and refused the offer of a pallet in the cave and with Barbarossa helping took a guard position below the swale at a point where anyone coming up through the narrow passage from the south end of the dish shaped killing ground below would have to pass. Unable to pull back the slide on his 1911 Colt Auto with his damaged hand he had traded one of the Cao Dai for a Smith and Wesson .357 Magnum six-shot revolver. His back against a tree and a large broadleaf plant in front, his position was well hidden. He passed out within a minute of sitting down.

299

Captain "The Snake" Trinh Ngo felt the night go from a not-so-good evening to a potentially wonderful night, reports from runners on the south end and radio reports from the north end of the noose he was tightening told him his simple plan was working. Trackers reported that ten to twenty enemy raiders were being herded toward the blind canyon on his map. A few men and a couple of dogs from the northern security teams had been lost to animal traps and mines but that was a small factor in the overall operation. For the most part his regular troops, he had co-opted two hundred men from the columns moving south, held back letting the Viet Cong, sappers and tribal allies stay in the lead, they were better at identifying dangers in the dark and leading the rest of the men to paths around dangers. Not recognizing in the lightless dark under the canopy that they were being led into channels.

Finally, an hour before dawn was due he received word that the men he was chasing were surrounded in the blind canyon, a deep bowl about fifty meters wide by one hundred meters long and only one way in or out without scaling the steep walls.

Too wily to follow the ghosts into the blind canyon in the dark (or perhaps afraid) and wanting to take prisoners, he ordered a team of his sappers to reconnoiter the edges of the bowl but hold off any attack until daylight. The sappers were soon back to report that they had heard faint sounds of digging and had caught a few flashes from a red-lens light; the "ghost demons" were trapped! Soon he would have proof that they were only men after all. What good luck to be able to engage them on his first day in the field!

In the remaining time before days dim light The Snake had his forces deployed on the narrow high grounds to the west and east of the bowl, weapons, including a couple of mortars, four or five RPGs, and several heavy machine guns and automatic rifles trained down into the depression waiting for his order to fire. A fifteen-man blocking force sealed off any escape from the north-facing mouth of the canyon.

Darkness turned to grey, and then a lighter grey light infused the air on the mountainside. A small explosion, probably a mine, went off to the east of the canyon; somebody had made a false step.

Nervous and excited, The Snake gave the command to spring his trap and the quiet morning was interrupted by the pop, whistle, bang of mortars, the clattering of machine guns and automatic rifles and an occasional basso/alto duet of RPG and grenade bursts. After a three minute barrage The Snake blew his whistle and signaled a bugler to play "cease fire", then waited, big questions preying on his mind: Had anyone heard or seen return fire? Why had there been no return fire?

As the Snake pondered these questions the ground beneath him heaved, causing the section of ledge he was laying on to slide down the steep slope into the canyon below. Planted explosives were being detonated and bringing down whole sections of mountain. The high ground surrounding the bowl was taking indirect machine gun and mortar fire and as his men scattered to escape to cover they were running into mine fields, deadfalls, and over-lapping gun fire. The Tango Bravo Sierra Killing Machine was in action and men were being wounded and dying in every direction, struck down by an un-seen enemy.

Silence slammed down around him leaving behind a ringing in The Snakes ears, eyes squinting against the sudden blue light from the open sky above the bowl he and several men had surfed down into on a section of ledge broken off from the canyon rim now above them. Not all the men on the rim had been so lucky, some had been killed outright by the blasts, others were half-buried and trying to crawl free, some completely buried under the landslide.

The experienced among the survivors on the high ground above the bowl knew they had two options when ambushed; charge the ambush party, leave the way they came in. But what ambush party? Where were they? As they tried to leave the way they had come in the dark hours before they found the few escape lanes had been mined behind them, they would have to pick their way out and down to the main trail below slowly and carefully.

The survivors down in the bowl began moving toward the north facing mouth of the canyon looking for a quick escape from the dangerous enclosure where just a few hours earlier they had thought to trap the enemy raiders, the raiders who had vanished into thin air again. As they began to file through the opening they were met by heavy machine gun fire, rounds ricocheting off the limestone walls sending deadly shards through the air, their own blocking force mistakenly keeping them penned in the bowl.

The Snake could see the men at the north end of the canyon taking cover from the fire coming through the opening and noticed but did not really understand the meaning of several aluminum mess tins and one "L" shaped flashlight hanging just above the ground on low bushes. Before he could start puzzling out the meaning of those hanging objects he spotted something more important, a narrow rift in the canyon walls at the south end, maybe another way out of the bowl. Signaling the five men nearest him to follow he began to climb up through the defile and back under the canopy at the canyon rim. Eager to find cover in the dark under the trees he moved up and out faster than the more cautious men behind him until he had a fifteen meter lead on them. He heard the ack, ack, ack and clank ratcheting sound of a machine gun being cocked and trying to turn and dive away (but which way?) saw something that made him freeze and the hair on the back of his neck rise. Then he charged.

Forced between two rock outcroppings and beginning to take machine gun fire, the five men following The Snake attempted to drop back down the passageway they had just climbed up. A couple of them may have made it to safety.

Sanchez woke up feeling miserable and confused, he hurt everywhere, head throbbing and ears blocked, he was seeing double and through a thin red haze, unable to tell how much of the night before was real and how much nightmare, bladder demanding attention. He stood up shakily, borrowed AK (he had lost his somewhere the night before, probably when the gas dump blew up right under his position) sliding to the ground, unbuttoned his fly and was having a piss when he saw a man charging at him. Still seeing double and unable to tell just which image was "real" he pulled his borrowed S&W .357 and cocking the hammer and firing single action (just like the cowboy sharpshooters of old) pragmatically put a round center of mass in each of the images he saw and one right down the middle for good measure.

Mortally wounded Captain Trinh Ngo, The Snake, was aware of the short red-bearded man removing the documents from his breast pocket when another figure appeared standing over him. It had red and black eyes set in deep black sockets and pale green and yellow skin with a sticky black beard and stiff tufts of hair sticking out in crazy angles from its head. Dressed in tattered rags of black and green the frightening figure looked like a wraith, a ghost, a demon. Was he seeing the Yeu Quai?

A still befuddled and confused Sanchez tried to answer the question he thought he saw in the eyes of the man dying on the ground in front of him, "I meloffautry", before the eyes dimmed and went flat.

Chapter 48

Hole In The Bucket

Huey, Louie, and Dewey were missing and the Lone Ranger was in a state of agitated worry.

Hayes had first met these three Cao Dai when we rendezvoused with Baphang for the first time high in the mountains in Houaphan Province and he began to understand in a short time spent with them that they were accomplished soldiers and mountain men, completely tuned in to their environment, very aware of everything going on in the forests and jungles where they lived and hunted and fought. If an elephant's stomach rumbled ten kilometers away they knew at once what sex and age the beast was. The smell or taste of a leaf could tell them who had passed a part of the trail and how long ago. A pile of dung offered an encyclopedia of information to them, a broken twig or crushed grass hummock was a billboard shouting a loud message. Skills honed by their association with the Yao and various Degar (mountain tribes loosely called "Montagnards" by the French and later the Americans).

And they were not only skilled trackers and hunters; they were also experts at small unit tactics, familiar with a wide variety of weapons, military and improvised, and the fine arts of ambush and counter-ambush. Without the assistance and mentorship of Baphang and his Cao Dai, especially these three and their Yao in-laws, it is a certainty that the An Lac Prics (a name we had for the Blue and Orange Teams) could not have lived as well or survived as long as we did in the mountains of the Annamite Range.

All three were believers in "Dai Dao Tam Ky Pho Do" (Great Religion: Third Period: Revelation: Salvation) or "Cao Dai" for short, a universalist religion that believes all the other world religions have "truth" and considers Shakyamuni Buddha, Confucius, Jesus, and Mohammad, among others, as Saints and Laozi as a Sage; they also venerate Sun Yat-

Sen, Joan of Arc, Victor Hugo, and Nguyen Binh Khiem as people who have brought some of God's Light to our world, as I understand it.

Circumstances did not allow the Cao Dai who had fled to the mountains with Captain Chan/Baphang to escape conscription into Diem's army to practice two of their main precepts, vegetarianism and non-violence, but they did not seem to carry any guilt over these lapses and were content to remain farmers, traders, and warriors in the jungles and high forests of Laos, at least until Baphang could find plantation land in Thailand where they would move with their wives and children and extended families.

The three that Hayes knew best and relied on most heavily were more Asian looking than some of their Cao Dai brethren and had all come from the same area, but not the same villages, on the coastal plain at the foothills north of Saigon. Like Baphang they had all been teenage soldiers, were multi-lingual, and considered both North and South Vietnamese as enemies (they also believed that the CIA may have had a hand in the assassination of their military leader, a prime candidate to be elected head of state in South Viet Nam, which explains the reluctance of all Cao Dai to align with American forces in the Central Highlands as the war progressed).

Our team all had nicknames usually based on characters in 1950's television shows and so these three had to have nicknames too and Donald Duck's nephew's names seemed to fit, in part because the names sounded phonetically somewhat like their real names, but also because to our Western ears whenever they chattered in Vietnamese or one of the hill languages it sounded to us like ducks in the park in the springtime – making new ducklings.

On a particularly hard day early in our training a Northumberland sergeant had told Hayes to reach into his imagination and put everything he cared about into a bucket and then carry that bucket to safety. He was to ignore heat or cold, fear, fatigue and pain, and carry the bucket forward, no matter what the obstacles. And the imagination tool worked for him, the bucket expanding to include all the Blue Team, a few of the Orange and Green BOGs (Blue, Orange and Green Teams), and some of the other people we lived and worked with, including our mountain top allies. So, our Lone Ranger, who always had trouble communicating his emotions verbally, carried around his feelings for his friends in an imaginary bucket and Huey, Louie, and Dewey were definitely in the mix, in the bucket along with a character we knew as Sanchez.

We never actually knew who Sanchez was working for, Sgt. Johnny Sorenson had long ago told us that Sanchez, or Chavez, or Murphy, or Vasquez or whoever he was at the moment did not belong to Special Forces, but Samuels and Kappas had vetted him somewhere and that was good enough for the rest of us.

We suspected he might belong to the CIA Special Activities Division, which would have meant he was S.A.D. but he told us that he reported to an office in Thailand called the "Special Operations Bureau" which made him a real S.O.B. and as we all agreed, "he is already a prick, he might as well be an An Lac Pric" and so Sanchez got put in Hayes's bucket after a lengthy ceremony one night that involved a lot of alcohol, some candles and feathers and a picture torn from a Playboy Magazine (as a reminder of all we were fighting for).

The two bad-asses, Hayes and Sanchez, linked up with Huey, Louie, and Dewey, began carrying out terror attacks on the traffic on the Ho Chi Minh Trail (whether these raids were authorized or not is still unclear), the five sharing a common goal even if their motivations were perhaps somewhat different; both Hayes and Sanchez wanted to demonstrate the effectiveness of harassing traffic on the Trail and make the case for putting troops in place to block access to the mountain passes from North Vietnam. Sanchez may have been following orders, Hayes's motivation was a little more complex, he was pissed off at the NVA, PAVN, and Viet Cong and somehow happy at the freedom he found in waging war on them. The Cao Dai just wanted to run all other Vietnamese, North or South, out of the mountains.

The five men made up the core of a formidable small fighting force augmented by varying numbers of additional Cao Dai, Yao, and Hmong tribesmen, the unit expanding and shrinking depending on the mission and location, the BOGs arranging and or supplying off the record logistical and tactical support. Tom Minor, our favorite Thai PARU, joined them on some of their missions; he was as pissed as Hayes at the Vietnamese intruders and had his own axe to grind (sometimes literally). Hayes had dubbed the small force "Team Blue Squared" (Tango Bravo Sierra, TBS); their prey on the Trail began to refer to them as Yeu Quai or "Ghost Demons".

Team Blue Squared had been in the mountains for many long weeks planning and preparing a killing ground for a combination ambush and air assault, laying false trails and mine fields, setting deadfalls and traps and placing explosives. They planned to lure an opposing force into this kill zone and during the confusion of an air raid on a North Vietnamese depot area down on a main branch of the Trail, spring the trap and make their escape to a pick-up point to the west.

The kill zone was designed along the lines of a fish weir; it would allow (relatively) safe passage funneled one way into the trap with death and dismemberment for traffic trying to escape. Deadfalls and other booby traps would be activated and mines placed to their rear after the "fish" had followed the lure to a dead-end canyon on the east side of a mountain where they would be subjected to indirect machine gun fire, a salvo of mortar rounds and small arms fire, and the detonation of planted explosives. The trap was designed to decimate the twelve to twenty or up to one hundred men that might continue to chase the bait Hayes, Sanchez and their team laid out even as the depot on the main trail was under air attack.

But as often happens the best laid plans "gang oft awry" and a few days before TBS was ready to spring their trap three transport trucks loaded with Thai military police and three USAF officers arrived at our "Camp Sammy" in the northern part of Thailand and shut down operations of our "Phantom Air Force" with the Fennecs (French versions of the T-28 trainer/fighter/bomber) that conducted our air support. The "regulars" were not going to allow the "irregulars" to manage any part of the non-war heating up in South East Asia and someone had tipped them off to the location of our little airport and its uses. There was no way for those of us in the field to get the message that this had happened, that there would be no air support for the ambush.

The trap had been baited; the supply lines along the main part of the Trail in this area poked with small hit and run raids and the raiders were pulling their pursuers along up pre-determined routes just as planned but there was no air strike to keep the focus on the storage terminals and instead of a couple of security patrols or perhaps a company of infantry the area was alive with NVA and Viet Cong, there were at least three hundred men in hot pursuit of the raiders, way more than the plan had anticipated. And instead of moving straight into the narrow bowl that made up the killing ground, the enemy took up positions surrounding the canyon and set up for a daylight assault.

Hayes had not had any contact from Sanchez or Tom Minor but knew from the sounds to his east and south that they had been busy and from the sounds and flashes of light to his east and north knew that the Cao Dai had done their job poking the beehive as well, but none of them had reached his position just below the ridge on the mountain above the bowl. Were they all running for their lives, could they be hiding from the swarm of men on the mountain side? He would have to hunker down and see what developed, reluctant to leave the field without drawing serious blood, unwilling to leave without knowing the disposition of the rest of his team. Where were those goddamn airplanes?

So, the Lone Ranger waited nerves on edge, fearful of the fate of his team and listened in the dark at the sounds coming up from every direction below him until the hour before dawn when it became very quiet, no night sounds of animals, no sounds from the humans he knew were under his position.

As the darkness of the forest at night gave way to the lighter darkness of the forest in the day he twisted the ends of buried wires on to the terminals of his small coffee grinder generator and spun the handle.

And was rewarded with a result much bigger than he had expected, the charges his team had laid above the bowl to create a small landslide must have been along a hidden fissure in the limestone formation beneath the shallow top soil, the entire shelf above the fifty meter by one hundred meter bowl heaved and collapsed down into the depression, dust and debris still rising when the sound of mortars and heavy machine gun fire reached his ears, at least some of the men on his team were alive and fighting!

The panicked men running upslope toward his position never saw him and succumbed to a few short bursts from the AK 47 he was carrying. Just for the hell of it he rolled a couple of grenades down the hill before he pulled the covers off the motion sensors that would detonate mines he had planted to cover his retreat and started for the team extraction point.

When he caught up with us at the old abandoned airfield he had been joined by a few of the Cao Dai and a couple of Yao, but I could tell by the white spots on his cheeks and the stiffness of his posture that something was wrong, then realized that Huey, Louie, and Dewey weren't in the little group.

In the past weeks and months he had been living under constant strain, hiding day and night, subsisting on poor food and little sleep putting together the TBS mission needs and had passed tired, turned left at fatigued and arrived at a state of weariness that hurt clear down in the marrow of the bone. He had tried hard to keep everyone on his team safe, to keep them all in the bucket and carry it on home. But sometimes the bucket sprang a leak and he would lose someone to attrition, distance or even death.

Seeing Sanchez alive, beat up but alive, and Tom Minor with him, was a huge relief. Seeing other Blue Team members even more relief, but he kept scanning the pass back toward the ambush site, hoping to see more stragglers appear. Then something tugged at the left corner of his eye and he saw three figures emerge from the green edge of the field in an unexpected direction, three men each carrying components of a ma deuce (MA-2 .50 cal machine gun); Huey, Louie, and Dewey, three little ducks in a row.

At that thought he started laughing and looking at Sanchez's yellow and green tattooed face and burnt beard and hair started laughing even harder. And kept laughing in fits and starts.

Laughter, the best medicine. Except he couldn't stop. Until Samuels appeared from the shadows inside a C130 and put an arm around his shoulders and walked him into the belly of the plane.

Chapter 50

The Man

It was understandable that the US Army Air Corp Colonel barely noticed the beggar in the faded blue and white striped burnoose and (probably) once-white turban, improvised crutch under one arm and carrying a battered press board suitcase held together with coarse twine; entire armies of Vichy French and German mechanized battalions had ignored the lame Moroccan Berber or Maghreb Arab or whatever they thought he was, never suspecting that the grubby beggar with the dark eyes, prominent nose, and walnut colored skin was a young man from the American West and part of the eyes and ears of Major Roy Ferrin's British Special Air Service "Desert Rats".

It was equally understandable that when the Colonel saw this same man again standing in front of his desk with a patchy moon-and-red colored jaw where a heavy beard had been close shaven the Colonel did not bother to look closely enough to stir even the faintest recognition, instead signing the papers put before him with only a glimmer of curiosity, "Why had orders come down from on high to send this young sergeant off to Officers Candidate School?".

The answer to that question was that the war-time organized U. S. Office of Strategic Services had decided that all their assigned military personnel forwarded to services in or with other countries should hold officer ranks. But the Colonel was too preoccupied with some face saving moves he was going to have to make to save his own career to dwell on the question.

The Colonels' courage as a fighter pilot was beyond question but his ability to make leadership decisions was in doubt. First, and probably against specific orders, he had dispatched the flyers from the Fighter/Pursuit Squadron he commanded in North Africa into combat in small numbers and far from their base of operations to engage in air-to-

311

air combat against a more experienced and numerically superior enemy that decimated his Squadron and took it far below operational status (or as some of the pilots under his command put it, "He got a lot of good men killed before they could become effective fighters".

And second, he had ordered another flying group under his command to avoid air-to-air conflicts and concentrate on ground targets only – then reported the pilots in this group as cowardly and lazy and of no real use to the war effort. Embarrassingly for him this group under another commanding officer showed great courage and achieved the highest marks performing bomber escort duties over heavily guarded targets (never losing a bomber) as the Tuskegee Airmen.

Years later and just after the cease fire that ended (most of) the armed conflicts of the Korean Police Action this same Colonel, now a General (but with no flying experience in Korea) took command of the 8th Bomber Group as they were being re-deployed to Itazuke Air Base in Japan and took the lead in the review board selecting candidates to be "riffed" (Reduction In Force) as part of the stand-down after the conflict. It is doubtful that he recognized the man who had stood before his desk in Egypt all those years before when he selected Lt. Colonel Kappas to be "riffed", much to the surprise and consternation of many officers who had served with Kappas and knew his skills and accomplishments in the air-to-ground operations in Korea. We knew it was our (the 8th COINs) great good fortune that Kappas took the option of staying in the service as a Senior Non-Commissioned Officer and we rarely noticed or remembered that he was maintaining his rank of Lt. Col. in the USAF Reserves. We knew him as father figure, military arts trainer, martial practitioner, pilot, marksman, wise old uncle, stern disciplinarian and sympathetic counselor; M&M Kappas was the heart and soul of our organization, he was "The Man".

As it became obvious to some of the people in positions of power in Washington D.C. and at the Pentagon that our involvement in South East Asia (SEA) was going to grow, just as some of them had hoped, the Joint Chiefs formed a planning commission and appointed the same General, as Director of Operational Requirements/United States Air Force (DOR/USAF); his brief would be to determine manpower and equipment needs for an increased operational presence in SEA.

General Lemay had already put his fingerprints on close air support, airlift, and anti-guerilla operations when he sent the very capable Major Alderholt on the scene to introduce a new short field aircraft, the Helio Courier, and energize the program to grub out landing fields on mountain tops all over Laos. He pushed further with the establishment of the 4400 Air Combat Training Wing at Hurlburt Field, Florida, and later the "Jungle Jim" school in the Philippines, where they were training the "new breed" of Air Commando; the General handpicked the commanding officers and even specified the Australian style bush hats and bloused boots for their uniforms. Later the name was changed to 1st Air Commando, and that made Kappas (and others) wonder about the credit due Air Commandos of Burma and other theaters in WWII and the Air Commandos of Korea and he decided the new wing might be called 1st to infer that General Lemay had come up with the idea out of whole cloth.

A few years later General Lemay's press officer issued a statement that said the new 1st Air Commando was labeled the "1st" to honor the actions of those previous units (?).

Elements of this new Wing were introduced to combat operations in Viet Nam in the fall of 1961 through their participation in "Farm Gate". Their role and duties in the field appeared very similar to those that might have been performed by 8th COIN members with one glaring exception; they were exposed to press media "ride-alongs" on some field ops.

At that thought Kappas let out a wry smile, in theaters where the 8th COIN were operating its members had stood next to the press corps without even being noticed. Good job, men.

The new DOR/USAF was a strong advocate for an all jet air force, belittling prop driven aircraft as "relics" despite evidence that the prop jobs were much more effective at ground support than any jet aircraft in the Air Force inventory at the time. But he would allow, after a sturdy prompting from the CIA and other sources with direct experience with air-to-ground tactics and operations that indigenous forces could continue to be trained and equipped with propeller driven war birds, including the Harvards (T-6) and Trojans (T-28) already fielded in some theaters.

Training indigenous pilots presented its own set of problems in SEA where many of the pilot candidates were semi-illiterate and had had little experience with operating machinery of any kind, for many of the hill people volunteering to learn to fly even the concept of a compass card was alien. And then there were language and cultural difficulties to overcome. Bravery and local knowledge might not be enough to turn the Lao and Mei (Hmong) candidates in Laos into effective air-to-ground pilots.

As the new directorate began to staff up the DOR/USAF in charge had his people begin looking through Air Force Active Duty and Reserve rosters to find the personnel who could create and manage a training syllabus to be activated at airfields in the U.S., Philippines, Laos, and South Vietnam.

The researchers knew that they had made a "find" when they scanned the USAF Reserve Officers roster and found the name of a Lt. Colonel with both combat flying and instruction experience in a variety of propeller driven aircraft. They got even more excited when they traced his service number and realized the reserve officer was currently serving on active duty as a senior NCO. And they knew they had found a great piece of news to take to the DOR/USAF when they discovered this same officer/sergeant was already serving in SEA and had experience with the local customs and languages.

It is questionable if the general recognized the name when he signed the papers reinstating the Reserve Officers' status and ordering him to report to Nellis Air Force Base for briefing and re-assignment.

Chapter 50

Smitty's Bar

When the six large scruffy looking bearded men came out of the fog and walked into the bar they saw four skinny kids with white sidewall haircuts dressed in tan uniforms and funny hats. Two were standing leaning on a coin operated pool table, one was chatting up three girls at the end of the bar closest to the door, and the other was sitting on a bar stool at a counter to the rear of the room.

The six were joined about a beer-and-a-half later by a tall man with longish hair and what Shakespeare might have described as "a lean and hungry look". This last arrival stopped at the bar for a moment then with a shot glass of whiskey in one hand and mug of beer in the other moved to a seat at the back of the room two spaces over from the uniformed kid sitting staring into space.

On our way back to Nellis from our latest TDY four of us were scheduled to stop in Hawaii and take a three-day training course at the Navy tower where they taught, among other things, departure from a submerged submarine. As part of the training we would enter a compartment at the base of the 100' tower and after the chamber was pressured up and flooded make our way to the surface using the latest in re-breather equipment. Part of the reason for this stop over was to get us, as M&M Kappas put it, "looking military, thinking military, feeling military" before we went back to our permanent party station, he knew we were all feeling a little down and thought the training might be a morale booster, the few days we would have in Oahu after the training wouldn't hurt our feelings either.

We dutifully shaved, got close haircuts (bitching and moaning about chicken shit), and had our uniforms pulled out of musty lockers and cleaned. Some re-tailoring was required as we had all changed shape in the field, some growing a little taller, all losing weight: what the hell, we would look our best and do our First Sergeant proud. Knowing he was coming along and would be there to observe might have helped with our motivation to look squared away for the Squids in Hawaii.

After a week with the Navy Kappas (now First Sergeant Kappas, we were military again) must have decided we were fit to be seen around military establishments because we were issued new travel orders and put on a plane, "sorry men no time for a weekend pass in Oahu", to the mainland where we would bus from San Francisco International up to Hamilton AFB to the north across the Golden Gate Bridge. Our plane had to circle for half an hour before landing at SFA due to foggy conditions and on the bus driving through the city we could only see shadowy images of people, buildings and cars, we didn't even spot one of San Francisco's famous streetcars. When we crossed the Gate all we could see from the bus windows were parts of the red bridge structure against an all white background. Damn, this was disappointing, we were all anxious for our first view of America in months.

Socked in, Hamilton was socked in and the forecast said it would probably stay that way for another day at the minimum so Kappas said we might as well be allowed to go to town for the rest of the day and just be sure to report back by midnight, he would go to the NCO Club for dinner and wait to tuck us in when we got back, he didn't want any of his flock to stray before we got back to Nellis.

The four of us decided to go back to Sausalito and took a bus to the little square next to the ferry docks, it was still foggy and we headed across the street to the No Name Bar for a quick drink, disappointed to see that they did not have a pool table, or any lovely young ladies hanging about, all they could offer on this dreary mid-week afternoon was liquor and backgammon. A bar patron gave us directions to a place up the road; pass the fire station and turn left one block, turn right and go a block or two and there would be a bar with pool tables. As for comely ladies, who knew, we would just have to go see for ourselves.

We walked through the patchy fog and had made the left and right turns and were looking for the bar when I leaned up against a building and started laughing and pointing at my companions, the two in front and one behind. Within half a minute of leaving the No Name Bar we had formed a line with men about three meters apart, Blaske in the lead followed by Cerone, then me, and an alert Hayes bringing up the rear. At the first corner Blaske had paused and looked around while Cerone passed him and went across the street at a diagonal, stopping at the next corner and waiting for Blaske to catch up and pass him while I crossed 15 seconds behind Blaske and Hayes watched from an almost invisible spot at the first corner.

We were doing our in-the-bush-leap-frog-patrol-walk ready for an ambush to appear at any moment in a little seaside town across the bay from San Francisco; as the realization of what we were doing hit me I could not contain my laughter. It took a moment before Hayes joined in then we were all laughing and pointing at each other while we moved on as a gaggle to find the bar.

Three ladies were in the tavern, not really comely but not ugly either, sitting at the end of the bar nearest the door and we were hardly in the room before Cerone had joined them and laughter was coming from that corner while Blaske and Hayes started pushing balls around a pool table. I took a drink from the bartender, prettiest girl in the place, and moved to a barstool at the end of the room where I could watch everything going on and practice my thousand-yard stare.

The bartender had just placed a second drink on the shelf behind my left elbow and I was about to turn and pick it up when the six men came in and with their "I'm a badass" noisy attitudes and body language told me what was probably going to happen in the next hour. They had already started making sotto voce comments like, "What falls out of airplanes? Chicken shit!" and making kissing sounds before the seventh man came in, got his drinks and took a stool two spaces over from me.

317

I went back to practicing my stare and watched and waited for the action I knew would happen: the six big men would pump each other up and bluster and attempt to bully for a while, then they would move into the "monkey dance" stage and start doing a little verbal, then physical pushing around trying to cow and intimidate the kids in uniform until a flash point was reached. The six big assholes would not even know the flash point had been reached before they were under attack; the question I was asking myself was who would open the action?

I knew Cerone could probably work his charm, tell a few jokes and defuse the tension in the room or maybe I could do something to stop things from going over the brink, after all we could not afford to have to meet any police today or do anything that might make us late getting back to Hamilton. And besides I didn't think we should cause any problems for the bartender. But Cerone seemed inclined to just see how things developed, he had traded seats with one of the girls at his end of the bar so that he could be in a better position if (when) a fight broke out and I wasn't through practicing my stare.

The bluster and buildup stage was ending and about to move into the monkey dance stage when Blaske walked to the bar, got some change and went to the payphone in the hall leading to the rest rooms. Who in the hell was he calling now? He was off the phone in a couple of minutes and went back, draft beer in hand, to lean on the wall next to the front door behind one of the pool tables next to the pool cue rack.

Hayes had moved to a spot on the other side of the door and was turned half toward the bar stool where Cerone was sitting and half toward the room with an expression that was part smile and part smirk on his face (not the scary blank I'm-going-to-kill-someone look he sometimes got in the field), he was looking forward to getting his kinks out with a little rough and tumble. I kept a flat face but smiled inwardly when I realized Hayes was closing off the exit, blocking the route of escape anyone might try to take while Blaske protected his flank.

Hayes really was the badass these wanna-bes thought they were and if roused could no doubt take out the whole room but he wasn't really worrying me; I was sure he would practice restraint and stay on the safe side of deadly force, he would simply dominate and perhaps leave behind a little blood and bruises. He was the only one of us that might let an opponent take the first swing.

Blaske's reaction I wasn't sure about, he liked the long gun in the field not just because he liked to see the results of solving the shot puzzle but because he liked to protect his team, providing cover when we moved in or out of hot spots. "Moms" Blaske could get junkyard dog mean if he thought any of us were in danger. Usually he was a counter-puncher but might take the initiative and strike first before letting any of the rest of us get hurt.

Cerone worried me though, if provoked into an attack he would likely not practice any restraint and would go full bore at any threat. In the Old West he would have been the gunfighter to fear, his reflexes might not have been as fast as Hayes' but he was quicker through the OODA Loop (Observe, Orient, Decide, Attack – a fighter pilots guide to survival put forth by Major "Forty Seconds" Boyd at the Nellis Fighter Weapons School and a system we adopted) and would probably be the first to fire, or in this case the first to engage. Yeah, I was pretty sure any action would start with Cerone. I was wrong.

One of the assholes in a leather vest, engineer boots, and greasy jeans, shirt open to show a hair covered tattoo, came down to the end of the bar where I was sitting, winked at the guy two spaces down from me and started making kissing sounds, probably sure that my immobility was caused by fear.

He hovered in front of me inches from my face surrounded by an ugly falang/white man smell of stale sweat, beef, beer and popcorn farts mixed with testosterone and adrenaline and a dash of gasoline and oil. Then he reached to pull the maroon beret from under the shoulder strap on my bush jacket.

Dave grabbed him in a firm grip, left thumb buried deep in the throat under the larynx, right hand squeezing his testicles, he ran the lout backwards until his head hit a support pole and the bigger man slid down moaning and gasping, specks of spittle and vomit on the front of his shirt. It took a huge amount of will power for me to prevent Dave from stomping on the groaning man's head or from kicking him in the temple, he settled for delivering a sharp kick to the idiot's mid-section. I had kept a part of my attention on the man two seats down from me and seeing that he was still sitting and did not look like he was going to be a threat I shifted my attention to the other end of the room where a ferocious looking Blaske (who knew he could look that mean?)was holding two men on the floor at bay with a swinging pool cue, Cerone was still seated (with a big grin on his face) and Hayes had two men on the floor near his feet, one holding his right arm at an odd angle and grimacing with pain, the other out cold (or faking it, staying down was a good idea for him).

The last man (of the six) standing wasn't really standing for very long, Hayes was holding the man at arm's length with his left hand, right hand balled into a fist held at the opposite end of his arm span and when he brought the two hands together there was a fountain of blood and another body slipped to the floor just as a man in a yellow baseball cap came in the front door and with eyes widened asked, "Did someone call a cab?"

I went back to the rear counter, gulped down my remaining brandy and soda then went to the bar and emptied my pockets of their sixty-three dollars and change as a tip for the bartender (bartendress?) who was giving me a strange look and pouring brandy into two shot glasses. Cerone was making his farewells and jotting down a couple of phone numbers (we might come this way again, who knew?) while Blaske and Hayes stood just inside the door waiting for us.

The bartender downed one shot and I downed the other and to her "who the fuck are you guys?" I replied, "I'm Tonto" and nodding to the other end of the room, "that's the Lone Ranger, the Cisco Kid and Pancho". I took another look at the man still against the counter at the rear of the room in time to see him raise two fingers to his forehead and smiling give a loud "Oo-Rah!"

Back at Hamilton AFB First Sergeant M&M Kappas wondered why we were back on base so early then seeing Hayes's blood splattered jacket and shirt and tie asked. "Are there going to be any police looking for you?" We shook our heads no and he asked, "Which of you started the trouble?" There were no, "the other guys started it" or other excuses that could be made. We knew that getting into a fracas off base was a big no-no, getting into a fracas off base and in uniform could be a serious punishable offense.

Four hands went up in the air.

Chapter 51

The White Envelope

After an absence of a few years it felt good to be back on the reservation camping under a tree he knew well, a day bag containing a large white envelope, a small black box, a windbreaker, two quarts of cold beer and sandwich makings parked between the roots at the base of the tree next to a thick wool blanket. It had been a long time since he had taken time to simply sit and think, to reflect on where he had been and where he expected to be going.

He thought he knew what was in the large white envelope with the "Tactical Air Command, Pentagon" stamp on the front and the red lettered "Top Secret" stamp across the sealed and taped flap. And he thought he knew what was in the small felt covered black box the clerk for the General's Aide had handed him. He was in no hurry to open either one.

When he had pulled up in front of the general store in Hon Dah and got out of the dusty rental car the old men sitting in the shade barely looked in his direction, acknowledging his presence with quiet nods and low approving grunts. No one asked where he had been, what he was doing back, how long he was staying, and they simply sat and waited for the answers to those questions to reveal themselves. He bought a few supplies; happy to spend a few dollars at the reservation store and nodding in silent reply to the old men got back into the car and drove to the base of the trail that would lead him to his camp spot. It felt right to be back.

With more than twenty-plus years in the Armed Services as an enlisted man, a junior officer, a senior officer, and finally as a senior NCO he knew as well as anyone that the military was a giant, clumsy bureaucracy filled with people anxious to maintain and improve their position/power/prestige even at the cost of the organizations fulfillment of its mission. The further up the food chain one looked the more jealous of their prerogatives the managers were likely to be. He knew too well that the military machine was a bureaucracy that would eat its own young.

And it wasn't just inter-services rivalry, the jealousy and competition for recognition, advancement, and funding raged on between departments and units in the same service. The transfer of power from one Presidential administration to another was always cause for waves of anxiety and change starting at the General Officer level and moving down through the ranks. As the Kennedy administration took the reins there had been, and still was (as Kappas sat under his tree) a scurrying for favor with the new "Boss".

Almost simultaneous with the start of the Kennedy Administration USAF Chief of Staff General White had retired and the new Air Force Chief was a man who did not particularly like the Tactical Air Command (TAC) or its mission, having famously said that, "Flying fighters is fun. Flying bombers is important".

General Lemay, new USAF Chief of Staff, was a heavy bomber man all the way but pressure from the administration and a view of some new (to him) realities forced him to reconsider the approach the Air Force would play in the newly emerging war zone(s) in Southeast Asia (SEA). Gen. Lemay's belief was that aerial and naval bombardments could end the war handily and that there would be no need for boots on the ground but political considerations and other factors made that unpalatable to the administration. In later years General Lemay insisted he had not said "We should bomb the little bastards back to the Stone Age", but rather had said, "We could bomb the little bastards back to the Stone Age".

TAC had already re-written its training syllabus for fighter pilots and was putting a new emphasis on training for precision air-to-ground operations and had developed a training program for ground based forward air controllers. Some of the pilots, aircraft, and air controllers were already operating in the field (including members of 8th COIN) in various parts of the world with favorable results. The problem for Lemay (after years of deriding such operations) was that he had had no part in establishing these programs; he had no "ownership" in the existing TAC successes, he needed to do something to get his fingerprints on anything positive, or with potentially positive appearances. He would have to be seen actively managing existing air to ground resources and/or starting new programs, or some combination of both.

The new administration was still giving an ear to those who counseled a limited involvement, low cost, high efficiency approach to the (mostly civil) wars in Laos and Viet Nam but many of the Admirals and Generals, including Lemay, were betting that the commitment would grow (some were pushing hard for a deeper involvement) and were positioning for the best place at the table.

Kappas had been involved with 8th COIN almost from its inception under TACs umbrella initiating a recruitment program for the training cadre and for new candidates. He had worked closely with Captain Samuels and Major Bohannon as they had written and modified the training courses for the candidates, chaired the candidate selection committee and personally overseen most of the early training. It may have been adopted but he still saw it as "his baby".

He had even insisted that it be called the "Eighth" Counterinsurgency Study Group, there was no 1st through 7th, there was no other group like it, the number eight came from the fact that eight is considered a lucky number in the Orient and he had known, or at least suspected that the bulk of the units' work would be performed somewhere in Asia. He was for the most part correct but could not project in the early days that there would be 8th COIN assets on assignments worldwide.

As the unit had evolved and proven its usefulness to certain officers in TAC five Captains, two Majors, and five senior NCOs had been added to the roster (none promoted internally, with one hilarious exception) and team names had been designed to identify areas of operations; i.e. teams assigned to Asia were named as colors (Blue, Orange, and Green operated primarily in Laos and Viet Nam), teams assigned to the Americas (Central, South, etc.) had numeric identifiers, and teams assigned to Europe, Africa, and the Mid-East had alpha identifiers. Kappas remained the First Sergeant of this far flung group, but kept Laos, where a lot was happening, as his main focus and relied on the other senior NCOs to keep the wheels turning smoothly and keep the teams as safe as possible on their missions (and keep the officers out of trouble).

In Laos and Thailand he assisted with pilot training of mercenaries and locals despite no longer being on any roster as a "flying officer", he still held his military licenses, and spent some time in the field in the northwest of Laos with an occasional foray into areas that are still classified. He also quietly managed our very own, paid for by the CIA through a couple of embassies, "Phantom Air Force" and planned and directed air assets for our "air ambushes".

He was a very busy man and though military doctrine might have dictated that his teams should have an officer or at least an E7 in charge in the field, and did in other areas of operations, in Laos Samuels was the only officer available with the right training and the confidence of the teams and he was already overworked. For some unknown reason (an early warning sign that things were not all rosy) requests forwarded for promotion of team members went unanswered and all that were available were E5s.

But Kappas had confidence in his men and their training and sent them into the field, sometimes singly, with full confidence in their ability to get the job done and come home alive. A few men were lost in various parts of the world and that hurt, each loss was taken to heart as a personal failure (he tried to conceal that fact), the losses in SEA particularly struck him personally.

Sitting under the tree and thinking it occurred to him that perhaps fatigue and overwork, and his personal enthusiasm for the job 8th COIN was doing, had made him ignore some signs that the unit might be in for some intra-service political difficulties. Jealousy of team successes might be at the core of some difficulties Major Bohannon was having with getting authorization and funding to recruit and train additional teams (the Major reported that many doors that had been warmly open to him were now closed, several General Officers who had proffered support for the Group in the past were either gone or unavailable). Colonel Van's abrupt departure from Laos and the subsequent news that he was no longer in the military had been worrisome and when operational control in Laos shifted from the Programs Evaluation Office to the Military Assistance Advisory Group the 8th COIN went into a kind of command structure limbo.

Captain Samuels still reported directly to the embassy and all 8th COIN personnel in Laos remained in civilian clothes (tech rep badges worn outside their shirts when in town or on base) and maintained a low profile, they just faded into the background, but still performed their duties in accordance with instructions that came to them through the embassy (as opposed to getting their orders from the new set of officers that came with MAAG).

It wasn't unusual for Kappas to be called back to the States for either de-briefing or to be briefed on new information, or for organizational and housekeeping duties related to the Group. So, it was no surprise when he received the cable instructing him to report back to Nellis but his reception this last time was out of the ordinary. The staff car that picked him up on the flight line took him directly to the office of the Base Commanders Aide where he was met by a Master Sergeant, who was an old friend and a man of few words, serving on the Commanders staff. The MSgt closed the door to his office and returning to his desk took two glasses and a bottle of Cognac from a drawer, pouring three fingers into each glass without saying anything. When both men had emptied the glasses, the MSgt handed Kappas a large white envelope and small black box, still without saying a word but flashing a big grin. As Kappas left the office the last thing he heard as the door closed behind him was the young Airman First Class stationed as gatekeeper saying, "Congratulations, Sir". Sir?

He had gone directly back to the flight line and checked out a "blue canoe" (Cessna 310) from the Aero Club and filed a flight plan for Show Low, Arizona, the nearest airport to the White Mountain Reservation.

It was a cold night under the tree on the White Mountain Indian Reservation and the man wrapped in a wool blanket woke before first light with a stiffness in his joints and a chill in his chest that made him regret his decision of the evening before to not make a campfire, he had wanted to watch the stars come up over the horizon without the distracting glare of firelight.

He stood, stretched, and moved off a dozen paces to have an early morning piss and relieving himself against the trunk of a vanilla smelling pine tree savored the clean crisp air of the mountains where he had spent a large part of his boyhood; perhaps he had been wrong not to keep a closer connection to this place and its people.

Returning to the base of the tree where he had slept he stood facing east to greet the morning sun and surprised himself when in a low voice he offered an ancient prayer as the orange/red orb rose to create another day. After accepting the sun's appearance and offering tobacco bits and breath in the directions of the Four Sacred Mountains, he completed his morning ablutions and prepared his breakfast. When he finished his breakfast, he would be ready to open the large white envelope and the small black box.

He opened a can of potted meat and made two large sandwiches, setting them aside while he used a "church key" (bottle and can opener, it would leave triangular holes in a can) to punch holes in the side and what had been the bottom of the empty meat can. He put the can, bottom side up over a lit heat tab burning on what had been the top of the can. On this improvised stove he carefully placed a canteen cup of water adding two packets of Nescafe instant coffee and an extra-large dollop of sweetened condensed milk.

Squatting next to his camp stove, hunger staunched with the two potted meat sandwiches and canteen cup filled with coffee ready at hand, he reached into his daypack and pulled out the small black, felt covered box and white 10 x 14" envelope sealed with red stamps on the front and back. He would open the box first, sure he knew what was in it, but strangely reluctant to confirm his conjecture.

He opened the box and looked for a long moment at the contents, then set it aside and with a razor-sharp para drop knife slit open the white envelope and scanned the documents enclosed, letting out a low "hah" each time he read the signature at the bottom of several of the pages. The officer who was a Colonel in Egypt when they first met, and who became a General he met again just after Korea, was touching his life once more. Reading the documents a second time and more thoroughly, he realized that even if he did not take this new assignment he would not be returning to the duties he had held for the past five years and more, that part of his military career was now closed to him.

Sitting under the tree he knew there would be those who would think he should be happy and he tried to connect with that feeling, but looking at the contents of the black box, at the two silver oak leaves it contained, he felt a chill that the now full risen sun could not warm.

Chapter 52

Xmas In The Desert

It was windy and cold at the old barracks on the dry lakebed at Indian Springs Auxiliary Airfield Number Two when they brought us there a few days before Christmas, the wind singing a forlorn song that we could not escape day or night. We could watch the fine dry sand filter in through cracks in the un-insulated walls and around every door and window; shine a flashlight at someone's breath plume in the below-freezing air and you would see a miniature universe of dust motes twinkling in the light. We were all coughing and sneezing within an hour of debarking from the series of transports that had hopped from Southeast Asia bringing us back to this part of the world.

Each man was issued a tick mattress, a fart sack, two thin wool blankets and two thinner yellow sheets, not enough to keep us warm in these temperatures and we were not happy to learn that the oil-fired boilers didn't have much fuel. We could see the lights brightening the sky to our south over Las Vegas and knew that just to the left of the glow was Nellis Air Force Base where our cold weather gear was stored about 90 miles away.

We spent our first night back shivering and bitching with three layers of tropical clothing on and wondering when they were going to send us back to our permanent party barracks at Nellis or ship us our cold weather gear, more blankets, and heating fuel.

On our second day in the desert other 8th COIN teams began arriving from other parts of Asia (colors), Central and South America (numbers), Europe, Africa and the Middle East (alphas). This was only the second time since early training that units from all over the world had been called back stateside at the same time, something big must be up.

We had a good laugh, or at least a chuckle, on the day when the name of one MSgt Seviers appeared on the posted roster, it took us awhile to remember who that name (and rank) could belong to; finally someone (Cerone I think) remembered a guy who had somehow vanished from our daily rolls when we had rotated (briefly) through Tachikawa Airbase, Japan. When he arrived at the security gate just down the road from the barracks (security gate deep in the desert with no fence on either side for about fifty miles) in a 1956 Chevy convertible even the most jaded among us were amused. It got even funnier when Hayes insisted he take off the jump pin he hadn't earned, the pathfinder patch he hadn't earned, and the maroon beret he hadn't earned. Seviers not only complied with Hayes' "request", he even "volunteered" to sell the Chevy to Blaske — who was panting and fawning all over the red and cream convertible. In exchange Seviers would (1) not get a beating from Hayes and (2) not have the scam he had been running for years in the Philippines (putting himself in for promotion and finessing the process way ahead of any time-and-grade schedule) exposed. And he could hang with us as long as he didn't try to pull rank (we all kinda' liked his stories and his Cajun cool).

There were never any brass bands when we left or when we came home from our overseas TDYs, no throngs of family or friends to tearfully bid us "farewell" or "welcome back". We quietly departed our permanent party station by bus, train, or plane and returned just as quietly.

There were no parades, no medal or awards ceremonies, no merit promotions (we were frozen at E5, most of us anyway), no public recognition or even acknowledgement of our service; although I believe that my mother may have received a letter from one or two Presidents thanking her for her sons' "service in harm's way".

There were no hero medals (although I had witnessed plenty of heroics) and no GI Bill benefits for "peace time GIs"; as "tweeners" between the end of the Korean Police Action in 1953 and the "official start" of the Viet Nam War in 1965 (they have been revising that date in recent years) when we left the service we would not be entitled to most Veterans Benefits for things like home buying, college tuition, or business loans, and we would not be awarded any points for consideration in placement in government jobs (some GI Bill benefits were reinstated and made retroactive for South East Asia and other "tweener" veterans in March of 1966, too late to be of use for many of us in 8th COIN).

On the bright side President Kennedy's Executive Order of December 4, 1961(retroactive to 1958) authorized the Blue, Orange, and Green Teams (BOGS) to wear the Armed Forces Expeditionary Medal (AFEM) with service stars and arrowhead devices and we were proud to wear our blue and white enameled Air Force Parachutist Badges and our Pathfinder Patches. Some teams with service in other parts of the world were also authorized the AFEM, some with and some without multiple stars and devices. That was enough; we knew who we were and where we had been, even if we were not allowed to tell anyone else.

General Orders posted on the bulletin board said that there would be no leaves or passes issued and we were all to remain on post until we were individually processed, which I knew would not happen until after the holidays, I'd seen this chicken shit before; the clerks and de-briefers that would process us were probably all off duty and enjoying the holidays while we waited in the desert. Hayes was sure we were being kept isolated (he said "quarantined") because "they" didn't want us talking to anybody at Nellis, enlisted or NCO, as our version of the realities in South East Asia and other parts of the world might not match the official line the generals were putting out. He was probably correct.

The small HQ (headquarters) shack where the dailies were posted was peopled by three airman clerks and a couple of nervous looking (I thought) 2nd Lieutenants, nobody we knew. A Major that none of us knew either wandered around "inspecting" and looking busy for the first few days we were there then disappeared back down the dusty road south in the direction of the main gate. A Colonel, also a stranger to us, with a lot of fruit salad and a certain air of swagger (must have been a fighter pilot) who appeared with a deuce-and-a half (two and half ton truck) full of warm clothing and new blankets following his staff car had MSgt Seviers (Seviers would not look in the direction of the BOGs) call everyone into a mid-morning formation on the lee side of what was designated as our "chow hall" and gave a short speech before dismissing us and disappearing in the same direction the Major had gone the day before. All I can remember of his speech was that he sneezed and coughed a lot - the warm clothing and fresh blankets were the stand-outs of the day.

I just said "fuck this" and volunteered for the detail that hauled garbage the fifteen miles or so down to the airstrip and hangars located by the main gate to the gunnery range, and next to the highway going north to Beatty or south to Las Vegas. At the airstrip I ditched the detail while they were on a coffee and (stale) doughnut break and let myself into a hangar where we had stored equipment after an exercise in the desert during a previous visit to the range. I lucked out and the BSA thumpers (one-cylinder 500cc dirt bikes) were still there and after some carb tickling and fiddling with the choke I was able to get one kick started and rode east across the desert through some rough terrain, staying in gullies and washes until I was sure I was out of sight of the airstrip tower then cut back south by west until I reached the highway just below the point where a road went up the east side of Mt. Charleston. I pulled onto the highway and merged with traffic, most of it cars with skiers and sledders coming off the mountain, hoping my plate-less motorcycle would go un-noticed in the holiday flow. I was heading for the "House With the Blue Fence" in Vegas.

Someone on the Blue Team, probably Blaske maybe Cerone, had had a similar but simpler plan; they had Seviers at the wheel of what was now Blaske's car show his MSgt stripes and bluff their way out of the main gate with Hayes riding shotgun and Blaske and Cerone in the back seat. The Air Police at the gate were too wrapped up in their own misery at spending the holidays in the dusty middle of nowhere to challenge the car full of NCOs "on a detail to requisition supplies" or whatever they said they were doing. They were already waiting with beer and whiskey when I got to the house. Maybe this Seviers guy was okay.

A serious cold snap moved in and we were all glad to be in our off-base home with the space heater roaring and providing a background noise to the non-stop beer, popcorn, and pizza party and card game going on in the front room. The only sour note came from the fact that none of our "Den Mothers" were there to greet us, four had reached the end of their work visa stays and had returned to England and the fifth was in Hollywood being prepped for a singing career. Bummer. Especially for Blaske.

On New Year's Day we decided we better get back out to the barracks in the desert before we were missed; permanent party clerks, officers, and the like would be coming back on duty and whatever "processing" or debriefing or whatever we were to undergo (the posted General Orders were not clear) would be starting soon and we did not want to be missing for the head count. We were AWOL but AWOL with a sense of duty.

I leaned the BSA against the rail on the back porch next to my old Triumph Trophy (might as well keep the bike around for a while), we loaded a couple of cases of beer in the trunk of the Chevy and heater on full blast, convertible top down, and a pitcher of Bloody Marys for refreshment, drove back up the Tonapah Highway to the gunnery range where our decrepit old barracks were waiting – we thought.

The Air Police (APs) at the gate just off the highway didn't even bother to check IDs of the occupants of the red and cream convertible, Blaske at the wheel, and we were on the dusty road north for less than ten minutes before we started smelling smoke and as we pulled the horizon hiding the old barracks closer we began to see thin tendrils of smoke and ash being pushed into mare's tails by a light breeze.

Two of the five barracks buildings in the desert compound were missing, smoldering ruins marking the scene where they had been. Neat stacks of footlockers, barracks bags, and other personal gear and equipment were lined up in the desert near where our barracks had been. Apparently, someone had carefully removed all personal items from the barracks before they accidently caught fire during the cold (really cold) weather of the previous few days.

A Colonel (he of the warm blankets a few days before) was there facing two straggly lines of grey-faced men, eight or ten fidgety APs sheltering behind him, no 2nd lieutenants in sight. MSgt Seviers jumped out of the convertible, followed by the rest of us moving a little slower (reluctant to put down our drinks) and started straightening the lines of men into an almost acceptable formation. While the troops were straightening up the Colonel looked around with a "nothing happened here" look on his face; that got some respect from the lot of us.

As the Colonel began addressing the assembled troops I found my mind wandering, trying to focus but being overcome by a sense of disaster, I could only pick out bits and pieces of what he was telling us; SMSgt Kappas had been reinstated as an officer and reassigned, Captain Samuels had been reassigned, Major Bohannon had returned to civilian life and joined his fathers' oil company in Dallas, none of them would be returning. All bad news, sad news I was having trouble digesting.

I started thinking about our friend Sgt Johnny Sorenson who had left the service for a job in Los Angeles, and Morrison who had taken an early-out to go back to college as part of a deal he had made with his father. Our armorer "Zero" had become a US citizen and was off to a new career at Edwards Air Force Base and TSgt Bobby Grimes hadn't come to our "reunion in the desert", where in the hell was he? No one knew where Sanchez had gone; he had just crossed the river into Thailand one day and never returned. I knew I was really going to miss the "Den Mothers" (a dark-haired one in particular) and that I might not see my friend Baphang again. Even "my buddy" Floyd had disappeared into the Golden Triangle with his Shan wife. I pushed my mind away from thoughts of any of the others we had left behind in SEA.

I shivered, not from the cold but from a sense of loneliness and loss; our world had shrunk to the four of us left on the Blue Team and a few acquaintances on the Orange and Green Teams. There was no one else on the planet with similar and shared experiences or that we could talk to about where we had been and what we had been doing without violating serious security constraints. There was no one left for us to talk, laugh, and drink and let our hair down with except the remaining 8th COIN members.

Then the Colonel gave us news that brought me back in the moment with a great shock. Ever since the Programs Evaluation Office had been closed we were all in an orphan unit, consequently 8th COIN was going to be de-mobbed (demobilized) and all personnel reassigned to other units. He continued talking but I didn't hear any of it, standing there in the cold looking around at my surroundings.

I had always liked the desert with its pastels and ever-changing colors, its stark light and brilliantly lit sunrises and sunsets. But now, ignoring the need to stay at parade rest facing forward, I turned and looked all around me and saw nothing but ugliness.

The desolation of our surroundings matching the bleak landscape in my heart.

Chapter 53

Dog Days

When Hayes stood up I knew I should remain in my seat but reflexes born of loyalty, comradery, and years of inter-reliance made me stand up next to him in the small space between the rows of folding chairs.

I had been daydreaming and had myself in a sunlit grove of trees next to a deep pool of clear water in a land where tigers still roamed and even God would need a map to find me, a dark haired girl with a brass buttoned blue jacket and colorful red, black, yellow skirt preparing tea off to one side of the glade, while the general on the podium, the Director of Resources Southeast Asia, droned on with his pep talk addressing the men of the Armament and Electronics squadron we were attached to while the four of us waited for the end of our enlistments to come closer.

When the voice went off half a meter above my head, "You're wrong. That's not how it works. Sir." I stood up fully awake in time to see a glowering general up on the podium and a couple of Air Police sideling our way. I didn't know exactly what had happened but knew the shit was in the fan now, Hayes had publicly challenged something the general had said, a breach of military etiquette that was not going to be overlooked, not by this particular general. Damn. A quick shake of my head kept Blaske and Cerone in their seats as the APs motioned Hayes and then me out to the aisle.

The general was warming the troops up for the conflict in South East Asia (SEA) upper echelons knew was coming and pointing out the benefits of an all jet Air Force and the new equipment pilots would be flying, and how important the maintenance side of operational readiness would be to future missions. And I guess that was all good, Hayes didn't have any beef with anything the general said until he started talking about air-to-ground applications with the new war birds. As the general pushed further and further into an area of our expertise Hayes found he was unable to swallow some of the bullshit and had felt a strong urge to speak out, a compulsive act.

After a night spent restricted to our barracks the two of us were standing in front of the general's desk at rigid attention early the next morning getting reamed. As the general's wrath wore down he switched from a tone of berating to one of lecturing; and Hayes did it again. As the general was condescendingly explaining to us how air-to-ground worked, Hayes took exception and interjected to explain how the interface between the forward air controller (they call them combat controllers now) and pilot really worked, and why the old prop jobs made better air-to-ground platforms.

A red-of-face, spittle on his lip general loudly ordered that Hayes be stripped of rank and put in the stockade for thirty days for insubordination and that I be punished by Article 15 of the United States Code of Military Justice (USCMJ) and stripped of rank for a period of sixty days. Perhaps the general didn't realize I had less than sixty days to go on my enlistment, or was he going to hold me over until I got my rank back? Not likely, I think he wanted to be rid of us, rid of all the old ex-8th COIN personnel, the only people at Nellis with recent live experience in the field and an awareness of what was going on in SEA; he shouldn't have to wait for long, there were only four of us left on his base. Members of the Orange and Green teams had either gotten discharged and returned to civilian life or re-enlisted and sent elsewhere to re-train in other fields. A couple of guys from numbered teams (Central and South America) had become part of the training cadre in the new First Air Commando Wing at Hurlburt Field in Florida, soon to be known as the 4488th Air Combat Wing, three from alphabet teams (Europe and Middle East) were assigned as instructors at the Jungle Jim School in the Philippines, I guess their desert experience made them experts at jungle warfare. None of the color team members (Asia), the ones with experience in Laos, Cambodia, and Viet Nam, had been recruited as instructors or as part of the NCO cadre for the new organization.

I wasn't particularly bothered by the demotion that was a regular occurrence for Cerone and I, we were constantly put up for discipline by First Sergeant Knight and recommended for promotion by the Non-Commissioned Officer In Charge (NCOIC) of the shop we were assigned to work out of on the flight line. Even the usually dapper Blaske had been ripped for slovenly dress and bad haircut a couple of times. The three of us checked the bulletin board in front of the operations shack to see what rank we were on any given day and finally just gave up and wore slick sleeve fatigue uniforms with dark patches where rank and insignia had once been. But Hayes had stayed out of sight training on the F105 Thunderchief (Thud) fire control systems (armament computers) and had thought he was immune to discipline by keeping out of the First Sergeant's sight.

His knowledge of the Thud's design purpose and mission capabilities was a large part of Hayes's disgust and disdain for the general's description of the role the plane was now being tasked to fill. The Thunderchief had been designed as a high altitude, fast delivery system for nuclear weapons and was well suited to that role, now the general was describing how useful it was going to be in low altitude ground support missions; Hayes knew that meant a lot of people were going to die, pilots and ground troops alike through this misuse of a weapons platform, the helplessness he felt at not being able to get this message across stung him, stung all four of us, to the quick.

Just the four of us from our original team now, our First Sergeant, Captain, and Major off to new adventures, a couple of us missing from fatal "training accidents", Morrison taking an early-out to enroll in a Pre-Med course at USC as his part of a deal he had made with his father when the Blue Team wanted help getting two little girls to safe haven in America. And our "known associates" were scattered, Sergeant Johnny Sorenson to the LAPD, My Buddy Lloyd had disappeared into the Golden Triangle with his Shan wife, and we had last seen Sanchez going across the river with his file case full of maps, notes, and photographs to support his, our, contention that boots and close air support in the passes of the

Annamite Cordillera could halt the flow of men and material down the Ho Chi Minh Trail.

Just the four of us, so of course we found ways to keep communications open with Hayes and make sure he had plenty of cigarettes to use as currency in the stockade. Reports we got back said that he was making good use of his time reading, arm wrestling all comers, and taking care of the guard dogs that were housed in off-the-ground cages in the stockade's fenced compound. Monday of his third week in the stockade we got a message from him saying we should be in a position to see into the compound during the monthly inspection due for the next Thursday.

We three on the outside were having car fun on our off-duty hours; Blaske washing, waxing, and caressing his red and white Chevy convertible, me collecting speeding tickets in a Jaguar XK 120 with a Buick V-8 under the hood and a five speed crash box, and genius Cerone having the most fun in a Triumph TR3 with hub caps that flashed the message "fuck you", "fuck you", "fuck you" when he drove at a certain speed down Officer Row. We would regularly form a three-car parade by the stockade in the early morning and yell and wave at Hayes while he "exercised" the guard dogs.

The designated Thursday arrived with desert spring blustery weather, a feeling of positive ions and the smell of ozone in the air with small thunderclouds quickly forming and just as quickly dissipating, some leaving wet spots on the ground as they passed, three of us on the bench seat of a USAF Ford pickup drinking coffee and waiting to watch the inspection, Hayes in view dressed in grey fatigues with the letter "P" stenciled on the back moving from kennel to kennel, never turning to face our way.

A patter on the pickup roof and the odor of wet, dusty alkaline soil announced a small rain shower was coming by just as Air Police staff and officers appeared in the stockade compound, some with umbrellas, all being careful to stay on the graveled pathways in the fenced in area. The passing squall and a certain incredulity made it difficult at first to see

339

what was happening across the road from our station, an odd sight through the blurred windshield and sweeping wiper blades.

The dogs were out; the guard dogs were on the loose and doing what they were trained to do, capturing intruders. We three in the truck were howling with laughter to see the pandemonium ensuing before our eyes, portly admin officers trying to avoid the dogs, the smarter or more knowledgeable among the officers lying face down on the wet ground and graveled pathways so the dogs would leave them alone, others less knowledgeable or perhaps more panicked trying to run or climb the fence and being pulled down by the dogs and the enlisted Air Police losing their white hats, and some getting bitten, while they tried to get the dogs in control.

The rattle of rain on the truck roof was getting louder but we thought we heard a whistle trill from somewhere in the compound and could see through the wet streaked windshield the dogs returning to the front of each of their kennels, sitting with tongues lolling, the picture of canine innocence. Standing at stiff attention in the rain, right pinkie finger raised in salute, was our boy Hayes. We couldn't make out the expression on his face from our position but guessed he was wearing a silly smirk, and could almost hear him saying, "That's one!"

Blaske and I were trying to figure out how he had trained the dogs in such a short time; Cerone wanted to know how he made it rain.

Chapter 54

Fear, Anger, and Guilt

Fear was always with us awake or asleep, a constant companion that could blow on the back of our necks at any time. Fear could make our guts watery, our knees weak; make a man's whole body shake out of control. He, she, it has an identity that could squeeze our lungs, blur our vision and dull our hearing. It could even stop a heart. Fear could freeze us in place when we should be moving or make us run madly out of control when we should stay still.

Fear could make us crazy, or do stupid things, or even kill one of us; it could come at us head-on in the light or sneak up on us in the dark, it always knew where to find us and when we would have our guard down. Fear is an unreasonable bitch; in order to survive it we had to learn to function in its company; we had to learn to accommodate fear and move on or it would cripple or kill us and maybe our comrades as well, in both combat and non-combat situations.

Fear would take many forms small and large: and no matter how long or how often we were exposed to it none of us ever knew for certain exactly how we would react when it ramped up, the same man who would storm an enemy position one day might hide somewhere with wet pants the next.

In the military environment even small fears can get ratcheted up to almost unbearable levels: Fear of not performing for your NCOs and Officers. Fear of letting your team mates down. Fear of letting your buddies know how really afraid you are. Fear of noise and confusion. Probably the biggest fear for the guys I knew; fear of being hurt and maimed. And somehow last on all my team mates' list; fear of death.

Training could not make any of us immune to fear but it could help us become inured to its' presence; to become accustomed to the constant pressure and still function. The message we got in training was that, "it's okay to be afraid, just don't let it stop you from doing what you have to do". Training and experience made us so accustomed to "Fear as a Constant Companion" that our conscious minds sometimes forgot it was there, familiarity can often build an ease with the circumstances of danger.

And we found ourselves in the circumstances of danger often, sometimes daily, sometimes minute by minute, second by second; sitting on a stick waiting to be inserted into hostile territory, walking through a claustrophobically narrow green tunnel with no visibility knowing every green leaf can hide a threat, sitting down at a strange café knowing the soup might blow up, entering a village compound hidden so deep in the forest it would take the gods three days to find us, and dozens of other situations we lived with day and night.

We knew that the many hours of training the military gave us and the circumstances we often had to live with taught us how to live with fear. But at the time none of us recognized that fear could be missed, that once habituated it could become a narcotic, that we could become addicted. I often hear people use the term "adrenaline junky" for thrill seekers; but that term misses the point, the adrenaline rush only lasts for a few minutes but being on edge and fearful can last for months, years, or a lifetime. I believe that for people who have been inculcated to living with feeling fear and stress over prolonged periods of time these feelings become a constant need, being without them makes the "addicts" feel unbalanced and they will seek out, consciously or unconsciously, dangerous situations. I know that held true for myself and my teammates and many other members of 8th COIN.

Anger was something else we had to learn to manage, we learned to push it down and hide it. The minute we got off the buses at boot camp we were hit with a barrage of verbal (and sometimes physical) abuse that required each new recruit to hold in his anger or be sent home. In training we learned that raw, naked anger would work against us unless controlled, we learned that suppressed anger could be used as a fuel to keep us moving forward in circumstances where we might quit or give up or not perform the (sometimes nasty) duties required of us without it. Suppressed anger, as in controlled rage versus plain rage, was often used to spur effective aggressive action and to bypass fear and shove aside guilt. And we learned to use a foe's anger as a weapon against him (them).

We learned, sometimes painfully, that the man who lost his temper in Close Quarter Battle (CQB martial arts) drills was the one most likely to lose the match; that the seriously skilled guys like Kappas and Hayes went into a state detached from any emotion when in any kind of combat, a mental positioning that a century before a Japanese Sword Master had named the "Mind of No Sword"; I believe meaning that the Mind is the ultimate weapon.

We all thought of Kappas as The Grand Master of CQB and gave him that honorific among ourselves. I'm sure he would have pooh-poohed the title as I remember once asking him how he had become such an accomplished martial artist and he snorted and gave me the look an eagle might give a lamb it is about to stoop on and said, "I'm not a martial artist, I'm a martial practitioner".

And so, with Kappas as our model we learned to use a flash of visible anger as a communication tool, to manage anger (real and unreal) at different layers but to keep the nasty, junk-yard dog mean anger hidden from sight until it was needed.

Closely intertwined with anger is guilt, another beast that doesn't let go, the two so closely wedded that they are sometimes indistinguishable from one another and are both able to push the unwary deep into depression, perhaps years after the events that triggered the feelings. In my experience all the veterans I knew needed to be on guard against the cocktail that results when anger, guilt, and depression mix. I surmise this is true for all veterans, but particularly those who have had to deal in death up close and personal; there is a certain detachment available in killing from a distance, i.e. dropping a bomb, strafing an area with a machine gun from above or firing an artillery round, that gets narrower when killing with a rifle or a handgun close enough to see the targets as individuals, and even narrower when killing with knife or bayonet or rifle butt, or garrote, or even bare hands.

We all had our own way of dealing with fear, anger, and guilt; some had religion, some relied on their confidence in the team and our leaders. Some just kept everything bottled up and did not allow themselves to feel anything that was not immediate and didn't share their thoughts on mortality or the right and wrong of what we were being asked. I thought that the abuse Hayes had lived through as a child had hardened him to a point where nothing would get through his shell (I was wrong). I had for some reason an absolute, perhaps naïve, confidence in my own luck (and Cercone's') and I had Dave.

Dave found fear exhilarating, anger a tool for the uninitiated, and guilt an abstract concept.

Dave was the cool guy, he was never afraid, never rattled, and would go straight to the crux of any threat dispassionately and with no hesitation. Caught in an ambush? Dave would charge at the exact right point in the enemy line. If my body was tiring and will slipping Dave would push me on with no regard to the physical or mental pain I was feeling. He had no sympathy and no empathy; water buff boy has to go? Dave would take care of it. Dave handled fear and anger for me, to Dave my guilt did not even exist.

He was two years ahead of me in high school, a gifted athlete (we could tell just by the way he moved through the halls) who never went out for sports and a good-looking guy who never seemed to notice the girls winking and blinking and swooning when he was around, he spent all of his time outside of school working with or just being around the father who had adopted him at around age eight or nine.

I didn't even know Dave knew I was alive until I ran afoul of two football playing brothers who were big bullies around the school, one had accosted me in the locker room after phys ed and I had dealt him some

344

quick pain and escaped before he could corner me. The rest of the day whispers went around the school that the Jones boys (not their real name) were going to catch me after school and "run me up the flagpole".

The "run me up the flagpole" reference came from an incident that had happened the year before when as a freshman I hadn't gone along with the ritual of upper classmen hanging the freshman boys (the small ones anyway) from their belts on coat hooks in the school entrance hall. As a big Irish, red-headed, letter jacket wearing, jock attempted to hoist me on a hook I took his action as an assault and refusing to be bullied waited until he lifted me to where our eyes were level and stuck a #2 pencil into the side of his neck just under his left ear. As I watched his mouth open and pupils widen in shock I broke the pencil tip off in his neck.

There was some blood, some shrill (girlish) yelling and cursing and a general consensus was established that I was too nutty to be messed with. And, oh yeah, the big Mick that had tried to hang me on the coat hook became a sort of friend and protector for the rest of the school year. And the Thompson twins (the boy set, there was also a girl set) and their tall friend Cal, who were already known around the school as berserkers, invited me in to their lunch circle.

But on the day the Jones boys decided to target me the Thompson twins were suspended from school for some mischief or other (a frequent occurrence for them), Cal was home caring for his alcoholic mother (again) and my big Irish friend had graduated the year before. I was going to have to get through the end of the school day alone. I thought about sneaking out the back door of the gym and cutting across the playing field to a back gate where I could make a run for home but pride stopped me from that route and after the last bell of the day I started for the front entrance doors.

As I came through the big double doors and started down the concrete steps I was looking at a ghoulish circle of high school kids eager to witness whatever humiliation I might be subjected to and at the outer edge of the circle leaning up against the elder Jones boy's '51 Ford were the brothers with big smirks on their faces. At the edge of my right peripheral vision I caught a glimmer of motion as Dave came up the sidewalk just before my total focus centered on my antagonists and I dropped my books to the steps and got ready to charge; determined to fight back at whatever cost. I knew I was about to get a beating but I meant to draw first blood and at least make them know they had been in a fight.

Before I could clear the bottom stairs a blur named Dave had pushed through the crowd and sort of skated or glided between the Jones boys spinning the older, larger one around and punching him hard in the right kidney and continuing his own spin to connect with an elbow to the side of the head of the younger brother. The younger brother folded up like an accordion and sank to the ground, the older swung an overhand right at Dave and found himself being accelerated at the end of his own arm and toward the side of his car. Dave reversed direction on the arm at the end of its swing and the whole crowd could hear the loud "pop" as a shoulder was dislocated and the older brother turned into a quivering mass on the ground next to the car. And all the time Dave had this ho hum detached look on his face, the same look I would see later on Kappas and Hayes and a few other seriously good fighters.

Ignoring the hushed crowd and the moans coming from the boys on the ground he beckoned to me and shaking his head said in a scolding tone, "You shouldn't get into fights at school" and "C'mon I'll give you a ride home". Just like a big brother.

I learned a lot from Dave and his Dad, regularly riding my bike (and later driving) the four miles out to his house with the barn in back where there was a full-sized boxing ring, weights, light bags, heavy bags, speed bags and wrestling mats. I learned about boxing and footwork, "If they're bicycling they're thinking, if they're gliding they're getting ready to jab, if they're gliding and planting they're getting ready to throw a hard punch or a combination" and enjoyed wrestling but liked the change of balance, timing and physics of judo the best.

I admired Dave and looked up to him as a friend and mentor and was devastated when he was killed in a head-on collision with a drunk driver on the narrow road along the river near his house. I kept my sad feelings to myself, unwilling to share my grief with anyone and sat silent and dry eyed in the pew next to his Mom and Dad at the funeral services.

But Dave wasn't completely gone, still isn't, he lived on as a memory and a voice in my head to be summoned at times of reflection or in times of peril.

Not that I was visited by his ghost or his soul entered my body or that I developed a dual personality or schizophrenia or anything all "New Age". It was simply that I formed a facet of my own personality to match a model of Dave's or of Dave's as I imagined it to be. The inner voice that I used (use) to coach myself when under stress sounds like Dave's voice and says the things I think/imagine Dave would say.

So "Dave", my memories of him and my imagined responses he would have to hazardous or noxious situations became a coping mechanism for me that allowed me to do things I might not otherwise have been willing or able to do. When the shit really hit the fan, when things were really dicey I became "Dave". The only problem was that the more I was forced to rely on this facet of my own personality the easier it became to access it, I developed a dark side that sometimes wanted out, that wanted the freedom to express itself whether my "goodie-two-shoes" side liked it or not. "Dave" could (still can?) and did get me in trouble more than once, especially when alcohol was around.

I had my coping mechanism and my team mates had theirs and the military had spent a huge effort and large sums of time and money to condition us to live with fear, manage our anger, and suppress our feelings of guilt.

But when we were about to return to civilian life the military spent no effort to detrain, untrain, or retrain us. Perhaps because our activities in the field were classified, perhaps because none of our upper echelon was left in place, or maybe there was just no reason to care about us; we were just another disposable asset.

No effort was made to teach us to live without fear.

No effort was made to teach us how to deal with our anger in the future or that it was sure to seep out.

No effort was made to teach us how to handle it when our feelings of guilt surfaced.

No effort was made to teach us to be wary of depression, what the warning signs are, and how best to deal with it.

Perhaps if Kappas had been there to help us transition back to civilian life, or Samuels, or Bohannon, or somebody we could trust.

Instead we all just self-medicated.

Chapter 55

A String of Pearls

There are memories that come to me in waking and sleeping dreams, memories of times I could not have had anywhere else, or with any other people. They hover just out of sight like a string of pearls hidden behind a haze of years, one pearl at a time coming up into shining focus then submerging back behind a twilight grey luster.

Navy Tower

The Navy Docs poked and prodded and finally released us into the tender mercies of the cadre in charge of training in the tower and after a rigorous physical training regimen we were handed back to the Docs, passing the second set of exams we were cleared to go to the next step. Late morning of the third day, satisfied that we had completed the training satisfactorily our Navy brethren locked us in the pressure chamber at the bottom of the tower and with a one-to-one instructor/trainee ratio flooded the room, opened the hatch and we did our slow ascent to the top using the "blow and go" technique, careful to exhale the entire rise and to never catch up and pass our own bubbles.

We must have performed well because we were "invited" to stay over two more days and take part in a SCUBA (Self Contained Underwater Breathing Apparatus) training exercise, Kappas thought it would be a good idea to have a refresher with the scuba gear so of course we all thought it would be a good idea too.

Not that we were training to be as proficient, or anywhere near that benchmark, as Navy Combat Divers, we were training to be able to exit submarines and perhaps make (relatively shallow) underwater approaches to beachheads or waterfront areas using scuba or self-contained re-breathing equipment.

The culmination of the scuba exercise was a dive almost to the base of the tower where we would buddy-breathe while we took turns removing the spring and ball bearing components from our two stage regulators and replacing them with components of a different color. This final test would require focus and control of fine muscular movement under pressure and had a real element of danger attached.

During the test I was probably sweating copiously, but who would know with all that water under, around, and over (over!) us. If I had been wearing a hat I would have tipped it to the Navy Divers who considered this exercise "kid stuff", in their training version they had to perform the same exercise in near total darkness, in tidal currents.

And so, I found myself with more than 90 feet of water over my head looking across at a man I knew could not even swim all that many months ago, each of us depending on the other to stay cool and collected (and safe) while we completed the exercise.

I swear Blaske was grinning behind his dive mask.

Thor's Hammer

We were at Angel Three Five (35,000') paralleling the California, Arizona border with a little more than a hundred miles to go when the radio crackled with the news that there would be well developed thunderstorms on our route back to Nellis AFB, Nevada. With no visible horizon and a smooth pilot in the front seat I had to watch the rear seat artificial horizon and heading indicator to see that we were making a one-minute turn to the east, then back north five minutes later. We would skirt the storm system and race it to our destination.

I was hitching a ride back from an emergency leave with my all-time favorite pilot, Captain Joe Finley, and was strapped in the back seat of an F-100F being lofted home on Talaria Wings (Mercury's shoes) when the bright stars above our path were swallowed by a deep black sky and we got the weather briefing. But I wasn't worried riding in a stout fighter plane with a real yank and bank fighter pilot in the front seat. A little concerned maybe, but not worried.

A wide swing up over a corner of Utah did not get us clear of the fast approaching storm front and with fuel tanks too near "bingo" to want to go to an alternate, or maybe he was just determined, Captain Joe decided to let ground radar thread us through the thunderheads, the on-board radar was strictly designed for air-to-air computations and would be of no use in reading the storm cells ahead of us.

Within minutes we were schussing down a steep mountain of air without being able to see the bumps or even our wingtips, the running lights and strobes turned off and dark visors pulled down to aid in keeping night vision while lightning flashed around us, nothing giving clues to the aircraft attitude, airspeed, and direction except the red glow from the sometimes-vibrating instruments. In my headset I could hear a series of grunts, the sound not registering for a moment until I realized it was the sound of both of us straining as our G-suits squeezed and massaged us under the g-loads the plane was taking. Between the grunts and under the sound of our engine and the air rushing past the canopy I began to pick out another sound, the Captain was singing "Danny Boy", the rhythm nearly matching the cadence of the sine wave we were traveling as we twisted between cells, guided by an airman on the ground somewhere in the dark ahead of us.

Our flight path took us back south and turned west again just as we entered a heavy squall line, the lightning blinding us intermittently even with sun shields down on our helmets, rain so dense it was if we were flying a submarine and the shot scattered sound of hail hitting our ride. I had my feet braced clear of the back-seat rudder pedals, hands clamped on to the shroud over the instrument panel in front of me, butt puckered in anticipation of hearing the siren wail that would tell us we had a flame out, sure that the amount of ice and water our engine was ingesting would choke it. If we had a flame out would we be able to get an air start? That was a theoretical problem I did not want the Captain to have to work out!

351

But our beautiful Hun flew on shuddering under the impacts of Thor's Hammer, bright strings of light streaming from the static brushes on the wings trailing edges, our bird pushed into the clear between massive columns of cloud lit from beneath by the bright lights of Las Vegas, lightning jumping from cloud to cloud and down to the ground. I could even see lightning flashes reflected on the water of Lake Mead just off to our starboard (right) side, we had popped into a clear space just over the Hoover Dam.

With all the ambient light I pushed up my sun shield and sat in awe at the show I was witnessing flying through the clear space between the brilliantly colored, lighting illuminated thunderstorms, starlight overhead again and Las Vegas an island of light beneath us as we circled to lose altitude. I heard the Captain ask ground control for a traffic report and heard the reply, "You're the only plane in the sky here tonight Captain".

Down at approach altitude the Captain made one more wide circle over the valley, reluctant to leave the show, before making a straight-in to Nellis. And I thought the approach controller was only half right: I felt like we were in the only plane in the world that night.

One Up

It was a sort of silly game we played, Hayes the originator. Whenever he did something he thought was "cool", or a first, or something no one else would be able to duplicate, something that would give him a "One Up" he would hold a pinkie finger up in the air and with a big grin say, "That's one!" or "Gotcha'!" or sometimes use the pinkie as a substitute for a middle finger. A habit we all picked up from him.

Throw a good dive off the three-meter platform, "That's one!" Shoot a one hundred on the pistol range, "That's one!" Win the morning foot race to the chow hall, "That's one!" and so on. Some of the firsts were spectacular, some just pedestrian, and some just in bad taste, most would not be funny to anyone not on our team. Sometimes just displaying a pinkie finger from across a room, or a parade ground, could start a series of choked back laughter, or outright guffaws, depending on the setting.

Late one night in the Rose Bar I had run into a girl I had seen dealing Black Jack at the Horseshoe a few times and when I offered to buy her a drink she accepted, her shift was over but she was still a little wound up, she said, and wanted to mellow down before going home to her apartment. In the next couple of hours I learned that she had bright eyes, a wicked, wry sense of humor and could maybe beat Minnesota Fats at pool. I also learned that she was a little stiff; wooden might be the right word, when we danced to a couple of slow tunes on the juke box. And I knew that it was just a matter of time before we became, in today's parlance, "friends with benefits". This happened three nights later.

Giggling over breakfast the next morning we planned a couple of fun activities (I was off duty for the next few days) and I told her the story of the raised pinkie and how it could send my team mates into howling fits of laughter. She thought my description was a little over the top but became a co-plotter and agreed to loan me an appliance (I said she had a wicked sense of humor).

Visiting the lads in the House With The Blue Fence with her as my guest for lunch I waited and let the boys all wonder what I had inside the barracks bag I had placed on a coffee table in the middle of the front room. When I felt the moment was right I reached into the bag and pulled out her appliance, a prosthetic, an artificial leg. Holding a pinkie finger high I exclaimed, "That's One!"

I was the undisputed "One Up Champion" for several months to come.

Chapter 56

Mail Call

Fruitcakes in red tins were a party from home, rum flavored cake with raisins and nuts and candied fruit and mysterious spices. Comedians like to make fun of them and people sometimes act like its cool to laugh about them but they were important to us and whenever Mom sent me one I would have to slice it thin so that everyone could enjoy the taste. Sammy's mother tried to have her cooks duplicate them, but the results never tasted the same as the ones from Mom. But one question about the fruitcakes went unanswered, "what are those chewy green things?"

Mom cookies and other goodies were treasures to be shared and whenever one of her brown paper taped, re-taped, and tied packages arrived someone would start a pot of "American" coffee and if we were in SE Asia perhaps have a couple of cafetheongs (strong Lao coffee, phonetic spelling) ready to brew while they waited for me to come to our shack.

On one outstanding day we opened a package with a wonderful aroma that got stronger as we peeled away the wrapping, inside was a confection that is hard to describe; sort of like a rolled jelly cake with a soft brown filling it was a date log and searching for a way to describe it Hayes, who never waxed poetical, said, "the recipe for this must have come down to your mom on the wings of angels". The bottle of brandy she sent with it added to our good cheer.

Blaske would get regular letters, often several in a batch, from a certain particular peaches and cream complected English showgirl, one of the ladies we called our "den mothers" in Las Vegas. The letters would be written in purple ink on a thin one-piece paper that folded to make its own envelope, the red, white and blue piping on the edges made them easy to spot, but we never could decide why she sent airmail letters from Las Vegas to a box at Nellis Air Force Base, located a just a few miles from the post office where she deposited the letters. To my knowledge he never wrote or received any mail from any family members, stubborn people on both sides.

Morrison's sister would send him letters with news from home, he was pissed to learn that his room had been converted into a library and home office, and his dad would send an occasional short note, usually asking (or berating) him about his future plans. His mom would send expensive but usually useless gifts like the long bright red thick wool scarf she sent him one summer. There was a girl from his high school days that sent him letters for a while but he stopped getting them after about a year.

Hayes would get occasional mail from his mother and a few letters a year from his older brother. One of the den mothers and a girl he sometimes dated in Las Vegas kept him up to date on what was going on there. He got a letter from his step-dad one year just before Christmas, read it, burned it, and never spoke about its contents until one alcohol-soaked night a couple of years later when he said, "The old prick is trying to make up to me. Fuck him".

Cerone mail could usually be picked out of the dispatch bag by a blind man. He got perfumed notes from at least three girls from his home town and more perfumed notes from everywhere we had ever been and a few places I had never heard of. Oh yeah, his mother wrote him once in a while too.

Letters to me from Beckstrom's sister would arrive one and sometimes two or more at a time, the postmarks always a month apart, the delivery dates subject to the whims of some clerks somewhere.

She had started writing to me a few weeks after I had visited the family farm with him while we were on leave during a break in our training cycles and continued writing once a month after his death, I suppose it may have been a way for her to keep some connection with an older brother she had loved dearly.

She would write about a cow that had her calf at the wrong time or place, but "both were doing fine now". She wrote about her dogs and the cat that refused to leave the barn when her kittens were born. She wrote about the fella' that took her to her first prom, and about how nervous her dad was to see her go off in a car with a boy. One letter described how excited she was to be going off to live in a college dorm. Newsy, chatty letters that never mentioned her brother or the pain she must have been feeling at his loss.

Some of her letters would contain newspaper clippings about events and news from around her home town and some had Kodak Process colored snapshots showing a pretty, clear eyed girl with wavy red-blonde hair smiling shyly at the camera. One contained a wallet-sized high school studio portrait that I carried for years before I lost the wallet somewhere in my travels after I was out of the service.

I wrote back a few times but never mailed the letters. Years later I drove through Minnesota near the county where the Beckstrom farm was located and tried to go by and visit, but the car I was driving would not turn down the road.

When I left Nellis for the last time I did not leave a forwarding address and I suppose she eventually stopped writing. But sometimes I like to imagine a box on a shelf somewhere at Nellis with letters that have arrived once a month for fifty years, full of homey gossip and peppered with minutiae about a sweet woman's life.

Chapter 57

On A Wing

A memory that visits me often is really a set of memories of quiet evenings that repeated over the years, most vivid from the time we were waiting for our discharges. Quiet nights in summer or winter spent sitting on the wing of a plane in the night dark somewhere on the flight line at Nellis with my friend Cerone.

Back at Nellis if Cerone and I weren't in training we usually worked as Fire Control Technicians repairing and calibrating gunsight and bombing computer systems for the F100 Sabre Jet series of aircraft and we usually managed to pull swing shift, the shift when less people were around to annoy us. Both night owls, we found the evening shift best fit our sleeping habits and gave us the free hours we liked best. Other Blue Teamers worked swing shifts at their various posts as well; we were all just geared to be awake at night.

We would go to the flight line a little earlier than our shift started and at the 7th A&E shack monitor the radio calls coming in describing problems that would be turned into work orders when the planes came in from missions over the gunnery range to the north. Sometimes we recognized called in complaints as bullshit, often that had to do with which pilot was reporting the problem, and sometimes pilots we knew were in the stack, we would go for their work orders first, ready before the planes had landed and the crew chiefs started their write ups. We cherry picked the stuff we wanted to work on and left the rest for the permanent party techs to cull through.

Boarding the flight line tram, we always carried two olive green canvas tool bags; one with tools, and in the other, depending on the season, two six packs or a thermos of coffee and a bottle of brandy. Might as well relax and enjoy our work. And we were good at analyzing the problems in the black boxes; we cleared more work orders without repeat write-ups than anyone else in the squadron. Not always, but often we would

357

follow the black boxes we had traded out back to the repair station and do the repairs to the electronics, curious about what failed and why. The NCOIC (Non-Commissioned Officer In Charge) of the repair station always signed our weekly evaluation forms with the notation "EWQ", Exceptionally Well Qualified; and in our final few months at Nellis recommended us for promotion on a weekly basis.

On hot nights the metal surfaces of the planes would still be radiating heat until midnight and the smell of the GPU (ground power unit) exhaust could get nasty so we would sometimes trade a couple of the married techs for the graveyard shift. The married guys would just hide in the air-conditioned repair station and work on housekeeping stuff until the NCIOC released them from swing shift to go to married quarters. It was a good deal on both sides and often resulted in a little something extra from Schlitz or Budweiser appearing in our lockers at the shack.

It was a cold spring during our last nights on the flight line and we would sit on a wing in the paling of the days light and listen to the sounds of the birds coming back from the range. First a barely audible high-pitched whine would echo off Sunrise Mountain to the south of the field, followed a couple of minutes later by the loud C-r-r-r-a-ack, C-r-r-r-a-ack, C-r-r-r-a-ack, C-r-r-r-a-ack, of four birds in formation coming over the field and ripping open the cold air above us. A louder whine and then the engine roar would get to us just after the planes had passed overhead and made their break from formation to circle and land at one-minute intervals. By the time they taxied up to park on the flight line it would be dark and cold while we waited for the engines to spool down, canopy open, and crew chief greet the pilot. On the, now rarer, occasions that we knew the pilot we would usually get a grin and a nod, the pilot ignoring the fact that we had forgotten to salute. One colonel did get huffy when we didn't salute him so Cerone and I picked up our tool bags and walked off to disappear in the dark, let him fix his own damn airplane, it wasn't broken anyway, we knew from past experience he just couldn't get the operational sequence of the systems right.

It was just the two of us sitting on a wing in the cold not talking, sipping our laced coffee and watching the stars march past one night; we really didn't mix with the other techs in the A&E squadron, Morrison long gone, Blaske working in the F105 Thud (Thunderchief) shop, and Hayes in the stockade, and the other aircraft work crews hiding indoors. Just the two of us sitting in the dark until a Ford dispatch truck pulled up and dropped off a passenger, Blaske had decided to join us and came bearing gifts, hot roast beef sandwiches and another thermos of coffee.

As the three of us sat there in the cold dark enjoying a sense of shared solitude a thought we all shared came to the surface, "Fuckin' Generals", three heads nodding in unison, "They don't even listen to the Captains and Colonels, they will never listen to guys from the field", three heads nodding again and then a question we had all been mulling over for months came to the surface, "Are you going to re-up?", "No", "Me neither, what about you?", this last directed at Blaske. "No". And then a statement directed at me, "If we don't stay in you know Hayes will get out". "Yeah, I know".

It was decided.

It was a nice early summer day at Nellis Air Force Base when we walked out of the main gate. The man behind the plate glass window in the dry cleaners next to the bus stop across from the gate saw what he probably thought were four confident young men in civilian clothes crossing the street to wait for a ride to downtown. Had he been able to see them a little closer he might have recognized that all four were a little nervous, suffering from undefined feelings of guilt, paranoia, and frustration. Low in morale, suspicious of authority, and vaguely disappointed.

The decision to leave the Air Force should have been an easy one with our unit demobilized, our leaders gone, and the likelihood that we four would be assigned to different units scattered throughout the organization. But, there was a reluctance on all our parts to leave the military environment we had grown used to; although none of us were good garrison troops, the training and experiences we had had making up our own rule book in the field precluded it, we understood and were comfortable with the military structure, civilian life was sure to feel alien to us for a while. And so, we all hung around The House With The Blue Fence for a few weeks.

Hayes was the first to leave, he had to clear up some details regarding his step fathers' estate and get ready to enroll in a university. Cerone was next, leaving to go to work with a small firm that supplied specialized electronic equipment and other services to governmental departments. Blaske would stay behind in Las Vegas and look for a job there.

I had no immediate plans or goals although my mentor for the United States Armed Forces Institute courses I took the entire time I was in The Air Force had suggested I could reapply for scholarships I had earned before going into service and complete course work for a degree at the University of Wisconsin. But I wasn't ready to commit to any path, I decided instead to hitch hike around the Pacific Northwest just to see whatever there was to see there.

I was glad to be away from the mosquitos and other biting insects and the leeches. Away from the sudden deadly threats and loud noises, the constant fearful tension and sudden adrenaline jolts. Away from the acrid stenches and dreadful fatigue the "strum und drang" of field operations.

But I knew I was going to miss the sudden deadly threats and loud noises, the constant fearful tension and electric adrenaline jolts. The days and nights of thirst and hunger. Miss the acrid stenches and dreadful fatigue; all interspersed with moments of exultation and sheer joy at being alive. I was going to miss all the nasty things we had all been complaining about. Except the mosquitos - and the leeches.

And I worried what would happen to our friends in the mountain villages who we all felt had been pulled into a war that they couldn't win. A war we were all certain was going to grow into a ravening beast.

As we parted company instead of being eager for new sights, sounds, and the taste of freedom from military discipline I was overwhelmed with a miserable feeling of being un-moored. Unable to sleep. Restless.

The nightmares would start in another year.

Chapter 58

Buster Leaves

The well cherished red and cream '56 Chevy convertible left the Tonapah Highway north of Las Vegas at a high rate of speed going airborne as it crossed the lip of the berm at the edge of the road, then the nose dropped and dug into the desert and the car pitch poled, flipped once and then rolled several times.

When the four men walked out the gate at Nellis AFB for the last time and into the civilian world the last echoes of the Programs Evaluation Office (PEO) and the last vestiges of the 8th Counter Insurgency Study Group (8th COIN) went with them. All four stayed and hung around the "House With The Blue Fence" for a few weeks until one left to prepare for college in the fall, one started a new job with an electronics firm with military contracts, and one left to wander restless for a few months, leaving Blaske alone in the house in Las Vegas.

He hadn't had any contact with his family since he had left to enlist, though he knew that the Air Force routinely sent letters to parents telling of completion of boot camp, assignment to permanent party stations and other information he knew they could have no idea of where he had actually been and what he had done in the years since he left home, his father saying "you are dead to me" and his mother tearfully turning her face to the wall as he left for the train station.

Proud of what he had accomplished and certain that enough time had passed for his father to forgive what the elder Blaske must have considered disloyalty and disobedience a few weeks after discharge he decided to visit home and attempt a reconciliation. But first he would send a Western Union telegram telling his father of his planned visit, no response expected.

He debarked from the cab in uniform, Class A Blues sharply creased, bloused pants over glistening boots with white paratroop lacings, pogie bait whistle passing through the epaulet over his right shoulder, blue and white enamel jump pin and winged pathfinder badge on his left breast over and under a ribbon bar, black and white silk scarf at his neck and 8th COIN flash on his maroon beret; even without the uniform his erect posture and bearing would have told an aware observer that here was a proud military man.

Feeling strangely nervous and uncertain he paid the cabbie and told him to "stand by", a link to the outside world as he was remembering a lesson from his training, "never enter a room without knowing where all the exits are".

With a quick shock he realized that the girl standing at the foot of the stoop talking with a young man with forelocks and a homburg hat was his sister looking all grown up. Then she saw him, he could see the recognition form in her eyes, and said something he could not quite hear before her face paled and the couple ran up the steps and closed the door behind them.

No one answered the door buzzer and after ten or fifteen minutes he went back down the stairs to stand on the sidewalk looking at the second story window where he had often sat gazing out wondering about the world beyond his neighborhood. Looking up he saw the white flash of a face that must have belonged to his mother, then the curtains were pulled tightly closed.

 Gut roiling, he got in the cab and directed the driver to take him back across the bridge into Manhattan and on to Grand Central Station, refusing to give in to the urge to look back over his shoulder as they left the neighborhood where all his boyhood memories resided.

Back in Las Vegas he found himself with a past he couldn't talk about and an uncertain future.

Mr. Binion, owner of the Horseshoe Club, had referred him to a company that was designing and building new electronic gambling equipment to replace all the mechanical/electronic hybrid slot machines currently in use all over Nevada. The circuitry design work was well paid and his employers seemed to think highly of him but he found it hard to stay focused and knew this was not the future he was looking for.

Lonely without his team mates and worried about them with them so far out of his sight and accustomed to a life in the NOW the man his team had admired for his stoic acceptance of discomfort and seemingly unending patience was feeling unmoored and disconnected. He needed a new purpose and was considering re-enlisting, perhaps trying out for Special Forces or the newly formed Air Commando Wing, certain that his resume and qualifications would make him an ideal candidate. Maybe he should take some college courses and reenter the services as an officer. Or perhaps he should go to Israel and join the Israeli Defense Force, which would be certain to garner his father's approval. But first he would go to England and look up the lovely Anne.

Three months after we walked out of the gate at Nellis and into civilian life the debris path the red and cream convertible left in its wake included broken glass, miscellaneous auto body parts, a dozen or so empty beer cans and a three-quarter empty bottle of Jack Daniels. The driver of the car lay in a fetal position several yards from the debris stream looking unharmed but not moving, a chain around his neck holding a rectangular metal tag that listed his name, blood type, military identification number, and the notation "non-denominational". In his shirt pocket was a letter written in purple ink on air mail stationary that began, "Dear Herbert..."

Epilogue

Remembering Day

The two women have never lived more than five miles apart in Orange County, California. After they got to "the world" in America both learned English, went to school, and married members of the Baptist church that their adopted parents had belonged to. And both raised their children in the same small community of repatriated Asians that came into the area during and after the Vietnam War.

Anyone looking at them would assume that they were twins and in fact their passports and driver's licenses and other documentation would seem to support that fact, but they knew that one was at least one or perhaps two years older than the other; the paperwork done to get them clearance out of an Asian country to the U.S. as orphans had been hastily and not entirely correctly done. Their exact ages would always remain a mystery to them.

Somewhere in their late twenties or early thirties and in response to questions their husbands, in-laws, friends, and children were asking they decided to hold a "Remembering Day" once a year. The American holiday "Veterans Day" seemed like an easily remembered and appropriate date. As the family grew and their children had children and cousins and friends were invited the event took on more and more ritual and meaning; not knowing the actual dates they even celebrated their birthdays on this day, never mind the dates on their documents.

Sometimes the "Crooked Face Man" would join them for the celebration, bringing along a child or two and whatever wife or girlfriend he was attached to at the time. Of course, they knew his name, they knew the names of all the people they were with during the time right before they came to America, they just preferred to identify those people by the names they made up as children before they learned to use the American words.

Arrangements for the event start a few days ahead of the big day; there is furniture to be moved, tables to be set up, and bedding to be aired for the overnighters, and food prepared to feed the growing number of guests. The lawn has to be neatly trimmed and hanging lanterns and other decorations hung on wire strands at whichever house they are using on any given year (they rotate hosting the event).

One food table is set up on a patio or in a sun room (depending on the weather) and loaded with a Pan Pacific/American/Asian array of foods ready for early afternoon arrivals. At one end of the table there may be a hotpot filled with a perfumed vegetable broth and thin sliced meat, at the other end there may be a bucket of Kentucky Fried Chicken, and of course there are eight kinds of noodles, two kinds of rice, hot peppers and pizza somewhere on the table. Something for all tastes, young or old.

The other food table is set up inside the house and won't be touched until the evening story telling has begun. Carefully prepared sandwiches of Spam and dill pickle on mustard and horse radish washed halved slices of a dark brown bread will be on a covered platter. There will be canned tuna and sardines, and Vienna Sausages skewered on toothpicks. There will be hot dogs, lima beans and ham, and a big bowl of popcorn. At one end of the table a slow cooking pot will be filled with a creamy beef mixture and parked next to a four-slice toaster, ready to make "shit on a shingle"- creamed beef on toast.

Cold bottles of Coca Cola, Seven Up, and Schlitz and Singha beer will be kept chilled in a bucket of ice. There will be a bottle of White Horse Scotch and a bottle of VSOP Brandy next to a seltzer bottle for those with a taste for stronger drink. Family members and guests will visit this table in a random ebb and flow during the evening story telling.

It gets dark early in November and by six or seven everyone has gathered around the two women, out on a patio in nice weather or indoors on cooler nights, lights dimmed to create the proper ambience. Well fed, burped and diapered even the youngest settle in quietly as the story telling begins.

Louise, the eldest of the two women, usually starts the tale by relating dim memories of an open space where a field of red flowers grew a short walk from their mountain home. Taking a path in the forest in the opposite direction would bring her to a sudden opening on the edge of a steep slope with farming terraces laid out row after row below. She would tell of collecting eggs from half wild chickens and of digging in the forest for roots. One or two of the children, sometimes prompted by a grown-up will ask, "What color were the chickens?', "What color were the roots?", "Did you have pigs?" the story telling an interactive affair.

Both women would tell of their grandfather, grandmother, and mother; details lost in the shadows of time, neither could remember their father who had left to fight with other men of their clan while the girls were still very young. But both could remember the day they left the village with Mother in front, girls in the middle and Grandmother at the rear as they marched single file on the red clay road, each carrying a bundle with cloth straps looped over and under their shoulders; Grandfather staying behind to watch over the almost deserted village. And they could remember crying when Mother cut off their long hair and dressed them in boys' pants and shirts the night before they started down the trail.

At this point in the story the two women will pause to look at one another and the entire room will give a collective sigh; a hard part of the story is coming.

Louise will tell how their Mother and Grandmother were taken off by strange men while the girls hid in an animal pen under a building. Then Lila will pick up the narrative and tell how "The Long-Faced Man" rescued them from under the building after it was set on fire, his own hat aflame as he kicked in the fencing and carried them off to safety. "Were you very scared, did you scream, MaMa?" "We were very frightened but we knew not to make any noise". "Did you ever see Mother and Grandmother again?" "No, we knew we would never see them again". Again, a collective sigh fills the room.

"The Long-Faced Man" carried them most of the day, probably afraid they would try to run away (but where could they go?), only stopping briefly around mid-day for food and water, his companion "The Monkey Faced Man" running ahead to scout the trail under the canopy.

Finally, they reached a clear spot where the trail they were on met a wider road and "The Long-Faced Man" deposited them on the ground in front of a noisy metal hut and motioned for them to get in. The girls had only seen airplanes way high in the sky and did not know what the metal structure was, only that it frightened them and clung to one another looking for a direction to run. "The Monkey Faced Man" and "The Light Haired Man" waiting next to the plane tried to comfort them and coax them through the door but they would not enter.

The girls did not understand English at the time but were practiced mimics and can still repeat the sounds "The Long-Faced Man" made when he pulled a fierce face, bugged out his eyes and pointing with his left arm shouted.

Now everyone in the room where the women are telling the story and who have heard it before will make a fierce face, bug out their eyes, and pointing shout, "Gityerbuttsintherenow!" the meaning very clear even if one didn't speak the language. Some laughter will follow the shout.

This is usually the point in the evening when the story telling has a pause and people get up to stretch, maybe use a bathroom, resettle little ones, and perhaps get something to eat from the buffet table. When the circle has re-formed Lila will take up the tale relating what happened when the airplane landed.

The two girls and their escorts disembarked the plane into a world full of people, noise, and confusion, but there to meet them was the "Crooked Face Man" who somehow with non-verbal communication, a big smile and large soft brown eyes gave them a feeling of security – they knew instinctually that this man would keep them safe from harm.

The women take turns telling about right after getting off the plane being in a food stall and eating warm rice porridge with the "Crooked Face Man", the "Light Haired Man", and the "Smiling Man" when the "Tall Nose Man" came into the stall. The "Tall Nose Man" looked around the stall and with a grimace said (here listeners will join in again), "Geezuzthosekidsstinkgetthemabathandcleanclothes"!

And it was true, they did stink after days marching without a chance to get clean, and both had soiled their pants during the terrifying airplane ride, the stains clearly visible even against the dark pants they were wearing. But neither understood what was happening when they were taken to the bath house in a compound behind a shack facing the flight line on the airport.

Lila likes to tell how it was dark when they got to the bath house and how they kicked and fought when they saw the big kettle of water with steam rising under the un-shaded light bulbs above and their escorts were trying to get them undressed. "Were they going to cook you and eat you, MaMa?", "Were they going to do unspeakable things to you?"

While the two girls were huddling together in a corner of the compound the "Crooked Face Man" called on a friend to help. His friend was a big bosomed woman, "Mynameisjane" who swept into the compound and shooed all the men out. Within minutes she had the girls calm and understanding that they were safe and were about to get cleaned up, shouting through the compound door, "theseboysyou'verescuedaren'tboys, theseboysaregirls!"

Later that night dressed in too big shorts and too big shirts they were in a little house with a raised floor and screens on three sides and two bedding pallets on the floor opposite the door. Through the screen they could see the "Tall Nose Man" sitting on the shelf in front of the door. At first they thought he was there to prevent them from escaping, but then realized he was there to protect them. And so it was for every night during their stay behind the little three-sided shack with the hidden spirit door opening into the compound where the Americans kept their supplies and tools of their trade.

Every night the "Tall Nose Man" would be there to protect and comfort them, to ease the fear when a nightmare struck, or hold them tight when a sense of loss and pain overcame either one or both of them; many nights he would spend with his back against the wall between the two pallets and a dark-haired head on each shoulder while he crooned a wordless tune of comfort and reassurance. It was during these nights that the "Tall Nose Man" gave the girls the names that they would take with them to America – Louise and Lily he called them.

At this remembrance of the "Tall Nose Man", even after so many years, both women find their eyes filled with tears.

The women have other memories to share like "Mynameisjane" bringing them girl clothes, and the day that the "Light Haired Man" and his pal "Smiling Man" came to the shack pushing a handcart loaded with a black box that was making a cloud trail as they pushed it along. Opening the black box, they revealed three round containers filled with delicious, cold, creamy mixtures, much to the delight of everyone at the shack that day.

They remember that as the men came and went from the shack whomever was there would spend time with the girls teaching them English and introducing them to American foods, and black and white movies where men chased each other firing pistols on horseback, with an occasional break for a song(?). Except the "Long Faced Man" who would sit drinking coffee or some beverage from a brown bottle but made no attempt to approach either of the girls, watching but not communicating.

And they remember the trips on the ferry across the wide river to visit at the big house where the beautiful lady lived. The lady who was instrumental in getting them the official clearance and paperwork they needed to be able to immigrate to America.

Until the day came that "Light Haired Man" and "Smiling Man" brought two brown valises and two small carry cases with visa wallets to the foot of a stairway the girls, dressed in school girl uniforms "Mynameisjane" found for them, would climb to board the big airplane that would take them to "The World". "Crooked Face Man" would travel with them and stay for a time while they got settled into a new life with the couple who were to adopt them.

Before they could board the flight "Long Faced Man" broke his reticence and hurried over to hold them both tight for a few minutes, both girls sure they saw his eyes watering before he released them with a light kiss on each forehead.

And that children, grand-children, friends and relatives was how they came to America.

Story telling over for the evening someone will turn up the heat on the slow pot of creamed beef and put bread in the four-slice toaster while someone else plugs in the coffee percolator and prepares to fry eggs in an electric skillet and other people fill plates from the remaining food on the indoor table.

Later there will be birthday cake and three kinds of ice cream - cherry chunk, vanilla, and chocolate.

 And canned peaches.

26285494R00231

Made in the USA
San Bernardino, CA
18 February 2019